D1641086

The Plays

of

Jessie M Page, PhD

BlankPages Press, Ltd.

i

For

LD and Ginger
and
our PT theatre days

The

Full Length Plays

Contents

Loose Women

A Play in Four Acts

©2008

Running Time: 90 Minutes
Three intermissions, 10-minute duration:
  End of Acts I, II, and III
Time: The Present.

Characters
(In order of Appearance)

CATHERINE: Mid-40's, tall, long black hair. CATHERINE: can absorb information, even upsetting information, without giving any of her feelings away.

ROSE: Mid-60's, robust, curly mop of greying hair. ROSE: gives nothing away.

EMILY:Mid-60's, petite, mane of white hair. EMILY is the caretaker, no matter what.

ZELDA: Mid 60's, long-bodied, short bright red (dyed) hair. ZELDA keeps everyone else on track, even when they're lost.

LJ: Mid-60's, scrawny and strong, head covered by a cap. LJ has seen just about everything during his years working on the Washington State ferries.

MARJORIE: Mid-60's, ample-bodied, eggplant-colored, styled hair. MARJORIE does not stand on courtesy. About anything.

Setting: The entire action takes place in the kitchen of Silas', a pub in the 1950's style situated in a small village on an island in the Pacific Northwest. Along the Left wall are the freezer and refrigerator, pantry shelving, and a door (interior) to the pub. Along the Right wall are cupboards, a door (exterior) leading to an alley outside, wall phone, light switches, and a largish window through which we see the edge of a green metal dumpster. Against the rear wall are the stove, griddle, ovens. In a corner stands a coat rack with a few outer garments hanging from it. In the cupboard and on the shelves are a minimal number of kitchen supplies haphazardly stacked or just lying about: cans of food, an old radio, keROSE:ne lanterns, candles, pots and pans, odd plates and flatware, cooking utensils including a carrot peeler, rolls of foil and wax paper, cotton towels, boxes of foodstuffs, and the like. A ceiling-fan-cum-light hangs from overhead. The lighting is flat, allowing for little shadowing.

Lighting and set changes are indicated at the beginning of each Act.

ACT I

Scene 1 (Morning, March 20)

Setting: Dawn, interior kitchen.

AT RISE: One small night light glows near the back door. We can just make out a folding chair, a folded-up Army-type cot with a blanket and weary pillow draped over it, a coat rack standing in a corner, and, at Center, a large butcher block table with two bar-type stools next to it. A cabbage is on the table, as is a dish of chopped onions and garlic. CATHERINE's face appears at the back window, hands cupping it, framing fright. Her knuckles knock on the glass. The face disappears. The back door is knocked on; the door knob rattled. CATHERINE's face reappears at the window. She is obviously in some kind of distress. As suddenly as her face appeared, it disappears. We hear a soft thud. ROSE enters from interior doorway, shuffling in men's slippers, pulling her faded flannel nightgown away from her body, rubbing her eyes. Her curly grey hair springs from her head as if in alarm. She makes her way to the butcher block table, picks up a cleaver lying there, and hollers,

7

ROSE: WHAT!! (*When she gets no answer, she starts moving for the door.*) This better be good, getting me outta bed in the damn dark. WHO'S THERE!! (*ROSE flings open the back door, swivels her head in both directions, sees something beneath the window.*) You there! HEY!!

ROSE disappears outside the building then reappears dragging CATHERINE's inert form by the feet. CATHERINE is dressed in a long skirt, droopy cardigan, hiking boots and socks. A back pack, still attached to one shoulder drags under her body. CATHERINE's long black hair trails out behind her in a fat braid. ROSE drags her prize to the middle of the floor.

ROSE: (*Cont'd.*) (*Dropping CATHERINE's feet.*) What fresh hell is this? (*Scratches her head; looks to the audience.*) Who said that? Whoever it was, she sure knew a thing or two about how mornings start.

ROSE straddles the recumbent CATHERINE; she tips her head, listening for breath, checks for a throat pulse, pulls up an eyelid, puts a hand inside her cardigan to check for heart sounds and chest warmth. O.S. we HEAR EMILY calling.

EMILY: (*off*) Yoo-hoo? Where you?

Scene 2

EMILY enters through the interior door wearing denim coveralls with MONDAY embroidered on the chest flap and a watch fob pinned to it, a denim work shirt under, sleeves rolled up, Juarache sandals, and a huge shoulder satchel. Her white hair is pulled atop her head with clothespins. She is greeted by the sight of CATHERINE's hiking boots peering out from beneath ROSE's nightgown skirts and ROSE's ample bottom waving in the air.

EMILY: (*Crossing to peer down at CATHERINE.*) I don't recognize her. Should I?

ROSE: (*Straightening.*) Not unless you're in the habit of identifying stray women.

EMILY: Where'd you find her?

ROSE: Hunkered down by my dumpster.

EMILY: What's she doing out there? (*Peering closer.*) She looks well tended.

ROSE: Uh huh, those boots alone set her back a penny or two.

She's wearing an expensive slip. No bra.

EMILY: What else do you know about her?

ROSE: Not a damn thing!!

EMILY: No need to roar, I'm just inquiring.

ROSE: Well, don't. It's too early in the morning for inquirings, especially with a peculiar woman on my kitchen floor.

ROSE and EMILY stare down at CATHERINE for a beat.

ROSE: (*Cont'd.*) Why're you here so early?

EMILY: I came to talk you out of it.

ROSE folds her arms across her chest and pouts.

EMILY: (*Cont'd.*) What're you going to do with her?

ROSE: You're the smart one, what would you do?

EMILY: Well, first, I think I'd get her up off the floor.

ROSE nods; EMILY opens up the roll-away cot, lays out the pillow, holds up the blanket. On ROSE's glare, she helps ROSE pick up CATHERINE, whose back pack drops to the floor. They drop CATHERINE on the cot; EMILY covers her with the blanket. They continue to stare at CATHERINE.

ROSE: Now, what.

EMILY: Now I'd throw some light on the tableau.

ROSE: You're reading them art school catalogs again.

EMILY: Well, I can't not read them. They come like presents in my mail box.

ROSE crosses to the wall switches in three steps, throws all the switches up. The kitchen is blazing.

ROSE: Next.

EMILY: Check vital signs?

ROSE: I did that.

EMILY: Identification?

ROSE: Haven't looked yet.

EMILY: Is she snoring or choking?

The women watch CATHERINE, who is indeed snoring, then ROSE pushes one of CATHERINE's shoulders, tilting her on her side.

EMILY: (*Cont'd.*) I suppose we should call someone.

ROSE: Who.

EMILY: Sheriff?

ROSE: Nah, he'd just put her in jail and we don't know if she belongs there, yet.

EMILY: Hospital?

ROSE: What for? She's warm.

EMILY: Newspaper?

ROSE: Not keen on folks knowing till we know. You know?

EMILY: Phone Company? Ferry? Greyhound Bus? Gas Station? Flower Shop? Motels? Bed & Breakfasts? I'm running out of ideas, Rose.

ROSE: (*Moving for the wall phone.*) That's okay, I got one.

EMILY: Who's getting the red flag?

ROSE: (*Dialing.*) Silas. If anybody'll know what to do with a stray, he will. (*Looks at CATHERINE.*) What do you think she is? (*Listening to phone.*) A runaway wife? Embezeller? College girl?

EMILY: (*Getting a closer look.*) Maybe just another lost soul. They wash up on this island all the time. (*Picks up CATHERINE's back pack and starts rummaging through it.*) Nothing in here but a change of underwear, cotton, a box of crackers, Saltine, half empty, toothbrush, maps… oh. (*Opens one of the maps.*) I wonder how she came to fetch up behind Silas' Pub? Look, this one's Colorado. (*Lets map fall to the floor, opens another.*) New Zealand! My, my. (*Peering at CATHERINE.*) I wonder where she was before, yesterday, last week? (*Sighs.*) Maybe she's been wandering the seven corners of the earth and Fate's brought her to us.

ROSE: Maybe she flew over from the mainland on a pound of cocaine. Focus, woman, we got ourselves a situation here. (*Pounds receiver against phone.*) Damn the man. He's never where he's supposed to be. (*Slams receiver on hook; stuffs fists on hips.*) Okay, he's out carousing. Who else.

EMILY: (*Still intrigued by maps.*) I know. Get Zelda down here. Here's one of Newfoundland. (*Rummaging deeper in back pack.*) But nothing else.

ROSE: Brilliant. And won't Margie just love being woken at, what the hell time is it, anyway? (*She dials another number.*)

EMILY: (*Consulting the watch fob on her chest.*) Six twenty two. A. M.

ROSE: Perfect. (*Dials, listens, then shouts into phone.*) Marge! ROSE:! You and Zelda! Get your skinny old behinds down here! Emergency!! (*Stares at phone in disbelief.*) She hung up on me.

EMILY takes the phone from ROSE, dials.

EMILY: Good morning, Zelda, it's Emily. Yes, I know. We're sorry for the alarm call, but we do have something, well, out of the ordinary, and need your help. And Marjorie's, if she'll come. (*Listens.*) It's a loose woman. (*Hangs up.*)

ROSE: Hell, how do you know she's loose?

EMILY: She's not tethered at the moment, is she?

They both look again at CATHERINE, who is now twitching in her sleep. EMILY kneels down by the cot, dropping the pack, rubs one of CATHERINE's hands. It seems to calm the younger woman. ROSE dashes out the exterior door and comes back lugging dilapidated cardboard boxes which formerly held alcohol bottles, chip packets, etc., all of which she puts on the butcher block table. The door slams behind her. The commotion agitates CATHERINE, who jerks in her sleep.

EMILY: Do you have to crash around so? You're waking her up.

ROSE: (*Starts tossing utensils into a box.*) About time, if you ask me. I have a sale to organize. She wakes up, she can help. I don't care what her story is.

EMILY: (*Getting up, getting her satchel.*) Here. (*Pulls out a white butcher paper wrapped package, plunks it down on the butcher table.*) Frank gave me a deal. Fresh butchered yesterday. Prime cut.

ROSE: (*Opening the packet; poking meat.*) Looks pale, like it was bled too long.

EMILY: It's extra lean.

ROSE: Uh huh. We can think about food later. Now, grab a box and start packing. Let's see…

EMILY: I do not agree with your leaving, so I prefer not to help. (*She puts meat in large pot, adds water, puts pot on stove.*)

ROSE: I've declared a moratorium on your preferring not to. Is moratorium the word I want?

EMILY: It's good enough, suspension of action.

Scene 3

ZELDA's voice is heard singing O.S. before we see her. She is wearing a

11

sou'wester over black tights and a thigh-length T-shirt which carries the
motto Fisherwomen do it at Dawn, day-glo socks underneath high-heeled,
red tap shoes. Her red hair is punked with gel. A large fishing creel is slung
across her chest. She enters via exterior door and ends up in the center of the
kitchen by the time the minor key verse of "Go Tell Aunt Rhodie" ends.*

ZELDA: She died in the mill pond/Died in the mill pond/Died
in the mill pond/A-standing on her head. (*Looks around.*)

I see nothing but your usual chaos, Rose, good morning, Emily,
and a body. Oh. Now that is worth mentioning. (*She takes a closer
look at CATHERINE.*)

ROSE: Where's Marge?

ZELDA: She's a sensible woman. Went back to sleep. Now
then.

ZELDA takes her creel and upends it on the butcher block; it contains herbs,
roots, grasses, a mortar & pestle, a bottle of aspirin, and a small thermos.
She grinds up the matter, puts the mix in a cup, and pours hot water over.

ROSE: Coffee, Emily?

ZELDA: (*Stirs her herbal brew and settles herself on the floor next to
CATHERINE.*) I'll have a half caf decaf latte. Leave some
room.

ROSE: You'll have Yuban and like it.

ZELDA: Emily, we need her sitting up.

EMILY props CATHERINE in a sitting position. ZELDA dips her fin-
ger in the hot drink and rubs it on CATHERINE's lips. CATHERINE
makes a small moan. ZELDA repeats the process until CATHERINE's
lips open on their own and she drinks a sip or two. ROSE starts wrapping
things in wax paper.

ZELDA: (*Cont'd.*) We can leave her to come back on her own,
now. (*She has trouble standing; EMILY helps her all the way up, brings
over a bar stool. ZELDA sits and watches CATHERINE. EMILY
watches ZELDA watching CATHERINE and looks again in the pack
as if for instructions.*) You might as well make me some breakfast,
ROSE:. (*She strips off the sou'wester and steps out of the tap shoes.*) It
looks rather like morning fishing has been tabled on account of
inclement, uh, arrivals.

ROSE: If you want breakfast this morning, Miss High and
Mighty, you can fix it yourself or lump it. I'm leaving. The pub

isn't opening today. Today, tomorrow, or any other day. No coffee clutches, no lah-de-dah breakfasts, or any other kind of breakfasts, no late night suppers, I've had it. And I want my extra key back, Miss Emily.

ZELDA: Clutch?

EMILY: I thought it was klatch. (*Turns on burner under meat pot.*) I'm keeping the key. You never know when it might come handy.

ZELDA: Surely not clutch? Isn't that something about wild birds? Clotch?

ROSE: I'm LEAVING!

EMILY: No. She's not.

ZELDA: In that case, I'll have corned beef hash, with two eggs sunny side up, and a Dos Equis.

ROSE: (*Handing ZELDA a box of cereal.*) I don't suppose you know how to pack a box?

ZELDA angles her hip at ROSE, who removes a bottle of Tabasco sauce.

ROSE: What's this?

ZELDA: A house warming present. For your next smelly apartment over a pub… (*Points upward.*) … or an Army cot in a kitchen… (*Waves her hand at the cot.*)

CATHERINE pulls in a huge breath of air and stretches, nearly falling off the cot. The other women's eyes swivel to her. She blinks a few times, focuses, and stares into ZELDA's eyes.

ZELDA: (*Cont'd.*) Don't worry, you're reasonably safe.

CATHERINE opens her mouth to say something, swoons instead, and flops down on the cot again.

ZELDA: (Cont'd.) Hmmmmm. (*She raises CATHERINE's knees and takes off one hiking boot and sock. She begins massaging the foot and ankle gently.*)

ROSE: Hey! The only reason I stuck around here was because of Silas and you know it!

ZELDA: We are all the masters of our own fates, and…

ROSE: Stuff it, Zel. Pack a box or get out of my kitchen.

ZELDA: Don't use words like stuff. Shows a lack of breeding.

ROSE: I'm going to show you a lack of breeding the likes of which you've never seen in about five minutes if you don't back off.

EMILY: Rose? Could I have a cup of tea, please? How's she doing, Zelda? (*ZELDA has her head down, examining something near CATHERINE's ankle bone.*) Zelda?

Scene 4

LJ walks in the exterior door. He is in his ferry worker's garb—shirt, vest, jeans, cap, boots—and has a grim expression on his face. He clears his throat to be noticed. EMILY does.

EMILY: LJ?

LJ: Miss Emily.

EMILY: What are you doing here?

LJ: We need one of you to come.

ROSE: Who's we?

LJ: Sheriff Nate Hooper, Sergeant Findlay Furst, me. Down to the ferry dock.

EMILY: LJ, I wish you wouldn't look so, well, serious.

LJ: It's serious business.

EMILY: Oh. Well, then. I'll come.

ROSE: I'll go with you, Em. You don't have to face whatever it is alone.

ZELDA: I'll come, too.

ROSE: You stay here. With the young one. (*She grabs a jacket off the coat rack.*) If she wakes up, set her to packing a box or three.

EMILY and ROSE exit quickly, noisily, with LJ via the exterior door.

Scene 5

ZELDA pulls up the folding chair, sits, and examines CATHERINE very closely, starting with her face, lifting her hair, turning her hands, returning to consider her ankle. CATHERINE finally comes fully awake. She sits on the edge of the cot, palms on knees, before getting up. The first thing she does is look around for her back pack. She opens it, removes the crackers, and munches on several.

CATHERINE: Is this a kitchen?

ZELDA: Yes.

CATHERINE: Is there any 7-Up in here?

ZELDA: Never seen any, but you're welcome to look.

14

ZELDA watches CATHERINE rummage through the frig and cupboards. CATHERINE comes up with a can of ginger ale. She pops the top and takes a large swallow.

ZELDA: (*Cont'd.*) How many months?

CATHERINE: Not quite three.

ZELDA: It'll pass.

CATHERINE: What, the baby or the nausea? (*CATHERINE suddenly gets up and starts prowling around the kitchen, absently touching things, putting a carrot peeler in her pocket, sniffing at the meat mixture which is burbling on the stove.*) This smells like old socks.

ZELDA: Turn off the flame.

CATHERINE: (*On the prowl again.*) Who are you?

ZELDA: Why don't we start with me asking you that question?

CATHERINE: Where is this place?

ZELDA: No, let's go back to who are you. Then we'll advance to where you are, maybe step back a bit and cover where you've come from, launch ahead some to where you're going. Like that. So. Who are you?

CATHERINE: (*Stops at the butcher block, whacks at a cabbage with a cleaver, puts the carrot peeler back.*) My name is CATHERINE.

ZELDA: Good start.

CATHERINE: Now you.

ZELDA: Zelda. My mother was startled by Fitzgerald's writing.

CATHERINE: And where I am is?

ZELDA: You are in the kitchen of Silas' Pub, in the town of Langley, on Whidbey Island, in Washington State, the Pacific Northwest, U-nited States of Am....

CATHERINE: (*Overlap; moving around butcher block.*)
In a bar on Whidbey Is... (She staggers, as if hit.) Oh, god, Whidbey Island. (*She sinks to the floor.*)

ZELDA: (*Looking down at her.*) What is it?

CATHERINE: I just remembered why I'm here and, oh, no, I'm gonna be sick.

ZELDA: Toilet's through there (*pointing*), on your left.

CATHERINE lurches up, exits interior door.

Scene 6

While CATHERINE is off stage, ZELDA, humming, slices up the cabbage, and slides the chopped onions and garlic into the meat mixture on the stove. CATHERINE enters interior door, her face pale. She crosses to sit on the cot. ZELDA steps next to her and pushes her head down.

ZELDA: Get your head between your knees.

CATHERINE pops her head up in protest.

ZELDA: (*Cont'd.*) Go on, do it.

ZELDA sits again and waits while CATHERINE has her head down. After a moment, CATHERINE lifts her head.

CATHERINE: I came here to find the father of this baby. To look him in the… I needed to look him in the eye, to help me decide about keeping it. I'm forty-four and this pregnancy is my first and where I've come from is my look-out, so is where I'm going. So if you don't mind, or even if you do, thanks for listening and whatever else you did, but I have to leave now.

(*She gets up and pulls on her back pack.*)

ZELDA: What about your mother?

CATHERINE: I beg your pardon?

ZELDA: Wouldn't your mother like a grand child?

CATHERINE: I don't have a mother.

ZELDA: I see. Father?

CATHERINE: Haven't got one of those either.

ZELDA: No, maybe not. (*Points to CATHERINE's stomach.*) Did you find him? Look him in the eye?

CATHERINE: Not yet.

ZELDA: What do you do for work?

CATHERINE: (*Losing patience.*) I appreciate you helping me. But nothing about me is your business.

ZELDA: True. What kind of work do you do?

CATHERINE: I write.

ZELDA: Babies like stories. (*She goes to stir meat mixture on stove.*) Have you got a vehicle somewhere? An actual destination? Anybody looking out their window for you?

CATHERINE: My van's across the Sound in a parking lot. Listen, I… This is nuts. I'm just going to leave now…

ZELDA: Well, then. If nobody's expecting you, why not stay

awhile? Help me cook? Have a little lunch? My friends will be back soon. Whatever happened down at the ferry dock should make a good story for a writer to chew on. Here. (*She holds out a wooden spoon and the dish of chopped garlic and onions.*) Sauté these in with the beef. Stir them up good.

CATHERINE: (*Hesitating at the interior doorway.*) I am hungry…

Scene 7

The exterior door bursts open. ROSE tumbles in, followed by EMILY, who is holding the sides of her face with her hands. The two look like they've seen a ghost.

ZELDA: Here they are now, and, from the look of them, with something big to say.

CATHERINE: But I'm leaving right after I eat.

ZELDA: These onions are not going to stir themselves.

CATHERINE: takes the dish of onions and garlic and the spoon from ZELDA and goes to the stove. Her pack she keeps slung over her shoulder. ZELDA shifts her attention to the other two, who have drawn up the stools and sit, like statues, at the butcher block table.

ZELDA (*Cont'd.*) There's a big table in the pub with some respectable wooden chairs. Go bring two.

CATHERINE: I am not going and bringing anything.

ZELDA: Do you want to hear this story?

After a beat, CATHERINE trots out the interior door and returns with the chairs. ZELDA takes one and sits on it, beckoning CATHERINE to sit on the other. They look expectantly at the other two, who still sit as if in a daze. ROSE breaks the silence.

ROSE: If I hadn't a seen it …

EMILY: Never in a million years …

ROSE: I always reckoned he'd go off with that good old bunch from the rifle club and get himself killed.

EMILY: He hated guns.

ROSE: That's why … it makes some kind of crazy sense, you know?

EMILY: But he didn't shoot himself. Or get shot. No shooting.

ZELDA: Who didn't get shot?

ROSE: (*Taking a moment to focus on ZELDA and CATHERINE,*

who, in spite of herself, is interested.) You're awake. Well (*turning to point*), there's a box over there...

EMILY: Rose! Oh, Zelda… honey, it's Silas.

ROSE: Explains why he didn't answer the phone, that's for damn sure.

ZELDA: From the looks on your faces, whatever this is, it's not another of his usual pranks.

EMILY: (*Getting up and standing behind ZELDA, hands on her shoulders.*) ccording to Sheriff Furst, he fetched up under the ferry cables round about three a m. Just wearing his old jeans. (*Pause.*) With the fly open. (*Pause.*) One tennis shoe on. (*Pause.*) No socks. (*Pause.*) Findlay figured he was drunk, wandering around on the fishing pier. Took a piss off the edge and fell in.

ROSE: I always figured he'd get himself shot. In the end.

ZELDA: Silas drunk?

ROSE: How's that gonna be for his obit? Silas Horner, pillar of the community, blah blah blah. Pillar. Huh! I could offer a few home truths about his pillar…

EMILY: Remember the time he went down to California to that Renaissance Faire, all dressed up like a hunched-back pirate? And he put the moves on that woman with a hump costume? Only it turned out hers was real?

ZELDA: I always liked the story of Silas losing his dead grandmother.

ROSE: The dead don't like it if you roll them up in a rug and leave them on the top of a Volkswagen van while you're taking a dump in the woods. They get cranky and disappear when that happens.

ZELDA: She was found, wasn't she? (*Beat.*) What was Silas doing on a fishing pier? He hated fishing as much as he hated hunting. And drinking. (*She stands, stretching out her back.*)

CATHERINE: You mean someone you know's died?

ROSE: You could say that. You surely could. (*She gets up and absently continues wrapping things up, only now it's food stuffs.*) Remember that time we all had us a fight over a Beatles song… something about who wrote Blackbird… and, Zel… (*ZELDA quickly moves next to ROSE, whispers something in her ear.*)

18

ROSE: (*Shrugging ZELDA off.*) …you said it was John, and you Em, you said it was Paul… but all along Silas said it was George, and…

ZELDA keeps on whispering. ROSE finally gets the message, shuts up, and shakes her head, no, in disbelief. EMILY, meanwhile, moves next to CATHERINE, and tugs on the younger woman's back pack.

EMILY: Tell me about one of those far away places you've been to.

DURING EMILY's and CATHERINE's brief exchange following, ZELDA clamps a hand on one of ROSE's arms and pulls her out of ear shot of the other two. ROSE resists; ZELDA keeps whispering; ROSE stops in her tracks. Looks in astonishment at CATHERINE.

CATHERINE: (*Small smile.*) Searching an unconscious woman's belongings is… oh, well, why not. (*She removes the map of New Zealand and shakes it out so both can look.*) Here. I've been to Auckland and Paraparamu (*NOTE TO ACTOR: PRONOUNCED LIKE PARACHUTE, PARA PAR AM, LONG A's*) and Dunedin (*NOTE: LONG E, EMPHASIS ON THE E*) on the South Island.

EMILY: (*Peers at map and tries to pronounce it.*) Para, parmua,…

CATHERINE: It's Para par am.

ROSE: (*Interrupting*) I, uh… (*She has to clear her throat a few times.*) Emily… uh… there's a… uh… oh, hell, I… uh…

ZELDA: (*Coming to her rescue.*) Emily? Something happened out in the pub when you were gone. I need help to set things right.

EMILY: But shouldn't Rose see to whatever it is? Besides, Catherine and I are just getting to know each other…

ZELDA has one of EMILY's arms in a vise grip.

ZELDA: Catherine isn't going anywhere… for a while. Come on, help me.

EMILY pats CATHERINE on the shoulder, smiles, and follows ZELDA out the interior door.

Scene 8

ROSE moves to sit on one of the wooden chairs. She folds her arms tight across her chest and stares at CATHERINE for a long beat.

ROSE: You have any other names besides Catherine?

CATHERINE: Is it important?

19

ROSE: I like to know who it is wakes me up by falling down on my dumpster.

CATHERINE: Catherine Page.

ROSE: Page.

CATHERINE: Nice last name for a writer.

ROSE: Oh. For a writer. Not your own, then.

CATHERINE: I never knew my own.

ROSE: Adopted, huh. By nice people, I'll bet.

CATHERINE: What difference does that make? (*She gets up and prowls again.*)

ROSE: None, none a tall, no problem. Nada. Zippo. Could not care less.

CATHERINE: (*Finds and puts back on her sock and boot.*) Uh huh. I'm sorry you all lost your friend, he sounds like he was an interesting character. But I really do have to leave. Now.

ROSE: What's he like, the daddy? (*Pointing to CATHERINE's belly.*)

Scene 9

LJ enters from the exterior door, followed by EMILY and ZELDA returning via the interior door. He solemnly puts a soggy tennis shoe on the butcher block, rests a gentle hand on the top of ROSE's head, dips his head in admiration to EMILY, hands a piece of folded paper to ZELDA, and exits the exterior door.

Scene 10

CATHERINE takes the opportunity to leave, to follow LJ out, but gets hit by another fainting spell. Down she goes. ZELDA, EMILY, and ROSE all look down at her, waiting.

ZELDA: We have an obligation on our hands.

ROSE: Can't we sing instead?

EMILY: (*Mulls, then offers.*) Row, row, row your boat/Gently down the stream/Merrily, merrily, merrily, merrily/Life is but a dream.

ZELDA: Stop it, you two. We have a decision to… oh, here she comes.

CATHERINE: (*Coming to.*) It's cold down here. (*Pause.*) I feel

20

unsettled.

EMILY: You look it, too. Sort of emotionally uncoordinated, if you get my meaning.

CATHERINE: Why aren't you crying? Washing away? Aren't people supposed to cry when someone you know dies?

ZELDA: He hated tears. "Gravestones cheer the living dear, they're no use to the dead."

ROSE: Nitty Gritty Dirt Band.

EMILY: I don't know why I should be crying. He thought I was crazy.

ZELDA: There was a time when he didn't. And even if he did, you didn't care.

ROSE: Look who's talking. The whole town gets up in arms over her sexual shenanigans—does she care? Nah.

ZELDA: And where were you the summer of fifty-seven?

CATHERINE: What are you all talking, or not talking, about? (*She extends a hand.*) Would someone help me up?

ZELDA: We are not talking. We're silly women making silly noises. (*She helps CATHERINE to her feet and to a chair. Her glare at the other two is fierce.*)

ROSE: (Spits it out.) The summer of fifty-seven Silas and I were shacked up on the Snohomish River.

EMILY: He said I was crazy as an uncaught butterfly, that time, on Craggs Peak.

ZELDA: (*Glancing at the paper LJ handed her.*) Well, well. Would you listen to this. (*Reading.*) I quote. No, I don't. (*She tucks the paper in a pocket.*)

EMILY: Zel… ?

ROSE: Damn his eyes! (*She throws a few pots and pans for emphasis.*)

ZELDA: I said, never mind.

EMILY scootches up to ZELDA, trying to get the paper out of her pocket. ZELDA pushes her away.

ZELD: (*Cont'd.*) Just some silly nonsense about asking the Three Graces to stand watch. Satisfied?

EMILY: Oh, good heavens. That sounds like he meant to…

ROSE: Damn his pecker! (*She throws a frying pan.*)

ZELDA: We have more important business on our hands! All

21

of us! (*Beat.*) Rose? Did you attend to it? (*ROSE: shakes her head, 'no'. ZELDA gives a huge sigh.*) As usual, wiser heads will have to prevail. Catherine:, sit down.

CATHERINE stands up.

ZELDA: (*Cont'd.*) Did you never wonder who your birth mother was? Is?

CATHERINE: (*Shrugs.*) She gave me up. Why should I?

ZELDA: Because she's here.

CATHERINE: Where?

EMILY: In this kitchen.

CATHERINE: (*Sitting down.*) What?

ROSE lifts her shoulders and lets them drop.

CATHERINE: (*Cont'd.*) You?

ROSE nods. Drops her eyes. EMILY and ZELDA watch CATHERINE, expecting her to swoon again. She does just the opposite, sitting up straighter, seemingly stronger, standing full up.

CATHERINE: (*Cont'd.*) You're my mother.

ROSE: For all my sins.

CATHERINE: No, you're not.

ROSE: You got a birthmark on your ankle, outside side. Shaped like this here island. Right?

CATHERINE nods, slowly.

ROSE: (*Cont'd*) I seen it after you slid out of me with your feet tucked up behind your head like an acrobat. Before I gave you to the nuns on Shaw Island.

CATHERINE: (Stunned.) What? After... huh... Before... You... Mmmm. Gave me to the...

ZELDA: We saw it, too, that morning.

EMILY: That's right, honey. You were born right here in this kitchen. We helped.

CATHERINE: (It slowly sinks in.) Well, ain't that a hoot.

ROSE: A hoot? You're calling me a hoot?

CATHERINE: The situation. That's the hoot. (*She starts to laugh, hooting.*)

EMILY: (*Goes to dampen a towel.*) An odd reaction.

ZELDA: Shock. Pure and simple. Catherine. Sit down and put your head between your legs.

CATHERINE is moving fast around the kitchen, picking up things and putting them down, laughing. EMILY follows, trying to apply the damp cloth.

ROSE: (*to ZELDA*) That's for fainting.

ZELDA: It worked before.

CATHERINE: (*Winding it up.*) And I suppose Silas was my father! That would make it perfect! What a great plot line! Pregnant 44-year-old goes back to the scene of the impregnation only to find her long lost mother holed up in a bar! And her dead daddy crab bait under the ferry dock! Fabulous! I can hear the roar of applause! Oscar! Tony! (*She gulps; looks a bit green, runs for the toilet, exiting interior door.*)

Scene 11

ZELDA, EMILY and ROSE stare at CATHERINE's retreating back. A KNOCK is heard at the exterior door.

ZELDA, EMILY, ROSE: CLOSED!

The three older women stand as if waiting for something. Then, ROSE returns to her packing. ZELDA starts to pack her herbs and potions into her creel. EMILY starts unpacking the boxes ROSE packs.

ZELDA: We'll need to organize the funeral.

EMILY: Funkhauser's.

ROSE: We'll have to find someone else. Didn't you hear? Funkhauser's been charging people to cremate their dead and all along he's been burying the bodies back in the woods and nobody knew till Janie Crain smelled something bad when she was hiking there and tripped over a bone.

ZELDA: Nonsense. Small town gossip. Never proved.

EMILY: Poor souls.

Scene 12

CATHERINE enters from interior door.

CATHERINE: (*Stalking up to ROSE.*) I don't believe it. Birthmark or no birthmark. What's a birthmark? I have decided, and therefore it is not true. We, you and me, we are not related.

ROSE: We are. Stay and we'll have a test. Or go. Take it or leave it.

CATHERINE: I'm leaving it. Right now. (*She exits the exterior door in a huff.*)

ZELDA: Pity. It would have been lively having a young one around.

Long pause.

EMILY: (*Taking ROSE in her arms.*) Honey? Could it be true? About Silas?

ROSE: I don't know… summer of fifty-seven saw a bit of action…

EMILY: … a butterfly…

ZELDA: Save us the sordid details of your ancient sex life,

ROSE:. (*Plunks her creel down on the butcher block table and sits.*) I am still waiting for that cup of coffee.

EMILY exits interior door, returns carrying three pewter mugs and a whiskey bottle. She puts the mugs down on the butcher block table and pours out. ZELDA is the first to swig down a hearty gulp. ROSE sits and stares at the whiskey bottle.

ROSE: You remember that summer, Em, so hot you could fry eggs on the sidewalk. Zel, you was off on one of them bone digs you used to go to? and Em was sailing with Margie and LJ up by the San Juan's. That left me and Silas, all on our lonesomes. (*She stands, digs in a box, retrieves a framed photo.*) When he asked me to marry him, up there on the river, I told Silas no, but said I'd run his pub if I could live upstairs. I was getting kind of cold in that drafty trailer. He liked the idea, remember, Zel? He could keep his pub but not have to be responsible for running it, he had an extra woman he could visit now and then when it suited both of us… and he could keep his shack a woman-free zone, the way he liked it. (*The other two laugh gently.*) And then what happens? He starts wandering off all over the place and before you know it I'm doing all the cleaning and the cooking and the bartending, trade's falling off because I can't keep up, bills coming due I don't have any right to pay… (*Pause. She takes a slug directly from the whiskey bottle.*) So now he's dead. So now I can leave.

EMILY: You can't go now.

ROSE: Watch me. (*She gets up. EMILY pulls her back down.*)

24

Turn me loose, old woman.

ZELDA: No need to be surly, Rose. Emily's right. You can't leave now.

CURTAIN

END OF ACT I

ACT II

Scene 1

SETTING: Interior, kitchen. Immediately following Act I

AT RISE: *CATHERINE enters from the exterior door. She walks as if in a trance to the table, looks at the wet tennis shoe, picks it up, drops it as if it burns her hand.*

CATHERINE: (*Speaking to the air.*) He wore shoes like this, last summer. No socks. But there must be millions like these…

(*She looks anxiously at the other three.*)

ZELDA, EMILY, ROSE: (*On top of each other.*) Oh, yes, certainly, millions, find them everywhere, can't turn over a rock without coming up with one of this kind… etc.

CATHERINE: Because if there aren't, and this was his, and he's this baby's father, and he's my father…

All the women stand still for a long, silent beat. EMILY breaks the moment. She finds a bottle of milk and pours some in one of the pewter mugs. ZELDA puts her arms around CATHERINE and helps her to sit on the cot. She pushes ROSE to sit next to the younger woman. After a moment, she puts ROSE's arm around CATHERINE's shoulder. CATHERINE and ROSE sit for a moment, then ROSE drops her arm and stands up. She returns to her packing in an absent sort of way.

EMILY: Catherine, come over here and have a drink of this, honey.

CATHERINE: What's the point? I can't keep this baby.

ZELDA: Why not?

CATHERINE: Why not? Why not? Are you out of your mind? (*Jumps up and prowls.*)

EMILY: A baby's coming. Does it matter why?

CATHERINE: I don't fucking believe this.

ZELDA: We don't swear in the kitchen, miss.

CATHERINE: Oh, that's rich. You don't swear in the kitchen,

25

but you don't mind that my baby might be the child of my father…

ROSE: Silas was a good man, in his way. (*She holds up the framed photograph.*) He drank too much and ran around with women too much, some said…

ZELDA: Can we help it if we live in a backwater, unenlightened village that can't see beyond its collective prejudicial nose? Noses?

EMILY: The man was a hound, but had a way about him that you couldn't stay mad at.

ROSE: (*Handing CATHERINE the framed photograph.*) And he wasn't my only summer of fifty-seven, so it's just possible he wasn't your daddy.

ZELDA: Well, now, Rose!

CATHERINE brings the photograph close to her face, then extends it a bit to see the image better. Her other hand goes, with a life of its own, to rest briefly on her belly.

EMILY: I know, that musician, what was his name? Up to his eyeballs in broken guitar strings?

ROSE: Wasn't no musician.

ZELDA: Findlay Furst!

ROSE: Pooh.

EMILY: Nate Hooper!

ZELDA and EMILY: LJ!

ROSE: Not LJ, or either of them other clowns, neither. I just want this young one to know Silas might not be her daddy. (*Picks up a box and looks in it as if for inspiration.*)

CATHERINE: (*Looking up from the photograph.*) Might not be.

ROSE: Pretty good chance not. And that's all I'm saying.

CATHERINE: But you do still say you're my mother.

EMILY: Honey, Rosie had her baby at a hard time, and it was even harder for her to give you up. See, she was orphaned herself…

ROSE: I'll tell this part, if you don't mind.

CATHERINE: (To no one in particular.) It's really him. Now he's dead… (*Puts a hand against her belly again.*) …what do I do about you?…

26

ZELDA: (*Mirroring.*) …what do I do about you?… That line…
what do I do about… (*to CATHERINE; sudden dawning*) You're
Catherine Page. You wrote that book, *The Forgotten Children*.
And someone's made a play out of it… what's it called?

EMILY: *The Forgotten Children.* I saw a review in the Arts section
of the paper… my word, you're famous!

CATHERINE: No, I'm not. (*She puts the framed photograph down
on the table.*)

ROSE: Well I'm damned. What's your book about?

CATHERINE: (*Standing eye-to-eye with ROSE.*) It's about girl
children who get left behind, or tossed out with the trash, or
dumped on a stranger's doorstep…

ROSE: I never done that with you, missy, so back off.

EMILY: She only ever wanted the best for you, honey…

ZELDA: That's the truth, sweetheart…

EMILY and ZELDA get busy stirring soup.

EMILY: She always wished she'd gotten to know you…

ROSE: You two stay out of this. It's between her and me now.
So what's it going to be?

CATHERINE: You tell me. Mother.

*ROSE looks in the box again, then at CATHERINE. SLOW SPOT on
CATHERINE and ROSE. Rest of stage drops to darkness.*

ROSE: Mother.

Scene 2 Late Afternoon Same Day

*A few changes are evident in the kitchen of Silas's Pub. On the floor, a
cradle is in the process of being constructed out of wood. ROSE's boxes,
filled and taped shut, are piled up almost obscuring the rear wall. The
center butcher block table has been replaced with a round wooden table and
five straight-backed chairs. On it are a tool box, a couple of saws, the pieces
for building a changing table, and an Indian cradleboard. CATHERINE
is talking on the telephone, quietly. She hangs up and moves to sit at the
table. Her thoughts are elsewhere. ROSE enters from interior door, dragging
another loaded box.*

CATHERINE: Can you give me a ride down to the ferry?

ROSE: Tomorrow, not today. I'm catching the 8:15 tomorrow
morning. Take it or leave it.

CATHERINE: Tomorrow's fine. I'll take it.

ROSE: Leaving here at 7:30. No later.

CATHERINE: I'll be ready. Can I bed down here tonight?

ZELDA enters from exterior door, bringing with her a dead owl. She crosses to the Indian cradleboard and puts the owl down on the table. She strokes its feathers.

ZELDA: I just love serendipity in action. Emily told me me she wanted something soft, and I come across this dead owl behind the dumpster. Getting to be a regular habit, us finding things out there.

CATHERINE: Things?

ZELDA: Special things. Important things.

EMILY enters from interior door. She crosses to the stove, consults the stew pot.

ZELDA: (*Cont'd.*) Things we want and need. Things of great value. Things…

EMILY: (*Spies and takes the owl from ZELDA.*) Just what we need. Down feathers. For the lining.

ZELDA: Might be something soft, cottony, in the lost and found at the laundromat we could use, too.

EMILY: (Starting out the exterior door.) We need to match colors.

ZELDA: (*To CATHERINE.*) If Rose is being difficult, you can stay with Marge and me tonight. (*She, EMILY, and the owl exit via exterior door.*)

Scene 3

CATHERINE: Perhaps that's better.

ROSE: Than what?

CATHERINE: I don't know, than us tripping over each other? Calling each other names? Finding out the truth about each other? Take your pick.

Mother and daughter shift their positions around the stage; never coming close, never going far away. ROSE breaks the moment.

ROSE: Well. If you want to use up some time, help me move these boxes (*Tries to shift one; it's too heavy for her alone.*)

EMILY returns via exterior door for the cradleboard.

ROSE: (*Cont'd.*) God, what do I have in here? Guess I should have labeled them. (*Pause.*) So this is what life comes down to, a stack of unmarked boxes. (*Pause.*) Isn't anyone going to help me?

CATHERINE: I will. Don't want us to miss that morning ferry.

EMILY: (*Quickly moving to her.*) You'll do no such thing! That baby needs a quiet start.

CATHERINE: This start is not going to finish. It's over tomorrow afternoon.

EMILY: But you can't!!

ZELDA returns via exterior door, the dead owl and some cotton flannel bits in her hand. She puts them down on the table.

CATHERINE: I can and I am. I came here to find the man who got me pregnant.

EMILY: The father of your baby!

CATHERINE: The man. I found him. He's dead.

EMILY: But you've found your mother! Rose? Honey? What've you got to say about this? You have to stop her! Zelda! Help me! We've got to stop this!

ROSE: Simmer down, Em, you'll make yourself sick.

ZELDA: (*Removing a rolled joint from a pocket.*) Here. Suck on this. It'll settle your nerves.

EMILY: I don't want to settle! Catherine, you can't stop that baby from coming, you just can't! I forbid you!!

ROSE: Em…

ZELDA: This is going too far… (*Puts joint on the table.*)

CATHERINE: The only way I'm going to keep sane about any of this is to have an abortion, which I'm doing, tomorrow, in a women's clinic in Seattle.

EMILY: When did you set this all up? (*EMILY is beyond furious.*)

CATHERINE: A little while ago.

EMILY: NO!!! You WILL NOT!!

CATHERINE: What other choice do I have? (*Touches EMILY.*) No, I mean, really. What other choice? (*Sits again.*)

ZELDA: (*Sitting at the table with CATHERINE.*) Let me tell you about choices. (*Pause.*) I had my first abortion when I was seventeen in the back of a liquor store in Ensenada, Mexico. Nineteen hundred and fifty nine. (*Pause.*) Very illegal. Very scary. And extra strange because I rode home flat out in the back of my boy friend's hearse. He used the thing for hauling surf board blanks up and down the California Coast. But that's another story. (*Pause.*) Had my second when I was thirty-two, compliments of Planned Parenthood, after they allowed as how I wasn't insane, just. Well. And my third. Now, here's another hoot for you. The city of the Angels gave poor women abortions and then sterilized them. For free. Sign up here, girls, and your worries are over. Your babies, too. Gave me an abortion and then sterilized me. No babies. Ever. (*Pause.*) Free? (*Pause.*) If you ask me, would I have done it differently? (*She waits to be asked.*)

CATHERINE: I'll ask.

ZELDA: Impossible question. I thought I had no way out, each time, and those were the choices I made.

CATHERINE: And now? If you could go back in time, now…?

ZELDA: We can't go back, that's never a choice, but we are here, right now, and Emily's building a cradle.

Scene 4

MARJORIE enters from exterior door. She is wearing an odd assortment of clothes that seem to stick to her as if they have just been pulled from the dryer and tossed on her body, and carries a plastic laundry basket full of more clothes. She takes in ROSE, fussing with her boxes, and the other three at the table. She crosses to them and sits.

MARJORIE: I declare, I'm going to have to fire Bitsy's ass.

ZELDA: What now?

MARJORIE: Can't leave that girl alone two minutes but she's gone and strangled someone's shirts in the dryer. Look at this mess!

They all look at the clothes stuck to her body.

CATHERINE: Why are you wearing them?

MARJORIE: I had to show somebody!

ZELDA: (To CATHERINE.) Marge is a lawyer in her other life, honey. A great believer in evidence, she is.

The phone RINGS. ROSE crosses and answers.

30

ROSE: Yeah? (*Listens.*) Sure, I'll tell her. G'bye, Bitsy. (*Hangs up; to MARJORIE.*) Bitsy said to tell you she can't work at the laundry tomorrow.

MARJORIE: Oh, great. What was her excuse this time?

ROSE: Her grandmother died.

MARJORIE: That makes her fifth dead grandmother this year. Something's going to have to be done.

ZELDA: (*At the stove.*) I vote we eat some of this good stew. That's what we do.

EMILY: Second the motion. (*She starts to dish up.*)

MARJORIE: (*Heading out the exterior door.*) I've got an imbecile to deal with. Save me a bowl!

EMILY: Go easy on her, Marjorie. She's young.

MARJORIE: And not going to get any older the rate she's going! (*MARJORIE exits.*)

Scene 5

ROSE: Poor Bitsy. I wouldn't want to be on the wrong end of Marge's wrath…

O.S. we HEAR a sudden slam of metal against metal, HEAR a high-pitched metallic scraping sound, HEAR a series of thuds, a crash, and a woman's VOICE screaming swear words. The women all leap up and start for the exterior door.

Scene 6

MARJORIE bursts in, blocking their exit. Her laundry basket is ripped and spilling out its contents. She looks very un-MARJORIE-like, frantic. The following exchange is rapid, overlapping.

MARJORIE: (*Shouting*) My God! Son-of-a-bitch nearly ran me down!

CATHERINE: Who?

ROSE: What was that horrible noise?

ZELDA: What's happened?

EMILY: Is anyone hurt?

ROSE: MARGE!! What the hell happened?

MARJORIE: (*Tossing down her laundry basket, straightening herself.*) I was very nearly killed is what happened!

ROSE: (*Running to look out window.*) But that sound…
(*Screams.*) My TRUCK!!! (*ROSE runs out the exterior door.*)
*CATHERINE looks out the window; follows ROSE out the exterior
door. EMILY pours MARJORIE a restorative drink; MARJORIE
gulps it down.*

MARJORIE: I was coming out of my laundromat with our
wash… sorry, Zel, but I think your black evening gown got
caught under the bastard's wheels…

ZELDA: (*Hugging MARJORIE.*) Never mind the damn gown.
A bunch of cloth, who cares.

MARJORIE: Before I could holler, watch it, this huge black
semi…

EMILY: Black truck? No one in the village drives a black truck.

MARJORIE: This was a 16-wheeler, at least, the thing comes
racing around the corner, crashes into Rose's pickup, slides it
along the curb like it was a toy, almost plows into me, the laundry basket gets snagged on the exhaust, this is all that's left,
and the fucker keeps on driving!

EMILY: I'll get Findlay on the phone.

*ROSE: returns via interior door on the trot, raging, beats EMILY to the
phone, picks up receiver, dials 911.*

ROSE: (*Yelling full throttle.*) Emergency! My wheels! No, not
seals! Wheels, you idiot! (*She bangs the receiver against the phone;
then yells into it again.*) My pickup's been killed! Get someone
over here NOW!!

EMILY: (*Takes the phone away and talks.*) Hello? I'm sorry, yes, it's
an emergency, of sorts, but I think Sheriff Furst can handle it.
Thank you. (*She hangs up and turns to put out bowls, etc.*)

ROSE: MY PICKUP IS DEAD!! (*She flops down at the table, puts
her head down, and bangs it not-so gently.*) Now what?!

CATHERINE enters exterior door; sits.

CATHERINE: Whole side's mashed in, sort of like a one-di-
mensional cartoon cut-out, leaning up against the curb. Looks
like something in a nightmare.

ROSE: It's my nightmare! That truck was my way out of town!

CATHERINE: Well, your horse is dead.

ROSE: But what do I do about my wheels!!

ZELDA: You say a few words over them, shoot straight, bury the corpse out at the dump, and give up all this talk of leaving. For once and for all. Here. (*Picks the joint up and hands it to ROSE.*)

ROSE: (*Nearly shredding all the joint.*) Stop that. I don't need getting stoned, I need to know what to do!

EMILY: (*Leaves off fixing the meal, sitting next to ROSE; putting hands on her face, focusing ROSE's gaze on hers.*) Last week, the doc said Harold could live another ten years. That day, I wished I'd had a gun.

ZELDA: Oh, now, Em...

EMILY: Truly. One of those Saturday night specials you hear about. There's nothing to him anymore, just sparrow bones and skin. At night, I watch his puny little chest flutter up and down, like a starved bird, like a miser hanging onto his gold, the way he breathes. And I wish I had me a gun.

CATHERINE: That's no solution.

EMILY: I know it doesn't make any sense, not when you look at it from a distance. But in those few hours I can call my own, in the middle of the night, I reach under my skirt with my fingers and rub myself, and I think of Harold dead. But I don't do anything about it. I don't get a gun, I get on with things. And you will too, Rosie. You'll put aside all talk of leaving and get on with the things right in front of you.

CATHERINE: (*To ROSE.*) I know it's none of my business, but what are you running away from?

ZELDA: Oh, honey, our Rosie tries on an escape every now and again.

ROSE: Nothing.

CATHERINE: Then forget it, like Emily says. Or buy another vehicle and go.

ROSE: Yeah. I'll get a four-wheel rig. Maybe in red. Purple? Forest green?

ZELDA: Remember when she started the grease fire, Em? That one could've been bad, but all that happened was she had to track Silas down to repair the back kitchen wall. (*Goes to stand next to ROSE; touches her.*) My all-time favorite has to be when she took Marge's dinghy out into the Bay, punched holes in the

33

hull, and waited for the thing to fill up so she could drown.

MARJORIE: Can you believe a woman living all her life on this island who doesn't know the tides?

ROSE: I didn't get out far enough before I got stuck on a shifting sand bar. Sat there for hours like a right fool in a boat full of water going nowhere. (*To ZELDA and EMILY.*) You two were no help, standing on the shore, laughing your heads off.

ZELDA: I think it's about time we started looking at all of this as a sign.

ROSE: Don't hand me that woo-woo, airy-fairy malarkey.

EMILY: No, Zelda's right. A sign. First, Catherine washes up on our shore…

ROSE: She landed…

CATHERINE: I fainted…

EMILY: Then, a truck comes roaring by. There's never ever been a big black truck in this village. Trucks don't come through here, we're not a thru-way to anywhere. But today one comes and… blam. You're grounded.

MARJORIE: Somebody needs to get Silas in the ground. (*To CATHERINE:.*) You have an appointment at the clinic in Seattle tomorrow?

CATHERINE: How did you know?

MARJORIE: It's an island thing.

CATHERINE: Yes, but…

MARJORIE: No buts. You need to call and cancel that and be here for Silas' funeral.

ZELDA and EMILY ad lib: Oh, yes, stay honey, we need you here, your place is here, etc.

ROSE: Leave the girl alone. She can make up her own mind.

CATHERINE: Girl?

MARJORIE: Girl, woman, Catherine the Great, you're staying. So are you, Rose.

ROSE: Wait a damn minute, don't I get a say here?

MARJORIE: No. (*To CATHERINE.*) What's the number of the clinic?

CATHERINE: (*Handing MARJORIE a slip of paper.*) But…

Scene 7 Three Days Later

A gaudy Christmas wreath hangs over the window. CATHERINE's back pack dangles from a chair back. CATHERINE enters, draped in a multi-colored serape over her skirt and cardigan. She is followed by ROSE, who is dressed now in a 1950's tea dress, hat with veil, gloves, and low-heeled pumps; EMILY, wrapped in an over-large man's full-length overcoat over her coveralls and sporting a carpenter's cap; ZELDA, who has added a turquoise feather-boa over her sou'wester, and MARJORIE, dressed in a modern skirted suit and 3-inch heels, all dark maroon. MARJORIE carries a dark maroon leather briefcase, a chart, and telescoped pointer. She also carries a square box covered in brown paper. She crosses to the table, puts these down on it, and sits. CATHERINE starts poking through the cupboards, looking for something.

MARJORIE: My laundromat won't run itself, so let's get on with the business at hand.

ZELDA: (Rummaging in the frig.) I'm not getting on with anything until I have some food. Rose? Why don't you have anything decent to eat in here?

ROSE: *(Picking up a box and moving it towards the outer door.)* I'm eating at the diner until I go tomorrow.

ZELDA: That wreck you bought won't get you any further south than the road out of town.

ROSE: I have faith. And a full set of tools

MARJORIE: Full set of holes in the head, more like it.

ROSE: Why, Margie, I didn't know you cared.

MARJORIE sticks out her tongue at ROSE and consults her watch.

EMILY: (*Drops her coat and makes to start working on the cradle on the floor.*) Rosie, honey, I need some more wood glue, but my truck's acting up. Pick me up some at True Value, won't you. They open at nine tomorrow.

ROSE: *(Moving another box toward the door.)* I'll be gone by eight.

CATHERINE: *(Her search fruitless.)* Anyone got a ferry schedule?

All the women remove same from pockets and hold them out. CATHERINE takes one from MARJORIE.

ZELDA: Well, we have to have something to eat, to mark the occasion.

35

MARJORIE: (*Consulting her watch.*) I vote we mark it by me reading his will.

EMILY: (*Crosses to the phone and dials; into receiver.*) Hi, Vern. I'm at Silas'. We'll be needing the works. Do you have some of that nice meatloaf? Oh, chicken fricassee. In Silas' honor. (*Turning to the women.*) Chicken fricassee suit everyone? (*No one nods, yes.*) That's fine, Vern, and some jello maybe, bread sticks, something green, and milk. Lots of milk. (*Listens.*)

ZELDA: Get some beer.

(*She takes the wreath from the window, settles herself at the table, shrugs off boa and sou'wester, and fiddles with the wreath.*)

ROSE: Tamales and a fifth of Wild Turkey™. (*She moves another box.*)

CATHERINE: (*Reading ferry schedule.*) Anchovy pizza and orange sherbet.

MARJORIE: That thing… (*Indicating wreath.*) …is the height of tackiness, Zelda.

ZELDA: Oh, but Silas would have appreciated it. Widows' weeds and all the trappings wouldn't have suited him at all. Live or dead.

MARJORIE: I suppose you're going to want to be laid out wearing red plastic boots, a see-through mini skirt and a coconut bra, with chartreuse feathers in your hair.

ZELDA: I had something silk and flowing in mind. Or maybe all feathers. For that particular journey.

MARJORIE: When are you going to write your will? Any woman past 50 needs a baseline of order to see her through the rest of her life.

ZELDA: Quit nagging, I'll get to it.

MARJORIE: Tomorrow. You'll get to it tomorrow. Rose, we should make an appointment for you, too. Get that will written and filed. No time like the present, as they say.

ROSE: You know what else they say, Marge? They say that the definition of flagrant waste is a bus load of lawyers going off the edge and there's one empty seat.

EMILY: (*Waving everyone quiet; back to Vern on the phone.*) I know, a sad day. (*Listens.*) Never was one to stand on ceremony, true.

(*Listens.*) Yes, thanks, Vern. And don't forget the milk. (*She hangs up and returns to her cradle project.*)

MARJORIE: (*Rattling the box.*) The grownups (*CATHERINE sticks out her tongue*) have decisions to make, or rather, you have his wishes to follow.

ROSE: Silas left wishes?

MARJORIE: Oh, yes. Quite specific ones.

ZELDA finds a bit of the joint on the table, puts it between her lips. MARJORIE snatches the joint and pockets it. ROSE takes off her gloves, exits interior door. CATHERINE rummages in her back pack to no avail; follows ROSE out interior door.

MARJORIE: (*Cont'd.*) (*Opening her briefcase and removing files.*) Now, then. (*Puts her reader specs on, consults pages, looks up.*) The gist is this.

ROSE returns via interior door bearing three whiskey bottles, two full, puts these on a cupboard shelf, and sits. CATHERINE follows, munching out of a bag of stale chips; also sits.

MARJORIE: (*Cont'd.*) Silas Horner was an extremely wealthy man.

ROSE, EMILY, and ZELDA all interject: Oh, yeah, right… must be a mistake… Silas loaded? Ha!, etc.

MARJORIE: Extremely wealthy, but only in land and property. No cash to speak of, except for what's in this old envelope. (*From her briefcase, draws out a very old, wrinkled #10 envelope, opens it, shakes out three dusty $100 bills.*)

ROSE: Land?

EMILY: Land?

ZELDA: (*Picking one bill up.*) What was he saving these for?

MARJORIE: In addition to this pub, Silas owned the land you and Harold live on, Emily, as well as the land me and Zelda live on. Plus he owns those 30 acres of second growth forest out by the grave yard.

ROSE: That son of a skunk!

ZELDA stuffs one $100 down her front, tucks one in EMILY's cap, and the last in ROSE's beribboned hat band.

MARJORIE: Son of a smart woman's more like it.

ZELDA: What?

EMILY: Wait, Marjorie, that's not right. Harold and I, well, he, brought our trailer over from the mainland years ago, and the land…

MARJORIE: Is held in trust by Red Fox Incorporated. Right?

EMILY: Ye-es… I've been paying a mortgage for over 30 years… about paid off… but how… I don't understand…?

MARJORIE: (*Sighs.*) It's a long story.

CATHERINE: When does it start?

ZELDA: Yes. Don't leave anything out, Marge.

MARJORIE: (*Holding up the chart which shows a family tree and snapping open the pointer.*) I'm hungry so I'll cut to the chase, which is this. Silas came from a line of smart, rich, whores.

The other women all get up to examine MARJORIE's chart, exclaiming, What?!, Who?!, etc., and over the names of Silas antecedents: Great grandmama, Liza Jones, grandmother, Wanda Lowe, mother, Susanna Horner, general ad lib. CATHERINE goes and surreptitiously digs in her back pack. She withdraws a small notebook and pencil and returns to sit at the table, keeping the notebook out of sight, in her lap.

Scene 8

LJ enters via the exterior door carrying a large take-out box filled with food cartons and two gallon containers of milk. He crosses to the table and unloads the box.

LJ: I was up to Vern's when you called, Miss Emily. Thought I'd see how you gals was holding up.

EMILY: We're doing fine, LJ. Thanks.

LJ: I'll leave you to it, then. (*He doffs his ferry worker's cap and exits exterior door.*)

Scene 9

During the following, the women move around, setting up their meal.

EMILY: There was the Horner fishing family. Now I always thought Silas was somehow related to them.

ZELDA: Oh, like one of those wrong-side-of-the-blanket Horner's. Could be. There's lots of them around, mostly up island, but they're around. Got those flat foreheads.

ROSE: But his forehead wasn't flat and he hated fishing. Now

38

I think about it, Silas always went quiet when asked about his beginnings.

EMILY: Didn't he go off Island to high school somewhere?

ZELDA: Navy, I think. He was gone a long time, I know that.

ROSE: Where'd the money come from?

Everyone settles down to eat.

MARJORIE: (*Around a large bite of chicken, taking her time with her story.*) Nobody knows about the money. But these were determined women. I can easily imagine them stealing what they needed and then taking a bit of extra, besides. Wanda... (*Points to the chart.*) ...was one smart cookie. She inherited her mother's whore house and...

CATHERINE: Where?

MARJORIE: The house? Up island. The family still lives in it so I can't tell you exactly.

CATHERINE: But you know.

MARJORIE: (*Winks.*) ...and turned it into a gold mine. I like to think of Wanda as the kind of woman who would refuse to darn a man's sock but be willing to wash his hair. For a price.

EMILY: That was Silas' mother?!

MARJORIE: (*Pointing to the chart.*) Grandmother.

ROSE: Women running their own lives, going against the grain. Sounds like every one of us sitting at this table!

ZELDA: Excuse me, I am nobody's whore!

EMILY: Oh, Zel...

CATHERINE: No, you're not, but I may be descended from a whole bunch of them.

MARJORIE gets up, exits the interior door. ROSE picks up the ashes box, looks at it as if it speaks to her. She hands it to ZELDA, who passes it round the table. MARJORIE returns.

MARJORIE: (*Shaking off her hands.*) Rose, you need some more towels in the head.

EMILY: You can pick some up tomorrow when you get my glue. Oh, some ten penny nails, too.

ROSE: I'm not coming back.

CATHERINE: But you are giving me a ride down to the ferry.

ROSE: Don't know about that, neither.

CATHERINE and EMILY: But…

ZELDA: Never mind towels or nails or ferries. Go on with the story, Marge.

MARJORIE: Rose, hand me something serious to drink and I'll get finished with this.

ROSE is on her feet, fetches the half-full bottle of whiskey from the cupboard shelf, brings it to the table, opens it, takes a slug before handing it to MARJORIE.

MARJORIE: (*Cont'd.*) Time I got back to my laundromat. Lord only knows what Bitsy's messed up over there now. (*Takes a large gulp of the whiskey and hands the bottle around. Consults papers once more, and continues her recitation while finishing up her food.*) Here's what it boils down to. Rose, the pub and the land it sits on is yours. (*Hands her the deed.*) Emily, the land is yours and Harold's.

EMILY: But that isn't possible.

ROSE: (*Handing back the deed.*) You mean, he wanted me to have this place all along…? I don't…

MARJORIE: (*To ROSE.*) Sit still. Wait for the finish. Then decide. (*Hands ROSE back the deed; then, to EMILY.*) Red Fox Incorporated was Silas, Em. He set the whole thing up. Kept it anonymous. (*Hands her a paper.*) So here's your deed of trust for all your land. And Zel…(*Handing her a paper.*) …here's ours. Plus our house.

ZELDA: You mean he owned us, too?

MARJORIE: His one wish is that we all make certain sure no one builds anything stupid on his 30 acres, so he put the land in trust in our names.

ZELDA: Define stupid.

MARJORIE: (*Ignoring her.*) He wanted that land to remain natural down through time.

EMILY: What if we wanted to make a special kind of park out there? Would that count as stupid? According to the…(*Points at the document MARJORIE is reading from.*)

ZELDA: What'd you have in mind, Em?

EMILY: I haven't had time to think about it, but, you know, put in trails, build an arbor…

CATHERINE: Are there any ponds out there?

ZELDA: Oh, good idea, a wetlands preserve.

ROSE: STOP INTERRUPTING!

MARJORIE: My turn again? Okey dokey. If any one of us doesn't want his gift, now here I'm quoting... None of the Graces... (*She looks up.*)...he includes me in this because I live with Zelda and I'm an honorary Grace... Back to quoting him...(*Continues reading.*) ...none of the Graces gets anything and all the property herein named is to be cleared of any and all buildings and set aside for wildlife preserves. Forever. End quote.

ROSE:, EMILY, and ZELDA interject ad lib: What?! No?! That's crazy! What if we change our minds? What if we can't agree?, etc.

CATHERINE: (*Scribbling in her notebook.*) Graces?

ROSE: (*Staring at her deed.*) This is some kind of something.

MARJORIE: And all true, legal and binding, I promise you.

MARJORIE starts packing up and preparing to leave.

CATHERINE: Wait... this constant reference to Graces... What is that?

MARJORIE: (*To CATHERINE.*) Ask the terrible trio here about the Graces. (*To everyone.*) Girls, we'll need to have a pow wow early tomorrow morning to make sure we all agree to accept Silas' gifts. If not... well, things might get messy. So be in my office, no, better come over to the laundro... I'll bring the files with me... at 8:30. Plan on spending the day if need be. If you all do something slightly left of center with his ashes this afternoon, I don't want to know about it. And if you make a night of it, Zel, don't wake me up when you get home. (*MAR-JORIE exits exterior door.*)

Scene 10

CATHERINE looks expectantly at the other three.

EMILY: I was the one in the middle, looking over her left shoulder at the painter. Euphrosyne, his Heart's Joy. (*EMILY strikes the pose of Bottecelli's famous painting, waggles her head for the other two to join her.*)

ZELDA: (*Taking up her position on the left of EMILY.*) He called me

Aglaia, his Brilliant one.

ROSE: (*Taking up her position on the right of EMILY.*) I was Thalia, Flowering his life.

For a moment, the three hold their pose, lost in a reverie of their own.

EMILY: (*Breaking the moment.*) Well, I swan.

CATHERINE: You what?

EMILY: Swan. You know. (*CATHERINE clearly does not.*) It's what you say when something's too big to handle. I swan. And this whole day… I'm not tall enough for many more days like this one.

ZELDA: (*Looking at her deed.*) Mercy, I never expected this. (*Waving the deed.*)

ROSE: Well, you two can swan and mercy all you like. I'm not having it. And I'm not having any more interferences. (*To EMILY.*) Is that the word I want?

EMILY: Not plural, try hindrances, or obstructions, that has a nice, determined sound, or meddling, there's a useful word. More of a concept, really.

ROSE: One of you meddlers take Catherine to spend the night with you. Bring her back here by 8 tomorrow. Now go.

EMILY: (*Picking up the ashes box.*) We're not taking Catherine anywhere. We're not going yet, either. We have to decide about burying Silas.

ZELDA: I was thinking about… you know the meadow in the east corner of his 30… somewhere around there might suit. What do you think?

ROSE: (*Handing ZELDA the ashes box.*) Here. Take it. Him. Stick him in his meadow. Toss him off the cliffs. Chuck him out of an airplane. Just take him. It.

EMILY: Not without you, Rosie. We can't send him off unless all Three Graces witness his leaving.

CATHERINE: (*To ROSE.*) What is it you're not having?

ROSE: What?

CATHERINE: (*Picking up the deed.*) Do you mean the pub, which you've been running for years, or staying with your friends, who seem important to you, or the memory of a man you once loved and may still, or not having me as your long-lost daughter, what exactly is it you're not having and are so desperate to run away from?

ROSE: I am not running away.

CATHERINE: Sure you are. At least admit it. Even if it doesn't make any sense.

EMILY: I always wondered what you thought you were going to find. Out there. That you don't have here. And where you're going.

CATHERINE: You can't out run yourself.

ZELDA: Now that's the truth. And, speaking just for me, I'm fed up with all this talk of leaving. You're always leaving, Rose, always going tomorrow. So you tell me. What is so great about tomorrow?

CATHERINE: It makes for good stories to tell about yourself, all this leaving tomorrow, but why? Is it just for the stories?

ROSE: Why're you all ganging up on me?

ZELDA: I'm just tired of skirting around the subject. Thought I'd bring it out. Put it on the table. Take a look at it.

ROSE: Well, put it back.

EMILY: You belong here with us, Rosie.

ZELDA: You have us and we're fabulous. Won't find any better anywhere else. So just don't do it.

EMILY: (Pointing to CATHERINE.) You, too. Both of you.

CATHERINE: No. She may belong here, but I don't. I'm a seeker. The nuns used to find me turning over rocks in their garden. When they asked me what I was looking for—I can remember this clear as daylight—I said, mommy's hiding somewhere. I have to find her.

ROSE: I am … not … running…

ZELDA: Didn't you ever ask the nuns questions about where you came from?

CATHERINE: I was the left baby on their doorstep. What was there to tell? Or to ask? But I sure used to ask myself questions. Like…(To ROSE.)…what could possibly have been so wrong in your life that could have pushed you to abandon me? Had you been raped? Was I the result of violence? Why, then, did you let me live, to carry that with me? Wouldn't I then be guilty

43

by association? Or, was it simpler? You just didn't want a kid around to spoil your good time? Or was it more complicated? And did you have some kind of secret hunch that we'd meet again, somewhere down the road? And that everything would be hunky dory?

ROSE walks out.

CATHERINE: (*Cont'd.*) Well, around about my thirteenth birthday, I quit looking under rocks. Real or imaginary. So I headed out. Went on the road.

ZELDA: What do you mean, on the road?

CATHERINE: Just that. I got on a ferry and kept on going.

EMILY: The nuns didn't hurt you, or anything?

CATHERINE: No, no. I just didn't fit there. Couldn't find anything under their rocks I wanted.

ROSE returns.

CATHERINE: (To ROSE.) Did you name me, first, before leaving me on their door?

ROSE: I couldn't put a name to what I couldn't keep.

CATHERINE: The nuns called me Catherine, after Saint Catherine of Alexandria. The patroness of unmarried women and scholars.

EMILY: I wanted to name you Trillium, in honor of the rare, forest flower.

ZELDA: I always favored Santolina Lavender, for trust.

ROSE: Saint Catherine preserve us.

CATHERINE: Sometimes, I feel some explosive thing coming, aching to get out of me and destroy anything in its way. Very un-saint-like. I call it the mean reds. (*To ROSE.*) You know what I mean?

ROSE: I'm acquainted with them.

CATHERINE: (*Still to ROSE.*) When I'm in the reds, I feel like I'm a symbol of everything in the world that eats mothers and daughters for breakfast.

ROSE: But you're not angry at me or hurt by me any more. Right?

CATHERINE: Bet your ass.

ROSE: Well, if you put it like that.

44

EMILY: There you go. That's settled, then.

CATHERINE: I haven't agreed to anything.

ZELDA: Okay, so here's what we'll do. We'll get on the bus, head out to Silas' 30, find a good spot to scatter him, say our words…

ROSE: I'm not saying any more words. Seems they just get me in trouble. Standing mum on the subject, any subject, from here on out.

EMILY: (*Putting on her overcoat.*) Zel? What about Seraphina? Marge didn't say.

CATHERINE: Who's… oh, never mind.

ZELDA: Seraphina is Silas's goat. (*She wraps the boa around her neck.*)

ROSE: Good milker, but has a tendency to go wandering and eating up people's rose gardens. Somebody's going to have to adopt her. I need a jacket. (*Rips open a box and pulls one out; puts it on.*)

EMILY: Catherine, honey, you're coming with us?

CATHERINE: I'd better. I think this crowd needs an adult. (*She shoulders her back pack.*)

All exit via exterior door.

CURTAIN

END OF ACT II

ACT III

Scene 1

SETTING: Interior, kitchen. The next morning.

AT RISE: The kitchen is dark. A hint of very early dawn light comes through the window, enough for us to see CATHERINE sleeping on the roll-away bed. She wears a flannel nightgown. She tosses and turns in a dream. CATHERINE sits bolt upright, rubbing at her eyes. She gets up, putting on ROSE's jacket for warmth. Full dawn light fills the kitchen before she turns on the overhead light. She exits interior door. Outside light continues to build into morning as EMILY enters, with her key, from the exterior door. She tiptoes over to the stove. From underneath her coat she produces a large stewing pan and a wrapped meat package, similar to the one we saw in Act I, although a bit smaller. She opens the package and puts

45

the meat (this time it is cut into chunks) in the pan. Adds some water. Lights the stove. Removes her overcoat. She's still wearing a shirt, coveralls, and sandals. ZELDA enters wearing tights, a short-skirted dress, work boots, carrying a large canvass tote, and humming "Blackbird."* She crosses to EMILY at the stove, and starts removing brown glass, dropper-topped bottles. Each has a label declaring its contents; tea tree oil, echinacea, willow bark, etc. The last bottle she produces is larger and has a screw-top cap.

ZELDA: What'd you dream about last night, Em?

EMILY: (*Sniffing stew pan; searching for salt, etc.*) The usual, dancing crutches and bed pans… but… I think Silas showed up.

ZELDA: He did me, too. (*Sniffs stew pan.*) Put some Tabasco in it this time. Needs some perking up, this does.

Scene 2

ROSE enters from interior door. She is dressed in jeans and a sweatshirt, socks, and carries one sneaker. She crosses to her boxes and starts digging in the open one for the other sneaker.

ZELDA: What about you, Rose?

ROSE: What about me what?

EMILY: Dreams. What do you remember from last night?

ROSE: I don't dream.

EMILY: Of course you do.

ROSE: Well, then, I don't remember my dreams anymore.

ZELDA: That's a shame, because Silas has started visiting.

ROSE: He better not come around my head any night soon or I'll send him back where he belongs. Aha! Gotcha! (*She's found the other sneaker, puts it on.*)

Scene 3

CATHERINE enters via interior door. Her hair is wound up on her head. She is wearing the clothes she arrived in, long skirt and sweater. She crosses to the camp bed and starts making it up. Sniffs the air in the kitchen.

CATHERINE: That smells even worse than before.

ZELDA: I told you, Em. Needs Tabasco.

ROSE: (*Crossing to look in stew pan.*) Is this that same meat? Looks worse than the last batch.

EMILY looks in the pan, then stands back and crosses her arms over her chest.

ZELDA: Harold?

EMILY: (*A huge sigh.*) It's Seraphina.

All of the women stare into the stew pot and then at EMILY.

CATHERINE: So that's why you wanted to know what Silas wanted done with her.

EMILY: Uh huh. If he'd wanted her to go to somebody else, it'd be too late.

ROSE: When was it too late? For Seraphina?

EMILY: She just wouldn't keep out of my roses. Lately the only pretty spot around our place, those flowers. I went out, after one of Harold's really bad days, and there she was. Chewing up my favorite Mr. Lincoln's. And there I was. With an ax in my hand.

CATHERINE: You didn't.

ZELDA: Handy with an ax, is Emily.

EMILY: Bled, stripped, gutted, butchered, packaged, and put in the freezer.

ROSE: You bury the bones good?

EMILY: Bonfire first. Buried the ashes.

ZELDA and ROSE nod their approval. CATHERINE is in a state of horrified fascination.

ZELDA: (*Pulling some loose blades of grass from the bottom of her tote; tossing them in the stew pot.*) Here's to you, Seraphina. You were a good old goat.

ROSE: (*Adding some sand she finds in a pocket of her skirt.*) Here's hoping you find some roses where you're going.

EMILY: (*Picking up some wood shavings from the table and tossing these in.*) And thanks for feeding us.

CATHERINE: (*Swept up in the moment, opens ZELDA:'s screw-cap bottle, and upends the contents (ground raspberry leaves) into the stew pot.*) Happy trails!

ZELDA: (*Stirring the mess with a wooden spoon.*) Well, if she gets pregnant where she's going, those raspberry leaves will keep her hip joints from freezing up on her.

Scene 4

MARJORIE enters from exterior door. She wears a dark shirt and skirt, grey blazer, and flats. She, too, crosses to peer in the pot and sniff the air.

ROSE: Uh oh, girls, hide your valuables. Margie has on her lawyer suit.

MARJORIE: Well, now you've gone and done it. (*Folds her arms across her chest and considers the women.*) Findlay's in an uproar, Nate says he's never seen the like and he's lived on this island all his life and then some, and LJ claims he wasn't on duty yesterday when there he was, bold as brass. Everyone saw him. And you. So what do you all have to say for yourselves?

EMILY: Join us for dinner?

ROSE: (*Moving for the exterior door.*) I was just on my way over to Findlay's to file a report about my truck.

MARJORIE: You put one foot in that Sheriff's office and you won't be leaving a jail cell, much less the island, any time soon.

ZELDA: That seems a little over the top.

MARJORIE: Over the top is throwing human ashes off a state ferry. In the middle of Puget Sound. When the boat's going full steam ahead.

CATHERINE: Did anyone actually see Silas' ashes going in?

ROSE: (*Nodding.*) Good question. (*To MARJORIE.*) Well, did they?

EMILY: We thought it was better to let him go out in the middle instead of when we were still at the dock.

ZELDA: That would've been messy. And much too public.

MARJORIE: The public, or at least a loud bunch of them, filed complaints on the other side. Mentioning grey ash and bits of something that looked like bone sticking to their clothes.

ZELDA: Oh, that's just made up.

EMILY: Surely the ashes don't stick… Oh, dear.

CATHERINE: Probably some tourist saw us and just decided to cause trouble. If it can't be proved…

MARJORIE: (*To CATHERINE.*) You're getting as bad as the rest of them.

ROSE: I'll go straighten out Findlay. This'll go away in no time. (*She exits exterior door.*)

48

Scene 5

MARJORIE: (Calling after ROSE.) It'd better! Zelda, how's about we take a day off and go play in Seattle. What'd'ya say?

ZELDA: There are still things that aren't settled here.

MARJORIE: Well, get it organized, then come on. We could leave as late as one o'clock and still have ourselves a time.

CATHERINE: If you two go earlier, can I hitch a ride down to the ferry? I need to be in Seattle by three today.

MARJORIE: Sure. Just come on over to the laundro... no, damn, I can't go to Seattle today, I've got to meet; oh, hell, who is it? (*Consults her diary in her briefcase.*) Lucinda. Lucinda's got a problem with her theft insurance. Honestly, you'd think that woman would have a good clearance sale once every decade or so to keep her inventory down, but, no, she makes things irresistible to ... what was I saying?

EMILY: That doesn't matter. What matters is what Catherine is saying. I thought you'd given up on this notion of an abortion.

ZELDA finds a kettle, starts water boiling. EMILY picks up the cradleboard and makes a few adjustments. CATHERINE shoulders her back pack and prepares to leave.

CATHERINE: You've all been very nice to me, and, well... I'm going for a last hike around town, maybe go back to where I first met, uh... Silas... Anyway. Take a look around, say good-bye... I'm not sure when or if I'll be back to the Island, so...

(*She gives ZELDA a quick hug; starts to give EMILY one, too, but it stopped by*)

EMILY: You ever have one of those moments when you know so clearly what to do about a thing that you move like someone else is pushing and pulling your body parts?

ZELDA: (*Picking it up.*) Yes. Your thoughts are razor sharp, and, like an arrow flying through the air for its target, you go straight and true until you land where you're supposed to be?

EMILY: (*Finishing.*) Well, that happened to me...

ZELDA: And me...(*Looks at EMILY.*) Even Rosie.

EMILY: (Nodding.) ...when you came to us, bringing someone new and fresh to look after and care about.

CATHERINE: Please, please don't get too attached to me. Why won't you listen. To me. I'm having an abortion in a few hours.

MARJORIE: Get it organized, Zel, before it gets away from you. Later. (*She exits exterior door.*)

Scene 6

ROSE enters via interior door.

ROSE: You look like you're ready to go.

CATHERINE: I'm going to hitch down to the ferry, pick up my van on the other side.

ROSE: (Shaking her head.) Did you get any sleep last night?

CATHERINE: Not much.

ROSE: Bad dreams?

CATHERINE: I'm not sure.

ROSE: Silas dreams?

CATHERINE: I'm not sure. (*Pause.*) Get it all straightened out with Findlay?

ROSE: I'm not sure. Where are you going to stay… after…

CATHERINE: I'll find a hotel, sleep it off…

ROSE: And then you'll be back on the road. (*CATHERINE nods.*) Where next?

CATHERINE: I don't know. I hadn't thought beyond coming here.

ROSE: Uh huh. Say. Out there on the road. You ever get lonely? (*Doesn't wait for CATHERINE to answer.*) I woke up this morning feeling lonely. (*Pause.*) Sometimes lonely comes down on me like the fog coming over this island. Settles in my bones and takes up residence there. Lonely could be my middle name.

CATHERINE: Do you have one?

ROSE: Nope. (*ROSE has something to say to her daughter. It takes her a beat before she is able to speak.*) The second I knew I was pregnant with you, I sort of blew up. I tore apart my trailer, stem to stern. I was scaring myself but I couldn't stop. I walked over to the back door, and put my fist through the glass pane. I stabbed the walls with a butchering knife; I made mincemeat of the kitchen counter with a mallet. I was just about to pull the front door off

50

its hinges when…

EMILY and ZELDA *(in unison)*: We showed up.

The following sequence happens rapidly.

EMILY: *(Putting her hands over CATHERINE's eyes.)* I pushed my hands over Rose's eyes…

CATHERINE: *(Startled, tries to push EMILY.'s hands away.)* What are you doing?!

EMILY: And kept on pushing…*(She's pushing CATHERINE.)* …until she staggered back and sat down, hard, on the floor.

CATHERINE: *(Sitting down hard.)* Stop it!

ZELDA: *(Quickly.)* I dragged her along to the bathroom and shoved her in the shower.

ZELDA Starts to drag CATHERINE, trying to continue this bizarre reenactment, but CATHERINE stops her with a glare and stands up.

ROSE: She turned on the faucets to full blast and said…

ZELDA: You drown your mad thing and then you make a decision. Do you hear me?

ROSE: I nodded, yes.

ZELDA: Whatever it is, I said, you make a choice, and you do it. Okay?

ROSE: Okay, I said.

EMILY: I striped down Rose's clothes, bundled them under my arm, and we left Rosie alone with her hot water.

Scene 7

MARJORIE: enters via the exterior door. She stands quietly by the door for a while.

ROSE: I don't know what comes over me sometimes. I'm like a drunk can't hold his liquor, or a bat without her radar, or a tree without its roots.

ZELDA: *(To CATHERINE.)* We know you're Rosie's daughter. You've got a way about you that comes from her.

CATHERINE: So what.

EMILY: So where is your anger? Why aren't we having to shove you in the shower? You asked us why we weren't crying about Silas. Now I ask you. Where are your tears? For this baby you're about to sacrifice to the knife?

51

CATHERINE: You have to stop. Now.

MARJORIE: (*Moving downstage.*) It seems to me Catherine has made her decision. Why won't you respect her for doing that?

EMILY: She doesn't deserve my respect for what she's setting out to do.

CATHERINE: I don't ask for it. For anything. From any of you.

ZELDA: Yes, you do. You came back to us.

CATHERINE: No, I didn't. I came back to make a decision.

ZELDA: Your protest doesn't hold water with me.

CATHERINE: I beg your pardon?

EMILY: Honey, your decision was already made. No matter what you told yourself you were doing when you came back here, you were following your own story. It's what we do. It's how we get through our lives.

ZELDA: And if you leave, now, you not only take yourself and that baby, but you take our stories and make them your own. That's theft. We can't allow that to happen.

CATHERINE: I don't believe this. What do you mean, allow?

EMILY: And your baby's stories. Don't they get a chance to be told?

CATHERINE: My baby's stories are my business, damn it.

ZELDA: What did I tell you about swearing in this kitchen?

CATHERINE: (*To EMILY.*) Your story is telling you its time to put your husband in a home.

ZELDA: That's definitely over the top.

CATHERINE: Maybe. (*Beat: to ROSE.*) You're awfully silent.

ROSE: (*Long beat.*) I think we'd both be better off on the road. Going our separate ways, like we've always done. I need to try myself, out there, and you, well I guess you know what you need.

CATHERINE: (*Frustrated beat.*) No. No, that's not, you don't… none of you…(*She stands and moves around during*) Going on the road means putting yourself on a line. It's a line that has no be-ginning, it has no end. Every once in a while a line leads away, and you follow that one for a while, seduced by its possibility, the unknown of it, until it peters out. Because it always ends in nothing. So you go back to your original line, and you follow it. One day you might stop to look back where you came from, look forward to where you think you're going. But it all looks the same. This line you've put yourself on has no real exits, only roadside stops, where you can catch your breath, but not get off. Going on the road is the opposite of freedom. You think tomorrow you'll find a better you out there, a free you, out there on the road. What you find is a mirage. The better you you wished for disappears in waves before your eyes. There is no better you. Just you on your line that you can't get off.

ZELDA: (Beat.) Get off here. We'll catch you.

CATHERINE: You're asking me to step into a reality I don't think I'm strong enough to carry.

EMILY: Babies are a feather weight.

CATHERINE: The incest. Name it. Somebody has to name it. Incest. That's the weight. My god, I may have fu—, had intercourse with my father. I may be carrying his child. Even the thought of this, the possibility of it, flattens me. (*Pause.*) Imagine what could happen, years from now, when she finds out. Or at her birth, some awful damage that I did to her. The damage.

EMILY: (*To ZELDA:, sotto voce.*) She. A girl.

MARJORIE: There are all sorts of damaging things we do to each other. Many of us survive in spite of ourselves. Some do it alone. Some do it in the company of friends and strangers.

CATHERINE: (*To ROSE.*) Did you ever have an abortion?

ROSE: No. Just you.

CATHERINE: Emily?

EMILY: My dreams of children never came true. (*The 'until now' is unspoken, yet clear.*)

CATHERINE: Ever since I've been here, I've felt like I've been inside a dream, like something I made up for a story, from the moment I first stepped foot on this island, even back then, and now.... The whole... thing... you, you're characters. You're fake fronts. You're another mirage of mine.

MARJORIE: No dream. No mirage. None of us gets off that easily.

ROSE: No fake fronts. What you see is it.

EMILY: We're not characters.

ZELDA: We're Island women, and we learned early on how to take care of ourselves.

EMILY: Maybe it's because we're separated from land, surrounded by water, like a baby in a womb.

ZELDA: Being island women makes us both scared to change much and real willing to change everything, all at the same time.

CATHERINE: (*To ROSE.*) You belong here, on your island. With them.

ROSE: Maybe.

EMILY and ZELDA busy themselves at the stove, concocting a healthy drink. MARJORIE exits interior door.

Scene 8

CATHERINE: (*To ROSE.*) Why were you mad about being pregnant?

ROSE: Because I knew I couldn't keep you. I wanted to tear apart the world. Because I couldn't keep you.

CATHERINE: Why not?

ROSE: No money, no job, no safe place, no ancestors to give you. Only my mad thing. Not enough.

CATHERINE: Are you sorry?

ROSE: What do you think? (*ROSE exits interior door.*)

Scene 9

CATHERINE: (*To EMILY and ZELDA.*) Is she, was she, sorry?

ZELDA: What do you want her to say? Yes, or no?

EMILY: (*Handing CATHERINE the concoction.*) You decide about that and then ask her again.

CATHERINE takes a swig absently, sits at the table.

CATHERINE: I have large, toy bear who rides in the passenger seat of my van. He's thirty-five next year, Bear, and very wise company. No matter where we're going, he never asks why. About anything.

ZELDA: Then don't ask her. Just take it as you get it. All of it. Us. The whole package.

54

EMILY: Like we're presents that came in your mailbox. And you can't throw us out. Come on, Zel, we need to get this poor owl de-feathered. (*She picks up the owl.*)

EMILY, ZELDA, and the dead owl exit through the interior door. They cross paths with MARJORIE returning.

Scene 10

MARJORIE: (*Sitting at the table with CATHERINE; she launches in without preamble, as usual.*) You've probably gathered by now that each of us has our roles in our little family of friends. Zelda is our tracker, she makes sure we get ourselves back in line when we wander off course. Emily takes care of us when we forget to take care of ourselves. Rose, now Rosie, she holds every woman's rage, and we've all had some down the years. I think Rose was born mad. All her ranting doesn't mean anything, though, and she only turns her anger inward, to herself. Does that sound familiar? (*CATHERINE reluctantly nods.*) Thought it might. (*Pause.*) Me, I'm the outsider, the girl who wouldn't grace Silas with her favors, the Grace who holds the frame for the other three. (*Takes a swig of the drink in CATHERINE's hand.*) I'm also the keeper of secrets and little known facts. The things I've heard. It's amazing what people tell you while they're waiting for their laundry to get done.

CATHERINE: Like bartenders.

MARJORIE: Better, because folks stay sober, or at least reasonably so for that two hours we're together. And they're not telling me things because they're scared or nervous like when they come to my law office. No, at the laundro, people, those who have a mind to anyway, those people drop their guards and show me their hearts. Silas was like that.

CATHERINE: What's your version of him?

MARJORIE: I knew him with a space between us, from behind my law desk and from behind the counter at the laundro.

CATHERINE: Then yours may be a truer assessment.

MARJORIE: There's no doubt in mind that you're Rose's daughter, DNA test or no DNA test. You hold her pride and her strength. Her impatience. I imagine once you get hold of

55

something, it's hard to shake you loose. Am I right?

CATHERINE: Tell me about Silas.

MARJORIE: I am. Silas Horner was a rake, a rogue, and a true charmer. Old fashioned words these days, but they fit him. The old women on the Island say he could charm eagles out of the sky before he was out of diapers. The Silas I knew…the grown man, also had in him a wandering streak. Sometimes that showed up in his conversation. He'd start off on one thing, wander off into new territory, and maybe wind back where he started. He was a great storyteller. But mostly his wandering moved his body around, around people he favored, around places. Keeping himself loose. Any of this sound familiar?

CATHERINE: (*Takes back the drink, swallows.*) This isn't bad, once you get going on it. I hope whatever else you're going to tell me goes down as easily.

MARJORIE: I've lived on this Island for thirty years. I may call myself an Island woman but, by Island logic, I'm a newcomer, just like you.

CATHERINE: Why doesn't anyone listen to me? I'm not stay… oh, what the hell. Go on.

MARJORIE: And Silas liked talking with me because we hadn't grown up together or shared a bed.

CATHERINE: Like talking with strangers on the road.

MARJORIE: That's it. That space in between stories. When you're loose, sometimes it's easier to tell those in between, those real stories. Silas told me lots of his, because he trusted me to let them lay in that space. So his stories go with him. (*Pause.*) But I can give you this. He was the kind of a man a woman, any woman, never forgets and always forgives. (*She takes and finishes the drink.*) Now here's two little facts for you to consider. One, Silas told me his one regret was that he didn't have a daughter. And two, this, straight from the mouth of a doctor friend, quote: If the parents are not carriers of genes that produce genetic disease, their offspring will be okay. End quote. (*MARJORIE stands, gives CATHERINE an affectionate kiss on a cheek, and exits interior door.*)

Scene 11

CATHERINE sits, stunned, motionless.

EMILY enters quietly. She carries the completed cradleboard. She puts it in CATHERINE's lap, touches CATHERINE's hair lightly, and just as quietly exits interior door. ZELDA enters, with a purpose. She holds a small leather pouch in one hand. She puts the pouch in CATHERINE's hands.

ZELDA: Put this under your pillow tonight.

CATHERINE: Is it legal?

ZELDA: It's for dreams that tell you which way to go. (*She kisses CATHERINE and exits interior door.*)

Scene 12

ROSE enters and sits down opposite CATHERINE. For a long beat the two regard each other.

ROSE: Whatever happens… (*She can't continue.*)

CATHERINE: (Beat.) Whatever happens.

After a beat, ROSE gets up and exits interior door.

Scene 13

CATHERINE gets up, carrying the cradleboard tucked under her arm, and, as if dreaming, wanders about the kitchen. She picks up an item here, gently kicks at one of ROSE's boxes, etc., and comes to rest in front of the cradle EMILY has almost finished building. With one extended foot, she prods the cradle; it rocks. Then stops.

CURTAIN

END OF ACT III

ACT IV

Scene 1

SETTING: Interior, kitchen. Seven months later, December 22

AT RISE: The kitchen has once again changed. The cradle is built, the owl feather and flannel-lined cradleboard hangs on one wall, and all save one of ROSE's boxes are gone. Silas' tennis shoe hangs by its laces from a nail on a wall. Candles and lanterns placed strategically around illuminate the set. The fold-up bed and bedding is gone. The table and chairs set is pushed back into a corner. A wooden rocking chair is placed center stage, with nothing close to it. CATHERINE sits in the rocker. She is wearing

57

a flowing dress and socks. She uses ROSE's last box as an ottoman and is gently rocking herself and the sleeping baby, wrapped in animal skins and soft flannel bunting, she holds. We HEAR the women's VOICES O.S. while she rocks.

ROSE: (O.S.) Rosie's Roost. What's wrong with that?

ZELDA: (O.S.) Nothing, if you're advertising a bunch of pigeons.

EMILY: (O.S.) Tea and Texts.

MARJORIE: (O.S.) Texts. Too hard to say. Texts. Texts. Texts.

EMILY: (O.S.) Or, Readin' and Sippin'. Or Books and Brews. Or…

ZELDA: (O.S.) How's about Tea for You?

ROSE: (O.S.) No good. Doesn't show any light on the books part.

MARJORIE: (O.S.) CATHERINE should decide.

Scene 2

EMILY, ZELDA, MARJORIE, and ROSE all enter from the interior door. ROSE holds one end of a banner that has nothing written on it yet. She is wearing a long peasant skirt and a hooded sweatshirt, and sneakers. No shoes. She carries a paint bucket and a well-worn, wide-handled house painting brush. EMILY holds the other end of the banner. She is now wearing a denim shirt and a long, circular denim skirt. Her feet are bare. She carries a similar brush. ZELDA follows, also carrying a well-used painting brush. She is wearing a thigh-length, colorful sweater, a long, full skirt, and is barefoot. MARJORIE comes in last, also carrying a used brush in addition to her ever-present briefcase, and is wearing a long, A-line dark skirt with a cream blouse. No footgear. Her toenails are painted. The women's voices are slightly hushed at first.

ROSE: (*Still holding her end of the banner; to CATHERINE.*) What do you think of Rosie's Roost?

CATHERINE: Doesn't say what it is.

ZELDA: (*Dropping her end of the banner and moving to look at the baby; to ROSE.*) See?

EMILY: (*Getting close to look at the baby in CATHERINE's arms; to CATHERINE.*) She has your chin. A good sign.

MARJORIE: (*To CATHERINE.*) Have you picked a name yet?

58

(*CATHERINE shakes her head, no.*) Well, what are you waiting for? She's a month old today. (*To ROSE.*) Catherine's obviously your daughter, Rose. Just as stubborn.

ROSE: No need to get snippy.

ZELDA: Time to name this place, give it a new start. Isn't that what the banner and paint is all about?

EMILY: Time to christen this baby girl.

CATHERINE: I agree, but I don't want her christened with sand, or wood shavings, or given a name I can't pronounce.

MARJORIE: Will champagne suit you? (*She produces a magnum from her briefcase.*)

ZELDA: Nice touch, Marge. But I was thinking more on the lines of something herbal. (*She produces a small, dropper-topped brown bottle from a skirt pocket.*)

EMILY: Let's take her down to the Bay and wet her head with salt water.

CATHERINE: It's two in the morning. We'll do no such thing. Rose? Anything to add?

ROSE: Tap water?

EMILY: I'm rather partial to Lilly.

ZELDA: I like Iris, myself.

ROSE: Victoria. Now, there's a name to be reckoned with.

MARJORIE: Sue is a useful name, no chance of anyone screwing with it.

ROSE: Sue? Sue? Sue becomes Susie, has blonde curls in ringlets, steals the other girl's valentine's day cards and ends up spending years in therapy on some quack's couch. Not my granddaughter, thank you!

MARJORIE: (*Taking legal documents from her briefcase and showing them to CATHERINE.*) You asked for it and here it is. You and Rose are now partners in this once-was-a-pub-establishment, and your baby owns title to the 30 acres. But I've got to have her name on this thing (*waving one of the documents*) before it's legal...

CATHERINE: I'm naming her Grace.

The older women all nod their delight and approval.

CATHERINE: (*Cont'd.*) That's a good start for a girl, don't you think? Grace. Grace Page.

ROSE: Okay. I've got it. We'll call it, Page's Place.

ZELDA: That's not bad. It's not good, but…

CATHERINE: No, we won't. I was thinking, The Five Graces Tea Room and Book Shop.

EMILY: Oh…

ZELDA: Perfect.

ROSE: Book Shop and Tea Room. Tea Room and Book Shop. (*On a look from CATHERINE.*) We'll figure it out.

ZELDA: Is that Graces with an apostrophe thingy?

CATHERINE: No, it's plural, not possessive.

EMILY: We're definitely not possessed. We're Island women.

The baby fusses as if to start crying. A sense of ritual shades the following. This is, after all, these women's version of a Christening.

MARJORIE: Here's to the fifth Grace. Island woman born.

She moves to begin forming a circle around CATHERINE and baby GRACE. The others follow. Baby GRACE begins a sleepy cry.

ZELDA: (*Thinks a moment, then sings in a clear voice.*) Blackbird singing in the dead of night/take these broken wings and learn to fly/all your life/you were only waiting for this moment to arrive.*

The other women join in as they remember the song. They are all singing, and begin slow dancing in a circle around CATHERINE:and baby GRACE, who both fall silent.

ZELDA, MARJORIE, EMILY, ROSE: Blackbird singing in the dead of night/take these sunken eyes and learn to see/all your life/you were only waiting for this moment to be free.

The older women repeat, "waiting for this moment to be free" like a chant, along with ad lib movements (i.e., bodies swaying, fingers snapping, etc. DISSOLVE SPOT to CATHERINE, gently swaying with baby GRACE, humming along, in the center of "this moment to be free."

CURTAIN
END OF ACT IV

*ASCAP Permissions Pending

Prop List

Act I
Cleaver
EMILY's watch fob, shoulder satchel, clothespins
CATHERINE's well-worn backpack and contents (underwear, box of crackers, toothbrush, maps)
Cardboard, grocery and alcohol packing boxes
White butcher paper wrapped meat package
Large pot
Water
ZELDA's hair gel, fishing creel containing herbs, roots, grasses, mortar & pestle, bottle of Aspirin, small thermos
Waxed paper
Cereal box
Bottle of Tabasco Sauce
ROSE's jacket
Can of Ginger Ale
Cabbage
Carrot peeler
Cabbage (on the stove)
Wooden spoons
Dish of chopped garlic and onions (on the stove)
Two wooden, ladder-back chairs
Soggy tennis shoe
Piece of folded paper
Damp cloth
Three pewter mugs
Whiskey bottle
Framed photograph

Act II
Bottle of milk
Framed photograph
Cradle pieces
Open boxes

Shut and taped packing boxes
Round wooden table, (add) three wooden, ladder-back chairs
Tool box
Couple of saws
Pieces of wood, i.e., cut up coat rack, for building changing table
Indian cradleboard (in need of paint and lining)
Fold-away bed
Goose-down sleeping bag (keep pillow from Act I)
Gaudy Christmas wreath
Silas' ashes box wrapped in brown paper
Four ferry schedules
MARJORIE's dark maroon briefcase; multicolored half-readers, wrist watch, file folders, papers, wrinkled #10 envelope, three old $100 bills, deeds, ripped-up laundry basket and contents
Joint

Three whiskey bottles, two full, one half-full
Packet of stale chips
Take-out box
Food cartons
Two, gallon containers of milk
CATHERINE's small notebook and pencil (in backpack)
ROSE's jacket (in a box)

Act III
Camp bed and bedding
ROSE's jacket (from Act II)
EMILY's second wrapped meat package containing chunks of pale meat
ZELDA's canvas tote; brown glass, dropper-topped bottles; one larger, screw-cap bottle, all labeled, leather pouch
ROSE's sneakers (one in jacket box)
Loose blades of grass
Wood shavings; Sand
Ground raspberry leaves (in screw-cap bottle)

Wooden spoon
MARJORIE's briefcase and business diary
Kettle
Dead owl
Drink concoction
Flannel or other soft cloth pieces
Cradleboard both unfinished and finished
Cradle (almost completed)

Act IV
Finished cradle
Candles
KeROSE:ne lanterns
Wooden rocking chair
One of ROSE's shut boxes
Sleeping baby
Animal skins
Flannel bunting
Paint bucket
Four used, wide-handled, house-painting brushes
Long banner
MARJORIE's briefcase, legal document, Champagne magnum
ZELDA's dropper-topped brown bottle

<u>Clothing</u>

Act I
CATHERINE: long skirt, droopy cardigan, hiking boots, socks
ROSE men's slippers, faded flannel nightgown
EMILY: denim coveralls, denim work shirt, Juarache sandals
ZELDA: sou'wester, black tights, thigh-length T-shirt, day-glo socks, red high-heeled tapless tap shoes
LJ: shirt, ferry worker's vest and cap, jeans, heavy work boots

Act II
CATHERINE: (add) multi-colored serape

ROSE: tea dress, hat w/veil, short white gloves, matching low-heeled pumps
EMILY: (add) oversized, well-worn man's overcoat, carpenter's cap
ZELDA: (add) turquoise feather boa
MARJORIE: hodge-podge of static-cling clothing
LJ: same as Act I

Act III
CATHERINE: flannel nightgown, outfit from Act I
ROSE: jeans, sweatshirt, socks, sneakers
EMILY: same as Act II
ZELDA: tights, short-skirted dress, work boots
MARJORIE: dark skirt, dark shirt, grey blazer, flats

Act IV
CATHERINE: long flowing dress, socks
ROSE: long peasant skirt, hooded sweatshirt
EMILY: denim shirt; long, circular denim skirt
ZELDA: thigh-length colorful sweater; long, full skirt
MARJORIE: A-line dark skirt, cream overblouse
GRACE: bunting

Secrets Among Us

©2011

ACT I
<u>Scene 1</u>

SETTING: MARGARET's house, dawn, late November

AT RISE: MARGARET enters from the stairway, wearing only a large, tattered beach towel, and singing "Good Night, Irene."* She crosses to the telephone and dials. Her actions are with intention, as if she has come to a hard won decision.

MARGARET: (*Into phone; pauses as appropriate.*) Helen? Good morning. How are you? Are you going to be in your office today? I want to stop by. I have something I want you to sign. That's it. Oh, lovely. Thanks. See you then. (*She hangs up and crosses to the valise and opens it. The suitcase is full of photographs. Black & white, sepia tinted, ragged-edged, 8x10's, snaps.*)

MARGARET returns to her song while she removes four edge-crinkled snaps, studies them for a moment, and puts these under the telephone. She gathers up a handful and tears them in half, in thirds, any-old-how. She repeats this action until she has a pile of confetti. She tosses this in the air, then exits via UC sliding glass door, dropping her towel as she goes. WYNONA enters via stairway carrying a purple terry-cloth robe. She glances out the picture window toward the sea beyond. The lawn between the window and the sea is covered in early-morning fog. Her gaze next falls on the torn-up photos. She opens the door leading out and calls OFF.

WYNONA: What do you call this?

MARGARET: (*O.S.*) For the party!

WYNONA: opens the robe and holds it close to the sliding glass door.

WYNONA: (*Calling.*) And which party would that be?

MARGARET: (*Her voice closer now.*) The one I've just decided I'm having. We're having.

WYNONA: Can't. I'm moving to Canada.

MARGARET: enters by stepping into the robe. Her hair is wet; bits of grass, etc., stick to her feet and ankles.

WYNONA: (*Cont'd.*) You should be giving up rolling around naked.

MARGARET moves to the dining room table, which is littered with papers.

MARGARET: (*Rummaging through.*) Where's that bill from the roofer?

WYNONA: We should be charging him for the mess he leaves every times he comes. And the work he doesn't finish. (*She picks up some of the torn-up photos.*) More importantly, what's the bill for this?

MARGARET: I don't know what you're talking about. (*Sniffs.*) What are you cooking?

WYNONA: Bean soup. You can put ketchup in it, if you have to.

MARGARET: Ugh. I'll just have coffee. In here.

WYNONA: I don't see you crippled up. Get it yourself.

MARGARET: If that's your version of a breakfast pep talk, I'm not having any.

WYNONA: You've got that hard look about you, the one that says, hands off.

MARGARET: Then stop looking at me.

WYNONA: Something's up with you, and I reckon it's coming from behind, not from what's in front.

MARGARET: You reckon, do you. (*She crosses to stand in front of WYNONA:, holds a hand over her head, measuring.*) You better be careful, Wynona, you're starting to shrink.

WYNONA: In your dreams. I've got a six-foot box on order and six feet I'll be when they put me in it.

MARGARET: You're five foot six if you're a day.

WYNONA: (*Slapping MARGARET's hand away.*) Unlike some 72-year old woman named Margaret. I know who shrinks because she eats too much ketchup. And does crazy things like rolling around on the lawn in the foggy foggy dew.

MARGARET: (*Laughing; surreptitiously taking a pill vial from her robe pocket, rolling it in her hand.*) I want to stay in town awhile today. That okay with you?

WYNONA: I thought we were doing the recycling. Got it all

loaded in the pickup. Besides, what do you need in town?

MARGARET: Things.

WYNONA: Things.

MARGARET: Yes. Things. I need things. We need things.

WYNONA: We do not need a single thing. Got food enough for the girls coming even if they drag along an army. Second, bought new bath soaps, as if the ones we have aren't good enough. Even washed out all the sheets and towels. And, it's not Wednesday.

MARGARET: I've decided we're too rigid. We need to change wash day to Thursday or Friday. Any old day.

WYNONA: Poo.

MARGARET: Poo? (*Turns away.*) My shower awaits.

WYNONA: You got a lover you haven't told me about?

MARGARET: (*Turning back.*) I have something I want to do. In town.

WYNONA: With this new lover of yours?

MARGARET: Poo.

WYNONA: Okay, okay, no more poo.

MARGARET: Oh, no, I think I'll grow to like it. Has a certain ring falling off the tongue. Poo-oo-oo. A nice rounding.

WYNONA: Put your tonque around this.

MARGARET again turns to leave.

WYNONA: (*Cont'd.*) Why have you invited Nora and ALLI-SON: here at the same time?

MARGARET: (*Stopping briefly.*) That's my perogative.

WYNONA: That's just throwing misery after trouble, if you ask me.

MARGARET: I didn't. (*She strides for stairway.*) And I don't. We're leaving in twenty minutes! (*She exits.*)

WYNONA waits to make sure she's really gone, then starts picking up all the photo bits and putting them back into the valise.

BLACKOUT

Scene 2 NORA's cottage, day

LIGHTS UP. NORA sits at her desk, deep in concentration, writing in a spiral-bound notebook. JANE perches on an edge of NORA's desk, filing a ragged fingernail.

JANE: Nora?

NORA: Hmmmmmmm?

JANE: (*Poking her nail file underneath an envelope on NORA's desk.*) What's this?

NORA: Uh huh.

JANE: Looks like news from Mags.

NORA: Fine, okay, salad's good, uh huh.

JANE: I thought we'd have fried cat for dinner.

NORA: (Looking up.) Where's George?

JANE: Outside, chasing a moose.

NORA: Mouse. He chases mouses. Mice.

JANE: (*Flips the envelope into NORA: 's lap.*) What is this?

NORA: (*Huge sigh.*) A summons.

JANE: Read it to me.

NORA: You read it, you're so interested.

JANE: But you know how to inflect her words. Almost as if she's standing in the room.

NORA: Heaven forbid. Give me that. (*Takes envelope, removes one sheet of paper, reads.*) Darling. I will expect you on Thursday next. The last train arrives at our station at ten o'clock. Take a taxi to the house. Mags.

JANE: I didn't know you were going up.

NORA: Neither did I.

JANE: How long will you be gone?

NORA: No idea.

JANE: What about your work?

NORA: I'll take my notebook. Besides, whatever this is, it's bound to be something my mother's blown out of proportion, as usual. We'll probably settle it in a couple of days.

JANE: I'll miss you.

NORA: No, you won't. You'll be too busy playing with your fish.

JANE: I take offense. I am Jane Copeland, capital P little h period capital D period. A serious marine biologist. I do not play with my fish. I dissect them.

NORA: Go and dissect some trout for dinner, then. Leave me

68

get back to my book.

JANE: (*Stands, looks over NORA's shoulder.*) How's it coming? (*NORA makes a rude noise. JANE gives NORA a kiss and turns to leave.*) Are you going to tell her? About us?

NORA: You know the answer to that.

JANE: Yes. And I wish I didn't.

BLACKOUT

Scene 3 ALLISON: 's boutique, day

LIGHTS UP. ALLISON is adjusting a garment on one of her mannequins. Her husband, RICHARD, stands very close to her, as if to keep their conservation for their ears only. He talks at ALLISON and through his teeth. She does not look at him throughout; if anything, she is timid, even fearful, not hard.

ALLISON: I'll only be gone a few days, honey. You know mom. She never writes and asks me to come unless it's really important.

RICHARD: I don't care where you go.

ALLISON: Don't be silly, Richard.

RICHARD: I told you I would leave, and I meant it.

ALLISON: I'll take care of it. I will. We'll be just the same, like we were before.

RICHARD: Leaving you is the only way I know to get through your betrayal. So suck it up. Be an adult.

ALLISON: I don't want to be an adult, Richard. I want to be married. To you.

RICHARD: We're done.

ALLISON: But I still love you. Surely that counts for something …?

RICHARD: We had one rule between us. Fidelity. All I ever asked of you was to keep that vow. And you broke it.

ALLISON: Richard…

RICHARD: You broke our marriage apart. You fucked another man.

ALLISON: Richard…

RICHARD: And you got pregnant by him. Sixteen years with me, barren, and you get pregnant like a bitch in heat.

ALLISON: I explained … I told you … it wasn't like that … you make it sound so awful … like a bad movie plot …

RICHARD: If it wasn't for me, you wouldn't have a life. Not the house, or your precious boutique, or money to go clinging to your mommy every time I asked you behave like a grown up. I've kept you, do you understand? Without me, you are nothing. I married you and made you something. Me. Richard, the ever faithful, the honest one. Remember me? (*Pause.*) I want you out of the house, my house, by the time I get back from Albuquerque. (*Pause.*) I want you out of this shop, my shop, by the close of business today.

ALLISON: You can't be serious…

RICHARD: Tomorrow my realtor puts a new lock on the doors. All the doors. (*Pause.*) As of now, you're on your own. So you'd better look to your own regrets, lady, because I have none.

BLACKOUT.

Scene 4 MARGARET: 's house, evening

The interior is growing dark. MARGARET and WYNONA enter from DR door. Neither turns on the lights as they are in the middle of a heated argument.

WYNONA: Your appointment with Helen isn't for another two weeks.

MARGARET: What the hell were you doing? Snooping on me? Stalking my every move? I come out of a building and you jump out of the bushes at me?

WYNONA: Not for another TWO weeks.

MARGARET: I heard you the first time. Now leave off.

WYNONA: Not until you tell me why you went into that medical center, into her office, when you told me to meet you in the park.

MARGARET: Why didn't you wait for me, like I asked? (*She flips on one lamp.*)

WYNONA: Because you've got that look.

MARGARET: Damn my look!

WYNONA: (*Snapping on the other lamp.*) Talk to me!!

MARGARET: I'm hungry.

WYNONA: Talk.

This time, WYNONA wins. MARGARET backs down and sits down.

MARGARET: I'm going to stop taking my heart pills.

WYNONA: I repeat. I'm going to Canada.

MARGARET: I mean it.

WYNONA: No you don't. (*Pause.*) Why?

MARGARET: Because it's time.

WYNONA: Time for what?

MARGARET: Just time.

WYNONA: I call bull shit.

MARGARET: Call anything you want. Call for a cab. Call, Ollie Ollie Owsen Free Free Free. Call, last drinks, gentlemen. Won't change anything.

WYNONA: I'll fix you a sandwich.

MARGARET: Eating won't change anything, either.

WYNONA: A bourbon and seven.

MARGARET: Still no change.

WYNONA: Our years and years and years and years of friend-ship don't count.

MARGARET: They count, of course they count, but no, no change.

WYNONA: The girls.

MARGARET shakes her head, 'no'.

WYNONA: (*Cont'd.*) You haven't thought this out.

MARGARET: I have, you know.

WYNONA: I don't know. Helen wants you to take a new pre-scription and you're pissed off? Is that it?

MARGARET: No.

WYNONA: Then, what? I think I have a right to know since you've obviously decided to kill yourself.

MARGARET: My right, my decision. Not yours. (*Long pause.*) I'm really hungry.

WYNONA: I really hate this.

MARGARET: Thank you.

WYNONA: And I hate you for making me hate this.

MARGARET: Nonsense.

WYNONA: Should I be concerned about your all or nothing stance about this?

MARGARET: No. I'm clear.

WYNONA: Lord, but you're tough. (*After a long pause.*) What can I do?

MARGARET: I just want your friendship. Your love.

WYNONA: You have both. No matter what.

MARGARET: Will you stay with me tonight?

WYNONA: Of course. I live here.

MARGARET: No. I mean, stay tonight, then go tomorrow.

WYNONA: That won't be easy.

MARGARET: I need some time alone with the girls.

WYNONA: And just where am I supposed to go while you and the girls are tearing up the house?

MARGARET: Canada?

WYNONA: They don't know yet, do they.

MARGARET: No. That's why I've asked them to come.

WYNONA: Helen doesn't know about this, either, does she.

MARGARET: Will you help me?

WYNONA: You're asking me to leave you alone to fix all of it, and then come rushing back at the midnight hour.

MARGARET: Will you help me?

WYNONA: (*Sigh.*) Call me when you want me to come home.

MARGARET: I don't know how long it'll take.

WYNONA: I hear Canada's nice this time of year. Think I'll go out to Alberta… (*Pause.*) Are you going to tell them about Sam and Charley?

MARGARET: I'm hoping we're all going to tell each other everything. Everything that matters, at least.

BLACKOUT

Scene 5 MARGARET:'s house, two o'clock in the morning
ONE TABLE LAMP GLOWING. MARGARET and WYNONA are sitting together on the sofa. They both wear long, flannel nightgowns. MARGARET has WYNONA's bare feet in her lap. WYNONA has her hands snugly wrapped around a chipped coffee mug. MARGARET drops WYNONA's feet and puts her head in WYNONA's lap. WYNONA

strokes MARGARET's head while MARGARET weeps. Intermittently, she speaks.

MARGARET: Father would tell me to not to give up my compass, and mother would sigh her breath away. (*Pause.*) Sam and me, we rolled like seals, Wynona . (*Pause.*) Charley, nothing I did could hold him, nothing, nothing. (*Pause.*) Nora. (*Pause.*) Allison. (*She sits up.*) There's still so much to do, Wynona. I have to get my girls on the same side.

WYNONA makes soothing noises.

MARGARET: (*Cont'd.*) I hope I have enough time.

WYNONA: Shhhhh.

BLACKOUT.

Scene 6 MARGARET's house. early the next morning.

LIGHTS UP. WYNONA stands by the DR exterior door, a suitcase at her feet, an embroidered tote bag in one hand. MARGARET stands next to her, wearing coveralls and boots, holding a white cardboard box with grease stains on it.

WYNONA: Fog's lifted.

MARGARET: I made you some cornbread.

WYNONA: If you made it, it'll only be fit for the sea birds.

MARGARET: It's like chocolate bars. You never know when it might come in handy.

WYNONA: In case I get a flat and need to brace up a wheel. (*She takes the box and stuffs it in her tote bag, then withdraws a comic book, and hands it to MARGARET.*) This might come in handy when things heat up around here. Pogo's a great one for putting things in perspective.

MARGARET: He's certainly kept me in good company down the years. Almost as much as you have.

WYNONA cups MARGARET's face with one hand, opens the DR exterior door, and leaves, calling behind her.

WYNONA: I love you!

MARGARET: (*Calling back.*) I love you, Wynona .

MARGARET watches WYNONA drive away. She stands still, then puts a hand in a pocket of her jeans and removes the pill vial. With purpose, she crosses to the valise, opens it, and empties the pills in with the torn photos.

She closes the valise and exits interior UL door.
BLACKOUT

Scene 7 MARGARET's house, late that night.

MOON LIGHT ONLY. The house is still. A car is HEARD to drive up to the house. The DR door opens suddenly; we HEAR the car drive off. NORA enters. She drops her Kelty Pak and sleeping roll on the floor, walks with familiarity to turn on one lamp. She looks around the living/ dining room, and shakes her head. Nothing changes here. She flops down on the sofa, weary. Another car is HEARD driving up. This time, voices are heard (O.S.) in a heated discussion. ALLISON enters in a flurry from the DR door. She marches in, sees NORA.

ALLISON: I'm short for the cab.

NORA: Christ, Allison.

ALLISON: Nora …

ALLISON: (Holds out her hand; NORA stands, digs in a pocket, produces rumbled dollar bills. ALLISON takes the lot and darts outside. We HEAR the car drive off after a beat; ALLISON returns.

ALLISON: (*Cont'd.*) What are you doing here?

NORA: Thanks, Nora. Oh, you're quite welcome, sister dear. Think nothing of it.

ALLISON: Thanks. So. What're you doing here?

NORA: Damned if I know.

ALLISON: I got a note, asking me to come.

NORA: Me too.

ALLISON: So what's it mean?

NORA: I don't know! Don't you have luggage? You usually come with half the contents of your house…

ALLISON dashes outside and returns with one large suitcase on rollers.

ALLISON: I really wish mom would have been more, well, explicit.

NORA: You could have called her. You know, picked up a tele-phone.

ALLISON dashes outside and returns with another large suitcase on rollers.

ALLISON: I mean, this is the worst possible time. For me to be gone.

74

NORA: Hi, Nora. How's things with you?

ALLISON dashes outside and returns with a third large suitcase on rollers. Finished, she sits opposite NORA.

ALLISON: Did you take the train up?

NORA: Uh huh. The ten-twenty.

ALLISON: Me too.

NORA: That's about right. We're both on the same train and don't know it.

ALLISON: Was it your idea? To take the train?

NORA: No, Mag's. Yours?

ALLISON: No, mom's.

A long silence spreads out between the sisters.

ALLISON: *(Cont'd.)* Mom asleep?

NORA: Do you see her?

ALLISON: Give me a break, Nora, I'm hungry. I'm not thinking straight. Do you think Wynona would mind if I raided the kitchen?

NORA: *(Standing up.)* I think you're going to do exacly what you like, no matter what anybody else thinks.

ALLISON: *(On her feet.)* Bound to be something in the freezer.

NORA: *(Long suffering.)* I'm going to bed.

BLACKOUT.

Scene 8 MARGARET:'s house, next morning.

A storm-filled dawn shows through the UC window. NORA enters from the DR door. She wears hiking gear and walking shoes. She is on her way to the kitchen when MARGARET enters from interior door UL.

MARGARET: Ah, there you are.

NORA: Good morning, Mags.

MARGARET: Have a good sleep?

NORA: Is Wynona here?

MARGARET: You never sleep well in my house, do you.

NORA: *(Beat.)* Does the condemned woman get breakfast?

MARGARET: I assumed you'd take care of yourself for breakfast, as usual.

NORA: *(Longer beat.)* I've been looking forward to Wynona's cornbread all the way up.

MARGARET: She's away.

NORA: Damn.

MARGARET: You'll just have to make do with me. (*She opens the breakfront and starts setting out linen mats, plates, etc*.) And how was your train ride?

NORA: Interesting, really. I met this huge woman named Crista Bell who…

ALLISON: enters via stairway. She is dressed in a long, flowing garment that engulfs her. MARGARET spins around and grabs her younger daughter in a bear hug. Releasing ALLISON, MARGARET touches her face.

MARGARET: Darling! You're so thin!

ALLISON: (*Pulling back a bit.*) I'm okay, mom. Really. There's just a lot going on.

MARGARET: We'll have plenty of time to catch up later. How about I bring you some breakfast. I've made eggs. A waffle? You always loved my waffles.

NORA: …who claimed she was related to Marilyn Monroe.

NORA sits; her breathing is a bit ragged. She takes an apple from the fruit bowl on the table and a Swiss Army knife from her pocket. She begins peeling the apple in one long strand.

ALLISON: Anything, mom. (*She sits across from NORA.*) I met the greatest porter on the train, mom. He kept bringing me things, and telling me all about his life, riding the rails, he called it. I gave him a twenty dollar tip when I got on. I remembered Richard saying, always tip first, not later … (*Her voice trails off.*)

MARGARET exits interior UL door.

NORA: (*Tossing bits of sliced apple in her mouth.*) I should think he'd be nice. Twenty bucks! I'll be nice to you for twenty bucks.

ALLISON: (*A whine creeps into her voice.*) Maybe he liked me. Is that so hard to believe?

MARGARET returns bearing a plate of eggs which she puts in front of ALLISON:.

MARGARET: Isn't this nice? My two girls together.

Nothing could be farther from the truth.

MARGARET:(*Cont'd.*) (*To ALLISON.*) Eat up, darling, The wraith look doesn't suit you. I hope you two can entertain yourselves a while, because I have some business to attend to. I'll be

home about two, and we'll have time for a lovely long walk before dinner. Seven sharp. I got a fine hen from Dabney's Farms yesterday. Nora, you're in charge of salad. And Allison, quit picking. Eat. (*She ruffles ALLISON's hair and heads for the stairway.*)
NORA: Mags?
MARGARET: (*Pausing at the stairs.*) Yes?
NORA: Why are we here?
MARGARET: (*Beat.*) I really do have to get dressed now. (*She exits.*)

Scene 9

NORA finishes her apple; ALLISON makes a feeble attempt with her eggs. She ends up pushing them around on the plate.
ALLISON: (Barely audible.) Richard's left me.
NORA: What?
ALLISON: Richard.
NORA: What about Richard?
ALLISON: He left me. Kicked me out. Of the house, my shop.
NORA: Say it again.
ALLISON: Don't make me. (*Pause.*) It's just like dad. They all leave me. Sooner or later.
NORA: He left? You're kidding.
ALLISON: I wish I were. Was. Whatever.
NORA: But I thought you're the golden couple. Forever entwined, like Lancelot and Guinevere.
ALLISON: A lot of people did. But that's a lie. It's ugly and stupid, and, and I'm ashamed, and mad, and I don't know.
NORA: Why did he leave?
ALLISON: It isn't my fault.
NORA: I didn't say it was. Just asking.
ALLISON: Well, don't.
NORA: Okay, I won't.
ALLISON: But listen. Don't say anything to mom.
NORA: You haven't told her? But you always tell Mags everything. Or at least, that's what she tells me.
The sisters sit in silence. NORA breaks it by standing and stretching.
NORA: (*Cont'd.*) I'm going for a prowl. (*She exits exterior DR door.*)

ALLISON sits, then, making an inner resolve, she gets up and goes to dial the telephone.

ALLISON: Hello? Regina? It's Mrs. Greenson. Is Richard there? He isn't? Oh. No, it's just, I, uh, can't remember where he said he'd be today. His club? No, I didn't try there. That's a good idea. What? Oh, no, everything's fine, just busy, you know, this and that. No, you don't have to tell him I called. I'm sure I'll catch up with him soon. Thanks. Bye. (*ALLISON hangs up, stares at the telephone, dials another number. Into phone.*) Hey, Mickey. It's me. Allie.
BLACKOUT.

Scene 10 A short while later
LIGHTS UP. The stage is empty. NORA enters from exterior DR door, crosses to the telephone, and dials.

NORA: (*Into phone.*) Hey. What're you doing? (*Listens.*) I'm fine, I'm… Jane, I still don't know why we're here, Allison and me. (*Pause.*) I came right out and asked Mags the reason and she avoided the question. I've only been here a short while and already I want to scream. It's just like it always is when the three of us are together in this house. Things seem so polite on the surface, but I feel this, this rumbling undercurrent of tension. It's like all my old childhood shit is trapped in this place and is flaking off in my face. What? (*Listens.*) No, I can't… there's all these damn secrets. Mags is lying about where Wynona's got to, I just know it, and Allison's got some shit going on with Richard, and I'm not talking about… as usual. I start off fine and then a sort of film drops over everything. I'm afraid I'm going to lose it here. And you're there. And that's about it. (*Laughs.*) Yeah, that's right! I'll remember that! (*Pause.*) Listen. I don't suppose you'd like to come up… Well, think about it, okay? Okay. Yeah. Love you too. Bye.
BLACKOUT.

Scene 11 MARGARET:'s house, evening
Through the UC plateglass window, we see a storm brewing outdoors. Inside, the table is set with heavy Georgian silverware, salt cellar, pepper

shaker, oil and vinegar pitcher, a crystal butter dish, lit candles in a holly centerpiece, china plates, crystal glasses, and a carving knife and fork. A fire burns cheerily in the fireplace. MARGARET, NORA , and ALLISON move from kitchen to the dining table ferrying tureens (vegetables, rolls), a gravy boat, serving utensils, and a decanter of wine, etc., on the drinks cart and in their hands. MARGARET carries out the browned hen on its platter. She places it at the head of the table, where she stands, and begins to carve. NORA surveys the table, opens a breakfront drawer, finds linen napkins, puts these around. ALLISON arranges the table to her satisfaction. All three women stand at their traditional places.

ALLISON: Everything looks great, mom. You really outdid yourself tonight.

MARGARET: Well, I hope so. Sit down. (*She sits; her daughters follow, ALLISON first.*)

NORA: Pass the beans, Al.

ALLISON: Trade you for the butter.

The whole scene feels like a well-rehearsed ballet choreographed to an invisible score until the dance is interrupted by an odd note.

MARGARET: I'd like us to say a grace before we begin.

NORA: Why? We never say grace. Saying grace would be a hypocrisy, don't you think?

MARGARET: Join hands, please. (*She waits until her daughters do this.*) We come together in reconciliation and humility, asking only that our faults be forgiven and that we remember who we are.

Both NORA and ALLISON experience inner struggles. NORA breaks a brief silence.

NORA: So, Mags, what's the occasion?

ALLISON: (*Taking a bite of hen.*) Mom, it's delicious!

MARGARET: (*After a beat.*) I have something to say.

NORA: You're selling the house. Again.

MARGARET: About twelve years ago, I developed a heart murmur. Northing very serious, but persistent.

ALLISON: (*Putting her fork down.*) You never told me that.

MARGARET: There was no reason to. It's my murmur and I got it under control.

NORA is having trouble breathing again.

MARGARET: (*Cont'd*) Then, a few years ago, it turned into a heart rhythm condition.

ALLISON: Mom…

MARGARET: I've been on a particular kind of heart medicine, Amiodarone, ever since. And then recently I've had to increase the dosage. My condition is getting worse.

NORA: Jesus.

ALLISON: But you can't be sick!

MARGARET: I've watched several of my friends die lately. Nasty, lingering deaths. Deaths without dignity or purpose. And I see people my age hanging on in misery and despair. Confined to a life of nothing but endless time.

NORA: Who died?

MARGARET: (Thrown off stride.) Wha… What?

NORA: I said, w-h-o d-i-e-d died, damnit.

MARGARET: (*Pulling her back up.*) Elsie Parmaleee down the street. Jason Kruger at the hardware store. Hope Maxwell.

ALLISON: (*Starting to shake.*) Hope? Hope's dead?

MARGARET: The point is that I have no intention of sitting in a chair with a failing heart for the rest of my days. It's getting weaker and the damn drugs might kill me anyway. I've made a choice and you two need to know about it. (*Pause.*) I've decided to stop taking my pills.

NORA: (*As if she's been slapped.*) You can't be serious.

MARGARET: Once I do that, we won't know exactly when I'll die, but it will come fairly quickly and I'll just go to sleep.

NORA: What do you mean, go to sleep.

ALLISON: (*Whispering.*) I don't understand…

MARGARET: I'll go to sleep. Naturally, quietly. And hopefully with both of you here.

NORA: You want us to witness this?

MARGARET: It isn't necessary that you understand what I'm doing, and I don't need or want your forgiveness. What I would like is for you to accept me and my decision. Support it. And me. If you can. (*She sits back in her chair, eyes closed for a beat.*) One more thing. I asked you both here not only for me. I want you two to get over the past, whatever hurts you think are still there between you, and be sisters.

Outside, the storm breaches. The power goes out in the house. The women are lit by candle and fire light, unflattering shadows are cast upon their faces. ALLISON stumbles from her chair. She kneels at her mother's feet and tries to hide in MARGARET's lap.

NORA: Do you plan on telling us when you're going to stop the pills? Or are you just going to show up dead one day?

MARGARET: (*Stroking ALLISON's hair; suddenly exhausted.*) I don't know yet.

NORA: So this is the reason for the summons. To casually tell us you're committing suicide.

ALLISON sets up a wailing, keening sound.

NORA: (*Cont'd.*) Well, it stinks. (*Yelling at ALLISON.*) For god-sakes, Allison, stop blubbering.

ALLISON cries harder.

NORA: (*Cont'd.*) (*To MARGARET.*) This isn't about you dying and us all being together in some, some sordid, happy families ritual. This is about manipulation, and hiding, and dishonesty. And suppression. Your heart. Your murmur. As thought we just don't count in your life. God. I can't breathe in here. Be sure to keep the tough stuff hidden, right? Don't let the kiddies see. Huh? Is that it?

ALLISON: Oh, Nora, stop!

NORA: What the hell do you expect us to do here? Roll over and say, okay, mommy, that's nice? It's swell that you want to kill yourself, we approve? Well, I DON'T! How DARE you! (*She stands so abruptly that her chair falls backward, rocks, and crashes to the floor; screams.*) TALK TO ME DAMNIT!!

MARGARET: (*Shielding a cowering ALLISON:.*) We'll talk later.

NORA: Oh, right. Sorry, I forgot myself for a moment. You're the one in charge. You dictate how and when and what to feel. (*Her anger sags; she steps back from the table.*) My whole life I've been reacting to you. Well, no more, lady. No more. (*She puts up her hands, as if warding off a frontal assault, then runs out the sliding glass door and into the storm.*)

CURTAIN

END OF ACT I

81

ACT II

Scene 1

SETTING: MARGARET's house, later that night.

AT RISE: ALLISON sits on the sofa, in a silk kimona. She stares into the dying fire. We HEAR a car skid up to the house followed by running footsteps and then pounding at the front DR door. ALLISON leaps up, terrified. Silence. The windows rattle in the storm's wind. The pounding picks up again, and a RICHARD's voice O.S. is HEARD.

RICHARD: (*off*) AL-L-I-SON!!!

ALLISON: (*Calling out.*) Mom!! It's Richard!

MARGARET appears on the stairway, hurriedly wrapping her bathrobe around her body. She dashes to hold ALLISON, to stop her from opening the door. Too late. ALLISON rushes to the door and opens it before any more pounds come. RICHARD tumbles in; he's drunk but not unaware of where he is. He fixes his gaze on ALLISON; at first he doesn't see MARGARET. He slaps ALLISON soundly across the face. ALLISON falls to the floor, her arms wrapped over her head. RICHARD stands over her, breathing like a tired bull.

MARGARET: (*Moving to her daughter; to RICHARD.*) Get out.

RICHARD: (*To ALLISON.*) Did you think you could get away with it?

MARGARET: Get out of my house.

RICHARD: This is between me and my wife.

MARGARET: It may be between the two of you, but you're not doing it here. (*She moves to stand in front of RICHARD as he makes a move toward ALLISON.*) You take one more step, and I'll shoot you.

RICHARD: With what? I blame you for this, you know. For her.

MARGARET: I. Will. Shoot. You.

RICHARD: (*To ALLISON.*) You'll be sorry. I'm the best thing that ever happened to you. (*He stumbles out the front DR door.*

MARGARET helps ALLISON to her feet and then to the sofa.

Once she HEARS RICHARD's car drive off, she returns to sit with AL-LISON:.)

82

ALLISON: It's not all his fault, mom.

MARGARET: (*Taking ALLISON:'s hands.*) Allison. Has he hit you before?

ALLISON: He says it's like something takes over him, and…

MARGARET: What did he mean, you'll be sorry?

ALLISON: I, I don't know.

MARGARET: Allison…

ALLISON: (*Starts hiccuping.*) It's not his fault, mom.

MARGARET: Do you remember, how you used to put on my hiking boots and go parading off down the garden? (*On ALLISON's nod.*) I used to watch you go. And worry for you. I still do. Put your arms over your head. (*ALLISON does; her hiccups abate a bit.*) You're never going to kick off my boots until you stop waiting to be rescued, and until you stop making excuses for people who hurt you.

ALLISON: Mom, you don't know what's happened.

MARGARET: You're right, I don't. But I can see the results of whatever 'it' is. Allison, you have to know that you are worth while. All by your self. You have to know this. No one else can know it for you.

ALLISON: I used to walk around in your boots because I wanted to be like you.

MARGARET: Oh, darling, we don't need a duplicate me. We need you, Allison, and the bits and pieces of Charley that you keep alive.

ALLISON: I wish you talked more about daddy.

MARGARET: (*Standing, with a bit of difficulty.*) Help your old mother up, darling. (*ALLISON does.*) Charley also loved tromping around in my boots, which was not a good thing. Do you understand?

ALLISON: Mom?

MARGARET: (*Starting to lead ALLISON to the stairway.*) Yes?

ALLISON: I'm hungry.

MARGARET: Does your face hurt?

ALLISON: No. I'm just hungry.

MARGARET: Put ice on it before you go up.

MARGARET drops her arm from ALLISON's waist and exits up the stairs to her bedroom.

ALLISON: Okay, mom. G'night.

ALLISON exits to the interior UL door a beat later, hiccuping gently.
BLACKOUT.

Scene 2 The next morning

LIGHTS UP. ALLISON enters from exterior DR door. She is dressed in
full English riding gear, including hat and boots, and carries a crop. She
looks flushed and happy. With her is MICKEY FINN, a sprightly Irish-
man, also dressed in riding togs, except that his reflect a working rider as
opposed to a weekend one. He stands at the door while she flings herself
into the room.

ALLISON: (*Taking off her cap.*) Oh, that was great, Mickey.

MICKEY: You still have a grand seat on ya.

ALLISON: And your stables! You've really come up in the
world. What happened?

MICKEY: (*Relaxing slightly.*) I don't rightly know. But horseback
riding became more popular and my ex got married all at the
same time. I ended up with so much money I didn't know what
to do with it.

ALLISON: (*Not listening to him.*) That's nice. Want something to
drink?

MICKEY: I'd rather you told me what's doing.

ALLISON: I just wanted a ride. And to see you. Of course.

MICKEY: You haven't wanted to see me in over ten years.

ALLISON: Well. Now I do.

MICKEY: Pull the other one, lass. (*He crosses to the easy chair and*
sits on the edge of its cushion. ALLISON begins pacing in between him
and the fireplace.) Seems a shame, you're wearing a groove in a
fine bit of carpeting.

ALLISON: (Stops in front of him.) Mickey, I'm in trouble. Big
trouble.

MICKEY: (*Taking her hands.*) I can see that, lovey. A woman
doesn't get a handprint on her face from doing the washing up.

ALLISON: pulls away and resumes pacing.

MICKEY: (*Cont'd.*) Come on, Allie. It can't be that bad.

ALLISON: It's worse. I've really done it this time. You remem-

84

ber I wrote and told you that I was worried about Richard? Well, about Richard and me, really?

MICKEY: Yes, I do.

ALLISON: You never answered that letter.

MICKEY: I thought it best not to. The last thing any man wants, lassie, is for his wife to be tellin' her marriage bed troubles to another man, especially an old lover.

ALLISON: Anyway, things got worse. And then, I had an affair.

MICKEY: They don't throw you in hell for that particular sin any more.

ALLISON: They do if you get pregnant by your illicit lover.

MICKEY: Oh.

ALLISON: Yes. Oh.

MICKEY: Does he, does Richard know?

ALLISON: And he's left me, and he's going to divorce me, and he's kicked me out of the house, AND my shop. (*Pause.*) Richard hates it when he's not in control of things, people. It drives him crazy. Bad things happen. (*She flops down on the sofa.*) I should've stayed with you, Mick. I can be more me with you than anyone else.

MICKEY: I'm still here for you, Lis. As a friend.

ALLISON: moves to stand in front of MICKEY. She puts a hand on his face and leans to kiss him. He backs up and stands.

MICKEY: (*Cont'd.*) As a friend. Come to the stables as often as you like. Ride. Take long walks. Work out your troubles. Spend time alone or we can have time together. I'd like that, because I'll always love you. But I won't be a casualty in your battle. Not again.

ALLISON: You say you love me and then push me away. What's that about?

MICKEY: Allison. Why did you come to me today?

ALLISON: To see you, talk with you, be with you.

MICKEY: I can't save you anymore. I won't.

ALLISON: (Starts pacing.) What am I supposed to do?

MICKEY: (*Turning for the DR door.*) I have a horse breeder waiting for me. Come to the stables and ride anytime. As a friend.

(*MICKEY exits.*)

Scene 3

NORA enters via UC sliding glass door. She looks as if she has been sleeping in a shed. She ignores ALLISON, who likewise ignores NORA, and sits on the easy chair, scowling at some inner vision. After a beat, ALLISON heads for the kitchen via UL door. MARGARET enters down the stairway. She carries a box of papers, which she dumps out on the dining room table. She sits and begins sorting through them. She doesn't notice NORA until NORA speaks.

NORA: Do I own you an apology?

MARGARET: Not necessarily.

NORA: I need some time to get used to the idea of what you're doing.

MARGARET: Time is the one thing we don't have.

NORA: But why?

MARGARET: Because it's my life, my death. (*Pause.*) I'd like you and Allison to speak with a counselor. Wednesday morning.

NORA: Christ. You're still telling me what to do.

MARGARET: Not for much longer.

NORA: See?

MARGARET: Nora? Allison's going to need your help.

NORA: ALLISON:'s a big girl now, Mags.

MARGARET: In my day, older sisters helped their younger sisters, no matter what.

NORA: I know. (*She rises wearily.*) But it isn't your day any more, is it? Isn't that what you're showing me? (*Pause.*) Okay if I take a shower?

MARGARET: Help yourself. I'm sure the water's heated up after Allison had hers.

NORA: I'm not going to any counselor, Mags. Not Wednesday or any other day.

MARGARET: Why do you object so much?

NORA: Because you insist.

Scene 4

ALLISON enters via UL door. She is chewing on a peanut butter and jelly

86

sandwich. She crosses and sits at the table with her mother.

ALLISON: Mom?

MARGARET looks up.

ALLISON: (*Cont'd.*) I'm going to have a baby.

MARGARET: Are you.

ALLISON: You don't seem too surprised.

MARGARET: I'm not, darling. I know you pretty well, you know. I could always tell when you were keeping a secret from me, and your uncharacteristically large appetite is a dead give away.

MARGARET gets up and hugs ALLISON who rises up inside the embrace. NORA sits at the table.

ALLISON: Well. Now you know. Are you happy?

MARGARET: I think it's wonderful, especially now that Richard's out of the picture. The worst reason to have a baby is to patch up a bad marriage. He is out, isn't he?

ALLISON: shrugs off the question.

NORA: Well, well, babies having babies. Ain't life grand.

ALLISON: Or, Nor, don't be mean.

MARGARET: (*Intervening.*) Are you going to be able to do this on your own?

ALLISON: Do I have to? Do it on my own?

MARGARET steps aside slightly.

ALLISON: (*Cont'd.*) Mom? Don't you want to see this baby? Be a grandma?

MARGARET: Darling. This is your baby. Not mine.

ALLISON: Oh, mom…

NORA: Remember who're your dealing with, Allison. Margaret, queen narcissus.

ALLISON: What?

MARGARET: Nora, behave.

The doorbell RINGS. NORA strides to open the DR door.

Scene 5

Jane stands on the stoop. She reaches to hug NORA, who steps back.

NORA: Jane.

JANE: Nora.

MARGARET: Doctor Copeland, isn't it? Won't you come in? Don't keep her standing on the doorstep, Nora. Invite the woman inside. (*She moves to shake hands with JANE.*) Did you drive up? Such a long drive, you must be exhausted. Would you like a cup of tea? Perhaps something stronger?

JANE: No, thanks. I'm fine.

MARGARET: (*Pulling JANE into the house; indicating sofa.*)Make yourself comfortable. I'll be just a minute. Come along, ALLISON:.

ALLISON, displaying no interest in JANE, happily follows her mother out the interior UL door.

Scene 6

NORA exhibits unease in JANE's presence; she puts distance between them.

NORA: Why did you come?

JANE: You asked me to.

NORA: I know I did, but I feel off balance enough in my past without my present life popping in…

JANE: I don't pop. So why aren't you happy to see me? Why no hug? Or is your mother still in the dark about us?

NORA: I'm not sure I am happy to see you or even what happy is, and no hug because yes about the dark. We're all in the dark.

JANE: I thought you needed me here. To spread a little light on the scene.

NORA: A phone call would have done.

JANE: But I needed to come.

JANE steps forward and holds NORA in an embrace. NORA finally relaxes; she's embarassed by tears.

JANE: (*Cont'd.*) Hey, what's this? Water works?

NORA: (*Stepping back.*) This, this is Mags. She's decided to kill herself. She's going to kill herself, soon, and she wants me and Allison here when she does it. I can't bear it. I just can't. I feel so terribly alone and afraid.

JANE: From what you've told me about your mother, I wouldn't have thought she'd ever do anything like suicide.

NORA: It's the ultimate control. (*Pause.*) She's dying.

JANE: Margaret? Dying?

NORA: It's a slow thing, and she won't… I don't want to talk about it now. Ah, Jane, I'm so glad to see you.

JANE: Do you want me to stay? I will.

NORA: Of course I do. But, no. Mags kicked Wynona out, so I guess I can't have you. We're doing this alone, us three.

JANE: I want to give you something. Here, let's sit down. (*She pulls NORA onto the sofa next to her.*) *I was going to give it to you later, after you got home, but maybe it'll help. (She puts a plain gold band in NORA's palm.)*

NORA: (*Staring at the ring.*) I could swear it's winking at me.

JANE: It's saying, wear me, wear me. (*Noticing the sad confusion on NORA's face.*) I thought you might say that. (*She produces a length of black silk cord from a pocket, slips the ring on it, knots the ends, slips the whole around NORA's neck.*) You can hide it. If you want. Or need to.

NORA smiles her gratitude.

JANE: (*Cont'd.*) I found out something yesterday.

NORA: You're changing the subject.

JANE: Ten seconds for me.

NORA: Go.

JANE: About my dad.

NORA: You found him? You know where he lives?

JANE: Yup. In the Veteran's Cemetery in Los Angeles. Viet Nam got him.

NORA: Oh, Jane, I'm so sorry. (*Pause.*) Let's make a pact.

JANE: What kind of pact?

NORA: I don't know. The moment just feels, big, you know? Like we ought to be pricking our fingers and taking an oath about something. Your father's dead, my mother's dying, I've got a ring. You know, a pact.

JANE: I refused to stick a pin in my finger when I was twelve, and don't relish doing it now. Even for you. (*Pause.*) I think the ring is our pact. Between you and me. As long as there is a you and me.

NORA pulls JANE's face close to hers and kisses her eyes, cheeks, mouth.

NORA: That's it sealed, then.

ALLISON: (*off*) But I don't want to go shopping, not yet.

MARGARET: (*off*) The Fall sales start tomorrow. We'll go then.

NORA and JANE break their embrace.

Scene 7

MARGARET and ALLISON enter via UL door. MARGARET pushes the drinks cart, which is filled with a high tea (tea pot, cups, sandwiches, scones, cake.)

MARGARET: Afterward, we'll make an appointment for you at the health clinic.

ALLISON: But I hadn't even thought about a doctor… I have one in Los Angeles…

MARGARET: (*To JANE.*) Will you pour, Dr. Copeland?(*She sits in the easy chair.*)

NORA gets up. The telephone RINGS. NORA answers; the call is for ALLISON.

ALLISON: I'll take it upstairs, Nor. Hang up for me, willl you? (*She runs up the stairs.*)

MARGARET: Nora, there's a rose bush in the back garden that needs to come out. You'll find the rake and shovel leaning against the back porch, along with a pair of boots and gardening gloves. Just make certain you get all the roots. (*Turning her back on NORA; to JANE.*) Will you have some of this pound cake, Dr. Copeland? My friend Wynona makes it with nutmeg. Very tasty. (*NORA, smarting from the dismissal, exits the window door.*)

Scene 8

During the following, we occasionally view NORA through the UC plateglass window wrestling with a stubborn, very dead, rose bush. JANE takes a piece of the pound cake and waits.

MARGARET: Has Nora: filled you in on things as they stand here?

JANE: Why would she?

MARGARET: I don't have time for the niceties of polite conversation. Even for you.

JANE: (*Pause.*) I repeat, why would she?

MARGARET: Because you are important to her. Possibly more

than even she knows. More tea? I'm glad she has you in her life, Dr. Copeland.

JANE: Jane.

MARGARET: Jane. For all her independence and strength, Nora needs to be able to let someone else take the reins now and again.

JANE: (*Taking a risk.*) The first thing I fell in love with was Nora's sense of self, her pride.

MARGARET: She gets that stubborn pride from me. (*Pause.*) I sometimes wonder if the girls will want to keep the house. The furniture, bits and pieces, cameras, things I called mine while I lived.

JANE: Do you care? If they keep things?

MARGARET: Yes, strangely enough, I do. I know it doesn't make any sense, after all, I won't be here to care, will I? They could throw the stuff into the Pacific Ocean and I'd never know. (*Beat.*) On second thought, they CAN throw the things into the ocean. It's the house. I don't want my house going to someone who won't understand it. (*Pause.*) Do you think you and Nora would ever want to come and live here?

JANE: I have my own house, Margaret, and I can't speak for Nora. I hope we'll be living together for a long time yet, but…

MARGARET: And Allison has hers. (*She gets up and looks out the picture window.*) My mother had her religion to sustain her for her short life. I could never buy it, or sit still on a church pew. But this…(*She sweeps a hand.*)…this continuance of nature. This, I can. (*She turns back to face JANE.*) Don't pick Nora up when she stumbles, Jane.

JANE: She won't let me. We have an agreement. We only pick each other up when we're asked.

MARGARET: That sounds very modern. Is it healthy?

JANE: It seems to be the only way we know how to work it.

Scene 9

ALLISON enters from the stairway. She has on her riding clothes.

ALLISON: Mom? Can I borrow the Chrysler? Mickey has a new mare he thinks I'll like.

91

MARGARET: The keys are in my Eleanor Rigby. (*On JANE's quizzical look.*) The basket by the door. (*To ALLISON.*) Just be sure you come home before dark, honey.

ALLISON: Okay. Thanks. (*She swoops up the keys and exits DR door.*)

MARGARET: (*Looking back out the window.*) Nora needs some help with that bush.

JANE: It's been, an experience, meeting you, Margaret. (*She opens the window door.*)

MARGARET nods her agreement; JANE exits. We see her approach NORA. MARGARET picks up the telephone.

BLACKOUT.

Scene 10 Late that night

MARGARET sits alone on the sofa, one lamp on. She has a book in her lap; she stares at nothing. A key is heard in the front DR door. WYNONA enters. She crosses and stands in front of MARGARET.

WYNONA: What's happened?

MARGARET: Allison is pregnant.

WYNONA: Hoo.

MARGARET: Wynona, how on earth am I going to hold to my intention. Now?

WYNONA: Want to take a look at it?

MARGARET: Yes. It's why I called.

WYNONA: Okay, then. (*She sits in the easy chair.*) What is the consequence if you choose to keep taking your medicine?

MARGARET: I go down hill. I end up a blob. I die.

WYNONA: What's the consequence if you choose to stop taking your medicine.

MARGARET: I still die, but I end my life the way I lived it.

WYNONA: And that is?

MARGARET: On my terms. (*Beat.*) My turn. What happens to ALLISON: if I don't live to see her baby born?

WYNONA: Allison goes on being Allison.

MARGARET: Okay, then, what do I miss by not being a grandma, even if only for a little while?

WYNONA: If you're dead, what can you miss?

92

MARGARET: Okay, let's try this one. How do I feel about ALLISON:'s news?

WYNONA: No fair. No feelings on the table. I can't get into your feelings, You can't get into mine. Just the problem, no feelings while we're looking at it.

MARGARET: (*Leaning to touch WYNONA.*) What do I do?

WYNONA: (*Touching MARGARET.*) You do what you do. Nothing more, nothing less.

MARGARET: But is it enough?

WYNONA: It has to be. There isn't anything else. Just your choice.

MARGARET: Damn. Double damn. (*Pause.*) Let's get drunk. Stay tonight, go back tomorrow before the girls get up. How is Alberta, by the way? (*She gets up and pulls a bottle out of the bookcase.*)

WYNONA: Alberta is Alberta. Any more questions for the table before we start intoxicating ourselves?

MARGARET: No. Yes. I don't know. Damn again. The table's just going to have to come up with a clear decision by morning, that's all.

WYNONA: You will come up with a decision, and it'll be the fourth best thing you've ever done.

MARGARET: (*Taking a swig and handing the bottle to Wynona.*) What're the other three, as if I didn't know.

WYNONA: Birthing Nora and Allison and opening your door to me. (*She takes the bottle and starts up the stairs.*) Come on, you can sleep in my bed tonight.

MARGARET: Giving birth, being a friend, dying. Hell of an epitath. Put it on my stone, will you? Here lies Margaret Finn. She gave birth, made a friend, died.

WYNONA: I thought we were supposed to toss your ashes to the sharks.

MARGARET: You are. But I also want a stone. (*She holds her hand out to Wynona; the two go up the stairs.*)

BLACKOUT

Scene 11 The next day, late morning.

93

LIGHTS UP. A grey sky outside. ALLISON enters from the stairway. She is wearing jeans and a sweatshirt. She takes a look around and starts moving furniture. She is struggling with the dining room table when NORA enters from exterior DR door, wearing her hiking clothes. NORA takes in the changed room.

NORA: What are you doing?

ALLISON: I've always thought the table should be more, over here. (*Pointing.*)

NORA: Why are you doing this?

ALLISON: Don't you think this is better? After I get all this moved around, I'm going to get a mop and tackle some of those spider webs…(*Pointing upwards.*) Honestly, you'd think mom lived in a cave instead of a house!

NORA: This is Mags' house, not yours.

ALLISON: It's my house, too.

NORA: No, it's not. You don't live here. Did you ask her permission?

ALLISON: Why should I?

NORA: You don't just walk into someone's home and start re-arranging it to suit you!

ALLISON: This is NOT someone's home, it's MINE. I grew up in this house! You left! You don't know!

NORA: Did you? Grow up? Are you never going to be able to think of anyone but your adorable self?

ALLISON: I was having fun until you came along. Go away. Go on, go hide in the woods like you always did because we're not good enough for you! Go A-WAY!

MARGARET appears in the doorway of the interior UL door, drawn up to her full height. Her voice is full of steel.

MARGARET: I know you two have things to work out between you. God knows I've waited years for you to put aside your differences. But I am going to ask you… No, tell you. Do not do it in my house. Not now. Not ever. I have enough on my plate without you two bickering at each other like the children you no longer are. Grow up or leave. (*She turns on her heel and exits.*)

ALLISON: (*Screaming.*) Now look what you've done! Mom was going to take me shopping, but you've ruined everything! You

94

always ruin everything!

NORA: Mother used to let me hold you when you were an infant. I should have dropped you on your head. (*She storms out the DR door, slamming it behind her. ALLISON drops to her knees and wails. NORA walks back in DR door.*)

NORA: (*After a beat, she slides down the wall and sits on the floor.*) I'm too goddamn tired for this.

ALLISON: I'm so scared, seems like, most of the time.

NORA: I guess we're all scared, in our own way.

ALLISON: I can't believe I won't be able to call her up on Sunday mornings.

NORA: Yeah. Goodbye takes on a whole new meaning, doesn't it. ((*She straightens her legs out in front of her, turns her toes out into a perfect balletic first position.*)

ALLISON: You've been working out? In the attic? (*NORA nods yes.*) I was always jealous of your dancing. I was too fat, unco-ordinated.

NORA: And I was the unwanted one.

RAIN is heard on the roof.

ALLISON: I sure wish my relationship with mom was more like yours.

NORA: God, no, you don't. Trust me. (*Pause.*) You know, it's funny, but I've always envied your freedom from adulthood.

ALLISON: That's a mean thing to say.

NORA: Maybe. But trying to be equal to Mags, or good enough for her standards, what I always thought were her codes of behavior, shit. Maybe it's all just my shit. I don't know. (*They listen to the rain.*)

ALLISON: Do you think we'll end up being friends? After…?

NORA: That's what Mags wants. (*She stands stiffly.*) I'd better get into some hot water before I turn into a board. (*She exits up the stairway.*)

Scene 12

On her own, ALLISON exits the interior UL door and quickly returns chewing a cracker. She surveys the room, then sits at the table. She looks down at her belly, cups it with her hands.

95

ALLISON: Your grandmother went around the world. Twice. Can you believe it? It's true. She was a photographer, very famous, and went everywhere taking pictures. (*Pause.*) I suppose I should tell you about your father, and the man I was married to, and the man I think I'm in love with, who might, if I play my cards right, end up being your daddy. But we can talk about them later. And when we do, I want you to remember that I loved you from the minute I knew no horse could keep you from growing under my heart. I tried shaking you out yesterday, Mickey has this new mare who's got a righteous canter, but, no-o-o. So I sat on the ground and decided that no one was going to take you from me, or me from you, no matter what. And I want you to know something else, a secret. I, yes, me, I am going to convince Mom to stay and meet you. She'll do that for me. And for you. (*Pause.*) Are you hungry?

Scene 13

MARGARET enters via interior UL door, pushing the drinks cart which holds a plate of sandwiches, a glass of milk, a bottle of beer. NORA enters from the stairway, toweling her hair dry. Outside, a new storm gathers power. ALLISON wanders to the table, where MARGARET is putting out the sandwich plate, etc., and starts nibbling. NORA exits to the interior UL door, returns with a glass of water. She sits at the table, takes a sandwich. MARGARET takes plates from the breakfront, puts these in front of her daughters, sits, drinks from the beer. NORA jumps as a big gust of wind whomps against the plateglass window.

MARGARET: Something wrong with your sandwich?

NORA: This storm's making me jittery as a cat in heat.

ALLISON: It's just the wind. It'll pass.

MARGARET: It's unlike you to get nervous in bad weather, Nora.

NORA: I feel like the damn roof's coming off. Aren't you scared?

MARGARET: No. I'm not.

NORA: You're right. It's not the storm. It's us.

ALLISON: You're not going to rage again, are you?

NORA: And what's wrong with that? At least my anger gets

things out, gets it all moving.

MARGARET: I've always hated your anger.

ALLISON: I was always afraid of you, Nor, you know, when you'd get mad at… things.

NORA: (*To MARGARET.*) If you'd not turned away from my anger, let me find out about it, perhaps it wouldn't still be so red. (*Pause.*) We're just pretending that things are as normal, aren't we, like we've always done. As though we're somewhere in our suppressed past, and not faced with the mother contemplating suicide.

ALLISON: That's not true, we've been talking.

NORA: Yeah. In code.

The wind picks up; the lights pull down inside the house, hesitate, then revive.

NORA: (*Cont'd.*) Mags? Please? Talk to us. A real conversation, all we do is jump at each other in bits and starts…or in speeches…

ALLISON: Not now, Nora. Not now.

NORA: Allie, there is no tomorrow on this one. You can't just pretend it isn't happening, damnit.

MARGARET: All right. Enough. Nora, what do you want to say?

NORA: (*Beat.*) I feel abandoned. And I think suicide's a cop out.

MARGARET: You're entitled to your feelings.

NORA: That's Wynona's therapist language.

MARGARET: Thus mine. (*Pause.*) I've always hated limits being put on me. I took control over my own life at a very young age. This house, the garden, my life. It's all getting ready to change. I cannot bear the thought of not being able to be on my own, take care of my simplest needs, indulge in my dearest pleasures. I do not want to experience anything different than what I have and am right now. So when I had to face myself getting weaker, dependent… I simply will not do it. I have had a wonderful life. I see no point in ending it dismally. And if that's a cop out to you, so be it.

ALLISON: But you don't have to be dismal! Not now!

MARGARET: When you reach a certain age, you realize that you've lost all the options you once thought you had. They're all closed down. And there is no future. You've living in it.

NORA: Open a new door, go exploring, like you used to, with your camera.

ALLISON: But what about my baby?

MARGARET: Your baby has its whole future spread long in front of it. Since this today is my future, and I like it, why should I risk it being any less than what it is right now?

ALLISON gets up and exits interior UL door.

MARGARET: (*Cont'd.*) (*Getting up, moving to the sofa, sitting.*) You know I love you very much, Nora. You were my first.

NORA: (*Following, sitting in easy chair; matter-of-factly.*) And I've always taken the back seat to Allison, your baby.

ALLISON: returns, joins her mother on the sofa. She is munching cookies. The storm suddenly swerves, leaving an unnatural calm in its wake.

MARGARET: Why don't you tell us about the ring, Nora?

NORA: (*Touching her chest.*) How did you know?

MARGARET: Unless you've recently sprouted a peculiar, ring-shaped growth on your chest, what else could it be?

ALLISON: Why hide it, Nor? If someone gave me a ring, I'd flaunt it. Maybe get a new outfit to go with it. Let's see. (*She reaches out.*)

NORA: (*Pushing ALLISON's hand away.*) It's from Jane.

MARGARET: And you felt the need to keep Jane a secret from me.

NORA: Sure. Keeping secrets is our family tradition, after all. Don't let down the side, et cetera.

ALLISON: I want to see. Does it have a stone?

NORA: No. Plain band.

ALLISON: Wow. So that means you're…

NORA: Afraid of commitment. Yes. And with all, all this, going on…

MARGARET: All this is even more reason for you to get on with your own life. You don't need, and shouldn't want, anyone's approval. Especially not mine.

NORA: I've wanted that from you forever.

MARGARET: Well, quit. Your wanting so much makes me nervous.

NORA: How do you stop a girl child from needing her mother's approval?

MARGARET: Ask a full-time mom the secrets of mothering, dear. Not me.

ALLISON: You know, we ought to have a picture of this, family grouping. Wait a minute. Wait. What are people going to say?

NORA: True to form. Don't you hear yourself?

ALLISON: No, Nora. I didn't mean it like that. Remember when I had to have Harry put to sleep?

MARGARET: You're equating me with a basset hound?

ALLISON: Mom! Of course not. But you remember how awful I felt and everyone said it was for the best and that made me feel even guiltier? If people say that about you, about what you've done, I don't think I'll be able to handle it.

NORA: What do people know anyway? Besides, this is our family secret. Just for us.

ALLISON: (*Chewing on the inside of her cheek.*) Okay. So. Are you going to marry Jane?

NORA: (*Turning the question.*) How's life in the fast lane?

ALLISON: (*Double avoidance.*) Mom? What would've happened if you'd talked to us first, gotten our opinions, before?

MARGARET: I can't answer that, Allison. Seeing backward is futile. The provence of fools. I may be many things, but foolish is not among them.

NORA: I need to know what's going to happen when you stop taking the pills.

MARGARET: My body will come to a stop. (*She smiles at Allison.*) Much like old Harry.

NORA: Details, please.

MARGARET: (*Triple avoidance.*) There's a particular photograph I want to take of this house before I die.

ALLISON: Oh, I wish you would, I've got some great memories of the old homestead.

NORA: Tell the truth, Allie.

ALLISON: I am, Nor. Great memories. From when I was little, and then after…(*She closes her eyes and drifts to sleep.*)

NORA: After I left. (*Beat.*) Mags, do you think I could use the attic for a studio? I need to get back to work.

MARGARET: Do you have an assignment?

NORA: No. It's a novel I've started. I don't have any contracts right now.

MARGARET: A novel.

NORA: Yes, Mags. A novel.

MARGARET: Do you think that's wise?

NORA: It may not be wise, but it's what I'm doing.

MARGARET: It might be better to wait until you have a regular job.

NORA: A regular job. We always get to this, don't we. You telling me I need a regular job. You never had a regular job, why do you think I can't make it as a freelancer? I'm making it! I support myself! Why can't you acknowledge me writing a novel?

MARGARET: Your short pieces are your strength.

NORA: There it is. You don't think I have the talent to write a novel.

MARGARET: At least wait until you have a year's worth of solid clients lined up, money in the bank, before you take time off to write a novel. There's no guarantee you'll get it published, for all your efforts, talent aside.

NORA: And you should know about guarantees, right, Margaret? (*She reaches over and shakes ALLISON.*) Allison, wake up. You don't want to miss this.

MARGARET: Leave her be. This is between us.

NORA: Oh, excuse me. Let's protect little Allie at all costs.

MARGARET: I am not going to debate this with you now.

NORA stands and starts to exit. She halts.

NORA: You always have protected Allison, haven't you, even against me. In point of fact, I frequently needed your protection, but never got it. You always assumed I didn't need it, I suppose. But then, you're very good at assumptions, aren't you. I don't need this, Allison needs that. All those assumptions of yours guaranteed Allison and me never getting close. And now you assume, just because you beckon, just because you're dying, that we'll embrace into sisterhood ever lasting.

MARGARET stands; NORA crosses to face her. Both women pull themselves up to full height.

NORA: (*Cont'd.*) (*Low voice that crescendoes.*) You asked me earlier how I felt about your impending death. About your choice. Choice. And I said I felt abandoned. You know how I know that feeling? Because I got it from you, a long, long time ago, when I was just a kid, when I expected guarantees. First I was pushed aside because of your career. Then because Allison came, then dad dying. And who blamed him? And now the ultimate one. The big desertion.

ALLISON jerks awake as NORA's voice rises. She stands, bracing the back of her legs against the sofa.

NORA: (*Cont'd*) Let's hear it for the woman who is in total control! She controls her children, her environment, and yes, even her death! Well, I have just one question. Why did you ever bother having children?

CURTAIN

END OF ACT II

ACT III

Scene 1 Immediately following.

AT RISE: The family is as we left them, a frozen tableau. MARGARET, tired to her bones, moves to the table and sits. Holding her spine erect, she takes a deep breath.

MARGARET: Charles Finn's death was a lie, Nora. He never died. He walked away. He walked away from me, from you, from Allison.

NORA: What are you talking about? We had a funeral in 1960. We all stood around his open grave…

MARGARET: The grave was already covered. He wasn't in it.

NORA: You planted a tree, and there was a sign.

ALLISON: 'Charley's Here.'

NORA: Flowers, people standing around. We ate after. All a lie?

MARGARET: If you want to discuss abandonment with me, know this. I am not the one who left you. Charles did. I did you a favor by telling you he was dead. I planted that tree in an abandoned graveyard and gave you a chance at a life. I will not be blamed by you. You are not my inquisitor or my judge.

NORA: He's not dead.

MARGARET: And he wasn't your father.

The silence that follows is a tangible, full-dimensioned, breathing, silence standing watch.

MARGARET: (*Cont'd.*) (*Saying the rest quickly.*) Sam was a drummer with a band that traveled through town and out of it. He was my first and favorite love. Look at your hands. They're Sam's. Charles married me when I was three months pregnant with you. He was your baby sitter, and Allison's father.

Before she can stop her arm from taking its swing, NORA's open palm slaps her mother's face. All three women are astounded by the action. MARGARET staggers backwards, then pulls herself tall again. NORA covers her mouth with her palm and runs up the stairway. ALLISON reaches out to stop her, then turns to her mother.

ALLISON: Mom?

MARGARET: Please, Allison. Not now.

ALLISON: Mom? If we didn't bury him, where is he? Is he still alive? Charley? My dad?

MARGARET: I don't know. Please. We'll talk about it later. Please.

ALLISON nods, then slowly exits up the stairway. MARGARET gingerly touches her face; she is relieved to feel its growing sting. She laughs out loud, sort of an odd response to recent events, but hers, nonetheless.

MARGARET: (*Cont'd.*) If you laugh at it, you control it. If you control it, it doesn't control you.

NORA enters with her backpack slung over one shoulder.

NORA: I'll be in Santa Monica. At the Breakers. The phone number's on the pad.

MARGARET: You don't have to do this.

NORA: Yes. I do.

We HEAR a car horn outside. NORA exits DR door.
BLACKOUT.

102

Scene 2 The following morning

LIGHTS UP. MARGARET: stands alone in the room, looking seaward out the picture window into a grey sky. WYNONA enters from DR door with her suitcase and embroidered tote bag. She puts these down and joins MARGARET. The two friends watch the world outside for a beat.

MARGARET: (*Turning.*) Did I phone you?

WYNONA: Details, details. I was sitting under a cedar tree by Lake Louise and suddenly had an urge to ask if you'd done any more weeping. So here I am.

MARGARET: I'm glad. (*They move to sit at the table.*)

WYNONA: (*Takes a chocolate bar from her pocket.*) Here. Your favorite Cadbury's, although why you like this imitation chocolate is news to me.

MARGARET: (*Unwraps and eats a hunk.*) Oh, this is good. As to weeping, I haven't any time for self pity. That one incident was a lapse in judgment and I'd appreciate your not bringing it up again.

WYNONA belches.

MARGARET: (*Cont'd.*) And stop making that noise. You'll fill up with air.

WYNONA: (*Another satisfying belch.*) The way I figure it, you're being terribly sensible. Am I right?

MARGARET: If you mean, am I taking care of business, yes, you're right.

WYNONA: Let's see then. You've seen the doctor, I know that. Told the girls, probably made an appointment with the lawyer. What else is going on.

MARGARET: Allison can't stop eating.

WYNONA: That's a good sign.

MARGARET: And Nora's gone to hide in the Breakers Motel.

WYNONA: An even better sign.

MARGARET: I wish she didn't have this need to, to run away when her life backs up on her.

WYNONA: Seems sensible to me. She listens to herself and follows her own advice. She's like you in that respect, you know.

MARGARET: I've never run away.

WYNONA: Not with your feet, maybe, but you've done your own kind of running over the years. Admit it.

MARGARET: (*She won't.*) When her marriage broke up, after she had her abortion… (*On WYNONA's double take.*) …oh, yes, I knew about that. I wonder what it is about the Breakers Motel in Santa Monica that appeals to her?

WYNONA: Someplace warmer? a narrow room, an unfamiliar stretch of beach? a place where she's anonymous, where no one can get at her while she does her brooding.

MARGARET: But she keeps going back. That beach is going to feel like home territory to her soon, if she keeps running to it.

WYNONA: Maybe she won't. Maybe this is her last time there. (*Pause.*) When did she go?

MARGARET: Yesterday. After she gave me this (*Shows WYNONA her cheek*).

WYNONA: (*Examining MARGARET's cheek.*) This looks like the beginnings of a long stay at the Breakers.

MARGARET: I hope not. She needs to be here. I don't want any loose ends. (*Pause.*) Speaking of loose ends, are you home for good? Or does Alberta still have you in its grip?

WYNONA: Looks like you're stuck with me. (*Pause.*) It seems to me you're forgetting the most important thing.

MARGARET: And what might that be.

WYNONA: You're forgetting Margaret. She needs some paying attention to. Margaret needs to get mean, red mean. She needs to sing the blues. Needs to get down to the black void.

MARGARET: You left out, needs to get green with jealousy because her best friend's going to go on living. (*MARGARET's chuckle turns into a gasp. She closes her eyes and reaches out a hand. WYNONA grasps it and holds on until the spasm passes.*) Don't let go of me.

WYNONA: Not until it's time. (*Consulting MARGARET's pallor.*) How's about I make you a cup of herbal tea?

MARGARET: Make that a beer and I'm with you.

MARGARET and WYNONA get up and exit interior UL door.

Scene 3

ALLISON enters via stairway. She is wearing vintage 1940's women's clothes. She crosses to the telephone, dials, listens and talks.

ALLISON: Hi. I'd like to get some information, please. What? Where did I? Oh, in the yellow pages. Anyway, can someone there… Hi. I need to know two things about getting a divorce. If my husband says he's going to divorce me but I do it first, can I get in trouble? And, if I have a baby, but it's not his, but I got pregnant when we were married, can I get in trouble? (*She listens for a beat.*) Okay, thanks. Goodbye.

ALLISON hangs up the telephone and exits via UC sliding glass door to the backyard. She stands there for a beat, then drops to the ground.

Scene 4

MARGARET and WYNONA, entering from the interior UL door on her heels, see her go down, rush out, and together bring her in. MARGARET's breathing is rough. NORA enters via exterior DR door wearing her backpack and carrying a beat-up wooden, hand-painted sign, 'Charley's Here', and watches. WYNONA puts ALLISON on the sofa.

MARGARET: (*To ALLISON, who is coming round.*) Can you tell us what's happened, baby?

ALLISON: I just found out I don't have to wait for Richard to divorce me. I can do it first. And I guess the thought of it made me kind of giddy, that's all, like I had no bones, or something.

MARGARET: (*Sighing.*) If you want to go down south to take care of things, I'll understand.

ALLISON: No, mom. I want to stay here with you. (*She sits up and hugs her mother.*) Hey! Hi, Wynona! (*She jumps up.*) I'm hungry. (*She grabs WYNONA by the hand and pulls her out the interior UL door.*)

Scene 5

NORA: How can she do that? One minute a noodle, the next a dynamo.

MARGARET: (*Sitting at the table, trying to slow her breathing.*) And?

NORA: (*Dropping her things, sitting opposite her mother.*) I cast it all away on a fish hook.

105

MARGARET: A fish hook. Do I need to know what that means?

NORA: I asked the cab driver to take me to Pioneer Cemetery first, then I was going to go on to the train station, head south. But once I got to the bone yard… I sat down and wrote.

MARGARET: (*Her breathing under control.*) Bone yard.

NORA: It came out of me in a flood of words, my sadness and fear of being abandoned by you, about Charley leaving, and all the left-over rage at being second best. The works. I think. (*Pause.*) I got up and walked over to the bluff and followed the path down to the beach. There, I saw a figure. It was fishing.

MARGARET: It?

NORA: I couldn't tell, it had a hood over its head.

MARGARET: A hood.

NORA: On a sweatshirt.

MARGARET: Oh. Yes.

NORA: I watched it fish. For the longest time. It looked so serene, like it knew something big, cosmic. Wonderous. What I wanted to do was take all my words and put them on a fish hook and send them into the ocean.

MARGARET: And did you?

NORA: No. I brought them back here to burn.

MARGARET: (*A beat.*) There's one last rose to prune. Care to lend a hand?

MARGARET stands, collects a pair of gardening gloves from her basket.

NORA: (*A beat of hesitation.*) Sure. (*She starts to follow her mother out the plateglass window door.*)

MARGARET: Remember, you nip the stem just above the third joint.

NORA: I seem to remember that roses bite back when you cut them.

MARGARET: Everything in life does. But if you do it with love, new growth comes. Let's see your technique. (*MARGA-RET exits via the UC sliding glass door; NORA follows.*)

Scene 6

ALLISON and WYNONA enter from the interior UL door. ALLISON holds a package of chips and is eating from them. WYNONA takes them away, sits ALLISON down at the table, and exits interior UL door. MAR-GARET enters via UC door and exits up the stairway. NORA enters via UC door and sits on the easy chair. WYNONA returns with nourishing food on a tray. She sets this out on the table. ALLISON gets up and stretches out on the sofa. WYNONA sighs, sits at the table and unashamedly listens to ALLISON and NORA talk.

ALLISON: It's not Richard's baby.

NORA: So that's why he left.

ALLISON: It was the straw. We were headed for doom, anyway.

NORA: Doom?

ALLISON: Richard never really loved me, not really.

NORA: What about the father then?

ALLISON: He's not important.

NORA: ALLISON:!

ALLISON: He never was. He was just my way of striking out. (*She rubs her belly.*) Now that Richard 's so conveniently removed himself, and I can divorce him first, this baby is mine. All mine. Do you think that's horrible?

NORA: I think this is going to come and bite you in the ass someday.

ALLISON: (*Frowning.*) I was sort of hoping to come home and have Mom take me and the baby in. I guess that's not going to happen. Now.

NORA: No.

ALLISON: Maybe she'll change her mind.

NORA: I wouldn't count on it. Haven't you noticed she's breathing funny?

ALLISON: Oh, Nora, I can't understand why anybody would want to stop their life from living. At the beginning or the end. *ALLISON gets up, returns to the table, tucks into the food WYNONA put out. NORA gets up and joins her. Nibbles on a carrot.*

ALLISON: (*Cont'd.*) I'm so glad I'm not throwing up anymore.

NORA: As are we all.

ALLISON: Gotta keep feeding bob, here.

WYNONA: Bob? You're going to call that child Bob?

ALLISON: Well, it's just thingamabob, now. But Bob's not bad. What do you think?

WYNONA: I think I'd better buy you a name-the-baby book.

NORA: (*To ALLISON.*) What are you wearing?

ALLISON: Don't you recognize it? I found all this stuff in a trunk in the attic. Wait! There's more! (*She leaps up and runs up the stairway.*)

Scene 7

NORA: That garment yours?

WYNONA: Margaret's, actually. My clothing era of choice is the nineteen fifties.

NORA: Wynona? Tell me about my father.

WYNONA: I don't know much.

NORA: His last name, at least?

WYNONA: We never knew. (*Pause.*) In the late fifties, lots of bands traveled up and down the coast, and even stopped in our little town. (*Pause.*) Sam was a drummer on one of those bands. Your mother and I went to their, well, you couldn't really call it a concert, more of a musical happening. She wore a slinky black number, her hair all up on her head, looked like a queen. She and Sam took one look at each other, like that corny song, seeing someone across a crowded room…

NORA: My mother, romantic?

WYNONA: (*Shrug.*) She slipped off her principles.

NORA: And here I am.

WYNONA: Yes. Here you are. The result of a wonderful fall.

NORA: Wynona.

Scene 8

ALLISON runs down the stairway now also wearing a white and navy satin jacket with the name, Tierras, embroidered across the left breast. She twirls for NORA and WYNONA.

ALLISON: Check it out! A pregnant queen of the hop! (*She starts singing, slow dancing with herself.*) In the still…

WYNONA: (*Chiming in.*) Shoo doo n shoo be doo.

NORA: …O-of the ni-ight…

MARGARET appears on the stairway, in a bathrobe.

MARGARET: Shoo doo n shoo be doo…

WYNONA: When I held, held you ti-ight…

WYNONA crosses, takes MARGARET's hand, the two dance, humming the song. ALLISON goes to her mother, takes MARGARET's hand, puts it on her belly.

ALLISON: Mom. Here's your grandbaby.

MARGARET: (*Pulling back from WYNONA.*) Allison. Nora. Listen to me. I stopped taking my pills.

ALLISON: No…

NORA: What?

WYNONA: When.

MARGARET: Three days ago.

BLACKOUT.

Scene 9 Afternoon, a week later

LIGHTS UP. MARGARET enters via exterior DR door. She is wearing an overcoat and gloves. She sheds her outer wear and sits thankfully on the easy chair. NORA follows, halfway out of her jacket.

MARGARET: It suddenly all seemed so distasteful, so impersonal. I just couldn't wait to get out of there. Poor Henry. I'd better phone and apologize.

NORA: I didn't like it much, either. (*She sits on the sofa.*)

MARGARET: You don't mind me making you executrix?

NORA: It sounds so grown up. I don't know if I'm ready for growing up yet.

MARGARET: We never know what we can do until we have to.

NORA: Why all the secrecy about the money? We were going to know, eventually.

MARGARET: Have I ever told you how much money I do or don't have?

NORA: Come to think of it, no.

MARGARET: When my father died and left me a legacy, I was very surprised. I'd no idea he had any money at all.

NORA: I see. A family thing.

MARGARET: Quite possibly. How much money do you have?

109

NORA: None of your business.

MARGARET: Indeed. A family trait.

Scene 10

ALLISON enters from stairway wearing her bathrobe.

ALLISON: What's a family trait?

NORA: It seems that none of us knows how much money the other has.

ALLISON: (*Sitting at the table.*) Well, I have vats of the stuff. Mutual funds, real estate investments, the works. All hidden away from Richard. And I don't care who knows it.

MARGARET and NORA share a look that momentarily excludes ALLISON.

NORA: Well, then, you must have been adopted!

ALLISON: No, I'm not! But I do feel like a movie.

Scene 11

WYNONA enters from UL interior door on ALLISON's line. She pushes the drinks cart which is loaded with a full tea service.

WYNONA: Sustenance for the returning warriors. (*To ALLISON.*) Funny, you don't look like a movie.

ALLISON: Oh, Wynona. You're so silly. The 'Red Shoes' is playing in town.

NORA: My all-time favorite flick.

MARGARET: You girls go. You too, Wynona. I think I'd just rather take it easy tonight.

NORA: On second thought, so would I. Maybe there's an old movie on TV.

MARGARET: I have a better idea. Nora, drag that old valise over here. Allison? What say we have a fire? Wynona, I'd love a cup of that tea. Maybe some bread and butter.

NORA does as bidden, ALLISON starts a fire that NORA has to finish building, WYNONA brings MARGARET her a cup of tea and bread on a plate. She puts these on the small table next to the easy chair. Settling ad lib dialogue during this action. MARGARET opens up the valise. NORA and ALLISON sit in front of it. WYNONA sits, crosses her arms across her chest.

110

ALLISON: What's all this? Mom, are these your photographs? Oh, what happened? Why are they all… torn up?

NORA: Quite a legacy.

WYNONA: A bad idea.

MARGARET: Carl Sagan, you remember him, the astronomer, he said that we're all star stuff, universally connected. I like that idea. (*She reaches in, grabs a handful of torn photos, and tosses them into the fire.*) Here's my offering to the stars.

NORA: (*To WYNONA.*) Is losing her mind part of this heart thing?

WYNONA: No, this is a clear Margaret thing.

MARGARET: I have truly loved three people in my lifetime. My one real friend. (*WYNONA gives her a nod.*) You two, Nora, ALLISON:. (*Pause.*) Parents keep secrets from their children in the name of well-intentioned love. I now think that's not such a good idea. (*She tosses in more bits; struggles for breath.*) Remember that, both of you, when you have your own. (*Pause.*) One more thing. I could not bear the idea of you three or anyone else see me turn into a sloppy, vomiting, incontinent invalid. What I've done was the only possible course for me. (*Pause.*) Now hand me those photos under the telephone, Allison. (*ALLISON does that.*) This one…(*Handing one to NORA.*) …is for you, Nora. It's the only photo I ever took of Sam.

NORA: From the story of my conception, it doesn't sound like there was time for photos.

WYNONA: Take the picture, Nora.

She does.

MARGARET: (*Handing ALLISON a photo.*) This is my favorite one of Charlie, him leaning in the front doorway. And these… (*She hands one each to NORA and ALLISON.*) …are the two of you. The only time I let Charlie use my camera, and he gave me this gift. I printed two copies, just in case. (*She reaches out a hand for WYNONA, who helps her stand.*) You go on to your movie, girls. I'm having an early night. (*She stands.*)

WYNONA: (*Leading MARGARET toward the staircase.*) Lean on me, old friend.

WYNONA and MARGARET exit up the stairs.

Scene 12

NORA and ALLISON remain, both looking at their photos, at each other, at the room, at the valise still full of bits. NORA reaches in a hand and tosses some in to the fire. ALLISON follows suit. WYNONA returns down the stairs, sees what the daughters are doing, joins them, tosses in a handful.

ALLISON: (*Her attention turning*) Isn't there a way to tell if it's a girl or a boy?

WYNONA: You can have an amnioscopy, which is the scientific method, or listen to an old wives tale that says, if the baby is growing out and in front, it's a boy. If it's spreading all around you, it's a girl. Me, I'd go with the amnio. (*Considering the drinks cart.*) Doesn't look like any of us wants a full tea time this afternoon.

NORA: (*Getting up.*) I'll take the cart back to the kitchen.

She tucks her photos in a pocket and exits with the cart through interior UL door.

Scene 13

ALLISON: Wynona?

WYNONA: What.

ALLISON: How would you like to come to California with me? We could rent ourselves a little bungalow, on a bus line, close to a market, libraries. It's nice and sunny there, you'd like it. And you could help at the birth, and help bring up Bob, like you did me.

WYNONA: I like it here. It rains. I keep well in the rain. I have people who depend on me, patients. And, if you believe in fairy tales, that baby is a girl.

ALLISON: Bobette, then? Please?

WYNONA: (*Considering.*) I've got three conditions.

ALLISON: What? Anything.

WYNONA: I'll come help at the birth.

ALLISON: Okay. And?

WYNONA: I'll stay for a few weeks, help you get started.

ALLISON: (*Flinging herself at WYNONA.*) Oh, Wynona.

WYNONA: You haven't heard my third condition.

112

ALLISON: Let's have it.

WYNONA: You'll hire a nanny. I'll come as a friend, stay for a little while, or I won't come at all. Now go find someone else to bother. I've got a cornbread to make up.

ALLISON: I love you. And you'll see. You'll like it so much you'll never want to come back here. (*ALLISON skips up the stairs.*)

Scene 14

WYNONA, alone, closes up the valise and puts it in a corner. She picks up NORA's backpack and Charlie's sign and does likewise. She is about to exit via interior UL door when NORA returns from that door.

NORA: (*Crossing to stand close to WYNONA.*) I don't know how to do this.

WYNONA: Yes, you do.

NORA: All this symbolic tossing of torn up pictures into the flames is too much for me.

WYNONA pushes NORA onto a chair at the table, sits next, and holds a hand.

WYNONA: But it is exactly right for your mother.

NORA: She's getting smaller, have you noticed?, shrinking before my eyes, dying in bits and pieces while I watch like some sad voyeur. And I feel bits of myself dying with her. (*Pause.*) What will the end be like? How will it look? Will it smell differently than a living day? What will she feel? What will I feel? If I feel any worse than this, surely I'll be allowed to explode, or maybe just implode into the emptiness that's becoming me. I don't know how to do this. I have to be the old Nora for a little while longer. And who is that? And what about all the stuff we don't have time to finish?

WYNONA: (*Letting go NORA's hand and standing up.*) You do the best you can. You finish up or allow time to heal old wounds. If it was me, if I was you, right now, I'd try.

NORA: Try what?

WYNONA: Just try. (*She exits to the interior UL door.*)

Scene 15

MARGARET comes down the stairs, carrying a letter writing set in a box.

113

She stumbles on the last step. NORA crosses to help her; MARGARET shrugs off the assistance and continues to the table where she sits and opens the writing case. She removes a sheet, a fountain pen, and begins to write. NORA follows and sits opposite. Then she moves to sit next to her mother. She starts to speak but is preempted.

MARGARET: (*Looking up at NORA; putting down the pen; pauses as appropriate.*) I make no excuses to you for what I have done that you may not have liked, or that caused you discomfort. I gave you what I knew how to give; I hope it was enough. If I have one regret about our early days together, it is that I could have given you a stronger father, a man you could have looked back on as your role model for all things male. As it is, you've had to find that out for yourself. I know that I never made you false promises, and that, sometimes, you would have liked me to. But it was not my nature. I have kept secrets from you. That is my nature. I know that part of me is in everything you do and are. But know this. Most of who you are is yours alone. Don't ever let anyone take that from you. If I have learned anything in this long life, Nora, it is that our uniqueness is all that we really have. (*Long pause.*) If I haven't said it enough, I love you. You're hard work, but I do love you.

NORA: (*Nothing left to say.*) Ditto.

NORA rises and exits slowly out the exterior DR door. She closes it quietly behind her. MARGARET watches her oldest daughter leave for a beat, then returns to her letters.

BLACKOUT.

Scene 16 Late that night

MARGARET sits in her easy chair, in almost complete darkness. Three candles are lit and flickering. MARGARET heaves a great sigh. Her head slumps to her chest. She slides part way off the chair. NORA enters via exterior DR door.

NORA: (*Calling.*) Mags? Are you still up? I'd like to… (*Sees her mother.*) …oh, no…

NORA rushes to the easy chair, kneels, puts her head on her mother's chest, listens, checks for breath, finds a feeble pulse. She puts her mouth close to her mother's ear.

114

NORA: (*Cont'd.*) I'm going to get help, mother, I won't be a minute.

NORA starts quickly up the stairs calling for ALLISON and WYNONA. ALLISON: appears first. NORA can only point in MARGARET's direction. WYNONA appears behind ALLISON; moves quickly over to MARGARET.

NORA: (*Cont'd.*) Can we please get her out of this chair? Off the floor…

WYNONA: Allison, come here. Make a chair with our hands. Hold one wrist with the other hand, there, that's right. Link up with me. Now. Lift her up. Gently, gently. Nora, get a blanket.

NORA rushes upstairs and returns in a beat with a quilt. ALLISON and WYNONA get MARGARET spread out on the couch. WYNONA checks that MARGARET is still breathing. NORA sits on the floor, hardly breathing at all. ALLISON takes MARGARET's shoes off.

ALLISON: I'll make some tea.

She exits through the interior UL door. WYNONA pulls the easy chair closer to the sofa, sits, takes one of MARGARET's hands. ALLISON returns from UL door carrying a tray.

ALLISON: (*Cont'd.*) Here, Mom. I made your favorite tea and brought some of Wynona's cornbread, too.

What she really brings is a mug with no water and a tea bag in it and a bowl of the cornbread batter. No matter. ALLISON sits on the floor next to NORA and rubs one of MARGARET's feet. NORA's head is down. MARGARET opens her eyes. She smiles at her daughters, and lastly at Wynona. Still smiling, she closes her eyes and lets go of her life on a sigh.

ALLISON: (*Cont'd.*) Mom, no… oh…

WYNONA kisses MARGARET's lips and pulls the guilt over MARGARET's face. She gets up and opens the UC sliding glass door. The wind comes in and sweeps around the room.

BLACKOUT.

Scene 10 One week later

LIGHTS UP. NORA sits at the table, smoking, drinking coffee. A full ashtray is in front of her. She's wearing the same clothes and hasn't slept much. Wynona enters from the interior UL door, carrying a coffee cup and rubbing her left hip. Passing NORA, she snatches the cigarette out of

115

NORA's fingers, breaks it, and puts the pieces into NORA's coffee.

WYNONA: This packing's no good for my sciatica. (*She sits at the table.*) I can recommend a good therapist in Portland who works exclusively with addictions.

NORA makes a rude noise. ALLISON enters from the yard via UC door. She is wearing an old pair of MARGARET's coveralls and her boots. NORA lights up a new cigarette. ALLISON kicks off the boots and crosses to the table. She mimics WYNONA's earlier actions re: drowning the cigarette. Sits.

ALLISON: I called Jane and told her you'd started again.

NORA: You really are annoying, sister dear.

ALLISON: Only because I love you, sister dear.

NORA: (*Starts to light up, catches the looks on the other two women's faces, surrenders the unlit cigarette to the coffee mug.*) Missing her is too hard. My whole body aches with it.

WYNONA: Takes time.

NORA: (*Growling.*) Shut up.

ALLISON: Nora!

WYNONA: I don't mind, everyone approaches death differently. The important thing is to respect ourselves while we're doing it. Not go picking up on bad habits. Treat ourselves with kindness. And let others help us.

NORA: I'm not used to letting anybody help me.

WYNONA: (*Smiling.*) Where have I heard that before? (*Pause.*) Your mother would have liked her service.

ALLISON: Great, wasn't it. All of her friends here, trading Margaret stories. And Red and Ellen playing her favorite songs.

WYNONA: I especially liked Red's rendition of "Take the A Train."

NORA: What're we going to do about the house?

WYNONA: I think you should sell it. Just make sure it gets sold to someone who truly loves roses.

NORA: Sell the house…

ALLISON: Whoa. Sell… Sell?

She and ALLISON look around, at each other, at WYNONA. The exterior DR doorbell RINGS.

116

Scene 18

NORA gets up and ushers in HENRY WINKMAN.

HENRY: Mrs. Greenson? Miss Finn? Ms Dell?

ALLISON: Mr. Winkman.

NORA: What are you doing here? Is something wrong?

WYNONA: Nora, ask the man to sit down. Honestly.

HENRY: No, no, I can't stay, nothing wrong, I assure you, Miss Finn. But something, rather, peculiar, uh… I just cannot apologize enough. There was an unfortunate, inopportune disagreement between the mail room and my secretary… (*He slips a hand in a breast pocket and withdraws an envelope. He hands it toward NORA who inclines her head toward ALLISON who opens the envelope, withdraws two thin sheets of blue paper.*)

ALLISON: It's addressed to Mr. Winkman, but it's for you, Nora. From mom.

NORA: Mags?

HENRY: It must have been mailed the day she died, from the postmark, see…(*Pointing.*)…there? She mailed it to me, and as you can see, one of those notes is also addressed to me. She wanted this to be a codicil to her will. (*Dramatic pause.*) But it never arrived on time for the reading of the will. (*Senatorial pause.*) And since I am still the attorney of record and this document is legally considered part of the estate, I was obliged to reads the contents.

NORA: I don't understand.

ALLISON: (*Reading one of the notes.*) Mags decided to leave the house to Wynona. That's what it says.

NORA: (*Taking the sheet, reading aloud.*) I leave the house to Wynona because she knows better than any of us what home truly means.

HENRY: I sincerely hope this won't cause you too much anguish? (*Doesn't wait for a response from NORA or ALLISON.*) I have one other missive, for Ms Dell. (*He withdraws a folded piece of paper from an inside pocket.*) My instructions, Ms Dell, were to deliver the codicil to Margaret's daughters and then this note to you.

WYNONA: (*Taking paper and reading aloud.*) I'm giving you the house, Wyn. I hope you don't mind. Yours through time, M.

117

HENRY: I wish you all much success in your lives. (*He tips his head, and scuttles out the DR door.*)

Scene 19

ALLISON: (*Getting hiccups.*) Wow! What do you think of that?
NORA: I think it's vintage Mags. And…(*To WYNONA.*) …I love the idea of you living here.
ALLISON: (*Hand on belly.*) She's coming to California with us.
WYNONA: The house is mine?
NORA: Maybe we better ask Wynona what she wants to do.
The sisters watch WYNONA, who is internally considering things.
WYNONA: I'm a northwest woman, Allison. I was born here and, like your mother, I'll die here. Margaret left me the house to remind me. It's quite a gift.
The telephone RINGS. NORA picks it up.
NORA: Finn, no, Dell House. (*Grins at the others; back into receiver.*) Hello. Oh, hi, Jane. How're you? Yeah, I know she did. Rat fink sister. Don't worry, between the two of them, they've got me off cigarettes forever. I'll tell you about it later. How's George? (*Listens.*) Three mice today. That's a record. Say, looks like I'll be home sooner than I thought. (*Pause.*) Would tonight be too soon? I'm still a mess, but if you can stand me… (*Listens.*) Okay. And thanks. See you soon. Bye. (*Hangs up.*)
WYNONA: (*To still hiccupping ALLISON.*) Hold you breath for 10 seconds. Then we'll try something more radical. (*Thinks.*) Have you got a house to go back to?
ALLISON: Uh, I don't know. I don't know what Richard's doing, there's the divorce… according to that lawyer… Richard threatened to take the shop away from me… I don't know.
WYNONA: I'll leave all that to you, but, instead of me having to go south for the birthing, why don't you move in here?
ALLISON: (*Throwing her arms around WYNONA and hiccupping wildly.*) Oh, Wynona!
WYNONA: I'll take that as a yes. All right with you, Nora?
NORA: (*She stands, looks around, as if for the last time.*) To me, this was always Margaret's house. So, yes, more than all right. (*Dials phone and speaks.*) Hi, I need a cab at 22 Cliffside. Thanks. (*Hangs*

up.) Well. (*She hugs WYNONA.*) Well.

WYNONA: Call when you arrive. Let us know you're safe.

ALLISON: I'm naming Bobette Charlotte, for Charley. (*She hugs NORA.*)

A horn HONKS outside. NORA picks up her backpack and 'Charley's Here' sign, and exits DR exterior door.

BLACKOUT.

Scene 20 (Months later, end of August)

LIGHTS UP. WYNONA sits at the table, tiredly sorting through papers. Cups, mugs, dish towels, a small blanket, a stuffed elephant litter the table top. NORA comes slowly down the staircase and joins WYNONA at the table. She picks up a mug, drinks, makes a face.

WYNONA: How is she?

NORA: Quiet at last.

WYNONA: Been a hard year, all things considered. No wonder she's edgy.

NORA: Nine months, three weeks, four days. Since Mags sent us her summons.

WYNONA: A hard old time. (*Pause.*) I've been sitting here with the past…(*Indicates papers.*)…and thinking. Just like your mother did, before she sent for you.

NORA: Oh, Wynona, not you, too. I can't take another…

WYNONA: No, no, no. I'm fine. Just thinking. When Margaret left me this house, she also left me with her past. And yours. My thinking now is, do we still want it?

NORA: I've never wanted it. But when Allison died giving birth… with Jane gone… this was the only place I knew to come.

WYNONA: And I'm so glad you did. This was a good place to run to. For you and Charlotte.

NORA: I've been calling her Lotte. (*Long pause.*) How could ALLISON: not know she had a bad heart? How could she put her child at risk? How could she? How could she be so selfish?

WYNONA: How could she die, you mean.

NORA: Hell. I guess I do. (*Pause.*) Did you ever find Charley?

WYNONA: His trail ran cold years ago. Time all of us stopped

119

looking. (*Pause.*) How's this for a thought. You adopt Lotte legally, I rent out this place and go back to Canada, you two come with me. We start over, a new family. There's too many ghosts here. Margaret's. Allison's. Even yours and mine. Wandering all over the place, bumping into each other. No room for anything new. Even the roses have given up, they won't grow for either of us.

NORA: Why not sell the house, then, like we were going to, before… get a real fresh start?

WYNONA: Because I've made out my will and left the house to Charlotte.

NORA: Oh. (*She gets up and paces.*)

WYNONA: It'll be up to her to decide, when the time comes.

NORA fetches MARGARET's old valise from its corner. She brings it to the table and opens it. She and WYNONA look at and lift up the remaining bits of photographs. NORA removes the empty pill vial and the remaining pills. She can't speak. WYNONA puts vial, pills back in the valise, takes the case to the fireplace, upends valise, and returns it, empty, to NORA.

WYNONA: (*Cont'd.*) Go on up and get Lotte. Bring her down here.

NORA: I just got her to sleep!

WYNONA: Go on, just bring her.

NORA, protesting, exits up stairway.

Scene 21

While she's absent, WYNONA takes a Pentax 35 mm camera with long lens and flash attachment from the breakfront. She is checking lenses, aperture, etc., when NORA returns carrying the sleeping CHARLOTTE.

WYNONA: (*Quietly.*) Sit at the table with her, no, over here, on the sofa, the light's better. I can prop the camera on the table, and… (*She sets the timer, sits next to NORA and baby CHARLOTTE*) …everybody say, Alberta, here we come!

NORA and WYNONA: Alberta, here we come!

The flash goes off. CHARLOTTE makes a sound.

CURTAIN
END OF ACT III

Serenäde

A Play in Three Acts

Running Time: Approximately 90 minutes
Intermissions: After Acts I and II

Cast of Characters
(In order of Appearance)

FATHER: 60+, handsome in a ravaged sense, tall, wild white hair.
MOTHER (MIRABELLE): 40, lithe, angular, dark hair and aspect. (Non-speaking)
GEORGE: 10-year old boy, red hair, large hands.
GEORGE at 23: Lean, hungry, mercurial, building narcissist.
SARAH: First wife, 26, part Native American who passes successfully as Caucasian. Dark hair, flashing eyes, strong willed.
BELLE: 1-year old daughter of GEORGE and SARAH. in a carriage.
GEORGE at 27: Struggling to find his music.
REBECCA: Second wife, 25, dark, petite, brooding.
 RED-HAIRED WOMAN: Ethereal, long-sleeved, long-skirted black dress, hair and dress float. (Non-speaking)
GEORGE at 30: On the upswing of his career.
EDNA: Third wife, 35 similar to REBECCA and SARAH.
GEORGE at 37: At the top of his career, yet beginning to have doubts as to his talent.
MELORA: Fourth wife, 40, light, blonde, ethereal.
BELLE at 14: Suggestion of MOTHER as she would have appeared at the same age.
GEORGE at 42: Beginning his downward slide; eager to find something to spur him on.
CLARA: Fifth wife, 45, similar to MELORA.
GEORGE at 47: Off balance; declining popularity.

VERONICA: Sixth wife, off-stage character.

GEORGE at 61: Settling in to his age with a young wife and possible acceptance that his musical career is fading.

PAULA: Seventh wife, 40, resembles BELLE.

BELLE at 40: The spitting image of MOTHER when she left GEORGE.

GEORGE at 71: White haired, slump-shouldered, disappointed by life.

JOYCE: Eighth, and most likely last, wife. Unlike any previous wife, MOTHER, or BELLE.

BELLE at 50: As MIRABELLE would have looked had she lived to 50.

Two middle-aged WOMEN (ACT III only; nonspeaking)

CASTING NOTES:

One actor plays FATHER

One actor plays 10-year-old GEORGE

One actor plays GEORGE at 23, 27, 30, 37

One actor plays GEORGE at 42 and 47

One actor plays GEORGE at 61, 69, and 71

One actor plays 14-year-old BELLE

One actor plays MOTHER (MIRABELLE) and adult BELLE

One actor plays SARAH, REBECCA, EDNA

One actor plays MELORA, CLARA

One actor plays PAULA

One actor plays JOYCE

One actor plays RED-HAIRED WOMAN (HIS MUSE, HIS INNER SELF)

Setting: The action takes place over a span of 61 years, in the parlor of GEORGE's ancestral home, a once grand English manor house situated near Lake Windermere in Cumbria (the North, Lake District, of England). As the play progresses, the architectural features and furniture change to reflect changes in GEORGE's financial status and emotional condition. A stairway leads to the bedrooms, etc. upstairs, UR. An interior door leads to other interior rooms, UL. A handsome fireplace graces the Left wall. Bookcases abut the fireplace on either side. An antique breakfront, filled with dishes and glassware befitting the decade and GEORGE's bank account balance is situated against the Right wall. A door, leading to the main hall and front of the house, is DR. The furniture and accouterments— an over-upholstered settee, easy chair, table lamp between, occasional tables, a working Victrola, and standing lamps—are secondary in importance to the piano, a grand, which remains on stage throughout the play. The floor is bare of carpeting.

Although divisive, a wall calendar can be changed to show the year of each scene. Changes in time can be also accomplished by shifting contents in bookcases, adding or subtracting wall hangings, paintings, etc., adding and subtracting antimacassars on furniture, changes in lighting, growing and shrinking piles of yellowing newspapers. etc. The number of scotch bottles increases during the play.

Chronology

GEORGE is born in 1929 in Windermere, England. The play begins in 1939; he is 10 (I-1).

MIRABELLE, his mother, 40, leaves him then, and is soon killed in London in the Blitz.

GEORGE marries his first wife, SARAH, when he is 20, in 1949. They have a daughter, BELLE, named after his mother, who is born in 1950. He leaves them in 1952 when he is 23. (I-2).

Weds second wife, REBECCA, in 1954, at age 25. Leaves her in 1957 when he is 28. (I-3)

Weds third wife, EDNA, in 1959, at age 30. Leaves her in 1960 when he is 31. (I-4)

Weds fourth wife, MELORA, in 1961, at age 31. Leaves her in 1967 when he is 38 and successful. (I-6)

Weds fifth wife, CLARA, in 1970, at age 41. Leaves her in 1972 when he is 43. (II-1)

Weds sixth wife, VERONICA, in 1975, at age 46. She is killed in 1976 when he is 47 and his popularity is declining. (II-2)

Weds seventh wife, PAULA, in 1984, at age 55 (longest marriage thus far). She is committed in 1990 when he is 61. (II-10) Weds eighth wife, JOYCE, in 1998, at age 69. She leaves him in 2000 when GEORGE is 71. (III)

Properties
Steinway Grand piano
Portrait of MIRABELLE
Red Shawl
Many liquor bottles

ACT I
Scene 1: 1939
SETTING: We are in the parlor. Morning.
AT RISE: Ten-year-old GEORGE. sits on the floor, playing with wooden blocks. O.S. we HEAR FATHER and MOTHER shouting at each other; their words are intelligible; their acrimony is not.GEORGE. tries not to listen; he gives up, and crosses to the piano. He sits on the bench and plucks out a classical tune. FATHER enters UR door, a scotch bottle dangling from one hand, his clothing askew.

FATHER. That's right, all he's good for is banging away on her stupid sodding piano, stupid sodding pillock. Give over, you. (*FATHER grabs GEORGE. by the back of his collar and flings him off the piano bench.GEORGE. scuttles behind the settee for safety. FATHER stumbles around the set.*) Bloody piano, should've thrown the bloody thing in the bleeding lake when she brung it here, effing woman. (*FATHER bumps into furniture, knocking things over, ends up falling onto the settee. He upends and drains his bottle.*)GEORGE! Show yerself, you great lumping coward! Stand up to it, boy! No mettle, that boy. None worth showing. Here! Bring us another! (*Waves bottle in the air.*) Be quick about it!

Scene 2
MOTHER (MIRABELLE) enters UL door. She is dressed to go out in a coat and hat and carries a hard-sided valise. This she puts down. She stands very still in the doorway while FATHER continues ranting.
FATHER. Ah! Stand tall, lads. Milady has entered the room. Giving us a rare glimpse of her even rarer beauty. Skin deep,

124

that is, chaps, beware, the ice queen cometh. Ha. Ha. There'll be no effing and blinding in milady's presence, nor any farts nor copulations. Take a good look, Georgie me lad. This time she won't be coming back. Good riddance to bad rubbish, I say. Put her out with the bins. Send her off to the tip. I say.

Sometime during FATHER's speech, GEORGE. dashes out from behind the settee and up to his mother. He grabs her around her legs, burying his head in her coat skirt. She puts a hand on his head, briefly. She pushes him away, not ungently, picks up her valise, and walks out the DR door. We HEAR her FOOTSTEPS receding, the front door SLAM behind her.

GEORGE. Mummy! (*Rushing toward door: FATHER grabs hold of him, stopping his flight.*) Mummy!! Don't leave me!

FATHER. We're well rid of her, laddie. Never where she should be. Where's my scotch? (*He boxes the boy's ears.*)

GEORGE. Mummy!!! (*SPOT ON GEORGE.*) Don't leave me here!!!

ABRUPT BLACKOUT

Scene 3 1951

LIGHTS UP QUICKLY. GEORGE, 23, SARAH, 26, and BELLE, 1, in her carriage, enter DR. They are dressed in mourning clothes. His is a black cape.

SARAH. But I don't want to go to the States, George I left there for a reason, you know. (*She parks the pram, removes BELLE, and sits with her on the settee.*) Besides, Belle's too young to travel.

GEORGE. (*Tossing his cape aside, crossing toward the piano.*) Nonsense, darling. She'll sleep right through the whole trip. That's all she ever does, isn't it, sleep.

SARAH. Be thankful she wasn't a fussy baby.

GEORGE. I am, I am, my dearest. Love you both to distraction. (*Sitting at the piano; playing a few chords; the piano is more important.*) I'm not sure about the ending of this bar. Allegro or pianissimo. What do you think?

SARAH. I want to get out of these fake widow's weedsGeorge Such a charade, really. Your father told me Mother Mirabelle died ten years ago. So why you still mark the occasion, I don't know. Where is he, by the way?

GEORGE. (*Plays a few more chords.*) But what do you think about this? (*Plays two more chords, one quick, one slow and quiet.*)

SARAH. I like the softer version, I think.

GEORGE. Yes, doesn't fit with the rest of the movement. (*Beat.*) But pay attention, Sarah, what sort of composer's wife you call yourself, not knowing allegro from pianissimo, not softer, for godssake, pianissimo, well, I don't know.

SARAH. I don't need to know the names of all the bits and pieces to love your music, George

GEORGE. I don't want you to love it, I want you to feel it...like I do...those bits and pieces, God, father was right, I shouldn't have married out of my class, those bits and pieces are the notes of my soul on paper, in this instrument, in all the instruments of the orchestra, as I make them come alive.

SARAH. Stop dramatizing, George You've wakened Belle. (*She bounces the baby who sleeps on.*) Besides, I don't know what you mean by class.

GEORGE. (*Fully preoccupied with his composition now.*) Class means my father told me to marry a woman with a title, sweetheart, for the panache.

SARAH. And my father told me to marry a plumber, hus-band dear, for the bucks. (*She stands, crosses to the piano, and plunks BELLE into GEORGE.'s lap.*) Certainly not a piano player with a dead mother complex and a drunken father falling down all over the place. You really should go look for him, you know, George.

BELLE all but slides off before GEORGE. catches her and wedges her into the crook of one arm.

SARAH. (*Cont'd.*) I'm changing, then off to my Women's Insti-tute meeting. There's a platter of cold meats on the sideboard if I'm late back.

GEORGE. Mmmmmmm.

SARAH. And don't forget to feed Belle. Five on the dot.

GEORGE. Mmmmmmmmmm.

SARAH. George!

GEORGE. (*Looking up finally.*) Something on the sideboard? I especially like this phrase. (*Plays it.*)

SARAH exits UR.

Scene 4

GEORGE continues finding his chords. He starts to make a few notations before he remembers baby BELLE. He rises, puts her down on the settee, and returns to his piano. This needs to be the action of a fully preoccupied man, not a careless or intentionally cruel one. FATHER shambles in UL. He is ten years older and has not aged well. He almost sits on BELLE as he falls down on the settee.

FATHER. George! Bring me my bottle! (*GEORGE ignores FATHER. Keeps on playing. Is hitting his stride, and is deeply engrossed.*) George. Bottle. Where's that slut of a wife of yours, George. You misplace her again?

BELLE wakes and starts wailing. The men speak over her noise.

GEORGE. Don't squash the baby, Father.

FATHER. I'll do what I bollocking well please. Mewling brat. (*He stands and staggers to the piano. He leans against it for support.*) This is my house, mine, you hear, you're not too high and mighty, too grand, for a good hiding. Get the strap. (*His tone changes to a whine.*) Get me a bottle, George. I'm fair parched.

GEORGE. My house. Mother left it me, not you.

FATHER. Fucking twat.

GEORGE stops composing. He rises, picks up BELLE and bounces her in his arms as he steps close to his father, brandishing a fist. BELLE raises her voice.

GEORGE. Don't call my mother that. Don't you ever…

FATHER. (*Swatting away GEORGE's hand.*) I could tell you some stories about your (*nasty emphasis*) mum, I could. Swanning off to London with her high and mighty society friends any time she damned well pleased, no thought about the rest of us. Bloody fucking cunt.

GEORGE. Fair warning, Father.

FATHER. You should be down on your knees to Hitler and his bombing blitz instead of mooning around like a sick dog, London and the sainted Mirabelle up in flames together, how fitting…

FATHER starts to say something else but is stopped as GEORGE's fist

127

connects with his chin. Down he goes GEORGE, still clutching the wailing BELLE, drops down on one knee to contemplate his father.

GEORGE. Father?

GEORGE puts BELLE down on the floor she quiets and puts his ear to FATHER's chest for a listen. We HEAR FOOTSTEPS returning.

Scene 5

SARAH enters DR.

SARAH. Had to come back, I've forgotten the minutes of last month's meeting… oh, good heavens, George, you've killed him.

GEORGE. I don't think so. Here. (*He stands up.*) You have a listen.

SARAH picks up BELLE and listens to FATHER's chest all in one smooth movement. A KNOCK comes at the front door.

GEORGE wanders back to his piano; SARAH goes to DR door. We HEAR her FOOTSTEPS going to the front door and returning. She holds an envelope which she puts on the piano bench next to GEORGE.

SARAH. Your ticket to America, GEORGE.

GEORGE. Our tickets! (*GEORGE leaps up from the piano and sweeps SARAH, still holding BELLE, into a dance pose. He twirls them around the room, gleeful.*) Just think how wonderful it'll be! America! Land of promise… I'll be famous beyond our wildest imaginings! Won't I… (*To BELLE.*) …you luscious bit of stuff.

SARAH. (*Pulling away a bit.*) If we go with you.

GEORGE. But I can't go alone…

SARAH. Of course you can. And you will. Belle and I will stay here and wait for you to come back. (*She puts BELLE on the settee with cushions bolstering her in.*) Feed your daughter, George, and do something about your father.

GEORGE. (*Not looking at any of them.*) He's all right. Just his usual state, I'm sure.

SARAH. Clean up your mess, George.

SARAH exits DR door. Once again, we HEAR her FOOTSTEPS retreating. This time, we HEAR the outer door slam shut.

GEORGE. (*Looking up at that sound.*) Mother?

ABRUPT BLACKOUT

Scene 6: 1957

LIGHTS UP SLOWLY. GEORGE, 27. and REBECCA, 25, enter DR, both in mourning clothes. GEORGE. flops on the settee. REBECCA disappears UL; GEORGE hums a few bars of a piece. REBECCA returns momentarily carrying a loaded tea tray.

REBECCA

I'm so glad I thought to prepare our tea before the funeral, George. (*She sits down on the easy chair, puts the tray on a table, pours out two cups, adds sugar and milk without consulting GEORGE. He, meanwhile, stares at her fussing with the tea things.*)

GEORGE. I don't know why you wanted to marry me, Rebecca.

REBECCA. (*As if her answer is the only possible one.*) You need taking care of.

GEORGE. No. I need understanding. As an artist. I still do.

REBECCA. (*Handing him a cup.*) Drink your tea, George.

GEORGE. (*Pushing tea cup away.*) I don't want a bloody cup of tea.

REBECCA. Temper, George. Temper.

GEORGE. Why won't you ever listen to me. I tell you I don't want tea, or a hot water bottle, or a different shirt on, and you just forge ahead as if I were speaking Martian or were a mute.

REBECCA. I'll excuse your mood, George. After all, we've just buried your father.

GEORGE. Nothing special about today, then. He's been as good as dead for years.

REBECCA. Well, the doctors did say that falling down the steps back then, that is what happened, isn't it, George, your father fell? Well, that blow hastened his death, is what the doctors said.

GEORGE rises abruptly, crosses to the piano, sits, plays a piece of his own. REBECCA joins him on the bench. It is a tight fit. While GEORGE plays, she can't stop herself from running her fingers over all parts of the instrument within her reach, as if her hand was a dust cloth. GEORGE pushes her hand away; she continues, smiling. This back and forth goes on for a beat. Then she starts straightening his hair, shirt collar, etc.

GEORGE. (*Jumping up.*) God's teeth, woman, leave it alone. A

129

man can't get any peace with you around, let alone get any work done. That's what killed father, you know, the need to get away from your interminable fussing!

REBECCA. Oh, George! What a mean thing to say! Now, you know that's just not true. I loved your father. He was just a big, old, gruff bear. I looked after him, kept him away from the drink.

GEORGE. That's just it. You keep us away from what keeps us going, keeps us alive. I haven't written a single note in months.

REBECCA. George! I always help you with your music!

GEORGE. You call fussing me about, helping. Strewth.

A KNOCK is heard at the outside door. REBECCA goes to answer it. She returns with a large painting wrapped in brown paper. GEORGE, meanwhile, paces, stopping to glare at the piano.

REBECCA. The delivery man said he wasn't sure about bringing this today, what with the old gentleman's funeral…

GEORGE. (*Taking the painting, ripping off paper.*) That's mine, not his. (*The paper off, George stares at his mother's image on canvas.*)

REBECCA. Oh, isn't she lovely. Who is it?

GEORGE. Was.

REBECCA. Hmmmmmm?

GEORGE. Who was it.

REBECCA. Who?

GEORGE. Mirabelle.

REBECCA. Mirabelle?

GEORGE. My mother. I had it done from a photograph.

REBECCA. She looks jolly. I wish I'd known her.

GEORGE. (*Propping the painting on the mantle and standing back to view it properly.*) None of us knew her, even those of us who thought we did.

REBECCA. (*Drinking tea.*) You never talk about your mother, George. Where is she?

GEORGE. Somewhere between heaven and hell, I'm bound.

REBECCA. (*Enough chit chat.*) I've got your washing done. Where do you want your new shirts put?

GEORGE. I don't care. Chuck them down the stairs if you want.

REBECCA. George. Honestly. Now. What shall we have for dinner tonight? (*She starts out the UL door.*)

GEORGE. I said I don't care. Oh, go on. Just leave me be.

REBECCA. (*Stopping by the door.*) I'll never leave you, George, nothing to worry about on that score.

SLOW LIGHTS DOWN

Scene 7

MUSIC is heard O.S. A waltz. SCATTERED LIGHTS; DREAMY. GEORGE enters (from anywhere) in a tuxedo, slowly dancing with RED-HAIRED WOMAN (HIS MUSE). She wears a long-sleeved, long- and full-skirted black dress; only her face and hands are visible. The two waltz around the room, faces close. GEORGE dips her, brings her up, they gently kiss. He twirls her, then drops to his piano bench, playing along with the waltz music. She leans against the piano, then touches his cheek as he plays. He segues into a piece of his own; she is entranced and excited. She drops to the bench, runs her fingers through his hair, they embrace passionately and kiss deeply. GEORGE pulls the woman to her feet; the two slowly waltz OFF.

LIGHTS FADE DOWN.

Scene 8: 1959

LIGHTS SLOWLY UP. EDNA, 35, enters DR. She wears a business suit, heels, and carries a lit slim French cigar and an alligator briefcase. She has a pronounced and noticeable facial tic. A pair of spectacles are perched on top of her head. Throughout the scene, she will hunt for these, patting herself down, etc., but never remembering they are on her head, until end of scene. She throws the briefcase in the general direction of the settee, kicks off her heels, and lays supine on the floor. GEORGE, 30, enters UL peeling an orange. He steps over her on his way to the piano, perhaps dropping a peel or two on her body. GEORGE is beginning to get recognition as a composer. His manner, clothing, and demeanor reflect a man on the way up.

EDNA. (*From the floor.*) It's our one-year anniversary today, Georgie. What's that one. Paper?

GEORGE. Rocks.

EDNA. One whole, glorious year.

GEORGE. I have done well, haven't I?

EDNA. Will I be your third and last? Third time a charm and all that? Poor old Rebecca. Suicide's such a stupid waste, don't you think. Well, I do. What happened, Georgie, you drive her to it? She couldn't take you gazing in your own reflecting pool any longer?

GEORGE. (*Not meanly.*) Shut up.

EDNA. What? What did you say, George..?

GEORGE. Shut. Up. Ed. Na. Clear enough?

EDNA. Oh, don't criticize me, George. Not today.

GEORGE. And what is so sacrosanct about today?

EDNA. No, you don't want sacrosanct. That's something preserved by religious fear against desecration or violence.

GEORGE. Feeling a bit on the violent side myself, at the moment.

EDNA. Sacred, George. That's the word you want. Any messages? Lord, I'm tired.

GEORGE. Sir Arthur telephoned.

EDNA. (*Jumping to her feet.*) George! That's marvelous! It'll mean a new commission, at least one, maybe more.

GEORGE. I told him I didn't want it. Won't take it.

EDNA. Nonsense, of course you want it. Where's his number? Where are my glasses? Here's what you do, George. You ring up Sir Arthur, the dear old fart, where are my glasses, and tell him you were in some sort of fugue state or something equally dire when last he rang and that you'll be delighted and honored and of course you accept the commission. What's it for?

GEORGE. He wants an opening march. (*He gets up and sits at the piano, plunks around on the keys.*)

EDNA. (*Searching for the telephone number.*) Didn't you write down his number?

GEORGE. What for? I told him no. I'm gaining importance now. I don't have to take commissions I don't want. A march. Pah.

EDNA. What for?

GEORGE. What?

EDNA. The march. What's it for.

GEORGE. Some muckety muck's hundredth anniversary in

132

some old boy's society, I think.

EDNA. Some imPORtant muckety muck's anniversary, George. That's what we need. Connections, leading to other connections, THEN you'll truly be an important composer in this country. Where are my glasses? Oh, hell, where's the *Who's Who?* That'll tell me how to get in touch with him.

GEORGE. Don't ring him back, EDNA..

EDNA. Don't be daft. Of course I'm going to ring him back. Oh, and by the way. Mother's moving in.

GEORGE. She is not.

EDNA. She is. Tomorrow. Tea time.

GEORGE. She can turn her broomstick around and go back to the cave she came from. Tomorrow. Tea time.

EDNA. Won't it be wonderful. While I'm at work in the film studio, mother can help you here. We'll be taking care of you day and night.

GEORGE. Flaming heck.

ABRUPT BLACKOUT

<u>Scene 9</u>

LIGHTS UP QUICKLY. This is a short scene, more of an extended beat, in which we see GEORGE., the composer, alone, in full artistic and boy-ish charm/glory/bliss, yet also further understand his loneliness———the paradox that is GEORGE..

Suggestions for the actor in this almost completely ad libbed scene are as follows: Use the piano as someone you wish to entice. Bring the music out of the instrument with passion, and all that passion entails. Your passion, even madness for your music, is what draws women. Let us see it fully blown in this scene.

Rise occasionally to regard your mother's portrait, to survey the room, rear-range books in the shelves, etc., all things an artist might do to counterbal-ance the intensity of making art as, in GEORGE's case, composing a new piece (definitely not a march). The actor needs to score the new work (mark musical notes on a score sheet), get enthused, play bits on the piano, grow frustrated, return to enthusiasm for the work, all like a ballet in move-ments of varying emotionality. By the end of the scene, GEORGE finds the chords to complete the first section of his new composition, a symphony.

133

He rises from the piano bench and crosses to stand in front of his mother's portrait.

GEORGE. You should have stayed. (*He exits UL.*)

SLOW BLACKOUT

Scene 10: 1966

LIGHTS UP SLOWLY. The set is at its best, reflecting success and comfort. MELORA, 40, and GEORGE, 37, are deep in an argument. They speak more with boredom than acrimony. Still, we know there is no love lost between them.

MELORA. Sarah was my sister, George. How dare you belittle her memory. You show nothing but contempt for the woman who was your first wife.

GEORGE. She wouldn't go to the States with me. I blame her for my failure there.

MELORA. That's absurd. You've no one to blame but yourself.

GEORGE. Your tiresome sister was only ever interested in herself. Look what she did to Belle.

MELORA. No harm has come to Belle, and you know it.

GEORGE. All I know is what's been relayed to me. Sarah kept Belle from me, kept my own and only daughter from me all these years.

MELORA. Don't be dramatic, George.

GEORGE. Sarah used to say that.

MELORA. And she was right. You blow everything up, clear out of any decent sense of proportion.

GEORGE. Do you see Belle here? Has she ever been here? Been allowed to visit me?

MELORA. Have you ever asked her to come? Did you ever visit Sarah? Even when she was dying?

It is a draw. The two retreat to opposite parts of the set; GEORGE to his piano, MELORA exits UL and returns with a bottle of soda. She sits on the settee, drinks from the bottle.

GEORGE. I wish you wouldn't do that, so classless.

MELORA. Always a concern of yours, isn't it, George. Class. What a snob you are.

GEORGE. And how tiresome you are.

134

MELORA. I suppose our getting married was a mistake.

GEORGE. Quite an understatement, wouldn't you agree.

MELORA. You certainly didn't marry me because I resemble Sarah.

GEORGE. I had high hopes the opposite might bring me luck.

MELORA. What did the other two look like, Rebecca, and, Erna?

GEORGE. Edna.

MELORA. Lord, what a name. And what a fool you are, George.

GEORGE. I am an artist. If all you see is the fool, I give you leave to vacate the premises. Poste haste.

MELORA. I would, believe me, your dubious charms wore off about two days after our wedding, but. Belle's due any minute and I won't leave her to your carelessness.

GEORGE. (*On his feet.*) Belle? Here?

MELORA. On the three-thirty train from London.

GEORGE. Good god, Melora, you could at least give a man decent warning.

MELORA. Why? You'd only run away.

GEORGE. That's not fair. I've never left.

MELORA. There are ways and ways of leaving, George, as I think you will agree. Oh, that must be her. (*A CAR is HEARD, the outer door SLAMS, FOOTSTEPS come along the hallway.*) Now remember, George, she's fourteen.

GEORGE. What's that supposed to mean…?!

Scene 11

BELLE, 14, enters DL. She is dressed as an apolitical American teen of the 1960s and chews gum. MELORA greets the girl with a quick hug and exits even quicker DL.

GEORGE. That's disgusting. Put it out.

BELLE. Why?

GEORGE. Because I asked you to.

BELLE. Why should I listen to you?

GEORGE. Because I'm your…

BELLE. What?

135

GEORGE. Hmmmmm. I need a drink. What about you.

BELLE. I'm fourteen.

GEORGE. Surely you drink something over there in the Colonies.

BELLE. Wyoming.

GEORGE. Wyoming?

BELLE. Where I live. With my mom and dad.

GEORGE. The… ?

BELLE. Robson's. And my sister. Judy.

GEORGE. Judy. How quaint.

BELLE. I like her. She's groovy.

GEORGE. I beg your pardon?

BELLE. Groovy, you know, with it.

GEORGE. With what?

BELLE wanders over to look at MOTHER MIRABELLE's portrait.

GEORGE. (*Cont'd.*) I was sorry to hear about your mother… about Sarah.

BELLE. She got run over by a guy calling her a nigger.

GEORGE. How utterly uncivilized.

BELLE. (*Shrugs.*) She was quarter Navajo. I'm an eighth. I'll have a coke.

GEORGE. What's that?

BELLE. Geez Louise.

GEORGE. What's that!?

Scene 12

MELORA enters UL. Both BELLE and GEORGE look to her for salvation.

MELORA. How are you two getting on? Fine? Good.

GEORGE. Melora, do you know what a geez louise or a coke is?

MELORA. Geez Louise, I imagine, by the look on Belle's face, is some sort of expression of exasperation, and coke is a fizzy drink. Belle, I've made the bed in the east room. Lovely morning light it gets.

BELLE. I'm not staying.

GEORGE. She's not staying.

MELORA. How alike you are! Your train doesn't go until ten tomorrow morning, dear, so of course you'll stay. And George, have you noticed the resemblance to Mother Mirabelle? (*Beat.*) In a moment of romanticism, George named you after his mother, dear. That's her, in that painting. See? Around the eyes, yes, that's the strongest bit. Now, then. Fizzy drinks all round?

GEORGE. Scotch, if there's any mercy left in the world.

BELLE. Got any beer?

MELORA. See? Peas in a pod, you two. Peas in a pod.

MELORA exits UL. In the beats before we see her again, BELLE and GEORGE regard each other as two wary cats might.

Scene 13

GEORGE.

She'll bring lemon water and biscuits on a tray. With a doily.

(*He crosses to a bookcase, removes a wide leather volume, pulls out scotch bottle and a shot glass. Pours a shot and downs it. Holds empty shot out to Belle, who nods. Pours her one, she takes a sip, starts coughing. MELORA pops her head round the door.*)

MELORA. All right in here?

GEORGE. Fine, fine. Too bloody fine.

MELORA. Goerge, don't swear in front of your daughter. (*She pops back out of sight. GEORGE and BELLE return to their wary circling.*)

GEORGE. You are, you know. My. Daughter.

BELLE. But you're not my dad.

GEORGE. No. Dad I am not. But I am famous, if that's any consolation.

BELLE. (*Lets that slide; to painting.*) What was she like, Mirabelle?

GEORGE. I don't know.

BELLE. That's dumb. How could you not know your own mom. Really dumb.

GEORGE. She left when I was ten.

BELLE. Where'd she go?

GEORGE. To war.

BELLE. Which one?

GEORGE. (*There is only one for him.*) W W two.

137

BELLE. I know about that, we studied it in history class. Was your mom a whaddya call it, WAC?

GEORGE. We had WRENS. No. My, Mirabelle, she got hit by a bomb and died.

BELLE. Wow.

GEORGE. Yes. Wow.

BELLE. Is that why you keep getting married…

GEORGE. You make it sound like a recurring ailment, gout, or lumbago, or something in the lungs…

BELLE. …cause your mom left and got killed?

GEORGE. Wow.

BELLE. Well. Anyway.

GEORGE. Mmmmmmmm. Indeed.

A long, uncomfortable pause. Abruptly, GEORGE moves to his piano. He begins to play. BELLE crosses slowly, leans on the piano, and listens. She does not understand his music, is quickly bored, moves away.

GEORGE. (Stunned) Don't you like it?

BELLE. I don't get it.

GEORGE. There's nothing to get, child.

BELLE. I'm fourteen.

GEORGE. Why do you keep saying that?

BELLE. Because you don't get it.

GEORGE. What don't you "get" about my music?

BELLE. Well, you couldn't sing to it.

GEORGE. (*Has met his match*) What kind of music do you like then?

BELLE. The Beatles. Stones. Turtles.

GEORGE. Good lord.

BELLE sings a verse of "I Wanna Hold Your Hand."

GEORGE. (*Cont'd.*) (*Covering his ears*) That's not music. (*BELLE launches into a verse of "Satisfaction."*) Sand to an ostrich! (BELLE. starts dancing around while she's singing. She stops after a verse of "House of the Rising Sun.

GEORGE. (*Cont'd.*) Well! So that's American music these days.

BELLE. They're all English groups.

GEORGE. Half of you is English, you know.

BELLE. Your half.

138

GEORGE. My half.

BELLE. My best friend back home is half German, half Mexican, and half Jewish.

GEORGE. How can anyone be three halves of anything?

BELLE. You aren't anything like I expected.

GEORGE. What did you expect?

BELLE. Well, either you'd be in mod gear (*GEORGE is bewildered by 'mod gear'*) or standing by the fire with a gun and a spotted dog, wearing a jacket, you, not the dog, with leather on the elbows, one of those weird cap things with the flaps over your ears, and those pants with those lumps on the sides. Oh, and long shining boots.

In spite of himself, GEORGE laughs; takes another drink.

GEORGE. What a picture I'd make, lord of the ha-bloody-ha manor! No, I'm a composer, a musician, an artist.

BELLE. I don't like art.

GEORGE. No one doesn't like art. No one sensible, that is.

BELLE. I can't make anything look like it's supposed to.

GEORGE. Then create something new!

BELLE. I'd rather listen to my records.

Scene 14

MELORA returns UL.

MELORA. I've just had the most MARvelous idea, George.

GEORGE. (*Another belt of Scotch.*) Hang onto your ear flaps, chaps (*winks at BELLE, who ventures a half grin*), Lady Melora has an idea!

MELORA. Stop drinking, Goerge. You know what you're like.

GEORGE.

Go on, tell us, MELORA. m'dear. What exactly am I like?

MELORA. No better than you ought to be, that's what.

GEORGE. Sod off.

BELLE. Sod?

MELORA. Never mind, dear. Your father's just playing silly beggars, aren't you, George.

GEORGE. Buggers.

MELORA. I'm sure it's not buggers.

GEORGE. The word is bugger. Buggers in the plural.

BELLE. What's a bugger? Buggers?

MELORA. (To BELLE.) Never mind about buggers. Beggars is a much nicer expression.

GEORGE. And if wishes were horses, beggars would ride.

BELLE. Sod?

GEORGE. Naff, if you prefer a more regional word. Same meaning.

BELLE. Naff?

MELORA. My idEa is that Belle come live with us.

GEORGE. What?

BELLE. What?

MELORA. For a year, to start, then we'll see how we go. It's all up to you, GEORGE.

GEORGE's response is to move to the victrola, select a record, put it on, and turn up the volume. GEORGE sits down and closes his eyes. BELLE, not knowing what to do with herself, sits primly on the sofa, waiting for the 'adults' to sort themselves out and give her instructions.

MELORA. (*Cont'd.*) The way I see it, you and I have reached an impasse. I mean, I was happy to step into the breach when you and Sarah split up and she couldn't afford to keep Belle and you didn't send her any money and I arranged for Belle to go live with the Robson's in Wyoming, I was happy to do all that. Now Sarah's gone and Belle's almost grown and, George, you can't see beyond yourself is the way I see it, and I can't see why you won't accept the fact that you're not as famous as you once were and get a post somewhere. Teaching is not much of a wage, but at least we'd have some steady dosh coming in instead of having to wait for you to be offered another commission. If you were more ambitious, but… Teaching, George. Teaching and taking care of your daughter for a while. That's for you.

GEORGE. Students tromping in and out of here? Touching my piano? Never.

MELORA. George, you're not listening. A post, George. At a school.

GEORGE. (*Shuddering and taking another drink.*) Like you said,

140

she's almost grown. What could I possibly do for her now?

MELORA. (*Throwing up her hands.*) It's not that I don't love you, George, heaven knows why but I do. But I think after another year, that's it for me. You'll have Belle and I'll go on to something new.

BELLE. (*Small voice.*) Can I go now?

GEORGE. Some one new, more like it.

The recording stops. GEORGE makes no move to put on another disc, even though it is obvious that the piece is unfinished.

MELORA. Maybe less than a year, George.

GEORGE starts a gentle weeping. He takes another drink.

GEORGE. I've never been able to finish it. Damnable thing haunts me. (*To BELLE.*) Is it any good? Is it?

BELLE. (*Very uncomfortable, yet well raised.*) What's it called?

GEORGE. Unnamed, unfinished, unsymphony. That's it, the great un.

MELORA. (Throwing up her hands.) Maybe more like six months, George.

GEORGE. Maybe you should start packing now, madame.

BELLE. (*Standing up.*) I really think I should go back to London now.

MELORA. Come along, dear, I'll show you to your room. (*She takes hold of BELLE's hand. BELLE resists.*) Oh, never mind him, we'll leave George with his great un. That's all he ever cares about anyway. His music.

MELORA and BELLE exit UR.

BELLE. (*off*) I'm leaving tomorrow. For sure.

MELORA. (*off*) Maybe that's best, dear.

Scene 15

GEORGE, alone, gets up, takes the needle off the disc, finds another bottle in the breakfront. Breaks the seal, unscrews the top, takes a healthy swig in salute to his mother's portrait.

GEORGE. They don't understand me, that's the problem. You know what I mean, don't you. If only once, just once, a woman came to this house and didn't try to change it, or me. At least in this room I have my music. They can't change that,

141

I won't let them. (*Salutes the portrait again.*) All I've ever wanted is to be understood. Isn't that what you wanted? You're gone, he's gone, and my music… my music. (*GEORGE flops down on the piano bench and picks up the last refrain of his unfinished symphony. This he repeats, searching for the next notes.*)

Scene 16
MELORA enters and listens.
MELORA. The last thing my sister said before she died was she wished she'd given you more time. But more time won't do it, will it, George? She was a dreamer, our Sarah. But not me. Me, I've decided to put Belle on the train tomorrow morning. And I'll be going back to the States with her. Miraelle's house, her piano, her painting, it's all yours again. Just like you need it to be. Isn't that right, George.
GEORGE is oblivious. MELORA watches him for a long moment, turns on her heel, and exits UR.

Scene 17
The ghost of MOTHER MIRABELLE. enters (from anywhere). She is wearing the clothes she wore when she left. She glides soundlessly over to the piano and puts a hand gently on GEORGE's head; it rests there for a beat, then slides down to one shoulder. Then, GEORGE finds the next phrase, the right phrase. The next section of his symphony unrolls before his eyes, through his hands, onto the keyboard.
LIGHTS DIM
CURTAIN
END OF ACT I

ACT II
Scene 1: 1972
AT RISE: LIGHTS FULL ON. The parlor has been the scene of a boisterous party. Empty bottles, full ashtrays, paper streamers draped over the piano and furniture, a table or two upended, the Victrola needle stuck in the center groove of a disc, someone's under garments tossed over a lamp-shade, etc. It is early morning and everyone's leaving, bumbling together in the hallway, staggering out the front door, struggling into coats and boots,

laughing and making goodbye chat. CAST MEMBERS alter their voices and overlap the following with laughs and giggles and rustlings to create the illusion of a crowd lingering in the hallway, leaving the house.

MALE VOICE (*off*) What a bash, eh? Nigel? Nigel? Where the hell's Nigel?

FEMALE VOICE (*off*) One hand down my nickers, last I saw him.

FEMALE VOICE (*off*) I can't tell you how wonderful it is that you're preggers, Clara.

MALE VOICE (*off*) Yes, old thing. Quite an accompish... accooompl... a coup (*he pronounces the 'p'*) to pull off.

FEMALE VOICE (*off*) In your dotage at that! Where's my gloves? Nigel? Have you got my gloves? Where's Nigel?

MALE VOICE (*off*) Our music man a papa at his advanced age! Still got 'em old boy, eh! Balls! Eh!

CLARA (*off*) Here are your gloves, Sissy. Attached to Nigel's belt.

MALE VOICE (*off*) Come on, ducks, let's move this thing along. I'm positively pissed. Somebody has to drive me home, darling. You? Come for a little nightie cap?

GEORGE. (*off*) Drive them away, Nigel. The wife and I have some private celebrating to do! Good night, good night, good night.

ALL VOICES (*off; fading away*) Good night, good night.

FEMALE VOICE (*SISSY; off; fading*) Could have bowled me over with a feather. George? Sexual? Somehow I just can't imagine him naked...

MALE VOICE (*NIGEL; off; fading*) Oh do come on, Sissy, for the sake of all that's holy.

The outer door SLAMS shut behind the last reveler. GEORGE, 43, and his wife CLARA, 45, enter DR. GEORGE has his arm around CLARA's waist; he is exuberant, she subdued. CLARA moves away from GEORGE and starts cleaning up.

GEORGE. Leave it! Leave everything and come dance with me!

GEORGE restarts the Victrola and the record on the turntable. It is a jazz number. He starts to boogie around the room, grabs CLARA up. For a mo-

ment she is entirely with him; then she starts to pull away.

GEORGE. (*Cont'd.*) You're right. Should be more careful. Here. You sit down. Put your feet up. I'll tidy everything away, don't you worry.

CLARA. I'm not worried, George, but…

GEORGE. (*Settling her on the settee.*) I know I've been a proper lout, inattentive, preoccupied, the lot, but now my symphony's almost finished…

CLARA. George, I need you…George., listen a moment…

GEORGE. Anything you want, my beauty. Imagine, me a father. (He is up, prowling the room in exuberance.) Had a chance, once, made a proper cock up… But now, now I'm rich… We're rich, my lady wife, concert halls around the world are ringing, offering the moon on a golden keyboard. Oh, Clara, thank you, thank you. I think this may just be my happiest day!

CLARA. Oh, dear.

GEORGE. (*Sits with her, takes her hand in his.*) I promise I'll be different from now on. I won't disappear into my music, well, I'll always play and practice, but… But you and this new baby… baby, imagine…

CLARA. I'm not.

GEORGE. I know, you're not sure I can be a good father. But I promise you…

CLARA. Don't promise, George.

GEORGE. But I want to!

CLARA. There's nothing to promise about.

GEORGE. Of course there is! I'm going to be a papa! Papa George! Or do you think it will want to call me pater? Father? Surely not Daddy? You won't let it call me daddy, will you, Clara? I don't see myself as a daddy, do you?

CLARA. Not a problem, George.

GEORGE. That's settled, then. How about a nightcap? (*He's up and pouring himself a brandy.*) I do see myself as exerting a positive influence unless, God, you don't suppose this child will want to grow up to do sport or be militaristic, or want to read maths at Oxford. You should really try to have a girl, Clara, I really do think I could be a better influence on a girl than a boy, after all, boys are such complex creatures, and…

CLARA. It's not a boy, George.

GEORGE. Well, then! (*Pours and hands her a brandy.*) Uh, how do you know? About, boy, girl…

CLARA. I just do.

GEORGE. Aren't you a miracle! Drink up, miracle girl! You can paint the box room pink for a nursery and start knitting small things, or whatever it is that women do when they're expecting.

CLARA. I'm not.

GEORGE. No? All right then, we'll get someone in. One of those nancy boys. Is that right? A decorator?

CLARA. George, sit down.

GEORGE. I'm too excited to sit… You'd think I'd be shit-scared, wouldn't you… But… Let's dance some more, better yet I'll play something… I'll start writing a, a lullaby, that's the ticket, never tried one of those before. Dah de, da da dum… (*CLARA tries to get him to sit next to her, but he's back on his piano bench, beginning to compose his lullaby. The notes, the rhythm, are wrong, somehow.*) Serenade, short a. The first in a new opus. Or maybe that should be Serenade, long a.

CLARA. There's no need for a new opus.

GEORGE. Of course there is!

CLARA. (*Sitting next to GEORGE*) There's no baby.

GEORGE. You're just nervous, new mother and all that. I'll find you a, uh, nanny, and, uh, helpers… how will I… maybe some of the church ladies will know of someone… how to arrange…

CLARA. (*Putting one hand over his on the keyboard, briefly, then, she speaks to the air, as if alone.*) No baby. It's strange, you know, how bodies work. Or mine does, at least. How they seem to know what's best. I never wanted a child, even when I was younger. I'm forty five now and want my life to belong to me, not some dependent creature pulling and pushing at me.

GEORGE. (*Starting to get it; slumps.*) But you said you were expecting…

CLARA. You were the one expecting, George. Going on at me, day and night, as if a baby were some sort of life-saving miracle. It's not. A baby is a lump of snot and shit and squalling demands. (*Pause.*) Last Sunday, during the Communion, we were singing a hymn I like. (*SINGS.*) "Come let us join our friends a-bove…". I took a deep breath, just before the line goes up. (*SINGS.*) "…That have… (*Her voice goes up and gets the high note.*) …ob-tained the prize…"* and I felt this sort of, of squeeze, like God had his hands inside my hips and was squeezing in, a pressing down sort of, a definite pushing out feeling, hot and wet between my legs, a trail of bloody slime ooze down my leg. (*Beat.*) Those good church ladies do know someone, George. (*She looks at him finally.*) Two of them got me to a doctor's surgery, where I was thoroughly scraped clean, and brought me home. (*Beat.*) All before lunchtime. (*Long pause.*) All without you noticing.

GEORGE. You'll have another. Baby. Yes?

CLARA. You're not listening. I don't want any children.

GEORGE. But I'm writing a lullaby.

CLARA. If I get pregnant again, I'll get an abortion. No lullabies.

GEORGE. (*Small crash on the piano keys.*) Then get out.

CLARA. (*Getting up, moving slowly UL.*) What do you want for supper.

GEORGE. I want you to get out.

CLARA. You're tossing me out because I won't have your children?

GEORGE. Out.

CLARA. Or are you throwing me out because you're afraid your music is drying up and finding a new opus is the only thing you really care about?

GEORGE and CLARA freeze. The red-haired WOMAN drifts through; lights and music strains (GEORGE's) follow her; GEORGE's inner vision follows her across and off stage.

SOFT BLACKOUT

Scene 2: 1976

146

LIGHTS UP. GEORGE, 47, is standing, listening to a voice on the other end of the telephone. He speaks and listens as appropriate.

GEORGE. Yes, this is George Blackstone... I'm sorry, I don't understand... Yes, of Blackstone Lodge, but what?... Yes, Veronica, my wife, yes... Well, of course she lives here, silly man, who did you say you were? Police? But what... No, she's not here right at this instant... Well, of course I know, she's not here. She's not here, is she? What do you want? Veronica? She's an actress, although what that has to do with anything... A performance, Covent Garden, yes, she's getting marvelous reviews... what? Nigel Winters? Yes, I know... what does he have to do with... an old family friend, yes... who did you say you were? Inspector Callahan? I see, Metropolitan Police, yes, but why... You what? Want me to what? I don't understand... Who the hell's Isadora Duncan? A dancer who died in 1927, all right, but what, yes, some sort of long scarf thing got caught in a car wheel... Veronica? Yes, she wears long scarves... (*Long pause for listening.*) I'd like to repeat this, if you don't mind, because it doesn't make any sense. You're saying that my wife, Veronica Blackstone, was found dead in Nigel's convertible roadster, evidently, that was your word, wasn't it?, evidently strangled when her scarf wound round the rear tire when the car started up... oh, the wind caused it to fly backwards... a windy night in London, as if that helps... and that she and Nigel were both drunk and he's in hospital in a drunken stupor, no, my word, Inspector, delirious about Veronica playing Isadora and what a lark when her scarf flew back, and she's in the morgue. And you want me to come to London to identify her. Have I got it right? No, no, I don't. I see. You'll send a car. Yes. I said, yes, Inspector. You'll excuse me? (*Hangs up. GEORGE grabs a bottle, sits at his piano, and whips off a short-abrupt, rich, multi-layered composition. Looks up at MIRABELLE.'s portrait. Plays through.*) What do you reckon? Pavanne for a Dead Wife? Number ten on the classical hit parade? Or, Sympathy for the Beleaguered Composer Husband, deprived of wife number six? Will I pass Henry by and take me a seventh? Ode to Everything in My Life Going Pear Shaped? Tell me. (Crash on the piano keys.) You tell me!!

<u>Scene 3: 1984</u>

LIGHTS UP. We HEAR GEORGE, 55, and PAULA, 34, entering from outside, moving along the hallway. They enter through the DR door on GEORGE's line.

GEORGE. You really are making excellent progress in class, Miss Darling. I don't quite see why you felt you needed a private tutorial, at your, um, level of musical acuity, although your interpretation of why Herrmann used a theramin in *Psycho* disturbed me.

PAULA. Say Paula.

GEORGE. Paula?

PAULA.

PAULA. Darling. Repeat after me. Paula…

GEORGE. Paula…

PAULA. Darling.

GEORGE. Darling.

PAULA. (*Knowing smile.*) I know I'm a good pianist. In time, I might even become a great composer. Like you. You're also a very good teacher. (*Beat.*) I want to get closer to the man.

GEORGE. (*Leading her to the piano.*) Next week we'll be studying the importance of timing in film scoring.

PAULA. (*She's playing the coquettish slut.*) My timing is impeccable. As is…(*She touches him.*) …my fingering.

GEORGE. When I signed on to teach at Trinity College of Music, no one warned me about students like you.

PAULA. I'm one of a kind, Georgie.

GEORGE. Ah, the film strip we'll be working with has timed blips in the upper right corner for the music cue.

PAULA. I'd like to work with your blips.

GEORGE. And, ah, our task is to make certain our down beat coincides with these blips.

PAULA. What about our up beats?

GEORGE. What?

PAULA. Up beats, George.

GEORGE. Professor Blackstone, I think, don't you.

PAULA. Isn't it a bit late for that? What with our down beats and our up beats and our timing and our fingering all coinciding so nicely. (*She sits at the piano and launches into one of his compositions.*) You act out the film, then, and give me my cues. When to go up. When to go down. When to go up. Down. Up. Down. Up Down.

GEORGE. Miss Darling.

PAULA. Paula.

GEORGE. Paula. Please.

PAULA. Please what?

GEORGE. Please will you stop larking about and... (*Beat.*) Well, hell, will you marry me?

ABRUPT BLACKOUT

Scene 4: 1987

LIGHTS UP. PAULA, 37, enters from UL, carrying a large basket. This she puts down and pulls things from. She is, from the look of things, starting to redecorate. Color swatches for wall paint, furniture fabrics, and the central piece, a fringed 1920s shawl in vibrant red shades that she tosses over the piano. She hums as she works, happily nesting. GEORGE, 58, enters the stairway UR, pulling on a threadbare sweater. He crosses toward his piano, kissing the top of his wife's head as he does so, moves the shawl away from the keyboard, opens it, starts to play, suddenly stops.

GEORGE. (*Indicating shawl.*) What's that?

PAULA. What's what, my darling?

GEORGE. That red thing. There.

PAULA. (*Coming to touch it.*) Isn't it dreamy? I found it at the church jumble sale last week and just couldn't resist the colors. Aren't they lovely? So bright. This room needs brightening up, I think. It's so... so brown.

GEORGE. Darling?

PAULA. Hmmmm?

GEORGE. Paula? (*She ignores him, continues holding swatches up around the parlor. He moves to her, holds her shoulders to get her attention.*) This room is off limits to any tinkering with its colors. Okay? Do say you understand. (*She nods.*) But this...(*He lifts up the shawl.*) ... will be the exception. Here. (*He drapes the shawl across her.*) Dance

149

for me.

She does, swaying sensually until a distant TELEPHONE BELL sounds. GEORGE goes off UL. While he's gone, PAULA packs up her swatches with much sighing. GEORGE returns UL, searches for a bottle and takes a hearty swig. PAULA takes the bottle from him, fixes him a proper glassful. Hands it to him during.

GEORGE. (*Cont'd.*) She's coming.

PAULA. Who is?

GEORGE. BELLE.

PAULA. Who? I don't recognize the name. Should I? Is this Belle person someone I should put on our list?

GEORGE. My daughter.

PAULA. I beg your pardon.

GEORGE. Belle. She's my daughter.

PAULA. Pardon?

GEORGE. I have a daughter, her name is Belle, and she's coming. Tomorrow.

PAULA. You have a daughter, her name is Belle., and she's coming tomorrow.

GEORGE. Oh, for heaven's sake, Paula. Yes, a daughter.

PAULA. Which, or whom, you never mentioned. (*Beat.*) How old is she, this Belle?

GEORGE. Well, I don't know, let's see… uh, she should be about…

PAULA. Whose daughter is she? That might help place her age.

GEORGE. What? Oh, she's Sarah's.

PAULA. Your… ?

GEORGE. First wife. Forty. That's it. Belle will be forty now. Gracious.

PAULA. You have a forty year old daughter who is coming here tomorrow. That's right isn't it?

GEORGE. Yes. I think a drink all round is in order. (*He helps himself.*)

PAULA. A daughter you never told me about, who is close enough in age to me as never mind, and who didn't have the courtesy to ask me if she could come, this same daughter is landing on my door step unannounced. Really, George.

GEORGE. She couldn't ask your permission as she, uh, doesn't know about you, you know, that we're married.

PAULA. This gets better by the minute. A forty year old woman is coming to this house to visit her father whom she doesn't know is married to a thirty-seven year old woman.

GEORGE. Do we have any cokes? I remember she used to like cokes.

BLACKOUT

Scene 5: The next evening

GEORGE, PAULA, and BELLE, 40, sprawl in the parlor; BELLE in the easy chair, GEORGE and PAULA on the settee.

PAULA. I thought tomorrow we might go into Hawkshead.

GEORGE. Count me out, dear.

PAULA. You adore Hawky.

GEORGE. Four students tomorrow. Four more pairs of hands committing artistic atrocities against my piano.

PAULA. Four more tuition payments, more to the point. (*To BELLE.*) Hawkshead is a typical Lake District village, complete with a proper tea shop-pe, newsagents, crooked alleyways, timbered houses, the Beatrix Potter museum. All served up cozy English fashion.

BELLE. I was hoping to go for a long walk.

GEORGE. Perhaps Belle would rather a day trip to London. Museums. Art galleries. History.

PAULA. The footpath down by the farm takes you right up to the top of Cunsey. You get a lovely long view of Lake Windermere from there.

GEORGE. The Underground. The Tower. Houses of Parliament. Soho. Covent Garden. My club.

BELLE. I had in mind something on the order of Wuthering Heights.

PAULA. Oh, that's the Yorkshire moors. Well, I suppose we could manage a visit to Howarth, where the Brontë family lived, you know. What club?

GEORGE. Hmmmmm?

151

PAULA. I didn't know you belonged to a club.

GEORGE. An inheritance. All the men in my family…

PAULA. Oh, a man's thing. Well, Belle won't want to see a bunch of old fogies snoring in stuffed leather chairs, will you?

BELLE. Well, I don't really…

GEORGE. Nonsense. Women visit all the time. On Tuesdays. Is the day after tomorrow Tuesday? We'll go then. She'll find it amusing at the very least. I'll ring up Nigel to join us for luncheon. He's always good for a laugh these days. Poverty seems to suit him.

PAULA. Is he living there now? How grim.

GEORGE. He says he likes vibrating to the pulse of London's once grand and noisy market district.

BELLE. I'd like to see Covent Garden, but, really, don't either of you go to any trouble on my account. I can entertain myself while I'm here. I was sort of hoping to spend some time by myself in London anyway. Maybe I can take a train down and stay in a B and B somewhere.

GEORGE. Well, that's settled then.

PAULA. London is stinky and sordid these days, if you ask me. Much better to stay here in the Lakes. I know, we'll go up to the stone circle at Castle Rigg. Have a walk round. Maybe catch a play down in Keswick afterwards. They've renovated their little theatre. Really quite good.

BELLE. There's some research I want to do. In London.

PAULA. Something connected with your work, dear? I don't think you told us? About your work? What is it you do?

BELLE. I type.

PAULA. Type?

BELLE. I have really strong hands. So I use them to type.

PAULA. What sort of things do you… type?

BELLE. Anything anyone throws at me.

PAULA. Well. How… extremely interesting.

GEORGE. (*Getting up; fixing drink.*) I'm for bed. I'm going into London on Tuesday, Paula's going off to the antipodes. You're welcome to join me, Belle, in civilization, fortify yourself with a lunch of meat, potatoes, and two veg before you launch into your researches. Paula?

PAULA. I'll be up in a minute, dear.

GEORGE. And I may stay the night. You could return on the train, Belle. Paula can fetch you from the station.

PAULA. Good night, George.

GEORGE, with a wave of his drink glass, exits.

Scene 6

PAULA. (*She takes up the red shawl and wraps herself in it.*) Your hands are rather like George's. Large. Spatulate fingers. (*She measures one hand against one of BELLE's.*) Mine are too small to reach above a solid octave let alone a twelfth like your father's. (*She drops BELLE's hand.*)

BELLE. You play piano, then.

PAULA. Yes.

BELLE. Do you give concerts?

PAULA. No, no. I'm in an orchestra that plays almost exclusively for commercials, or that music you hear in posh elevators. (*She hums a few bars.*) Oh, but you wouldn't recognize that, would you.

BELLE. So your talent is anonymous.

PAULA. Well, huh. I... huh.

BELLE. Like mine.

PAULA. I suppose. (*Long pause.*) At least I have a steady income.

BELLE. As do I.

PAULA. I'm not bothered about fame.

BELLE. Being in the background isn't so bad.

Another long pause.

PAULA. I know so little about you, nothing really.

BELLE. What would you like to know?

PAULA. Um, married?

BELLE. No.

PAULA. Ever?

BELLE. Once. Briefly.

PAULA. Children? (*BELLE shakes her head, no.*) Any bad habits?

BELLE. I chew my fingernails when I'm nervous. Which I suppose is a good habit. For a typist.

153

PAULA. What kind of food should I... I didn't know what to get in...

BELLE. Meat and potatoes and two veg sounds fine.

PAULA. You can't have that for breakfast.

BELLE. Whatever is available is fine.

PAULA. Cereal?

BELLE. Fine.

PAULA. Omelettes?

BELLE. Fine.

PAULA. Toast and jam?

BELLE. Fine.

PAULA. Ham? Sausages? Scones? Orange juice?

BELLE. I've never had a crumpet.

PAULA. Neither have I. (*She drapes the shawl around BELLE's shoulders, and starts to lead them both UR.*) Then we should.

BELLE. Fine. (*Pause.*) Or high tea. I've never had a high tea. Cucumber sandwiches.

PAULA. With the crusts trimmed off. Lemon curd.

BELLE. Bovril.

PAULA. Vile stuff. Full of yeast and masses of vitamins (*NOTE TO ACTOR: 'vit' as in bit, not bite.*).

BELLE. Clotted cream.

PAULA. I have some in the fridge.

BELLE. Salad cream.

PAULA. I actually know how to make that.

BELLE. Steak and kidney pie.

PAULA. I will not make that.

(*She rubs at her temples. The women exit.*)

Scene 7 A week later, late afternoon.

BELLE sits in the easy chair, reading a book. A loose pile of papers are at her feet. She occasionally bends over, consults one, returns to her book. GEORGE enters. He has about him a slightly disheveled look, as if he's been running or tossed together. He fixes himself a drink. Holds up the bottle in BELLE's direction. She shakes her head, 'no'. He plops down on the settee.

GEORGE. Alone, are you?

154

BELLE. Paula's gone to her yoga class.

GEORGE. Ah. (*Beat.*) Anything laid on for tea?

BELLE. Will you explain tea to me? Seems to be all sorts of times in the day for tea.

GEORGE. If you're working class, your last meal of the day, taken around six P.M., is your tea. "Fix me me tea, Soph." If you're upper class, low tea and high tea are both served at four o'clock. Low simply means you had a large luncheon and take a biscuit or two with your tea. High means you had a smallish lunch, and need more sustenance. Sandwiches, cakes, gateau, sweets and savory, fish or meat paste, clotted cream, jam. Then there's elevensies, just in case your breakfast won't hold you over until the mid-day meal, and consists of creamy tea and a digestive biscuit or two. To say nothing of the little something one must have before retiring so one doesn't wake hungry in the night. Someone once said, or wrote, I can't remember which, that we English survive because of or in spite of our tea. (*Beat.*) How or when the aristocracy takes their tea, I haven't a clue.

BELLE. What are you?

GEORGE. Are all Americans this blunt?

BELLE. I don't know about all. It's a large country. My friends and I speak plainly to each other, yes.

GEORGE. Upper middle, I suppose.

BELLE. Which means you take your tea… when.

GEORGE. I don't take tea.

BELLE. Yours is scotch, instead. No cookies.

GEORGE. Cookies?

BELLE. Biscuits.

GEORGE. Ah. Yes. No cookies. (*Beat.*) How long are you staying?

BELLE. My return flight is next week.

GEORGE. I have a concert in November. In Ipswich. I'm conducting my Fourth Symphony. Once upon a time called the great Un.

BELLE. I'll be flat out of money by October. I need to get back to work.

GEORGE. Cash in your ticket.

BELLE. Can't. Non-refundable.

GEORGE. Stay. Don't worry about money.

BELLE. Really. Whose will I be using?

GEORGE. (*Waves away her question.*) I'd like to have you stay. Longer.

BELLE. When I read your letter, I couldn't believe it. Out of the blue after twenty-five years.

GEORGE. Twenty six.

BELLE. You counted.

GEORGE. (He shrugs this off, also.) You're good company for Paula. She gets lonely with just me… and has odd headaches… I thought, perhaps, someone her own age… a girl… and then when you rang up…

BELLE. Oh, and I thought you wanted to see me.

GEORGE. I did. I do.

BELLE. I've been here a week and I've seen you maybe ten minutes.

GEORGE. Surely more.

BELLE. Okay, fifteen.

GEORGE. (*Waving away this implication.*) What's all that *(indicating papers)* in aid of?

BELLE. Before she died, Sarah wrote and told me about a distant Welsh cousin of hers.

GEORGE. The Welsh are crazy.

BELLE. You're part Welsh.

GEORGE. One-third only. What's Paula planning for dinner?

BELLE. I'm cooking.

GEORGE moves to sit at the piano. He begins to play.

BELLE. (*Cont'd.*) That sounds familiar.

GEORGE. I played it for you when you were last. You didn't like it then.

BELLE. (Listens for a beat.) It's disturbing.

GEORGE. What do you mean?

BELLE. I mean, I feel edgy, out of whack. (*Beat.*) Could you play something else?

GEORGE. There isn't anything else.

Long pause.

156

BELLE. And that sounds familiar.

GEORGE. Beecham once said I was the new Stravinsky, another musician, that I was the English Rachmaninov. (*Beat.*) My symphonies have been called more substantial than those of Malcolm Arnold, more approachable than either those by Robert Simpson or Tippett; more melodic and far better structured than those by George Lloyd, and possess a wonderful color not found in the symphonies of Edmund Rubbra. Yet the symphonies of those five composers are available on commercial recordings. Mine are not. (*He lifts his fingers from the piano.*) More than a bit deflating, that. Hard to think about writing something else, let alone something new. (*GEORGE rises. Raises his drink glass in salute to his mother's portrait.*) Four Emily Songs. Chorale in F Flat. (*He moves abruptly to the piano, where he sits and recites as he plays.*) I'm Nobody! Who are you?Are you—Nobody—too? Then there's a pair of us! Don't tell! they'd banish us—you know! How dreary—to be—Somebody! How public—like a Frog—To tell your name—the livelong June—To an admiring Bog!* (*He lifts his hands from the piano keys.*) That's all I have. Rather slow going, I'm afraid. (*Turns to BELLE.*) What do you think?

BELLE. I think you should finish it.

GEORGE. What if I don't? Can't?

BELLE. That would be a shame, I think.

GEORGE. Do you.

BELLE. Yes.

GEORGE. Well. Then. Another? (*Indicates drink; BELLE again shakes head 'no'.*)

BELLE. And I think you should finish it now, while it's fresh in your mind.

GEORGE. You do.

BELLE. When I get half way through typing a big manuscript, I push on for another couple of pages. That way I keep the momentum going to get the thing done.

GEORGE. Interesting approach.

BELLE. Don't knock it till you try it.

GEORGE. My muse and I have a different rhythm.

BELLE. Lubricated with scotch?

GEORGE. Don't knock it till you try it.

BELLE. Touché.

GEORGE. Paula's awfully late.

BELLE. (*Rising; starts to move UL.*) I'll start supper. Or is that dinner?

GEORGE. (*Walking behind her.*) Depends what time you serve it and how big it is. Come on, I'll slice something.

BELLE. I thought I'd write to the crazy Welshman.

GEORGE. Your second cousin, he would be, is part of the clan that owns property and plays golf. You should meet him. He has magnificent eyebrows. He rides to his pub for a nightly pint on the back of a prize Hereford bull.

GEORGE and BELLE exit UL.

BLACKOUT

Scene 8: 1988

LIGHTS UP SLOWLY. BELLE enters UR. She carries a suitcase and a knapsack. These she puts on the floor by the DR door. BELLE HEARS the outer door SLAMMING shut and footsteps running up the hallway. The DR door flings open. PAULA stands in the doorway, breathing hard, hair flying, clothing askew. She's frantic, disjointed, somewhat incoherent. A Mad Hatter's Tea Party atmosphere ensues.

PAULA. Is he here?

BELLE. The cab? No, I…

PAULA. No, not the cab. Him.

BELLE. Him? Who?

PAULA. Him.

BELLE. Paula, what's wrong?

PAULA. He's not here?

BELLE. Do you mean George?

PAULA. Tell me.

BELLE. Tell you what. Paula, come sit down…

PAULA. Where is he?????

BELLE. You want a drink? Brandy. Brandy's good for shock. God, I don't believe this is happening again. Not now. No, hell. No, water. Water? Would you like some water, Paula?

158

PAULA. He's with them, isn't he.

BELLE. Who? Paula, you're not making sense.

PAULA. You bloody well know who bloody who.

BELLE. No, I… Do you mean George? Where George is? I don't know. I packed, called for a cab, came down, and you ran in. That's all I know.

PAULA. He's with THEM.

BELLE. Who? Tell me who, Paula. (*Yells.*) GEORGE!!

PAULA. (*Sick laugh.*) You won't want him. (*She begins darting around the room.*)

BELLE. I want someone. (*Chasing PAULA.*) Paula, please sit down. I am not equipped to handle a flipped-out stepmother. I have a nice, quiet, uneventful life. I type, meet with my book group at the library once a month, take walks with my dog, go on a two-week hiking vacation in the Rocky Mountains every year, run errands, shop at the health food store, an ordinary life, with ordinary routines, predictable days and nights. Nothing to prepare me for… PAULA, STOP!

PAULA. (*Sounding almost reasonable.*) He told me to stop larking about and marry him, so long ago. And, you know, I was curious. He had tremendous appeal, you know. Never knowing what was behind his screen, that's what drew me to him. You know. (*She slows, stops, stands staring inward. BELLE drops into the easy chair.*)

BELLE. Screen? What screen? You're not making any sense, Paula.

PAULA. But he didn't mention them.

BELLE. Oh, God, Paula, not now.

PAULA. He didn't stand up in church and say, I promise to love, honor, and cherish, drop the screen, and to bring my whores into the marriage bed.

BELLE. No, Paula, I'm sure he didn't.

PAULA gets hold of a bottle of scotch and starts drinking from it.

PAULA. To be fair, and we must always be fair, mustn't we, so English, fairness, to be fair to him, he didn't start straight away.

BELLE. You shouldn't drink with your pills.

BELLE easily takes the bottle from PAULA who now seems more inter-

ested in taking off her clothes. BELLE keeps trying to get PAULA to dress up, not down. By the time GEORGE enters, Scene 9, she is down to a teddy and bloomers.

PAULA. His whores.

BELLE. Not the whores again, Paula.

PAULA. He didn't bring them in bodily, you know, (*giggle*) there wouldn't be enough room for us all in that antique bed we sleep in. That bloody bed. I blame it all on that sodding bed.

BELLE. How about putting some of this back on now.

PAULA. I told him and told him and told him to buy us a new bed. He just walks away and crashes around on his effing piano. He disappears behind his screen. Hasn't written anything new in years, you know.

BELLE. (*Trying reason.*) He played me a beginning, to some poetry. Here, put this back on.

PAULA. Four Emily Songs. Dead as a dodo and just as useless. I just wanted a new bed!

BELLE. I'm sure you did.

PAULA. He doesn't go to any club, you know. He goes with whores and then comes home and makes me smell their sex on his fingers, in his mouth, on his prick.

BELLE. Paula, I don't want to hear this.

PAULA. You think I don't know my own stink? (*She swipes two fingers across her crotch; thrusts those fingers under BELLE's nose; BELLE recoils.*) I'm sweet, like oranges. They're foul, dead fish rotting.

BELLE. Paula, I can't… you have to stop behaving like this… Come on, let's tidy you up. George will be here soon, you'll see. You'll take your medicine and have a nice cup of tea and a good laugh about how you chased me off with your story about the whores.

PAULA. (*Suddenly sly.*) I pity you, if you don't believe me. GEORGE.. is a thief, he took my youth and soiled it with the whores, this house is contaminated…(*Sudden switch of mood.*) Take me with you.

BELLE. What? No, I, I can't…

PAULA. Take me to America. I'll start over over there (*another giggle*). Wait. Hold the taxi. Just give me a minute to pack… I'm taking this…(*PAULA grabs up the red shawl and dashes up the stairs UR. BELLE stands, as if waiting for the next assault.*)

Scene 9

GEORGE enters UL door, quietly, almost tiptoeing, as if he's been listening behind the door.

BELLE. Where the hell have you been?

GEORGE. At my club.

BELLE. She's completely lost it this time. Thinks I'm taking her to the States with me.

GEORGE. Are those her bags by the hall door?

The DOORBELL RINGS. PAULA comes running down the stairway UR. She is still in her underwear, with the scarf tied around her head and trailing behind her. She carries a small beaded purse. The DOORBELL RINGS again.

PAULA. I'm ready!

GEORGE. Paula, put something on, for mercy sake. Who's that at the door?

BELLE. Oh Christ. (*BELLE goes out the DR door. We HEAR her mumble something. She quickly returns.*)

GEORGE. I need a drink.

PAULA runs toward BELLE, then on out the DR door. We HEAR the outer door SLAM.

BELLE. What you need to do is take care of your wife. And what the hell is her story about whores? True?

GEORGE. Are those your bags or hers?

BELLE. Mine.

GEORGE. You can't leave.

BELLE. George, I've been here over a year, and I can't help you any more. You have to grow up and do it yourself. She's your wife, not mine. Whores? Shit, how cliché. Clean up your mess, man. I have a cab waiting.

BELLE picks up her bags. She hesitates at the DR door, returns, gives GEORGE a quick kiss on the cheek, then starts to exit. PAULA comes running back, passing BELLE without a glance, and up to GEORGE.

PAULA. Georgie, where've you been? I've such a headache, and… Why am I standing here in my underwear?

161

BELLE exits the DR door. We HEAR her footsteps recede; the outer door SLAM behind her.

Scene 10: 1990

PAULA sits, splay-kneed, on the floor. Scattered about her are the swatches we saw her with in ACT II earlier. Torn or cut-up bits of the red shawl litter her head and body like rose petals. She holds a large butcher knife and is slowly slicing off her hair in hunks. She rises, circles the room.he stops to stare at MIRABELLE's portrait, considers stabbing it, but finds a better target in GEORGE's piano. She pets the thing like a lover then jams the point of the knife into the keyboard. GEORGE enters DR door, carrying an overcoat and accompanied by two pleasant looking WOMEN, dressed in sensible suits. The women move to stand on either side of PAULA., gently flanking her. We can tell they have done this sort of thing before. GEORGE gently wraps the coat around PAULA's shoulders. She shrugs it off. They repeat this a few times until GEORGE holds the coat on with his hands while he talks to her.

GEORGE. Darling, you remember Mrs. Symms and Mrs. Gordon, from the church. They've come to take you for a ride. To Hawky. Isn't that nice?

PAULA. Georgie? Where's Belle? I want Belle.

GEORGE. She had to go home. You remember. Back to America.

PAULA. I'll be beautiful in America, Georgie. Famous, too. A famous pianist.

GEORGE. Of course you will, darling.

PAULA. You'll come to my concerts and wish you hadn't gone with the whores.

GEORGE. Wild horses, Paula. Now, hold your coat tight. It's cold outside today.

PAULA. I want a crumpet with clotted cream. And salad cream. And Bovril.

GEORGE. Anything you want, you just ask these good ladies. Anything at all.

PAULA. See you in America, George.

GEORGE. Goodbye, darling. Goodbye. (*Beat.*) Bloody hell.

The two WOMEN gently, smilingly, lead PAULA out the DR door. We

162

HEAR all their footsteps recede, the outer door CLICK shut. GEORGE, left on his own, surveys the wreckage of his room. He pulls the knife from the piano keyboard and tries out the keys. The sound is unharmed. The key action may be sluggish, but the piano is unharmed. The following has a dream-like quality, yet is absolutely real to GEORGE.MIRABELLE enters from UR, moves to GEORGE, touches his shoulder, he sits. MIRABELLE continues to touch him as he plays a piece of his symphony. The RED HAIRED WOMAN dances across stage from UL. She dances alone for a beat, then pulls GEORGE up into a dance. His music continues playing.

MIRABELLE joins in the dance. The two women alternately touch GEORGE, touch each other, dance alone. The actor playing PAULA joins the dance (sashaying in from DR door).

The actor playing SARAH, REBECCA, and EDNA enters from UR wearing a piece of clothing from each woman. She joins the dance. Above it all, GEORGE's music swells and sways.

LIGHTS DIM

END OF ACT II

CURTAIN

ACT III

Scene 1: 1998

SETTING: We are in the parlor. Morning.

AT RISE: GEORGE, 69, enters from UL, carrying a tray on which are a sandwich on a plate and a glass of milk. He sits on the settee and contemplates his meal. He decides to open a bottle of scotch instead and settles down for some serious drinking. GEORGE has a distinct air of failure about him; a seediness in dress and grooming, a slump to his shoulders. His hair is mostly white and worn long. The parlor looks neglected, yet his piano is still clean and dusted. All color seems to have gone from GEORGE's soul, his room, his life. GEORGE sits at the piano, massages his fingers, and starts practicing scales. Up and down, scales. The DOORBELL RINGS OFF. It RINGS several times before GEORGE rises, goes off DR. We HEAR mumbled voices before GEORGE. returns, followed by JOYCE. JOYCE is now a spry, confident 70-year-old, her hair is grey and carefully styled. She wears riding clothes, carries a riding crop. She strides into the parlor before GEORGE in full voice.

JOYCE. I simply couldn't believe my eyes. George Blackstone! Why, I thought you'd moved away yonks ago. Gone to the States, I'd heard. But then, that was donkeys wasn't it. Some time in the good old dark ages! And there you were, sitting like a pukah sahib in Sissy's conservatory… my goodness, what a good likeness that is of MiraBelle! George, you simply must tell me everything. Leave nothing out, not a jot! And you could offer me something liquid. I'm dry as a desert. Isn't this grand!

GEORGE. (*On her heels.*) Uh, scotch all right?

JOYCE. Gin for me, dearie. Gee and tee if you can manage it.

GEORGE. I can manage scotch. Neat.

JOYCE. (*Peering up at MIRABELLE's portrait.*) I always thought her a most intimidating woman. Beautiful, in an icy way.

GEORGE. Uh, Joyce? (Handing her a drink.)

JOYCE. But then I suppose she'd have to be, married to that bully of a husband.

GEORGE. What are you doing here? Did I invite you?

JOYCE. It's a social visit, George. Unannounced. Just thought I'd pop in after my ride. Do you ride? Grand hobby. You should, you know. Keeps you fit. And, frankly, darling, you look like hell. More than the years can account for.

GEORGE. But what do you want?

JOYCE. Still all the social graces of a slug. Never did grow out of the shy boy, eh.

GEORGE. I'm a famous composer, hardly a boy.

JOYCE. Incidental, George. Incidental. A full life requires growing up, leaving home, striking out.

GEORGE. I've struck out. Uh, no, I don't mean out, but I've struck, oh, hell, Joyce.. Why are you here? No, don't tell me. Finish your drink and go. I won't mind. No one will mind. You just slope off like a good girl. Go back to your ponies and… I presume there's a husband in the wings?

JOYCE. Hardly a girl, certainly, a woman. A widow, actually.

GEORGE. Say, I didn't see you at Sissy's. God, what was that? Some sort of…

JOYCE. Tribute dinner.

GEORGE. Who for?

JOYCE. George, are you quite sure you're all in one piece? You look rather done in.

GEORGE. Leave it. (*Handing her her drink.*) What sort of tribute?

JOYCE. A funereal tribute, George, to my dearly departed husband Wilfred. The one who made me a widow. (*She's roaming.*) You have in your parlor the recently bereaved widow of his lordship. And not much else, by the look of the place.

GEORGE. Good lord. (*Fixes himself another drink.*)

JOYCE. A recently bereaved widow who inherited half the country.

GEORGE. Would I know him?

JOYCE. I thought you did. Why else were you there?

GEORGE. Sissy's idea. What was his line?

JOYCE. Radial tires. Horses. Aeroplane parts.

GEORGE. What, no woolen mills?

JOYCE. Oh, he bought those out decades ago.

GEORGE. Good lord. (*Considering JOYCE.*) Radial tires and horses and aeroplane parts aside, why are you here? Come to lord it over me, did you? Local girl makes good, local boy in a ten-year slump.

JOYCE. Do you remember that day at Rydall Water?

GEORGE. I still have my faculties, Joyce.

JOYCE. Well, do you?

GEORGE. I remember many days at Rydall Water. With you.

JOYCE. One in particular. The day we pricked our fingers and held them together and vowed to love each other for always and ever.

GEORGE. Romantic sod me.

JOYCE. I wasn't. I'm not. Completely practical, me, even at thirteen. I told you that I was going to marry well. Do you remember? Under a spreading chestnut tree?

GEORGE. I remember you saying you wouldn't ever marry me because I wouldn't end up rich.

JOYCE. That's right. Romantic to the bone, you, George. Oh, talented enough, but not enough ambition. That's always been true. I knew even then that someday you'd come to this. Talent galore but no oomph. I knew someday you'd be sitting alone in this house as it slowly falls down around you.

GEORGE. (*Attempt at protesting.*) I… don't… uh… nothing wrong with this house… sound as bells…

JOYCE. Don't interrupt, George. I haven't much time. Now then, where was I. Oh, yes. House falling down, or closing in, whichever way you like to look at it. Reaching the end of your musical genius, having nothing left that matters. I'm right aren't I? I hadn't reckoned on all the wives, heavens, seven? Isn't that a bit extreme, even for you? But never mind, they fit in my little scenario of George, the boy-man I once knew. Even the last wife is gone, yes? I am right. Yes?

GEORGE. (Drawing himself up.) Paula is, sensitive, that's the word, sensitive. She's having a rest. Somewhere quiet. I don't take kindly to your précis of me, Joyce. Thanks for coming and all that, but I'd really rather you left now.

During the remainder of this scene, GEORGE and JOYCE move closer to each other until their faces almost touch. She does touch him occasionally, with her hands, here and there. He is passive, resisting now and then, but eventually he succumbs, we sense, out of fatigue rather than willingness. In other words, JOYCE wears GEORGE down by the end of the scene. A cautionary note: JOYCE is not a bully, but a woman on a rescue mission. This may make her a bit brusque; never hard or unsympathetic. Likewise, George. is not a complete pushover. He is, however, tired and almost welcomes JOYCE coming to his rescue. The seduction, such as it is, is mutual.

JOYCE. George, this is not a time for pleasantries, however small.

GEORGE. You call this pleasant?

JOYCE. And no pretenses at happy families. Paula is sequestered in a funny farm, a very exPENsive funny farm, where she will live to a ripe old age and die without ever knowing where she is.

GEORGE. Joyce…

JOYCE. No, it's time to stand up to things, George. And I'm just the girl to help you do that. There's a lot to organize. House renovations, the grounds are in an appalling state… How much are you paying to keep her there?

GEORGE. What?

166

JOYCE. I imagine the fees are exorbitant. Well, we'll have to change that, somewhere less bucolic will suit just as well. I mean, the woman is completely gaga.

GEORGE. You will not touch Paula.

JOYCE. I have no intention of touching her.

GEORGE. I want you to leave.

JOYCE. Now then. Have you started collecting your pension?

GEORGE. I'm hardly creaking. Hardly ready for the nacker's yard. My work is performed all over the world. Royalties come through here every month.

JOYCE. And who does your accounting?

GEORGE. I do. Musicians are not complete morons, Joyce. I resent that implication even more. Time to go.

JOYCE. Do you even know your net worth these days?

GEORGE. Off limits. You know where the door is.

JOYCE. I have decided that you are worth saving, George, in spite of your present condition. I'll marry you if you promise not to dribble on the toilet seats, or womanize, I'll leave you if you do that one. And no whinging. Start working again. Invent some new composition so we don't have to dine out on your past glories. No more failures, George, not with me in the house. Now. As to this house. I'll have my lawyer draw up a contract. I want equal title to this house. Better yet, since you're obviously a loss at all matters practical, we'll put it in my name. Then you really won't have to grow up. You can just sit in here and play your music for mum and I can play lady of the manor, a role I am very good at. Fair do's, George? I think so. Yes.

GEORGE. Did I ask you to marry me?

JOYCE. It's the only solution that makes any sense. I have money, you are months away from the bailiffs, I need a home…

GEORGE. What happened to your inheritance? Desert and swamp land, I think you said.

JOYCE. The place belonged to his family, not to mine, it's mortgaged to the hilt. I'd have left him if he hadn't conveniently popped off. So you see…

GEORGE. One of my former students is organizing a concert… income… commissions…

167

JOYCE. Pie in the sky, George. You need an infusion of capital now. You need to get your face out of the scotch bottle. You need me.

GEORGE. But do I want you?

ABRUPT BLACKOUT

Scene 2: Two weeks later, midnight.

The parlor is dark. JOYCE enters, UR, carrying a torch (flashlight). She stubs her toes on something.

JOYCE. Damn and blast! Power outages in this day and age! You'd think we were living in… what in hades is this? (*JOYCE angles her torch down to the floor. She has been stumbling into GEORGE, who lies face down in a pool of his own vomit.*)You'd better be just dead and not drunk, George Blackstone. I am not going through all that again. (*She nudges him with a toe. He groans.*) I've arranged for three new students tomorrow, George, so pull yourself together. Honestly, I don't need the agro, or you legless. You're letting the side down. Up you get. (*JOYCE. shines the torch on the portrait for a beat.*) I blame you for what's become of him. Thankfully I'm tough enough to out do what you've done. (*Beat.*) Not done. (*JOYCE. extinguishes her torch and flounces out of the room. GEORGE. moans again.*)

BLACKOUT

Scene 3: 1999

LIGHTS UP. GEORGE and JOYCE sit in the parlor. He is at his piano, cleaned up, shaved, looking healthier. He is working on what appears to be a new composition. JOYCE reads through an accounting ledger; what she sees there gives her pleasure.

JOYCE. (*Closes the ledger; satisfied sigh.*) We've done it. Managed to keep afloat AND make a profit. Selling off that extra bit of land to Jonas Morton was a stroke of genius, if I do say so myself.

GEORGE. That was Sarah's favorite place. Even more than her room upstairs.

JOYCE. Sarah?

GEORGE. First wife.

168

JOYCE. (*Uninterested in wives.*) We need to get someone to organize your Fall concert.

GEORGE. David handles all my bookings. He'll set it up.

JOYCE. He's a bit long in the tooth. I think we need someone new, someone younger. Get some fresh blood on the hunt.

GEORGE. (*A tone.*) I don't need anyone new. Not in charge of my concerts. That's my music, my business, Joyce. Hands off.

JOYCE. Still too much hands off around here, you ask me.

GEORGE. No one did. Does.

JOYCE. All right, then, David stays in the loop. What's he got booked for you next month?

GEORGE. A revival. My chamber pieces.

JOYCE. London?

GEORGE. York.

JOYCE. I hate York.

GEORGE. Don't come.

JOYCE. I always come to your concerts.

GEORGE. Skip one. Not the end of the world.

BLACKOUT.

Scene 4: Two months later.

LIGHTS UP. JOYCE prowls around the parlor, ticket stubs and a theatre program in one hand. She is agitated in the extreme. We HEAR the outer door SLAM, footsteps down the hallway, and GEORGE enters, DR. He carries a small suitcase. He goes up to her, moves in for a peck on her cheek. She backs away. He hangs onto his suitcase.

GEORGE. Hello, darling.

JOYCE. How dare you.

GEORGE. Hello, not darling?

JOYCE. I told you. No dribbling, no whinging, and no womanizing.

GEORGE. I have become the most circumspect of urinators, have not uttered a single whine or whinge, even when fully entitled.

JOYCE. And women?

GEORGE. Ah.

JOYCE. (*Waggling tickets in his face.*) What do you call this?

169

GEORGE. (*Looking closer.*) Looks like train tickets.

JOYCE. Two tickets. Not one, but two.

GEORGE. Yes, I see two. Any tea ready? I'm famished.

JOYCE. Both first class.

GEORGE. Bread and butter? Finger sandwiches?

JOYCE. Return tickets from York.

GEORGE. Never mind, I'll wait until supper. What's on? (*Sniffs the air.*) Do I smell…

JOYCE. Two first class return tickets from York. Last train. Side-by-side tickets. Whose ticket is this, George?

GEORGE. I don't know, do I.

JOYCE. Whose ticket.

GEORGE. (*Takes the tickets, tears them up.*) I must have picked up an extra by mistake. You remember, I came back late from the concert. No, maybe the second one was David's. You know, I think something's burning.

JOYCE. I called David.

GEORGE. Ah.

JOYCE. He returned by motor. Said you wanted to go off alone. Said you were accompanied by a bosomy blonde in a black dress.

GEORGE. Ah.

JOYCE. And I said I'd leave you if this ever happened. Prepare to be left.

GEORGE. Nothing new in that.

JOYCE. But know this. This house is in my name. This time, if I go, when I go, you lose everything. You'll be out in the street. Will your blonde slut take care of you like I have? Will she?

GEORGE. Joyce… Two out of three indiscretions?

JOYCE. This is the one that cracks it. You have a month, no, I'll give you three, to remove yourself from my house. (*JOYCE starts to exit UL.*) And take your piano and that woman's portrait with you. I don't ever want to see either of you again in my lifetime. (JOYCE exits.)

GEORGE stands, stunned for a beat. Then, still holding onto his suitcase, he reaches for the telephone. He dials. Operator? Give me the United States. Wyoming. Sheridan Wyoming.

170

BLACKOUT.

<u>Scene 5: 2000.</u>

LIGHTS UP. GEORGE, 71, at his lowest ebb, sits at the piano which, now, is covered in dust. The keyboard lid is still raised, however. He stares at his piano—in longing, in disgust. He does not hit it or cause it harm. Rather, he feels betrayed by it. He sits without motion. We HEAR the outer door open, shut, footsteps cover the distance from there to the inner door UL. GEORGE does not look up as BELLE, a healthy 50 and the exact spit of her grandmother had MIRABELLE lived to 50, appears. She does not carry luggage, but is wearing a long skirt and duster. She stands in the doorway, waiting, for a significant beat, to be acknowledged.

GEORGE. Took you long enough.

BELLE. I once told you I had a life. That, at least, hasn't changed.

GEORGE. I needed you.

BELLE. I'm here now.

GEORGE. I needed you last year. And the year before that.

BELLE. Let it go, George. (*Beat.*) What's the situation with the house?

GEORGE. Joyce's solicitor did a bunk with her money, so she fled and left it. All. Left it all.

BELLE. Have you seen Paula?

GEORGE. She's dead.

BELLE. I'm sorry. I liked her.

GEORGE. Died from lack of attention, I was told. Simply folded in on herself and withered away. All Joyce's fault.

BELLE. And Joyce is?

GEORGE. Gone. Long gone. I told you.

BELLE. But where? Is she liable to pop up again? Demanding things? She sounds like the kind of woman who might return to the scene.

GEORGE. I needed you to come.

BELLE. The message you left was that things had gone pear shaped, again, and would I come? Brighten up the place a bit, those were your exact words. When I wrote back, asking for details, I never heard from you. Not for a whole year. I'm here because I'm curious. Thought maybe you'd died.

GEORGE. Not quite.

Finally, BELLE moves from the doorway and comes closer to her father. She can see he's a wreck and notices the dusty piano, runs a finger across it.

GEORGE. (*He finally looks at her.*) So you come if I'm dead, not if I'm alive.

BELLE. Your eighth wife. Clearly not one of your housekeeping successes, huh.

GEORGE. Why did you stay away so long?

BELLE. What happened with this one, George?

GEORGE. She caught me with my pants down around my ankles.

BELLE. Nasty.

GEORGE. Metaphorically. The woman was an ice cube in bed. And she thought you were cold.

GEORGE gets up and we see he now uses a cane. His back is bowed a bit from osteoporosis; he leans slightly on one leg, favoring the other. He crosses to the mantle and stares up at MIRABELLE's portrait.

BELLE. Thought I was…?

The RED HEADED WOMAN enters down the stairway, as if floating. BELLE cannot see her. GEORGE is aware of her presence as one is aware of a memory rising to the surface. She hovers close to GEORGE during the following.

GEORGE. (*Speaking to the portrait.*) I remember the touch of your hand on my forehead, late at night, when you crept into my room. And the smell of your silk scarf as it brushed my face when you leant in to kiss me. Butterfly kisses with your eyelashes. Never a kiss with your lips. Why? Why not? (*GEORGE backs away from the portrait.*) Why did you let him? Kick me about? Throw me down the stairs? Oh, yes, down the stairs. I landed just there. Once, too afraid to move, I closed my eyes and waited, wishing you would come and give me your butterfly kisses. HE came, with a boot, or a cane. Like this one. IS this one. Do you find that ironic? (*GEORGE moves to stand behind the settee. RED HEADED WOMAN goes to stand next to him.*) I do. (BELLE, watching this odd performance, silent until now, speaks up.)

BELLE. Did you ask me here just to freak me out? Because you

172

are, George, you really are. So quit this, whatever you're doing, and talk to me.

GEORGE. (*Looking at BELLE.*) Why didn't you stand in his way?

BELLE. George…

GEORGE. Get between him and me somehow.

BELLE. GEORGE!

GEORGE. Why did you leave me with him?

BELLE. Dad!!

This seems to shake GEORGE into the present.

GEORGE. Belle?

BELLE. Yes, Belle.

GEORGE. (*Walking out from behind settee.*) Is that you?

BELLE. Yes.

GEORGE. You're here.

BELLE. Yes.

GEORGE. Why?

BELLE. You sent for me.

GEORGE. Sometimes I can't…

BELLE. (*Moving to her father.*) Here, sit down, Dad. We'll talk.

GEORGE. … I hear the notes, like voices… calling… but I can't reach them…

BELLE. (*Close enough to touch GEORGE.*) Maybe I can help.

GEORGE. … I hear the voices, like notes… (*GEORGE listens as if hearing once again while the RED HEADED WOMAN floats out from behind the settee, up the stairs, back down, as if carrying GEORGE's parents' voices.*) Why didn't you take me with you? I was a nice little boy. You'd have liked me. (*BELLE starts to touch her father; he raises the cane; she halts.*) That night you left. I heard you yelling at each other and came down here. Then your voice came…

BELLE. Dad, George, I'm not MiraBelle.

GEORGE. I sat at the piano to play, to hide your voices in my music… (*He sits at the piano; does not open the lid.*) But he found me. Even music couldn't save me then. Can't save me now. (*GEORGE leaps up from the piano and scuttles behind the settee, miming himself as a young boy in ACT I.*) I crouched down behind here, so he wouldn't catch me…(*He disappears behind the settee. The RED HEADED WOMAN stands behind BELLE whose confusion is becom-*

173

ing alarm.)

BELLE. Dad, please, I don't, George, this won't… why… damnit, George...

GEORGE. (*In his father's voice.*) No effing and blinding in milady's presence. No farts. Copulations. This time she won't be coming back. Take a good look, bad rubbish, out to the tip. She won't be coming back.

BELLE. (Moving up to the settee, peering over.) Should I call someone? (*GEORGE pops up, stares at her, moves quickly out from behind the settee, lunges at BELLE, falls at her feet. The RED HEADED WOMAN drops to the floor next to GEORGE.*) George, please, you're scaring me…

GEORGE. (*Wrapping his arms around BELLE's legs; burying his face in her skirt.*) Mummy! Mummy!! Don't leave me!! (*BELLE pushes at his hands, pushing him away. He falls to the floor. She, frantic, looks around for the telephone, cannot find it, starts to rush off UL. GEORGE drags himself to her, clutches her again, begins to sob.*) Don't go!

The RED HEADED WOMAN moves to GEORGE, puts her arms around him, gather him up, pulls him to his feet. He stands, head down, awash in grief. BELLE makes her escape.

Scene 6

BELLE. (*O.S.*) I think something's wrong with my father. Please come. Quickly. I'm by myself… and …What? Oh. Blackstone Hall. (*BELLE returns, finds a bottle, opens it, moves toGEORGE to hand it to him. He knocks the bottle out of her hand.*) George, come sit down. Please.

GEORGE starts prowling the set, tears pouring down his face. We are as if watching GEORGE melt. BELLE attempts to stop him moving, but he keeps going. He flings his body behind the settee and out in front of it, to the piano, away from it, and suddenly stops. He fixes his attention on his daughter. GEORGE moves surprisingly quickly to BELLE's side. His piano hands grab her around the throat.

GEORGE. This time you stay.

BELLE is too stunned to react at first; then, she is in a fight for her life. GEORGE's face is rage-filled. BELLE is the younger and stronger of the two, but GEORGE's rage is fearsome. During, BELLE grunts, groans, and screams as appropriate. GEORGE is silent in his attempt to strangle this woman. The RED HEADED WOMAN stays out of the fight. Instead, she circles the pair struggling on the floor, watching, hovering above the outcome.

The actors playing the wives enter from various points: SARAH, REBECCA, and EDNA; MELORA and CLARA; PAULA, and JOYCE, and join the RED HEADED WOMAN, watching. They, however, are not silent. BELLE cannot hear them; they are a chorus for GEORGE only.

SFX NOTE: Backdrop of GEORGE's symphony or other piece played under.

SARAH, REBECCA, EDNA (*As SARAH.*). Clean up your mess and stop dramatizing, George. (*As REBECCA.*) You need taking care of, George. I always help you with your music. (*As EDNA.*) Don't criticize, George. Not today.

MELORA, CLARA (*As MELORA.*) You've no one to blame but yourself, George. What a fool you are. (*As CLARA.*) You wouldn't listen, George. Play me no lullabies.

PAULA. The mystery of trying to find out what was behind your screen. Your mystery. Anyone there?

JOYCE. Not enough ambition, George. Talent, no guts. Haven't got the bottle to go the distance.

The WIVES silence, back up, begin to slip away in all directions. GEORGE wins the struggle with his daughter/mother. BELLE goes limp. GEORGE sits up, then stands and walks to his piano, leaving BELLE on the floor. He opens the keyboard lid and immediately, without needing to think first, begins to play a new piece, a Pavanne, a piece filled with rich, beautiful, haunting minor chords; a piece worthy of stilling nightmares.

BELLE is motionless on the floor. The RED HEADED WOMAN touches her lightly (not felt by BELLE), moves to GEORGE, stands behind him as he plays, then slowly drifts away and off, back up the stairs from whence she came, UR. GEORGE finishes his Pavanne with a glorious final chord. He lifts his head, smiling. His head is held high; his burden lifted. He closes the keyboard lid, and, without a backward glance, exits down the hallway. We HEAR his FOOTSTEPS receding, and then the outer front door SLAM.

CURTAIN

Three Graces

A Play in Three Acts

©2004
by Jessie M Page

Running time: Approximately 90 minutes
15-Minute Intermission between Acts I and II and (possibly) a
5-minute intermission between Acts II and III.

Three Graces is dedicated to

The women of my generation who still
keep their stories silent

Author's Note: This is a memory play. The NARRA-
TOR, a woman in her early sixties, is reflecting upon the oc-
currences and consequences of her three abortions, the first
of which was dangerous and illegal. She provides a gateway
from the audience to the other characters, those in her past,
including herself, as she considers a predominant theme, that
of abandonment--of self, by other. Another theme throughout
is that of nonattachment.

These are people, the NARRATOR. included, who frequently talk past each other, who frequently do not answer direct questions, but move instead into their own fragile egos.

This play is not concerned with casting blame; rather, its
intention is that of giving voice to experiences long held silent
and secret.

Characters

All the actors wear black clothing, including shoes, with the
exception of CAROL, whose clothing and hairstyles change to
reflect her emotional landscape over time and the time in her
history, and the THREE GRACES, who wear white dresses

and are barefoot. The NARRATOR changes from black garments to white for the final scene. The women wear skirts, "officials" adding white smock coats. The men all wear long-sleeved black shirts and pants, the "official" men add a suit coat and tie, or, as appropriate, a white jacket. Characters in order of appearance are as follows.

NARRATOR.: A young-looking sixty-two year-old woman; she can pass for a youthful fifty. Tall, medium build. Dark hair. She is, even though lyrical and poetic, somewhat fumbling her way through her words, rememberances, and recognitions.

CAROL: CAROL is the NARRATOR at three earlier ages: Nineteen, thirty-two, and thirty-five. (Played by one actor, peferably two.)

JOAN: Nineteen and thirty-five, sturdy build, thick long dark hair. Whiskey voiced.

MOTHER: English; blonde; a held-together woman; twenty-nine, forty-eight, sixty-three (Played by two actors, possibly one.)

FATHER: Thirty-three, also English, tall, lean, hungry-looking, sloppy red hair.

COUPLE: A MAN and WOMAN, early 30's. Can double for COUNSELOR #1 and COUNSELOR #2, NURSE, ATTENDANT (no lines), DOCTOR, or ANESTHESIOLOGIST (no lines).

BILL: A rangy, lean, blonde-haired man who wears his hair long. Twenty-nine; soft spoken, gentle.

FRED: Twenty-seven; aggressive, handsome, well-built, impressive voice. Dark hair, very short. Tight-lipped; mean when crossed.

177

JIMMY: Twenty, extremely thin, long blond hair, musician sen-sibilities.

COUNSELOR #1: Male, middle-aged, tired, balding. Can be doubled as above.

COUNSELOR #2: Woman, 30's, energetic, trying hard. Can be doubled as above.

ATTENDANT: Male or female. Average build. Can be dou-bled as above. (no lines)

GRACE #2: Thirty years old, very thin. Her face, body, cloth-ing, all of her appears as a ghost, as insubstantial.

ZEKE: Mid-forties, elegant in his voice and carriage. Highly sensual. Thick dark hair.

NURSE: Matronly, motherly, can be doubled as above.

DOCTOR: Male, fifties, abrupt in manner, voice. Can be dou-bled as above.

ANESTHESIOLOGIST: Can be doubled as above. Male.

DOUG.: Almost forty; small-boned, compact, 5'8" max, imp-ish, greying hair.

CATHERINE: Forty-three years old. Tall, slim, blonde. She carries a brief-case, symbol of authority, yets seems unsure of where to put her body, how to use her body in space/the world.

GRACE #3: Is twenty-seven years old, in a wheelchair. Her body is rounded, her hair dark. She has a keen intelligence about her and not a whisper of self-pity.

Properties

Tall wooden three-legged stool.

Two wooden, ladder-back chairs

A hospital gurney

White sheets

The chairs and gurney are on stage throughout, perhaps deep Up in a shadow to begin, and are moved about by the actors as needed. The stool is the sole property of the NARRATOR.

Folded letter

Manilla file folders

Briefcase

Guitar

Medical white coats

Matchbook

Pen

ACT I

<u>Scene 1: Present</u>

AT RISE: NARRATOR walks on FULLY LIT stage, bringing her own stool. She puts the stool to one side of the stage, extreme D, and stands by it (if there is an apron, this is where she places her stool throughout the play).

NARRATOR. Funny the things you miss once you give them up, isn't it? (*Holds one fist up.*) Do you remember writing your name with missus in front of it on your notebook cover? All through school, my notebook covers were dusty blue, a sort of nubby fabric, imperfect for drawing on with an ink pen. But I did it. Writing my name with Missus in front. Missus Mike Starbuck. Missus Carol Bruderlin. Missus Prince Charming. And remember making a fist to see how many babies you'd have? (*Looking at her hand fisted.*) We folded our fingers over and counted the creases made between our bent pinkies and our palms. I have three creases. (*Showing audience.*) The second one is faint, but there are three. Three babies. (*Long pause.*) You'd think my creases would have faded long ago. When each never got its start. (*Long pause.*) You know what's true about abortions? They aren't linear things, a girl doesn't say, I'm going to get an abortion, without all the rest of her story clanging in her head, even for nowadays girls who talk about abortion like it's a birth control choice. (*Pause.*) Now, us late 1950's girls, girls born after the mayhem of World War Two, we did not talk. We held onto our silences. We did not share. We hinted, or lied by omission. Not revealing private matters was the norm. Those of us 1950s girls who inherited our first menstruations as a curse, we did not chat about our abortions. We drank Sanka™ or Maxwell House™, black, smoked Marlboro's™, and kept our mouths shut. (*Sitting on stool. All slows down.*) I meet women of my age today who, if I ever allude to having had even one abortion, will nod, knowingly, and lower their eyes. At least, we engage in a slowed-down exchange: Me: I had one.

WOMAN'S VOICE O.S. Me, too.

NARRATOR. Here?

WOMAN'S VOICE O.S. No.

NARRATOR. Ah.

180

WOMAN'S VOICE O.S. Hmmm.

NARRATOR. At most, we hold a moment of silence between us, as if in a shared reverie after a bereavement. For those of us who had to scurry down to Mexico or up to Canada in secret when we "got caught," who had to keep our mouths and hearts silent, there is no forgetting our abortions. We girls of the 1950s were not encouraged to live our choices. But some of us impatient ones struck out anyway. Sometimes the turns we took looked like we were running away. More often, though, we ran toward, encountering a vast emptiness, like a hole in the ground. Behind us, girls came galloping along eager to learn from the leaps we took. Frightened of the unknown ahead and the future nipping at our heels, we ran faster, kicking dust over our aberrant moments. (*Pause.*) Still we do not forget—the decisions to, the hiding from, the cutting away, the aftermath. We do not lose sight, even if we've put blinders on it over the years. (*Sliding off stool; moving about the stage.*) The other day, I was chatting with my favorite clerk in my favorite store, you know how you do, and she said, Saturday was my birthday and I'm thirty now, and we kept on talking, you know how you do, about was it a quiet or a noisy day, was it raining then?, have you tried the cherries yet?, and all the while some little dark thing was building in the back of my mind. (*Pause.*) Later, I took a walk with a friend and she said, out of the blue she said, I'd like to be your daughter because... (*Pause.*) That small dark thing took on some bulk with her words, I'd like to be your daughter. She could be my first or second daughter, she's the right age. The right height. The right heft. And that girl in the store could be my third daughter. She's the right age. And me? I'm of the age to have started all this. Except for what I gave up and dropped into silence. (*NARRATOR shifts her position, or performs a tiny dance step, sits. Then, continues addressing audience.*) Social workers and psychologists and doctors and well-meaning friends, they all say, in their ways, tell yourself you had no choice, times were difficult, don't blame yourself, call it an act of God, that child decided not to be born to you, and my personal favorite, you were courageous to do what you did. Bullshit. Courage had

181

nothing to do with it.
LIGHTS soften.

Scene 2: 1959
NARRATOR. In 1959, Joan had the courage.
JOAN. enters, carrying a guitar. She moves one chair to center and sits.
NARRATOR. To pick up the phone, to put the thing in motion. All I had to do was go along for the ride. Not think, not feel, not say. Just leave myself and go along. (*Pause.*) Isn't that what I'm best at? Have always been best at?
CAROL. enters, moves the other chair such that she is facing JOAN. LIGHTS FADE on NARRATOR, FULL on JOAN and CAROL.
JOAN. I know about a man in Mexico. (Picking up her guitar.)
CAROL. Oh.
JOAN. (*Tuning guitar.*) Do you want me to call?
CAROL. Yes. No.
JOAN. You have to go when he's ready, not when you are.
CAROL. I don't know what to do.
JOAN. (*Strumming minor chords.*) He doesn't speak English and charges two hundred dollars.
CAROL. I don't speak Mexican.
JOAN. His embryos are sent to UCLA, he's that good. (*JOAN begins the chords for "House of the Rising Sun" on her guitar. Singing; full-throated blues; basso.*) There is a house in New Orleans/They call the rising sun/It's been the ruin of many a poor girl/and God I know I'm one.
CAROL. (*Echoing.*) And God I know I'm one.
LIGHTS UP to include NARRATOR in scene.
NARRATOR. As if it were happening now, I feel myself sitting with Joan in her dark room, one strong hand of hers curled around the heavy black telephone receiver…
JOAN. mimes telephoning, talking into the receiver.
NARRATOR. (*Cont'd.*) …her husky voice whispering the Spanish words that could never be erased, the other hand resting on her guitar, her dark eyes swinging to me occasionally, asking, telling, revealing nothing, showing all. Wisps of black curls, whole hanks of thick waves, floated down her neck. I focused

182

on that neck, those curling hairs, and willed myself to fall a little in love with her confidence, with her guitar, with her floating hair. I equally steeled myself so I would not hear her hang up, or see her eyes search mine as she said,

JOAN. Next Wednesday, two o'clock. (*Pause.*) Do you want me to come?

NARRATOR. Or hear me say,

CAROL. No.

SPOT on NARRATOR.

NARRATOR. Abortion isn't an isolated thing, it doesn't happen all by itself. Abortion happens to a woman in her body, in her beliefs about herself, in her stories, in who she has to talk to, or not talk to. So we need to know why Carol is sitting in Joan's room, in 1959, setting up her first, very illegal, abortion. What part of her story brought her here, to her first lover, her first sex, to one friend, with one baby growing underneath her ribs. (*Standing.*) A whole hell of a lot of a girl's story goes into deciding about abortion. Like mine did. My story is, I was left. I was raped, I was beaten. I was lost, then found. I've been halfway around the world and back again. The other half frightens me. (*Some movement.*) I've been ignored, forgotten, betrayed, hobbled, and tossed aside. I've been beautiful and sad ugly. I've been rescued. I've vanished and reappeared. I've had money and I've been broke. I stole money from my mother and a candy bar from a store, once. The candy bar I returned half eaten. (*Movement stops.*) I'm much like you. I've lived stories that, woven together, make up the fabric of a life. This piece of my story is more or less awful or intriguing than yours. Yours may be shorter or longer, less or more convoluted… but somewhere in yours is a piece of mine, somewhere in mine a whisper of yours. (*Moving to stand R.*) United States. 1940. A young British couple, on visitor's visas, decides to seek residency in America. The wife gives birth to a girl. The family must remove themselves to Cuba, to await approval, before they can immigrate through Ellis Island. But the family doesn't go.

BLACKOUT

Scene 3: Present & 1940

LIGHTS FULL. NARRATOR watches from her stool as MOTHER, 29, walks onto stage from L, carrying a newborn baby in a blanket. FATHER follows. A COUPLE, MAN and WOMAN, enter from R.

MOTHER. We have no choice, you know.

FATHER. It's best. Really. We might not make it back from Cuba.

MOTHER. War makes it hard on everyone.

FATHER (*To COUPLE.*) If we don't get sent back to England, we'll return for her.

MOTHER. If it's possible. Some day.

MOTHER hands the baby to FATHER who hands the baby to the COUPLE. MOTHER and FATHER watch the COUPLE, oohing over their new baby, walk away; his arm around her waist. MOTHER and FATHER exit opposite, not touching. Long pause.

Six Months Later.

The COUPLE, carrying a noticeably larger baby in a different blanket, enter from R, stand C, wait. FATHER and MOTHER enter from L, go up to COUPLE.

FATHER. (*Taking baby; to WOMAN*) We shouldn't have left her.

MOTHER. (*Taking baby.*) We have a train to catch.

COUPLE exits R. MOTHER and FATHER and their baby exit L. LIGHTS DIM.

Scene 4

NARRATOR. (*On stool.*) I suppose the reasons for my having had three abortions and one husband might be linked to my very early beginnings. Being left by my parents when I was born because, well, I'm not sure of what this because truly is. Later, my father left, for reasons I still don't fully understand, when I was about two.

MOTHER enters stage from C. Sits on one of the chairs. She reads from a letter in her hand.

MOTHER. I can't live in the States anymore. I'm going back to England. You stay here and take care of Carol. Good bye.

MOTHER looks at both sides of the brief letter, drops it from her hand. Puts a hand to her mouth. Exits.

NARRATOR. Even so, I lay my love of dancing in the curve of my father's fingers over piano keys. (*Rising; slowly dancing during speech.*) Strange that I remember that curve so clearly; the length, breadth, and shape of his hands easily spanning a tenth is vivid. His hands were pink with blood passion for his music, from the effort he expended creating notes that rose and fell in between the spaces of our brief lives together. He left, returning to England, following those passionate hands I cannot recall ever touching me, in kindness or frustration or hatred. As if born of music, I, like Athena, rose fully formed from my father's hands while they caressed cold ivory piano keys. (*Sitting again on her stool.*) Even now my muscle memory senses that eruption, as though I burst forth on the wings of a mighty war cry. Why didn't I take up my gold armor and spear and strive out to tame life's wild horses? I suppose, because, unlike Athena, I didn't consider myself the daughter of only the Father, because mine absented himself and his music from my life early. Too early. (*Long pause.*) Subsequent leavings: my mother. always leaving to go to work because she was our sole support, remarrying when I was seven and having a baby right away, her leaving that marriage, and the three of us—one woman, two girls—leaving New York to venture to California when I was eight. Me leaving my mother.'s and half-sister's cocoon of secret togetherness for school and dancing classes. (*Leaves stool to move.*) Dancing was the first place I found to speak myself by expressing my body all through space. I was encouraged to dance in a red house that perched on a hilltop in West Los Angeles, Rudolph Valentino's house once upon a time, now Miss Rindlaub's. Miss Rindlaub forged our bendable bodies to her wooden cane's wishes: she was a swordswoman with that tool of encouragement. And at Brentwood Elementary School, I was encouraged by Miss Simms and her mouth harp to become a cellist. Miss Simms, an intense, thin woman, wore her hair bright red; it matched her lipsticked mouth and varnished nails. Her mouth harp was silver; I imagined it in a fantastical sexual congress with her lips when no one was watching. Miss Simms had about her the air of something hidden, waiting to leap out and flame. Did she want me to become a cellist because she could imagine me spread-legged, my thighs clutching a curvaceous wooden object that could make music to fill the bones and blood with longing? I'll never know: this was, if it was, her dream, not mine. Miss Rindlaub held my dreams in her cane. For a while.

(Long pause. NARRATOR sits on her stool.)

MOTHER, carrying a briefcase, enters wearily from C. Sits on one of the chairs. CAROL, age 10, dances across stage in a world of her own. MUSIC CUE: "Les Sylphides."

CAROL dances up to her MOTHER, who distractedly allows a hug, then gets up and exits. CAROL continues dancing for a minute, then runs after MOTHER.

NARRATOR. *(Cont'd.)* Dancing was my way of leaving. In dance I found a world of sweat, stretched muscles, bleeding and blistered toes, gasping lungs …pure physical exhilaration. No thought, no emotional tuggings, no wondering where was father, where mother, just the lovely feel of satin ribbons against my ankles, or bare feet on a perfectly sprung wooden floor, of costumes like masks. *(Pause; possible shift in position.)* I am reluctant to hang my abortions on all the leaving, them leaving me, me leaving them, us leaving each other. This sets too solid a ground for victimhood… for casting blame about like apple seeds. Yet, yet, there is no doubt that abandonment, by other, of self, explains much. Especially why I was such a handy target in high school. I mean, who can stand up for themselves when they know they are only worth being left?

BLACKOUT

Scene 5: 1956

SETTING: University High School, Los Angeles. LIGHTS FULL. NARRATOR watches as CAROL, sixteen, enters wearing cardigan sweater buttoned up the back, a cotton dickey, dangling encapsulated mustard seed on a gold chain, aqua poodle skirt with zig-zag rick-rack stitched on, saddle oxfords and white socks. She carries books. She is walking as if at school, also as if away from some disturbing thing. VOICES follow her from O.S.: all MALE, hushed but loud, loaded with implication.

VOICE #1. Hey, Lips.

VOICE #2. Where ya goin', Lips?

VOICE #3. You take good care of those lips. They're mine.

VOICE #4. You be home tonight. I know where your window is.

VOICE #5. Come on over here, Lips, you know you want to.

CAROL. (*Stopping: to audience.*) They only do it because I won't kiss any of them. I think. I think that's what lips means. (*CAROL hurriedly starts to exit. VOICES follow her.*)

VOICE #1, VOICE #2, VOICE #3. Li-i-i-pp-p-p--s-s-s-s!!!!

VOICE #4, VOICE #5. Yee-a-a-a-a Lll-i-i-p-p-p-s-s-s-s-s!!

CAROL. (*Jerking to a stop: to audience.*) Like snake hiss, all through my senior year, following me all over school, even down the phone, once.

MALE VOICE (*O.S.*). (*Sultry.*) Lips.

CAROL exits at a run. LIGHTS DIM.

NARRATOR. (*Up and dancing slowly.*) Somehow, then, my father paid an unexected visit to Southern California. He was at the top of his profession: composer for the Sadler's Wells Ballet in London. I can see us leaning against a large boulder on the beach of Santa Monica, ...and I can hear his voice telling me that, because of my long legs and vivid stage presence, he could get me an audition. He was in a position to help me have something he thought, we both thought, I wanted. (*Pause.*) Why didn't I say yes, I'll come back to England with you, I'll follow you, your music, my yearnings of daughterhood? (*Sits on stool.*) If I sit very still, I can remember the band of tightness I felt wrap around my chest, my need to push off from that boulder and move away down the beach, my desperate wish that he'd take the offer back and not make any more promises he probably wouldn't keep. You see, I only knew him as a man who offered the moon and delivered dust. (*Pause.*) What if I had said yes, packed my toe shoes and flown away with him? No answer exists for this question, yet I feel the tug of this girl to this day. I said no to my father, but yes to another man, one who taught jazz as choreographed by Lester Horton, in a small

187

studio space somewhere in downtown Los Angeles. (*Pause.*) The other dancers were all fully adult; I was still on the edge. Their body confidence awed me. In that awe, I lived my shyness and hid my dancer. I gave her up, not knowing, then, that giving dancing up would cause a hole to grow in that core place of myself I called me. (*Pause.*) I left dancing for sex, for my first lover, Bill, when I was seventeen. Bill. A lean man who, year-round, wore Clark's Desert Boots, Chino pants, and sweatshirts with the sleeves cut off above his elbows.

CAROL enters, followed by BILL. The two sit on the gurney, engrossed in each other.

NARRATOR. (*Cont'd.*) Bill, an illiterate surfboard maker by trade, already had had his wife and two children. I had my first diaphragm, fitted in me by a woman doctor who looked so like Eleanor Roosevelt I felt blessed with a fleeting greatness each time she laid hands on my body. Bill took my virginity with tenderness and with love. That night, I opened to him with more than my legs, hips, mouth.

CAROL and BILL, on the gurney, drop into a sweet, passionate embrace.

NARRATOR. (*Cont'd*) I dropped down into the sacred center of my selfhood, that place needing no words, questions, answers, or reasons, and found little there. Once my first foray into sex stopped, when we rested against each other on his lumpy bed, I began to weep.

BILL holds CAROL as she cries.

NARRATOR. (*Cont'd.*) Why? Without knowing or understanding or describing, I sensed that I had just lost something valuable and possibly irretrievable. A feeling filled me; a feeling that, somehow, the act of sex removed me from my self. (Pause.) I was nineteen so I ignored the feeling and continued to visit his bed. One day my periods stopped.

BILL and CAROL stand and move apart. The gurney becomes a table on which BILL sands/paints his surfboards. CAROL stands and watches, exits by end of her speech.

CAROL. I was scared. Too scared except to tell him, Bill, I'm pregnant. To wait for him to tell me he'd welcome it, to watch for a smile cross his face. But my first baby did not charm him.

When I saw the usual delight in his eyes vanish at my timid announcement, as I watched him turn his spare back to me to bend lovingly over his surfboards, caressing the blanks with his paints and lacquers, I prepared myself to sacrifice our baby to the abortionist's knife. How to begin? Who to tell? Who to ask for help?

HALF BLACKOUT.

CAROL moves to sit on one of the chairs. JOAN enters, sits on the other chair. They do not face each other.

JOAN. Next Wednesday, two o'clock. (*Pause.*) Do you want me to come?

NARRATOR. Or hear me say,

CAROL. No.

NARRATOR. Ten days until next Wednesday. I allowed myself one question: Is this what it feels like, is this what your mind does, when the doctor says you have a month left to live? Presented with this query, my mind simply threatened to spin me out of any knowing orbit, so I focused instead on counting minutes. (*Pause.*) Waiting for the bus to take me to my job at the real estate office in Beverly Hills took anywhere from three minutes to ten. I counted each one off in seconds, running these across the inside of my eyes. At sixty seconds, I turned down the smallest finger of my left hand. The next sixty, and my fourth finger went into my palm, and so on. Sitting at my desk, waiting for the soda crackers and 7-Up™ to soothe my jumpy tummy, I began counting off the hours until lunch. Then through lunch. Then after. Then whole days. Counting kept me from recalling school girl gossip … girl babies spread around their mother's navel … boy babies stick straight out. I grew thicker, a girl baby, counting the seconds until shreds of her would end up … where? In a jar? On a slide in a laboratory? Down the drain? The latter seemed most likely. (*Pause.*) The haze of my life became a fog which settled around my feet, obliterating the moment I was fired from my job because I could not concentrate and kept losing $20,000 bank deposits; suffocating my sleep. Until.

BLACKOUT

Scene 7: 1959

LIGHTS FULL. CAROL and BILL sit on the chairs, facing forward. They stare straight ahead. BILL is "driving." NARRATOR. is on her stool.

NARRATOR. In 1959, Joan had the courage, and Bill had a Hearse that he used for hauling surfboard blanks up and down the California coast in the pre-freeway days. That Wednesday we used it for a—how do I remember it—surreal, unreal but too real, trip to Ensenada, Mexico.

BILL. Everything's going to be all right.

CAROL. Uh huh.

BILL. No, really. Everything's going to be fine.

CAROL. Nothing's going to be all right or fine ever again.

BILL. It's best.

CAROL. Stop the car.

BILL pulls over. Looks at CAROL. She waits for some signal from inside her body.

CAROL. (*Cont'd.*) No, guess not.

BILL. Okay?

CAROL. No.

Long pause. BILL continues driving.

BILL. What did Joan say?

CAROL. Even UCLA's heard of him.

BILL. So he's safe?

CAROL. Safe?

BILL. If UCLA says he's okay.

CAROL. I didn't say UCLA said he's okay.

BILL. But I thought…

CAROL. Just drive.

Long pause.

BILL. What else did she say?

CAROL. Two hundred dollars.

BILL. What?

CAROL. It'll cost two hundred dollars.

BILL jerks the wheel around. They sway as the "hearse" returns.

BILL. Shit. Why didn't you tell me?

190

CAROL. I thought you'd know.

BILL. Why? I've never done this before, either. I've only got fifty.

CAROL. (*Pointing.*) There's a bank, next corner.

BILL. Wrong one. (*Long pause.*) Maybe he'll take a check.

CAROL. You think so? How about that one?

BILL 'stops' the car; gets out; exits SR. Meanwhile, CAROL stares outward. BILL enters SR, climbs in, stuffing bills into his wallet, gets the car going again. Silence for a beat.

BILL. I got extra, so we'll have enough for lunch. And dinner.

CAROL. I'm not really hungry.

BILL. You will be. (*Pause.*) I really like that design your mom came up with for my logo, the way she made my name look like a wave. She's quite an artist.

CAROL. Uh huh.

BILL. You think she can help me get them printed up? Decals for the boards, first. Then an invoice? Business cards.

CAROL. Where are Vicky and Chuck?

BILL. Huh?

CAROL. Where are your kids?

BILL. Why does it matter where they are?

CAROL. Just something to say.

BILL. With their mother, with Sandee.

CAROL. I thought she was back in Camarillo. Again.

BILL. They let her out last week. She's not really crazy, just gets nuts every now and then.

CAROL. Your ex-wife scares me.

BILL. She's harmless. Really. Quit thinking about her.

CAROL. Yeah, but it's just the idea of… never mind. (*Pause.*) Your kids scare me. They're so…

BILL. They scare me.

CAROL. Loud. (*Beat.*) How much longer?

BILL. Couple hours to the border. Why don't you take a nap?

CAROL. What, and miss all this?

BILL. It won't be so bad. And, hey. We've got enough money for a bottle of Mexican tequila. The real stuff with the worm in it.

CAROL.
Oh.
BLACKOUT

Scene 8: Two hours later.
LIGHTS UP. CAROL. sits alone in the 'car', her head bowed. BILL en-
ters SL, 'opens the passenger door' and waits. CAROL doesn't move. BILL
has to reach in and pull her out. He does this gently but firmly.
BILL. Come on, Carol.
CAROL. (*Standing by Hearse.*) Just don't make me look. I don't
want to see. (*She puts a hand over her eyes.*)
BILL. I won't.
CAROL. (*Grabbing at BILL's sleeve.*) Bill? Don't tell my mother.
BILL. Why would I?
CAROL. Because she loves you. You and your surfboards. So
don't tell her.
BILL. Let's go in.
CAROL. (*Uncovering her eyes and looking around.*) Where are we?
BILL. Here.
CAROL. But where?
BILL. Come on, Carol.
CAROL. This is a liquor store?
BILL. Around back. Joan said around back. There's a door
there. She said. In a yellow wall.
CAROL. What color door?
BILL. What color…? It doesn't matter.
NARRATOR. It mattered. The color of the door mattered.
The building was white. The sign over the liquor store was
hand-painted in red. The wall was yellow. These things mat-
tered. To me. Even now I can feel those colors. (*Pause.*) Seems
like I stood there, seeing those colors, for an eternity, until
BILL. We're not standing here any more. We're going in.
CAROL. You go in.
BILL. Carol…
CAROL. You go in. I'll stay here.
BILL. You're coming in. We're both going in.
BLACKOUT.

<u>Scene 9</u>
SETTING: The Abortionist's.
LIGHTS UP. BILL sits on a chair. Head and hands hanging low. He looks at nothing. Silence. (NOTE: These sounds can be prerecorded if desired.) NARRATOR covers her ears when the sounds CAROL makes come. A sudden O.S. YELP (CAROL O.S.) breaks the silence. BILL's head jerks up. More silence.

NARRATOR. (*Overlaps O.S. sounds*) Until the moment I felt Doctor Arguilles' forceps tug and pinch my vaginal wall, felt my cervix groan wide, felt the cold metal table underneath my buttocks.

An O.S. MOAN comes. BILL stares off. By the third O.S. GROAN, BILL is on his feet, pacing. He moves up to a "wall" and puts his ear to it. Hears something that agitates him. BILL (overlapping following speech) paces. Sits. Stands. Waits.

NARRATOR. (*Cont'd.*) Until I saw the yellow walls in that room behind a liquor store blaze indifference on our tableau of mustachioed Mexican man, pale white girl, argentine metal table, mottled porcelain catch basin filling with my blood and pieces of my Catherine.
BLACKOUT.

<u>Scene 10</u>
SETTING: On the Highway and at the Drive-In. LIGHTS UP HALF. BILL sits in the front "seat" of the Hearse. CAROL lies in the "back" (on the gurney). A long silence while BILL drives.

BILL. I'm glad to be back on this side of the border. Aren't you? (*Nothing from CAROL.*) What was that, pinching? I heard you. You said, well, called out, well, pinching. What was that? (*BILL swivels his head to look back at her. CAROL isn't talking; he focuses on his driving.*) I'm hungry. (*Beat.*) We're in Manhattan Beach, Jerry's Drive-In. Hey, they make a good chicken fried steak. That's for me. And spaghetti. You like spaghetti. We'll eat, then I'll get you home and in bed by midnight. Okay?

CAROL. I can't go home tonight. Take me to Joan's.

BILL. (*Stopping the hearse; HONKING the horn.*) What do you want with your spaghetti?

193

CAROL. Nothing.

BILL. (*HONKING again: leans his head out the "window".*) Jeez, but they're slow tonight. I'll go place our order inside. (*BILL gets out of the 'car' in a hurry and exits UC.*)

FLASH BLACKOUT.

NARRATOR. Our food came on heavy diner plates on brown plastic trays. Bill. passed mine, spaghetti in meat sauce, through the window. As I watched, stunned by a two-ton silence, pieces of red-smeared spaghetti fell off my fork onto the black carpeted floor next to me in the back end of that Hearse.

CAROL. I wanted to name her Catherine. There's majesty in that name, Catherine. (*Pause.*) Now she's in pieces in a bucket in Mexico.

NARRATOR. Pieces of lies began to form in the "and" counts of my hushed breathing, in the spaces separating those beats that fall in between the solid counts and hesitations, in the composition of a life.

CAROL. And a-one. Tell your mother you have the flu.

NARRATOR. And a-two. Tell the unemployment office you looked for work today.

CAROL. And a-three, tell yourself this trip to Ensenada, Mexico, to the yellow-walled room behind the liquor store, to the rendezvous with Doctor Arguilles' scalpel, tell yourself, and a-four, it did not count.

NARRATOR. Happens every day. Just happened to happen to you today. And a-five.

CAROL. Tell Bill, no. To anything else.

NARRATOR. And a-six, seven, eight, eight beats to the bar. Tell yourself you will forget about it.

CAROL. In no time.

BLACKOUT.

Scene 11

SETTING: Present. SPOT ON NARRATOR, on her stool. During NARRATOR's speech, MOTHER, 48, enters UC and stands, waiting to interrupt.

NARRATOR. But abortions don't let you forget.

(*Steps away from her stool, moves C.*) They haunt the back of your mind, fragments of memory like old songs you heard once but can't remember the words to. (*Pause.*) After Bill rode away into the Malibu sunset in search of the perfect wave, I sacrificed a whole hunk of myself on the altar of belonging to another man. The one I married.

LIGHTS UP. MOTHER moves down stage, brings one chair with her.

MOTHER. You're leaving some things out.

NARRATOR considers MOTHER; leaves her stool and steps into SET-TING: MOTHER's house. MOTHER arranges chairs to face each other. Sits. Waits. NARRATOR crosses to the other chair, stands behind it.

NARRATOR. I covered the bases.

MOTHER. You left me out.

NARRATOR. I mentioned you.

MOTHER. Yes, that you didn't tell me. (*Beat.*) Why not?

NARRATOR. You were busy living a life that didn't include me was how I saw it.

MOTHER. I was busy making a living for you. In the 1950s, women alone were truly alone. We didn't have day care centers if we didn't have husbands and had to work. We had ourselves to count on, to figure things out, to make life work. We did what we had to do.

NARRATOR. But you and me, we both had an idea of what teenage grace should be.

MOTHER. Teen age is a time of innocent grace.

NARRATOR. How could I tell you I'd fallen out of that grace by getting pregnant? (*She sits.*)

MOTHER. You took me out of your life with your silence. Abortions are about mothering, you know. The mother needs to be there, somewhere.

NARRATOR. Maybe abortions are about the absence of mothering.

MOTHER. A woman who wants to be a mother would never consider an abortion as a choice.

NARRATOR. When a woman's mother has been absent most of her life, maybe she can't think of anything else. If she gets pregnant.

195

MOTHER. If you die before me, I'll have no idea what friends of yours to notify, what colors you liked, or which flowers you would want at your funeral.

NARRATOR. If I even want a funeral.

MOTHER. We're strangers.

NARRATOR. (*Standing, moving chair so the women both face audience.*) Estrangers, entitled to be close, yet mutually rejected. I read that somewhere. It fits, don't you think?

MOTHER. Do you look back at 1959 and feel shame?

NARRATOR. Yes, but not how you might think. My shame is our separation, yours and mine, shame like a fire stoked by indifference.

MOTHER. Mine is, too. We were both found out.

NARRATOR. Found wanting.

MOTHER. (*Turning to face NARRATOR.*) Wanting. (*Pause.*) You should have stayed married to FRED..

MOTHER exits during
BLACKOUT

Scene 12: Present & Past Mixed

LIGHTS UP to include NARRATOR returned to her stool and full stage.

NARRATOR. (*To audience.*) Remember the middle-class white girls of my generation: we believed that Donna Reed and Harriet Nelson and Lucille Ball and the wives they played knew the truth about marriage—husband decrees, wife agrees (or tries to trick him into thinking she has agreed). And we believed, or thought we did, or tried to believe even though we did not or were not sure, that marriage was our promised land.

FRED enters, interrupting her speech.

FRED. You're still leaving things out.

NARRATOR. (*Glowering at FRED.*) I didn't want you in this.

FRED. How can you leave me out?

NARRATOR. We didn't have children. You didn't want any. You had too many hangups about the word father to consider taking it on for yourself.

FRED. We didn't have the right house, the right connections. There wasn't enough money for babies.

196

NARRATOR. Not enough heart, more like it.

FRED. For both of us, then. You can't leave me out of this. I'm part of you, who you are now.

NARRATOR. You told me I walked like I had a stick up my ass. I've never forgotten that.

FRED. But you need me to make sense of everything that went before and all that followed.

NARRATOR. What arrogance. How dare you presume to be that important in my life. (*To audience.*) Well, to be fair, he is. Important to this story, at least. (*Long pause.*) The first time I saw the man I would someday refer to as my ex-husband, so tall, handsome, cruel yet elegant, a sliver of a reminder of those dark dangerous boys from high school?, he took me to the apartment he shared with three other college guys.

FRED. I was digging graves to put myself through art school at UCLA, and then this guy in one of my classes tells me he'll fix me up with the prettiest girl I'd ever seen.

NARRATOR. Our first date was like something out of a well-rehearsed seduction scene. (*To FRED.*) Admit it. Red lights, candles, cheap red wine, steaks.

FRED. I was ready to get married, so if I wanted to convince you to marry me, I had to impress you.

NARRATOR. Oh, I was impressed.

FRED. You danced for me that night. Naked.

NARRATOR. You told me to dance for you.

FRED. Like you had no choice?

NARRATOR. That's how it seemed.

LIGHTS DIM on FRED.

NARRATOR. (*Cont'd.*) (*To audience.*) He watched me dance and fucked me under the glow of a red lamp. (*Pause.*) The word fuck is important. I don't remember ever feeling, or saying to myself, we are making love.

FRED. Never?

NARRATOR. (*To FRED.*) I felt like you were always doing something to me, as if I wasn't there. Not really. (*To audience.*) That was the beginning of us, of our eight years. Long before we met, I'd already put myself aside. So I let my soon-to-

197

be-ex-husband mold me into the woman he wanted. Maybe I thought, hoped, he knew how to put me back together? (*Pause.*) In truth, I walked into that relationship fully masked. Me? I was going to build a perfect movies marriage, lights up on the cliff, violins in the background, subdued lighting so the warts don't show. I wasn't going to repeat the only kind of marriages I grew up with, where people walked off in different directions, leaving broken leafy bits of themselves scattered about the landscape. No.

HALF BLACKOUT. CAROL enters and takes a chair.

Scene 13: 1954 & Present.

NOTE: This scene is played with tension, not anger, between the two.
LIGHTS FULL.

CAROL. (*To FRED.*) I kept slim for you on secreted diet pills, wore my long hair tied back for you, cooked full-course meals for you and your friends, all the while working full time, did not speak unless and until spoken to, made breakfast and then went back to bed on Sunday mornings so you could fuck me. You peed on the toilet seat and the floor and I cleaned it up. I never said boo, not to you, or asked for your help, never offered to clean your wounds.

FRED. Wounds? What are you talking about?

CAROL. Your father abandoned you, you grew up hard on the streets in San Antonio, you had a way about you, sometimes, like a dog that's been thrown out of a moving truck.

FRED. What a silly girl you are. Come here.

FRED holds open his arms. CAROL rises and steps into his hug, then steps back.

FRED. (*To NARRATOR.*) What about the times back packing? (*Sitting; as if reading a topo map; to CAROL.*) Honey, did you make your list? (*CAROL exits, returns with a list, hands it to him.*) (*FRED reading list.*) We'll need two extra pairs of socks, another butter tube, three more dinners, and pick up a flask for me.

CAROL. Why?

FRED. We're going up Tuolumne Falls. It's a longer trip, but there's a lake up there that looks good.

198

CAROL. No, why the flask?

FRED. I'm tired of carrying a full fifth.

CAROL. I always pack your Bushmills. In and out.

FRED. An extra roll of film, and make sure my shirts are back from the cleaners. We won't be back until late Sunday night and I've got a staff meeting Monday.

CAROL. I've only got a week off.

FRED. Tell your boss you're taking two. I'll call him for you, if you can't do it.

CAROL. No, I'll…

FRED. And pack your diaphragm. I'm feeling horny.

NARRATOR. (*To FRED.*) Remember the time we had to cross a river on a log and I couldn't unless I sat down and scootched across and you yelled at me?

FRED. (*To NARRATOR.*) A child could have crossed that log on her feet. (*Pause.*) What about all those photographs?

NARRATOR. They were damn good. I remember a closet full, that closet by the stairs, pictures of all those backpacking trips we took up in the Sierra. Boxes and boxes of photos. Such gorgeous country. And you had a beautiful sense of design. Do you still have them? The pictures?

FRED. Do you still have your Kelty pack?

NARRATOR. You were good. With a camera. Not with me.

FRED. (*To CAROL.*) When's dinner?

CAROL. I was home late tonight, so…

FRED. Why?

CAROL. My boss kept me late, we're working on a proposal, and then I had to stop at Gelson's.

FRED. What for?

CAROL. Bushmills.

NARRATOR. (*To audience.*) Here's where it all comes apart, moments like this one, where Fred's history and mine collided, where his need to control his world—and my recognition that I was only worthy of beatings, belittling, and mopping up urine—blew up in our faces.

FRED. (*Still to CAROL. Snarling.*) Fucking the box boys, more likely.

CAROL. (*Trying to move beyond the potential danger.*) I'm going to need more money this month.

FRED. You have a salary.

CAROL. Our expenses went up lately.

FRED. Your expenses, you mean.

CAROL. (*Softly.*) No. Your film, your cleaning, your Bushmills, extra food for dinners for your boss. Yours.

FRED. Those dinners are my ticket to something better. A decent house. With decent neighbors, people who appreciate a better life.

CAROL. (*Evenly.*) We don't have enough money for the life we're living. We're putting up a false show. To everyone else, we're the golden couple, we're Rob and Laura Petrie, but there's no money to cover it. I'm bouncing checks. You're bouncing checks. I'm borrowing money just to keep our account even.

FRED. Who from? Who are you borrowing money from?

CAROL. Uh, from our savings, to start with. Then I had to ask Mother…

FRED. I told you we're never talking to your mother again. She's crazy, her and all her arty friends.

CAROL. She said no anyway.

FRED. You went to see her.

CAROL. No.

FRED. I don't believe you.

CAROL. There's nothing not to believe, I phoned.

FRED. I saw you checking out that guy at the park yesterday.

CAROL. (*Very soft.*) What? Guy? What guy? I don't know what you're talking about.

FRED. Extra money for a motel maybe? Going to shack up with that park guy? And let's not forget your good looking boss.

CAROL. No, I… I'll go get dinner ready.

FRED. No. Come here.

CAROL. No, I don't want… I'm cooking pork chops…

FRED moves for her.

CAROL. (*Cont'd.*) …the way you like them… no, please…

FRED grabs CAROL, slaps her face, and pins her down. Simulation of brutal, forced sexual encounter, a rape. CAROL is silent throughout; this is awfully familiar to her.

NARRATOR. (*To audience.*) Weren't we a pretty pair. A full-blown dangerous bully boy and a victim goddess, each depending on the other to keep our wounds open. I think we nearly annihilated each other with our stories. (*To FRED.*) Do you agree?

FRED. (*To NARRATOR.*) I called it marriage.

NARRATOR. (*To FRED.*) Today it's called rape. Or, that catch-all wimpy word, abuse. I hate that word.

FRED. (*To NARRATOR.*) I loved you. (*Pause.*) Maybe too much.

NARRATOR. (*To FRED.*) You loved the idea of me, Fred. That's how you wanted me. A carefully controlled composition frozen in photographic emulsion. (*Pause.*) But you could only see my picture, not me. That's why I had to go. (*To audience.*) I left him all the things, all the photographs, and walked out.

CAROL leaves stage; FRED also exits, uttering one line toward CAROL's and NARRATOR's directions.

FRED. (*Exiting opposite.*) You'll be sorry. I'm the best thing you'll ever find.

LIGHTS DOWN on stage.

Scene 14: 1969

SPOT on NARRATOR on her stool.

NARRATOR. I hated to think he was right. So I went hunting.

LIGHTS UP. CAROL enters, sits on a chair, and mimes preparations (using the fourth wall as a mirror).

NARRATOR. (*Cont'd.*) Each night I went out to the bars in the Marina Del Rey, in Manhattan Beach, in Hollywood, each night demanded many hours of preparation, of sluicing down, polishing, refining, the outer me. My choice of garments became as important as breathing; I was, after all, wearing sex like a cloak. I was also wearing long, curly hair, false eyelashes, a zaftig body fully toned, 36Ds, long curvy legs, red 3-inch spike heels, and a come-fuck-me attitude. I practiced first by watching the women who came late to the meat market bars, left their coats with the bartender, circled the room, had maybe one watered down drink, selected their prey, and left with it. I studied these women as if playing their part, this part, was

201

my entire reason for being. Soon, I became a high priestess of instant seduction. I dropped all of my girlfriends and went on a sex spree. I turned into my own version of a dangerous girl, and started collecting men.

CAROL, satisfied with her look, exits. LIGHTS dim such that the following "parade of men" is very much a background to NARRATOR's spotlighted speech. During the following monologue, actors dressed completely in black, including black hoods, so we do not recognize their faces or gender, walk slowly, in single file, across the stage, L to R, and continue crossing in rhythm with NARRATOR's words until a few beats after her monologue is complete. Occasionally, one of the "men" may move closer to her, pop up over her shoulder, bump into another "man," several may huddle around her in a clump, then break up and resume their solemn walk, etc.

NARRATOR. (*Cont'd.*) Like the restaurant manager who needed to trim my pubic hairs with his nail scissors before he could get hard. The CIA agent, he said, who said my box stunk but never accepted his part in creating said stink. The acrobat who gave me acid and standing-up head. The boy who hated 69: the old man who loved it. The black man who believed the myth that dark skin color makes for bigger cocks and better lovers. The yellow man who surprised me with his tenderness and by not being circumcised. The red man whose long black hair marked my pink skin with his tracks. The white man from my high school days, who did not remember me, whose cock I pulled so hard he cried out in pain, who, watching me leave his sex bed, begged me for more. Two men in a Seattle walk-up after too much cocaine. A couple of women, just because. (*Changing tempo.*) Doing "it" in pick-up truck beds, in double beds, in queen-sized beds, in clean beds, filthy beds, on floors, in alleys, standing up, lying down, frontwards, backwards. Doing it to Ravel's Bolero, in sync with the Beatles, on a Malibu mountain top the night men walked on the moon. Doing the infamous "it," the it once reserved for marriage beds, the it still not called the sex that it was. Fast sex. Sloppy sex. Cruel sex. Kind sex. Dry frantic sex. Oily sweat sex. Hard, fast, dangerous sex. Sweet sex. Silly sex. Sex on toast, with breakfast, over drinks, under hangovers. Sex that was reserved for sucking, or licking, or fingering. Sex that was relegated to fucking. Lemon scented sex with an English engineer. Sex with men who worshipped at the vestibule of my vagina. (*Slowing down.*) Sex with men who hated women—can't we always tell? Favorite sex with a youngster who lived in a Venice Beach walk-up apartment complete with a pull-down Murphy bed, who later asked me to sail around the world with him. (*Pause.*) I didn't go. I took Jimmy home, instead.

Scene 15: 1969 & The Present

LIGHTS to HALF, soft. CAROL enters and sits on the (gurney) bed. JIMMY enters and sits next to her; he's shy with her.

CAROL. I don't usually do this. Bring men here. This is my mother's house.

JIMMY. I like your room.

CAROL. See, I got divorced, the papers came, the trial... Can I call it a trial? I stood up and sat in the witness chair and said he raped me and beat me and I don't want to live there anymore and the judge said okay you don't have to, go sign papers with the clerk, and I watched the clock when he said you don't have to, and it all was done in three minutes. All those years. Gone in three minutes. And now I'm back here, in her house. Like I'm being punished.

JIMMY. My room is kinda dark. Good to sleep in, but I can't get much thinking done there.

CAROL. I changed my mind. Let's go to your place.

JIMMY. My folks are having a party tonight.

CAROL. How old are you?

JIMMY. Twenty.

CAROL. How'd you get served?

JIMMY. The bartender at the Surfrider is my cousin. From Arizona.

CAROL. Shit. (*She gets up, exits, returns.*) I've got my period. I've never done it during... not even my husband... so, thanks for...

JIMMY. I don't care. (*Putting one hand on the back of her head.*) You're beautiful.

CAROL. You don't care?

JIMMY. We've got a gig next weekend, in Malibu. Will you come? With me?

CAROL. You don't care. Wow.

JIMMY. I'm vocals and lead guitar. (*Singing: a sweet, clear voice.*) "Love isn't lying/it's loose in a lady who lingers/saying she is lost/and choking on hello"

CAROL. (*Singing.*) "They are one person…

CAROL. and JIMMY. (*Singing.*) They are two alone/they are three together/they are for each other."*

CAROL and JIMMY slide down on the "bed" in an embrace.

NARRATOR. I drifted into Jimmy's world and happily stayed there until it was time for me to step into thirty and for him to discover twenty one. (*Pause.*) I have one photo of us, a close-up. *NARRATOR looks at CAROL and JIMMY. They sit up, put their faces together and look at her, then directly at the audience.*

NARRATOR. (*Cont'd.*) Our heads touch as we look right into the lens. In both faces I see—from this side of the camera and the years—what I felt about us then, a look of hesitant possibility about the eyes, a sort of slightly open-mouthed, oh. He wrote songs to me; I wrote songs asking questions. With another friend of his, we wrote a song for a movie, one of those loaded with confusion and outrage about the Vietnam War. But, as much as I adored this man, we really weren't for each other. We simply couldn't be. Our lives got lost in our escape routes of music, foreplay, afterplay, and marijuana smoke. Just too far apart, us.

CAROL and JIMMY slowly exit. LIGHTS down. SPOT on NARRATOR.

NARRATOR. (*Cont'd.*) Later, trying out San Francisco for a time, a true poet, a follower of Ferlinghetti, brought me to tears of longing after our sexual rollings. "Why do you cry," he asked, holding my head against his bare chest. I could not answer, could not reassure either of us. I was awash in an emotional waterfall that had no words. My separation from myself was crying crocodile tears. (*Changing tone: all business.*) Now then. The poet of medicine, he liked me to wear skirts and no underpants to dinner in Italian restaurants, so he could finger me and then smell me on his fingers while he ate scaloppini. He called me his virgin whore, and tossed me aside when I asked why he kept a large sheep dog in a small cage beside his bed. (Pause.) Three different men the weekend I turned thirty-two, in the Malibu Hills beneath the shadow of the Dominican Monastery Cross. (*Pause; shift in tone.*) My reasoning tells me I must have known: the tender part of me asks, pleads, why? Why put yourself on the rack again?

BLACKOUT *or* CURTAIN

END ACT I

ACT II

Scene 1: 1972

SETTING: A Planned Parenthood Clinic in Los Angeles.

AT RISE: Thirty-two year-old CAROL sits on a chair, waiting.

The other chair is placed so that we know a desk is in between CAROL and the COUNSELOR who will enter after a beat carrying a manila folder under one arm, cross to sit, and fold his hands in his lap (to mimic on a desktop).

COUNSELOR. Sorry I'm late. Staff meeting. (*No response from CAROL.*) So many meetings these days. Just when I think I've got a minute to myself, up comes another meeting. The cost of doing business, I suppose, eh. Well, what can I do for you? Birth control pills? Do you have a doctor's prescription?

CAROL. No.

COUNSELOR. No? Well, you look a little bit old for birth control counseling, but we've got a group starting next Monday I can get you in. (*Looks in file.*) That's right, next Monday, seven o'clock, at the Venice office. Where do you live?

CAROL. Santa Monica, but that's not…

COUNSELOR. (*Closing file.*) That'll work fine, then. You get there early, say, six forty-five, get yourself checked in, take a look at our brochures, did you see our brochures in the outer office?, look at those. (*Consulting watch: standing; extending hand.*) Nice to meet you, Miss…

CAROL. I don't need a group.

COUNSELOR. Oh? That's too bad. We find that the group

205

dynamic is most effective for girls in discussing birth control methods.

CAROL. I'm not a girl and I don't need a group. Or a counselor.

COUNSELOR. Then I'm sorry, I don't quite understand why you're here?

CAROL. I'm pregnant.

COUNSELOR. Oh. (*Consulting watch again; exits SR. COUNSELOR enters quickly SR, a female COUNSELOR close in his wake.*) (*To SECOND COUNSELOR.*) I didn't get a termination file on this one.

SECOND COUNSELOR. That's because I haven't done an intake on her yet. (*To CAROL.*) We'll need to schedule an intake interview for you, Miss. Will you come with me out to the receptionist's desk?

CAROL. No.

SECOND COUNSELOR. No? Perhaps we'd better sit down and talk about this.

CAROL. No. I've been sitting out there, at the receptionist's desk, for two hours. I called last week, I said I needed an abortion, the woman on the phone made an appointment, here I am. I don't want counseling, I don't want a group, I don't want to sit down, I don't want you to hold my hand, this isn't my first time, I know what I'm doing, I want my abortion. Isn't that what Planned Parenthood is for? To give women abortions when they need them?

SECOND COUNSELOR. Yes, certainly, but not without extensive counseling, or unless there's some physical reason why a woman cannot carry her baby full term.

CAROL. It's not a baby. Yet.

SECOND COUNSELOR. (*To COUNSELOR.*) I can handle this, Richard. You go on to the meeting and I'll catch up later. Give me the file. (*Taking file: to CAROL.*) Let's sit down.

COUNSELOR exits: CAROL and SECOND COUNSELOR sit facing each other.

Scene 2

SECOND COUNSELOR. (*Cont'd.*) Would you like a drink of

206

something? We've got a coke machine and a coffee machine that works sometimes.

CAROL. No, thanks. But thanks for asking.

SECOND COUNSELOR. My name is Mary.

CAROL. CAROL.

SECOND COUNSELOR. Carol. You said earlier that this isn't your first abortion. Is it your second pregnancy?

CAROL. Yes.

SECOND COUNSELOR. Are you married?

CAROL. No.

SECOND COUNSELOR. Were you the first time?

CAROL. (*Sighing.*) No.

SECOND COUNSELOR. Tell me about that first time.

CAROL. Not much to tell. I screwed up, he didn't want a baby, we went to Ensenada.

SECOND COUNSELOR. Mexico. In a clinic?

CAROL. A room behind a liquor store.

SECOND COUNSELOR. You had an abortion in a room behind a liquor store in Ensenada, Mexico. When was this?

CAROL. Nineteen fifty nine.

SECOND COUNSELOR. Any repercussions?

CAROL. How do you mean?

SECOND COUNSELOR. Did your periods change? Any heavy bleeding? Or pain anywhere in your abdomen? Your pelvis? Lower back?

CAROL. Oh, that kind of repercussion. No, nothing like that.

SECOND COUNSELOR. And you got pregnant again.

NARRATOR. (*To audience; softly.*) I'm surprised I didn't explode from the pressure. Today I'd tell her to get stuffed. But then, my thirty-two-year-old biological imperative was crashing into my desperate shame at having fallen even further out of grace.

CAROL. I don't need a lecture from you.

SECOND COUNSELOR. Part of my job is making sure that an abortion is the best decision you can make right now.

CAROL. That's why I'm here. I'm not about to go sneak down to Mexico again when Planned Parenthood tells me they'll help me with my decision. You'll help me. You won't tell me I'm no good or stupid or careless, you'll recognize me as an intelligent adult making her own choices. You won't scold me into keeping this might-be baby. Your mercy is supposed to be pure, not dangling off a punishing hook.

SECOND COUNSELOR. And the father of this child? (*CAROL doesn't answer.*) You could give this baby up for adoption if you don't feel equipped to be a mother. You might marry again, and want another child. The chances of getting pregnant decrease with each abortion.

CAROL. Really?

SECOND COUNSELOR. We think so. And with all the birth control choices available to you, there's no reason to get pregnant anymore.

LIGHTS DIM: SPOT on CAROL, standing C.

CAROL. (*To audience.*) She's going to make me tell, that I don't know who the father is, that I've been sleeping around because I'm trying to find something in myself and I think seeing myself in men's eyes will tell me what it is. And then she might tell me, no, we won't do this for you, you're on your own, out, get out. She's going to ask me, where is the father? Where is your father? Where are your parents? Where is your minister, your teachers, people to tell you how to behave? Where is your morality? Where your conscience? I'm going to be found out, I'm a bad girl, shame threatens to leap out my throat and scream. My rage won't help me here; I have to be silent and say what these people want to get what I want. I'm not finding anything in myself, I'm losing myself. No reason to get pregnant, she says. No reason? No reason not to dare to hope for someone to cling to, to love?

SPOT on CAROL fades; slow DIM on stage; SECOND COUNSELOR exits. NARRATOR enters and takes up her position on her stool.

Scene 3: Present & 1972

CAROL executes slow dance steps in the background during part of NARRATOR's following speech.

NARRATOR. Once, when I was about twelve, I went to a friend's house for a swimming party. I knew my dancer's body looked pleasing as it arced off the edge of the diving board and plunged into the cool blue water below. This day, I climbed up to the high board, settled my body into itself in readiness for the dive to come, took my steps out to the end, and, in the instant I leapt up, realized a wasp, sunning itself on the end of the board, had stung me. That trip down to the water seemed to take a lifetime. As my body plummeted to the bottom of the pool, the sting gathered its power and, when I surfaced, howling in pain, reached its zenith. My second abortion feels like that suspended time in the air in between the diving board and the pool. I am as if suspended in air, with one foot screaming, except I can't feel or hear it any longer. I am as if untethered, unattached to my life. (*Long pause.*) What I do remember comes in thumbnail sketches of a whole yet to be filled in.

LIGHTS UP on stage. NARRATOR rises, stretches, and situates herself to stand far R, out of the action, but within the circle of light. CAROL sits on one of the chairs and mimes driving.

NARRATOR. (*Cont'd.*) I don't remember where the place was, but I drove up tree-covered hills into a residential neighborhood. A sloping driveway…

CAROL stands, walks C and looks at

NARRATOR. (*Cont'd.*) …a neutral-zone waiting room with the requisite out-dated magazines on wood-grain side tables. And then nothing until

CAROL stands, walks over to and reclines on the gurney.

CAROL. I am lying on a gurney, waiting my turn in a white hall, slightly doped up, but not enough that I can't see a …a transparent bucket on a trolley being pushed out of double doors across from me, across the hall.

An ATTENDANT pushes the bucket on to stage from R.

CAROL. (*Cont'd.*) The bucket has a vacuum tube and nozzle attached, just like the one on my upright Hoover™. The bucket is filled with something red and fleshy. Some other woman's left overs. Did she cry?

NARRATOR. Why couldn't I?

CAROL. Did she feel her tears, her loss, her gain?

NARRATOR. Why didn't I?

CAROL. The sight of that bloody bucket killed any feelings I might want, or, more likely, want to also kill. Soon—how long is soon when one is doped up, waiting for the surgeon's blade, lacking awareness—my semi-conscious mind turns the sucking machine and its bucket into a grotesque cartoon and watches the whole business roll past me on little wheels. Long after it passes, I can hear the bucket traveling down those sterile white halls as if on blistered wheels.

O.S. bucket squeak-burp-squeak-burp-squeak-burp-squeak

CAROL. (*Cont'd.*) Until I shut my eyes and clamp down my mind.

NARRATOR. Heart feelings long gone—if I considered it at all, I imagined my heart as the size of a shrunken pea's shadow, flushed away as waste. Until.

CAROL. All thinking, feeling, knowing, touching, in front of, behind, me, nothing, except, until…

O.S. bucket squeak-burp-squeak-burp-squeak-burp-squeak

CAROL. (*Cont'd.*) I am wheeled through a pair of swishing doors, and gratefully vanish under the full dose of sodium pentothal. Fully numb. Nothing left.

NARRATOR. We were rendered unconscious for our abortions then, just as our mothers had been for birthing their babies.

CAROL. After.

NARRATOR. I sat in a chair in the waiting room, that nondescript, depersonalized medical place of anticipation, of dreams lost until

CAROL. I am offered orange juice, but can't drink anything, just feel one thing suddenly, the need to get out—of the place, of my skin. (*CAROL stands, sits on a chair, and starts "driving" furiously.*) I drive somewhere by myself. Hard. Long. Fast. After.

NARRATOR. I never told anyone what I had done. Not anyone, until now. Memory does not tell me the season; was it fall? I am left with three distinct sense impressions of that time: crisp, fresh air touching my face once I emerged from the clinic; a white, endless corridor with no point of perspective, and

O.S. bucket squeak-burp-squeak-burp-squeak-burp-squeak squeak-burp-

squeak-burp-squeaking

NARRATOR and CAROL. Until.

They exit during

ABRUPT BLACKOUT.

LAZY SPOT follows GRACE #2 drifting across the stage in a floating white gauze dress.

GRACE #2. She can't remember any more, or the most more of that day, because we never touched. Our souls didn't connect, or someone forgot to throw the switch that makes women mothers and daughters, or because… Because she was afraid of what she was doing? Because she never grew up? Because attaching to someone was too dangerous? Because all that leaving in her story cut her from herself? Nothing there for my soul to hook on to with any grace, so I'm still out here, floating, part of her but not. She didn't name me. She couldn't. How could she name what was lost before it was found? I'm her ballet of what might have been, a piece of love found wanting, a melody with no ending note.

GRACE #2 concludes her dance and floats off.

BLACKOUT.

Scene 4: Present

LIGHTS UP. NARRATOR. enters and sits on her stool.

NARRATOR. After that, I went back to dancing, sort of. I had this little route, from my job at MGM, to Woman's World, to my apartment in Century City. Woman's World took me back into my body with weights, Dancercise classes, steam room sweats.

CAROL enters and walks, naked, across the stage under NARRATOR's speech.

NARRATOR. (*Cont'd.*) Inside the health club, women's gazes followed my toned-up body as I walked, naked, from locker to steam to sauna to massage table. Their attention to my body let me know I was ready. For a true love.

CAROL. saunters off.

NARRATOR. (*Cont'd.*) True love came to us 1950s girls as a package deal or not at all. The first requirement was a prince, and I found one gliding around the sound stages of MGM Studios. I beheld ZEKE. as a starving woman beholds a crust: I salivated. I all but lay down on the back lot for his attention. And I got it.

Scene 5: 1974

SETTING: An office at MGM Studios.

LIGHTS up FULL. CAROL enters carrying file folders. She sits on one of the chairs, and begins "working." ZEKE enters.

He straddles the other chair facing her.

ZEKE. Hi, beautiful.

CAROL. Hi yourself.

ZEKE. Did you miss me?

CAROL. When?

ZEKE. Didn't miss me at dailies? On the set?

CAROL. I've been too busy to pay attention to you coming and going. (*Rising; filing; returns to sit.*) Where've you been?

ZEKE. Sick.

CAROL. There's a nasty flu going round.

ZEKE. I didn't have that.

CAROL. No?

ZEKE. I had my own version. A highly specialized fever that kept me up nights.

CAROL. What did you take for it?

ZEKE. I called my doctor in the middle of the night and she came and gave me a B12 shot. Now I'm as healthy as you see me.

CAROL. She. Of course.

ZEKE. Of course.

CAROL. What do you want, ZEKE.?

ZEKE. Ah, business. My untouchable beauty wants to talk business.

CAROL. I am not untouchable.

ZEKE. No?

CAROL. No.

ZEKE. Good. (*Takes her arm.*) Walk with me over to stage nine. One of your actors is getting fussy about his contract. I need you to soothe his feathers.

CAROL. He's not my actor. Get one of the producers.

ZEKE. They're all at lunch.

CAROL. Why do you think I'd be any good at soothing feathers?

ZEKE. I think you're good at lots of things.

BLACKOUT.

Scene 6: Later that night.

LIGHTS up low. CAROL sits on one of the chairs, reading at "home." A KNOCK comes. CAROL rises to greet ZEKE who enters bearing a bouquet of flowers. He stands as if at the doorway, testing his reception for this unannounced visit.

CAROL. Ah.

A beat, and then ZEKE hands the bouquet to CAROL and swoops her into a passionate embrace and kiss, all in one smooth movement. He leads her to the "bed" (gurney). LIGHTS DIM further. SPOT on NARRATOR on her stool.

NARRATOR. Zeke made love to me that night. Not sex, not fucking, but love, as if he had been hiding in my closet for years watching me masturbate. Or as if he was performing for an audience only he could see, or perhaps to a panel of sexual contest judges. In any event, he instantly claimed mastery over a body he was touching, seeing, smelling, for the first time. I could hardly breathe. When he left...

ZEKE rises, touches CAROL briefly, exits. CAROL stands, then mimes NARRATOR's words.

NARRATOR. (*Cont'd.*) I stood very still in the doorway, watching him go, trying to hold him with my yearning. Gently I bathed, softly I put myself back in my bed, smiling I drifted into a dreamless sleep. I can feel that smile on my face even now, feel the hope it held that this man, this beginning, was my way back home, whatever that meant. (*Standing, moving DR.*)

CAROL rises from the gurney and exits.

NARRATOR. (*Cont'd.*) I didn't see him for a week. I was crazy for him. So I did the unthinkable. I called the studio personnel officer for his home address, saying one of my boss producers

213

needed it. And I went there. One night, past midnight. *BLACK-OUT during which ZEKE enters and lies down, sleeping, on the gurney.*

Scene 7: A week later; night.
SETTING: ZEKE's apartment. A bedroom. LIGHTS UP. CAROL hovers at CL. An O.S. KNOCK comes. ZEKE gets out of his bed (off the gurney), answers door, finds CAROL on the doorstep. Reluctantly ushers her in.
NARRATOR. (*Cont'd.*) (*To audience.*) I ran to Zeke for some of his perfect, unattached loving. But our second roll in the hay was a big mistake, on several fronts. I was the one who pushed for the date, if you can call it that, which he, quite obviously, did not want.
CAROL. I know this is crazy, but…
ZEKE. No, no. It's okay. Just late.
CAROL. I know.
ZEKE. You want something to drink?
CAROL. No. I just want to go to bed. With you.
ZEKE. Wait a minute. (*ZEKE goes off, returns with a condom packet. He frowns at it.*)
NARRATOR. (*To audience.*) He was the one who was prepared with one holey rubber which he used reluctantly.
ZEKE. I don't know how old this thing is.
CAROL. Where's your bed?
ZEKE. In here. It's one of those adjustable kind and it's stuck in the knees up position.
CAROL. So am I.
NARRATOR. (*To audience.*) I was the one who insisted we fuck in his broken mechanical bed. It was not a repeat of our first coupling. Positively dull by comparison.
CAROL and ZEKE slowly exit, CAROL leaving the stage first. SPOT on NARRATOR.
NARRATOR. (*Cont'd.*) A few days later, I was canned. The studio didn't pick up the pilot, so the series wasn't a go, no need for our production company, no need for me. No chance of seeing Zeke, of bumping into him by accident, of calling him to our offices on some pretext or other. No job, no man, I felt

like I was standing on quicksand. Time to move and start over. Joan offered me a room in her Topanga Canyon house, I gave notice, and organized a sell-it-all-up-and-get-out-of-town sale. To be held on my front lawn that weekend. (*Pause.*) Like ghosts, Fred, my now ex-husband, and Bill, my first lover, appeared on that lawn on Saturday, about two hours apart. My now ex-husband Fred arrived with a woman in tow. He circled my life spread out on the lawn and bought a ten-cent item. She, not he, handed me the dime. Bill came because that's what happens when the gods and goddesses of all that's sane and holy take the day off, and because strands of my life were floating backwards as well as forwards.

Scene 8: Front Lawn Sale
LIGHTS full. CAROL enters, sits on a chair. After a beat, BILL arrives. He wanders around the "sale," then comes and sits on the "ground" next to CAROL.
BILL. What's this all about?
CAROL. First my ex-husband and now you. You tell me what it's all about.
BILL. No. I mean this. You're selling everything you own, looks like.
CAROL. No, just what doesn't belong to me anymore.
BILL. What does that mean?
CAROL. It means I'm moving on.
BILL. And leaving us behind.
CAROL. Well, I don't know who us is, but, yes. That's my plan.
BILL. Where are you going?
CAROL. Up Topanga Canyon.
BILL. L.A. finally got to you, huh.
CAROL. Something like that.
BILL gets up and wanders around a bit. Returns to her side.
BILL. How long is the sale?
CAROL. I'm calling it done tomorrow at five o'clock. I've still got packing to do.
BILL. Okay. What you don't sell I'll buy.
CAROL. What for? These're girl's things.

215

BILL. I'll be back tomorrow five thirty. With a truck.
BLACKOUT

Scene 9

The next night, BILL's apartment. LIGHTS UP. CAROL and BILL sit on his couch, (the gurney) passing a joint back and forth.

CAROL. I'm sure glad you didn't come back for all that stuff with the Hearse.

BILL. I got rid of it once the freeway opened and I didn't have to spend the night down in Dana Point anymore.

CAROL. Is your shop still on Pico?

BILL. No. Venice.

CAROL. Still making surfboards.

BILL. And other things.

CAROL. What other things.

BILL. Money, for one.

CAROL. Money? When you say money, you mean…

BILL. Money. Bucks. Big.

CAROL. And still you live like this? In one room? When we knew each other, at least you had a one-bedroom apartment.

BILL. I like my life tucked in close around me these days.

CAROL. What else do you make?

BILL. Not so much as make, but I got into a sort of wholesale business.

CAROL. Sort of.

BILL. Yeah. (*He rolls another joint.*) How about some wine?

CAROL. No thanks. This is enough. (*Taking a toke.*) What's your business?

BILL. I buy tanks.

CAROL. Fish tanks?

BILL. No, tanks.

CAROL. Like Army tanks?

BILL. Yup.

CAROL. Why?

BILL. People pay a lot of money for U.S. made tanks.

CAROL. You're a gun runner?

BILL. No, just tanks. And they don't really run. More like

216

crawl.

CAROL. Good grief. I can't get my head around this.

BILL. Why not?

CAROL. You and tanks? It doesn't fit. You're such a…

BILL. A what. Dope? Idiot?

CAROL. No. A sweet guy. (*Beat.*) Are you happy?

BILL. Happy enough, I guess. (*Long pause while the two sit and smoke.*) What about you? Are you happy?

CAROL. I don't know. I mean, what is happy? What does happy look like? How does it feel?

BILL. Were you happy with me?

CAROL. Mostly I was in awe. I couldn't get over… that you liked me. All those girls hanging around in the surf shop and you picked me.

BILL. I didn't just like you. I loved you.

CAROL. I never knew that.

Another pause.

BILL. I was a dope, you know.

CAROL. About what?

BILL. You. I never should have let you go.

CAROL. That was a long time ago.

BILL. When I saw you today, sitting on that lawn, and… Right now it feels like yesterday.

CAROL. Bill? Are you crying?

BILL. No. It's just the grass. Good weed always makes me tear up.

CAROL. You are. You're crying.

BILL stands and holds out his hand. CAROL takes it and he leads her off. LIGHTS DOWN half. SPOT on NARRATOR on her stool at apron.

NARRATOR. We smoked more weed, he cried over us, I felt my heart turn over, he climbed up to his bed and held out his hand. I went there. That night stands out in my memory as some of the sweetest, sexy love I have ever made and received. That night holds a special tenderness because he had been my first, years before, and still held a piece of me in his heart, years later. (*Pause.*) And I, in the next month, held a piece of one of these two—ZEKE or BILL—in my womb.

217

Scene 10: JOAN's house.

NARRATOR. (*Looks at stage, catching the memory.*) Each dawn, in the back room of Joan's house, I awoke from a series of Persephone dreams in which my body was raped and dragged into Hades.

LIGHTS UP on stage, DOWN on NARRATOR. JOAN and CAROL enter, in conversation. The women cross to sit on chairs.

JOAN. What do you want to do?

CAROL. I don't know.

JOAN. You should talk to your mother.

CAROL. I can't.

JOAN. You shouldn't be alone with this. Not again.

CAROL. Talking to her just opens up all those lousy doors, all that... I can't...

JOAN. You have to put the past aside. You need help. You need her help. You need her to know she still has a chance to be a grandmother.

CAROL. I'm in my third month. I don't even know if I can get an abortion.

JOAN. Then talk to her. And soon. And then, we'll figure something out. There's always room for another baby here.

LIGHTS DOWN on stage, UP on NARRATOR.

NARRATOR. Dear Joan, surrounded by love and people all her life, so sure of herself and her choices. So unlike me. I cried for days, knowing this was my last chance to mother another being of my body. Endless tears, splashing into Joan's stainless steel sink, draining away to the sea. I was now 35 and felt I had fallen so completely out of grace as to be completely invisible. Wavering between tentative motherhood and invisibility brought me...instead of closer to a decision, deeper into a hell of my own design ... a place where continued inactivity produced extreme anxiety, so much so that I took to physically vibrating at high frequencies, until I took the decision away from my shattering self, and put it onto the prospective daddies. Bill I told first, hoping his kindness in bed, under the influence of marijuana, would spread out and envelope me and my growing fetus and I could slow down and stop awhile with him. I said,

218

Bill, I'm pregnant, and he said, I had a vasectomy three years ago. Zeke went straight to the point. He handed me $200 in used bills in a downtown bar where no one would recognize him. (*Pause.*) Then I did what Joan said I had to do. I went to my mother.

BLACKOUT.

Scene 11: MOTHER's house.

LIGHTS UP full. MOTHER, 63, and CAROL sit on the chairs, facing each other. NARRATOR observes from her stool.

NARRATOR. The potential of that meeting, the possibilities, would she? wouldn't she? throb in my memory. Beneath my grown up words, I hear the baby girl Carol calling, Mommy! Look! See what I made!

MOTHER. (*To CAROL.*) I won't offer you a cup of tea. You're always in such a rush when you stop by.

CAROL. I have a job that keeps me busy.

MOTHER. I've never understood what your work is.

CAROL. I've told you. I'm an administrative assistant. I assist others do things.

MOTHER. Where are you working now?

CAROL. For an architect.

MOTHER. You're not in television anymore?

CAROL. Films. I was in films.

MOTHER. What happened to that?

CAROL. It doesn't matter.

MOTHER. Well. How are you?

CAROL. I need your help with something.

MOTHER. I won't give you any money.

CAROL. It's not money I need, well, not directly.

MOTHER. What, then?

CAROL. I'm pregnant.

MOTHER. Pregnant.

CAROL. Yes.

MOTHER. And you want me to take you in. Help you raise the baby.

CAROL. Well, I was sort of thinking…

219

MOTHER. What about the father?

CAROL. Not possible.

MOTHER. Why not?

CAROL. He just gave me the money for an abortion.

MOTHER. You say that so easily.

CAROL. It's anything but easy.

MOTHER. I don't believe in abortion. Girls shouldn't be so silly as to get caught. You shouldn't have been so silly as to get caught.

CAROL. Then you'll help me?

MOTHER. You know I admire you. Tremendously. But I don't understand you.

CAROL. That's all I ever wanted from you.

MOTHER. It's very difficult when all of your choices are so silly. Like this one. No. I won't help you. This is your choice, getting pregnant with no husband. It's like football.

CAROL. Football.

MOTHER. Girls today wanting to play football. As if they were boys. Why do girls want to do what boys do? Boys are such fragile creatures who turn into more fragile men. Why do girls want to emulate that? Abortions and playing football. Both absurd conditions for a woman to put herself in. Girls should stay off the football fields and in marriages.

CAROL. You didn't. And what good are husbands when times get tough? Yours sure as hell didn't stick around.

MOTHER. That was different.

CAROL. How.

MOTHER. We were married before you came along. It was war time. The world was in chaos. And your father tried, but he couldn't find himself in this country. So he left.

CAROL. I feel like I've been punished for his leaving all my life.

MOTHER. No. That's silly thinking. You're an adult now. You have to live with the consequences of your actions. Just as I have. All these years.

MOTHER stands and exits, taking the chair with her.

CAROL. Mommy? Look! (*Low.*) See what I made. (*CAROL rises and exits, taking the other chair with her.*)

LIGHTS DOWN on stage. SPOT on NARRATOR.

NARRATOR. (*To Audience.*) I couldn't turn and show my father. He was busy making music and collecting wives in England. But why didn't I even try? (*Turns to face the past.*)

LIGHTS full.

Scene 12

CAROL enters, R.

CAROL. Daddy? Look! See what I made!

FATHER enters, CL. The two have no chairs; the distance between them is palpable and much more than their physical one.

FATHER. Hello, darling.

CAROL. Tony.

FATHER. Lovely to see you. Are you staying long?

CAROL. No. I, I have something to tell you.

FATHER. Did I write to you about the New Zealand concert? My agent is rather hopeful. She thinks it could lead to a performance in America. Somewhere in Arizona. Where is Arizona? Somewhere near you, isn't it?

CAROL. I'm going to have a baby.

FATHER. Well, that's nice. Isn't it? Are you pleased?

CAROL. I'm going to need help. I can't do this on my own.

FATHER. Oh, I have every confidence in you, you're my daughter after all. But a warning, darling, if you'll allow me. Children are difficult, you know. They have teeth that need taking care of, and get awkward diseases. They're rather demanding of one's time and attention. And, if one isn't careful, of one's career.

CAROL. I don't have a career.

FATHER. Well, then, that's all right then. How is the hotel? I did warn them you'd probably want en suite? But they're used to Americans and their showers and do a lovely pub lunch. I take most of my mid-day meals there. And of course you're welcome to take your evening meal with us. All right? Darling?

CAROL stands with her arms open, looking at the audience. What is there to say? CAROL and FATHER exit opposite sides of stage.

NARRATOR. That's pretty close to the mark, knowing us now.

221

And it didn't occur to me to go to him, then. Dare I wonder what would have happened if I had, and he'd said, yes, come, deliver, create? Again, no answer. (*Pause.*) Instead, I went back to the Topanga house and wept into Joan's welcoming sink. When I had finally exhausted my soul's misery, I took Zeke's $200.00 and once again offered up my unborn beauty. (*Stands.*) This pregnancy carries the most weight, both in my memory and at the time. So much so, that what happened next doesn't surprise me. (*NARRATOR exits.*)
BLACKOUT.

Scene 13: 1975 & Present
SETTING: A Planned Parenthood Clinic in Los Angeles.
LIGHTS UP. NOTE: There is about this scene the ethereal, especially when CAROL "leaves" her body as the abortion begins. Thirty-five year-old CAROL sits on a gurney, alone. A NURSE enters, gently pushes CAROL down to a supine position, and administers a relaxing shot. CAROL's eyes stay bolted open. NURSE exits. CAROL is agitated, beginning to panic. The NURSE enters, sees CAROL still wide awake.
NURSE. How ya doin', honey?
CAROL. Not so good.
NURSE. It'll all be over in a little while. You'll see. (*She pats CAROL.*) You just give in to the medication and you'll be back awake and ready to go home in no time.
CAROL. I'm really frightened.
NURSE. Why, honey, nothing to be frightened about. Dr. Glen is about the best there is. You just close your eyes, go on, do it.
NURSE smiles, pats CAROL again and exits. DOCTOR, ANES-THESIOLOGIST, and NURSE enter and move the gurney into the 'operating theatre'. CAROL is draped appropriately; her eyes are still wide open. DOCTOR looks into her face. Turns to NURSE.
DOCTOR. Jane, this girl isn't close to unconscious yet.
NURSE. I don't understand it, Doctor, I gave her the pre-op half an hour ago.
DOCTOR. Well, I can't operate like this.
NURSE. We have a waiting room full. (*Peers into CAROL's face.*) She should be almost gone by now.

DOCTOR. (*To ANESTHESIOLOGIST.*) Can you put her under anyway?

ANESTHESIOLOGIST. It's a risk. I'd rather she was dopier than she is now.

DOCTOR. We can't wait. (*To CAROL.*) You don't have to do this, you know.

CAROL. (*Crying; the drug kicking in.*) I have no choice.

DOCTOR. Are you sure?

CAROL. (*Softly.*) No. I just have no choice.

DOCTOR. Okay then. (*To ANESTHESIOLOGIST.*) Start the drip.

LIGHTS down. SPOT on NARRATOR and on CAROL on gurney.

NARRATOR. At this point, I got the hell out. I left my body. And drifted up to a corner where the wall and ceiling met.

CAROL rises from the gurney and begins to slowly, curiously, drift around them as DOCTOR, NURSE, ANESTHESIOLOGIST, in slow motion, go about the business of performing an abortion on the 'body' that remains on the gurney.

CAROL. (*Circling the medical team.*) I'm here but I'm not here. I've slid beneath the surface of my mind and there's all this busy-ness going on, sucking out of life, saving life. Weird. I don't know where I am and I know exactly where I am. Do I feel anything? Ghosts don't feel, do they? Am I a ghost? Of myself? Listen. Isn't there a hum inside these walls? Who is that? All the other killed babies? Or is it me, my heart beating? Am I still breathing? This is kind of nice, being out here instead of in there, in me. What if I just stopped breathing—oh, they've stopped. (*CAROL places herself back on the gurney just as DOCTOR says*)

DOCTOR. Watch her in recovery. We may have a jumper on our hands.

The MEDICAL TEAM exits.

CAROL. (*Propping herself up on one elbow: to audience.*) He was right about jumping, just wrong about when I would. I jumped right under his hands. So maybe my, what'll I call it, psyche, had to get out, before it, too, was killed.

NARRATOR. Or perhaps some wise corner of my soul needed

223

to observe this third abortion from a distance, without attachment to emotions, so that it, and I, would never forget. (*Pause.*) How odd, then, that I very nearly did. (*Standing.*) Months later, still in Joan's home up on the Canyon hills, breathing in an elixir of eucalyptus and sun-baked dust, I wrote a letter to Zeke. I described, in detail, how, from my ceiling vantage point, I watched his baby being violently sucked out of my womb, down my vagina, and carelessly discarded into a container marked, BioHazard. A hard letter, this was, the kind one writes but never sends. I sent it. Signed. (*NARRATOR exits stage.*)
LIGHTS UP full. Hold.
BLACKOUT.

Scene 14: Six years later.
LIGHTS UP on stage and Apron. NARRATOR enters, not carrying her stool. She stands at apron.
NARRATOR. I went back to dancing for a while. I moved around the country, dancing. For a while I stopped in Boulder, Colorado. There, I fell into something with a painter who drove cab for a living. Doug had great stories, was a true Irish romantic. One day we drove into the mountains, to a bar in a relic mining town. I had no idea this day would be one of those turning points we all bump into, sometimes.
NARRATOR turns to consider the stage and watch as CAROL enters carrying one chair. She turns it and sits straddling. DOUG enters with his chair and sits straddling next to her. They face each other, easy in each other's company.
DOUG. See those bottles up there, above the bar?
CAROL. I was noticing.
DOUG. They're souvenirs, sort of.
CAROL. Souvenirs of what?
DOUG. Love. See, people come to this bar, couples, from all around the mountains, and put their names inside those bottles.
CAROL. And there they stand. Not washed out to sea, but stuck in a bar in Colorado forever.
DOUG. I think of them as waiting. For some day. You want to?
CAROL. Sure, why not.

224

DOUG takes a matchbook from a pocket, CAROL hands him a pen; they write their names.

DOUG. Oh, wait.

CAROL. What.

DOUG. You're supposed to put down a date you'll meet here again. Like a promise.

CAROL. Okay. How's about June tenth, two thousand and two?

DOUG. Great. (*DOUG writes the date down.*) Now all we need's a couple of beers.

CAROL. Henry's. Light. No. This feels like an occasion. Make it a Dos Eckies, glass of ice with lime slice on the side.

DOUG. (*Signaling as if to bartender.*) Make mine a Coors. (*To CAROL.*) So we have a date. June of two thousand and two. Seems like a far way away.

CAROL. (*Looking as if out a window.*) The day is drawing in. Look. And we're sitting here.

NARRATOR. (*To audience.*) Warmed by our illusion of some-day coming together again. Perched on a stool in this moose head bar on an unpaved mountain road in Colorado, I tell Doug a truth as it hits me, as it rolls out of my mouth.

CAROL. (*To DOUG.*) It's not 1952 anymore, when all I had to worry about was my crinolines falling down around my ankles in the halls of high school. It's not even 1958 when my smile changed. Sex with strangers is too sad, too weepy, it's lost its glory. I don't understand it anymore. Mostly, I don't under-stand me with men. Aphrodite is in dust motes around my feet, so I'm going to take some time off. Off the whole sex thing, until it makes some sense to me.

DOUG. I'll miss you. But I'll see you, June tenth, two thousand and two. Won't I?

CAROL doesn't reply. The two stare as if out a window.

NARRATOR. We held hands until the pale December sun slid behind a mountain peak and the sky filled our eyes with night.

SLOW BLACKOUT during which DOUG and CAROL exit.

LIGHTS very DIM as NARRATOR moves to lie on the gurney.

NARRATOR. (*Cont'd.*) (*To audience.*) A year or so later, Dr. Art

Eulene started performing tubal ligations on poor women at a Japanese clinic in downtown Los Angeles. He later became a known commodity because he hosted a medical tv show. But when I returned to California and met him, he was just the man with a miracle. (*Pause.*) I woke up from that procedure staring into a face full of compassion and softness. An IV dripped sustenance into a vein in my hand for hours. (*Pause.*) Other faces came and looked gently into mine. The big white doctor came himself and assured me that all was now well. No more babies. No more. No more. No more. (*Standing by gurney.*) I walked away from that clinic numb, sort of, yet also in a state of what I can only call psychic euphoria.

NARRATOR moves in a walk, then in a slow dance, and gently exits.
BLACKOUT OR CURTAIN.

END ACT II
*Crosby, Stills, Nash, "Hopelessly Hoping"

ACT III
Scene 1. Present
LIGHTS UP full. NARRATOR is once again at apron, with no stool. She talks with the audience, as if expecting answers to her questions.
NARRATOR. So that's the story. Three babies. (*Holding up a fisted hand.*) Three possibilities. (*Opens fisted hand; palm is flat, extended.*) No babies. No more. (*Pause.*) Could no more also mean no more craving after false intimacy from others? Was this peculiar emotional imbalance actually one of balance, finally? Although I wasn't aware, at the time, that I was trading one creative potential for another, is it possible that my aborted girls stepped aside so I would one day find voice to write anything down? If so, I salute my dead baby girls for giving voice to this little enterprise. (*Executes small dance step on each 'and' count.*) On occasion, someone asks me, "Do you have any regrets about not having had children?" I never know how to answer. I stand like the Heron, watching, waiting, and notice pieces of my self re-membering, in those "and" counts of my life. And a-one. I inherited tremendous female fears that made me too selfish,

226

too afraid, to pass those along yet again. And a-two. I may have killed each of my three girls in an attempt to kill off parts of myself. And a-three-four. In a true sense, my abortions have killed me in psychic ways, the graves of which I am yet uncovering and in another, much of my awakening life, those early years, was a walking around, a treading in someone else's reality, one filled with improbable promises. And a-five-six-seven-eight. My body has grown older while a shade of my essential self remains, like those aborted babies, unborn, its voice stilled before it was ever heard. (*Sitting on the floor.*) Not so much do I regret the abortions: still, still, the tying of my fallopian tubes was an act of complete abandonment. I carry grief for this betrayal, for the absence of my three girls. I care about my three girls, my trilogy of lost potential, as I care about the eagle rising, the wave cresting, the reed unfurling, about my soul finding its own dance. I care about all the men I've slept with, fucked with, rolled with, loved with, even the ones I was embarrassed to let see my far-from-compleat body… especially those who thought they glimpsed my spirit laying lighthouse beams down an intermittent path across a sea of dreams. (*NARRATOR rises, turns her back to the audience, and heads upstage as if to exit. She halts, center, turns to face audience, and says*) Funny the things you miss once you give them up, isn't it? (*Moves downstage.*)

Scene 2.

NOTE: A sense of reunion, of completion framed in beauty, needs to prevail throughout the scene. MUSIC SOFTLY UP ("Flower Duet," Lakme looped, or "Sail On," Chris Young); continues until curtain. LIGHTS diffuse. A SPOT like a lighthouse beam slowly spreads from L across stage behind NARRATOR.

NARRATOR. (*A confidence; a whisper to Audience.*) Do you ever wonder who they'd be? Who you'd be? If only… if…

She turns just as the lighthouse beam finds her. She stands in reflection of what might have been. GRACE #1 enters the lighthouse beam, L. This is CATHERINE, 43 years old. She hovers on the edge of the light, then moves fully into it. She proceeds down its length to C. She and her might-have-been mother view each other across a small distance.

227

NARRATOR. Catherine.

CATHERINE. Who I might have been is very much on your mind, isn't it.

NARRATOR. On the minds of all of us who had to let you go, let you all go, once upon a time.

CATHERINE. What you might have wished for me is also once upon a time, isn't it.

NARRATOR. Am I allowed to mourn the loss of you?

CATHERINE. Imagine yourself revisited, in those days, when you were less certain than you are now, a woman who can write this.

NARRATOR. Certainty is not in this writing. Far from it. Hearing it, seeing it, my writing is but a reflected submersion. The self I went digging for here, the self I had hopes of finding, seems abandoned still.

CATHERINE. (*Insistent; for them both.*) Imagine yourself striding along the halls of industry, a manager ahead of her time, a woman pushing up against a glass ceiling of unfairness, imagine yourself wearing high heels. And a girdle, if not of cloth, then of fact and wrapped around your dreams. Imagine yourself afraid to reach out for love. Imagine yourself finding love and losing it. Imagine yourself nineteen years younger. That's all. That's what you lost, yourself nineteen years younger with whole pieces of my father, your first lover, wrapped up in a new package called Catherine.

NARRATOR. I am stunned, facing you.

CATHERINE. And you are right. We were your potential, your possibility, a possibility turned another direction.

NARRATOR. I feel lonelier than before, ever before.

GRACE #2, 30, the wraith with no name, enters down the lighthouse beam as if floating. She encircles NARRATOR and CATHERINE.

GRACE #2. (*Fluttering broader, around stage.*) I am your ballet, your ballet, your ballet of what might have been, a sumptuous waltz, a gorgeous glissade, a frantic leap, a furious pirouette, an entrance and an exit, the overture and the coda all wrapped up in one Red Shoes dream, I am your piece of love found wanting, found wanting, wanting, a melody, your melody with no

228

end, no ending, no ending note. No ending note.

GRACE #2 stops moving. Drifts up close to NARRATOR., circles her, hovers close enough to touch but does not. A long beat before GRACE #3, 27, begins her slow wheelchair roll along the lighthouse beam. She wheels herself in front of the other three and addresses audience.

GRACE #3. Let's imagine me as a girl, growing up in the late seventies. A shade of flower power fading away, a sort of in-between time. Mine was called the groovie generation, heralding-in the microchip, women's lib. A time of transition. Let's imagine she named me Ruth and I changed my name to Chloe or Star Fire. Then imagine, what? What shall we imagine? Anything is possible. It's possible that I'm in a wheelchair. It's possible that I'm not. (*She stands and pushes chair off.*) It's possible, knowing who I came from, that I'd be the rebel. I'd be the one to strike out, in transition, in trying to escape the generations behind and terrified of those coming up. Transition, moving from one moment to the next, like on a tightrope that isn't hooked up anywhere that I can see. Our Narrator opens up a dialogue with us. To what end? To assuage guilt? To find a point of reconnection with herself? With us? Why would a woman, this woman, do this to herself? To bridge a gap? To become the place that tightrope hooks on to? (*Pause.*) The answer is simple, just not easy. She wonders, always, about the possibility of grace in her life. Where did she leave it? Put it? Who stole it? Can she ever get it back? Were we her last chances? (*Turning to face NARRATOR and GRACES.*) You said it earlier. You know it. We are your voice. We are you.

The THREE GRACES arrange themselves around NARRATOR. None of them touch her or each other.

NARRATOR. (*To audience.*) I have a greeting card I keep in a special place with other sacred objects …shells, feathers, stones, drawings. Written on the front are the words, "If it's the last dance." Also on the front is an illustration of the shadow of a Harlequin executing a Toulouse Lautrec-type kick. (*She does this.*) On the floor extending out from the shadow's foot is its figure. Just the reverse of what one would expect. On the inside, the card reads, "Dance backwards."

229

NARRATOR begins a slow "backwards" dance. The GRACES each, in turn, dance in their own "backwards" fashion. Slowly, the NARRATOR and her GRACES, moving backwards, form a loose circle that shrinks and widens, shifts and flows, then they drift back along the lighthouse beam to its point of origin L, and off the stage.
LIGHTS DIM then
BLACKOUT OR CURTAIN.

END ACT III

The

One Act Plays

Contents

Four O'Clock in the Tuileries

© 2004 Jessie M Page

Characters

DORIS CLAYTON-JONES: 58, short, stocky, fully grey hair, stubborn as a mule, generous to a fault, one grown daughter who does not understand why her mother lives in Paris in a small flat. DORIS never goes anywhere without three pairs of glasses dangling from her sweater front: one pair magnifies, one pair for distance, one pair sunglasses. DORIS' pronunciation of French is appalling. Her attempts are written here phonetically.

LUCILLE RAMSEY: 63, tall and willowy, hair still dark auburn, tends toward dreaminess and unreal expectations of her self and life, never married, no children, living on a pension in a pensionne in Paris. Never goes anywhere without her woven shopping bag/basket. LUCILLE's pronunciation of French is elegant, a bit of the American high-school variety.

GERARD: Dashing and handsome silver-haired artist.

MISTRESS: Gerard's, plump, 20's/30's, hair dyed the color of orange and burgundy, favors extremely high heels, tight jeans, skimpy tops.

GIRL IN BLACK: Another of the café regulars, 20's, dressed in black leathers complete with full-length zippers that are frequently half unzipped, chains, studs, dog collar, very heavy metal, hair dyed flat shoe black and punked.

BOY IN WHITE: GIRL IN BLACK's steady companion, also 20's but looks younger, dresses in all-white cricket clothing, down to his shoes, hair flaxen. The two make a separated harlequin.

GARÇON: The waiter who circulates the three café tables.

Setting
An outdoor café in the Tuileries in Paris, afternoon. Three circular metal tables, with two metal chairs each, form a loose vee (down C, up R, up L). A bare tree is up C.

ACT I
AT RISE: The tables are empty of people. On the one R, a plain shoe box resides. BOY IN WHITE and GIRL IN BLACK are in a living statue pose facing each other, connected, but not touching. They stand directly in front of their table, up R. A begging tin cup is on the ground in front of them.

Scene 1: 4 pm
LUCILLE enters, SL. She leisurely walks past GIRL IN BLACK and BOY IN WHITE, places a few coins in their cup. GIRL IN BLACK and BOY IN WHITE bow slightly. We know they are real. LUCILLE now steps purposefully to the center table and arranges herself—clutch bag, coat, hat, straw shopping bag/basket. Folds her hands in her lap. Waits. Notices the shoe box on table up R. Starts humming. BOY IN WHITE and GIRL IN BLACK release their pose, strike a new pose further R, facing away, as if to other customers. LUCILLE rises, circles the R table, ever more curious. Darts back to center table just as DORIS enters from opposite direction. DORIS is talking as she joins LUCILLE and eventually sits.
DORIS: You always get here before me, I never get here before you, we sometimes get here together.
LUCILLE: The last one's the lie, obviously. (Pointing at R table.) But look.
DORIS: What is it?
LUCILLE: A box, wouldn't you say? A shoe box?
DORIS: Likely not a hat box.
LUCILLE : No. Wrong shape.
DORIS: Did you open it?

LUCILLE: No. (Pause.) It wasn't here yesterday.

DORIS: Or last week.

LUCILLE: A new addition.

DORIS: Should we open it?

LUCILLE: I don't know. What if it contains explosives?

DORIS: Or spiders.

LUCILLE: A box of spiders? Here in the Tweeleries? Putting spiders in a box isn't very French. Would you say? Perhaps love letters? Or postcards to long-dead ancestors.

DORIS: Scorpions?

LUCILLE: Perhaps buttons. Perhaps a whole box of antique buttons.

DORIS: I hate antiques, I love buttons, I'm ambivalent about boxes.

LUCILLE: All lies. You love antiques, your house is full of them, you hate buttons, you say they're never the right ones, and I know you want to know what's in the box. What about, small stones and shells. Gathered by virgins in the moonlight.

DORIS: A French August full moon. Hot. White. Ripe.

LUCILLE: A moon so hot and ripe it blinded all the virgins and turned them into street beggars, their box of lovely stones and shells forgotten in some Paris alleyway until a Romany gypsy found them, carried the box aways, then dropped it and forgot it here. In the Tweeleries. At tea time, no, just before tea time. Lunch, perhaps, or after a late breakfast of rough bread and beautifully sliced ham.

DORIS: Maybe it's just another box of blasted hopes. (Pause.) Another old woman begging. I saw another one on my way here.

LUCILL: Too many now. So sad.

DORIS: There but for the grace of whoever and some sound investments go you and I, go you and I, Lucille.

LUCILLE: Whom.

DORIS: Which?

LUCILLE: Whomever.

DORIS: Where?

LUCILLE: Doris?

235

DORIS: Have you ordered?

LUCILLE: No. Garçon hasn't appeared yet. Do you suppose it's money? In the box?

DORIS: Someone plopped down a box of money on a café table? In the middle of Paris? (*Calling OFF.*) Garkon! Doo thé… (pronounced tay) See voo plate! Honestly, he's taking his own sweet time today.

LUCILLE: I'd like it to be money. In the box.

DORIS: Why? You don't need any. You've bags of the stuff. Garkon!

LUCILLE: Actually, no, I haven't. No bags.

DORIS: But you said!

LUCILLE: I said to start up a conversation.

DORIS: That was nine years ago! Picture it. (*She waves a hand around.*)

LUCILLE: I was wearing a blue suit, unsuitable for Paris, bien sur, but that's all I wore for days out in Manhattan.

DORIS: You looked like a fish out of water, you did. So I helped.

LUCILLE: You said, sit down and take a load off.

DORIS: See? I helped. Still am, for that matter. You'd've been a news item the way you were going about it.

LUCILLE: I found my way, in time. And my French is better than yours. C'est ça!

DORIS: (*Considering LUCILLE.*) So you're not rich after all! Are you broke? How fascinating. I've never known anyone who was broke. Well, there was the Langston's back home, losing all their money on the horses, but I wouldn't call them broke, I mean they had…

LUCILLE: Not broke, or broken, no. Just beent a bit. I have a small pension. It's a small pension, nothing grand. I get by. But I find the idea that it might be money in the box comforting. Don't you?

DORIS: I hate money, actually. Actually, the whole idea of money terrifies me. I don't understand how it works. So let's talk about something else.

LUCILLE: Alors. (Indicating with a nod of her head.) Regardez.

DORIS puts on her distance glasses.

Scene 2: Immediately following

The women watch as GIRL IN BLACK and BOY IN WHITE turn facewards, break their pose, and return to the table R with the shoe box on it. BOY IN WHITE pushes the box to one side. Both sit and prepare to smoke. Seeing this, DORIS immediately exchanges the distance glasses for magnifying ones and removes two small, battery-operated, face fans from LUCILLE's woven shopping basket. Table clamps are affixed to the fans. DORIS mounts one on their table, aimed at the couple's table. The fans point outward. She flicks it on. Smoke will now be blown back to the smokers and not to DORIS and LUCILLE's table.

GARÇON enters, takes the couple's order, nods at the women, exits slowly.

LUCILLE: What if I wanted something different today?

DORIS: (*Glasses back on her chest.*) You can't have anything different. We have tea together every day. Here. At this very table.

LUCILLE: But what if…

DORIS: Sundays no exception.

LUCILLE: But what if I wanted something different?

DORIS: All right, then. What would you have?

LUCILLE: When?

DORIS: Now. Something different. You said you wanted something different.

LUCILLE: Yes. Different, like, like that holiday we took to the Pyrenées.

DORIS: (*Thinking.*) We kept getting lost. Kept ending up facing the wrong direction, scattering ourselves all over the countryside. Like a box of stray buttons.

LUCILLE: But we got there. Eventually. What was the name of the village? I'm trying to remember the name of our village. With the abbey. Where we stayed.

DORIS: Ellie something.

LUCILLE: No, that's not it. Let's see. A… (Pause.) B… (Pause.)

237

C…

DORIS: Start further on.

LUCILLE: R… (*Pause.*) S… (*Pause.*) T…

DORIS; T, that's right, but it had a funny…

LUCILLE: Twee-er.

DORIS: …spelling. Spelled with an H and a U. Lordy, what made you think of that?

LUCILLE: I was trying to remember the woman's name, Madame Whatsit who committed suicide while we were there.

DORIS: Ah. (*Looking at the box.*) The shoes.

LUCILLE: Yes. Remember? She left a note. The Mayor posted it on the church wall.

DORIS: She left a note! I do remember! It said, Bury me on my dancing slippers!

LUCILLE: In, Doris. In my dancing slippers. Dans, in, not sur, on.

During the next exchange, GARÇON slowly enters with two tea pots, cups and saucers, cream pitcher, sugar bowl, spoons wrapped in paper napkins, all on a circular brown tray; more slowly sets out LUCILLE and DORIS' tea things. BOY IN WHITE and GIRL IN BLACK rise, slide over the tin cup, and strike separate poses behind the table they were sitting at.

LUCILLE: (*Cont'd.*) I always wondered what it was that made Madame Whatsit reach for her slippers, make that decision, decide to put on her best shoes and turn her face to the wall. (Looking into the tea pot.) Maybe she was slowly losing her mind, or her will to live, or she lost her favorite box of something.

DORIS: Maybe she lost hope. (*Pause.*) Think I'm too old to take French lessons? I mean, it's embarrassing. I've lived here almost ten years and still sound like a damned American tourist.

LUCILLE: One is never too old for anything.

GARÇON exits as if being summoned.

LUCILLE: (*Cont'd.*) (*Pouring out.*) She was right, you know, to insist on special shoes. One needs special, no, just the correct, shoes, when one commits suicide, so one can tiptoe beautifully into my next, better, life.

LUCILLE takes the distance glasses from DORIS's front and puts them on. Focuses on the box.

DORIS: I wouldn't tiptoe. I'd get me some high-heeled pumps and strut on out.

GERARD and MISTRESS enter and take their seats at table L.

LUCILLE: I just think I'd like something different. (*Pause.*) And a pair of antique lace gloves. (*Swiveling to nod in GERARD's direction.*) Ah, Monsieur…

DORIS: C… (*Pause.*) D… (*Pause.*) E… F…? G…?

LUCILLE: G. Gerard. (*Removing glasses; calling to him.*) Bonjour, Monsieur Gerard. (*To DORIS.*) Or is that his first name?

DORIS: Is that his third mistress in nine years or his fourth?

LUCILLE: His ninth in four years, perhaps.

LUCILLE waves prettily at GERARD; MISTRESS scowls. GARÇON returns, bringing a tray containing a bottle of water, a carafe of wine, two wine glasses, two glasses containing beer. He places the beers on the R table, and BOY IN WHITE and GIRL IN BLACK strike a new pose, closer to LUCILLE and DORIS's table. DORIS takes a sip of tea; grimaces, pours it back into the pot. GERARD and MISTRESS prepare to smoke. LUCILLE takes another fan from her bag/basket, mounts it on the other side of their table, switches it on. DORIS fusses with her glasses, drops one. LUCILLE pours out DORIS's tea again. The whole has a ritual feel to it. Their movements are unhurried; the pacing is natural and this movement without dialogue extends just a beat longer than the audience might expect.

DORIS: I'm not sure I like the way we're talking today, Lucille. Tiptoeing, and lace gloves, mistresses, shoes, suicide…

BOY IN WHITE and GIRL IN BLACK strike a provocative pose, sex simulated.

DORIS: (*Cont'd.*) Oh, that's a new one. Worthy of a sou, I think.

LUCILLE: It's Euros now, Doris. Sous and francs long gone. Like elegance. And grace. Like women wearing lace gloves to tea, or satin shoes…

DORIS: Give them a Euro or two then.

LUCILLE: My check hasn't come yet this month. You give them.

DORIS: I've only got a five.

GIRL IN BLACK and BOY IN WHITE move over to GERARD and

MISTRESS's table, strike a new pose.

LUCILLE: Put your purse away. I heard Gerard sold a paint-ing last week. He'll take care of them.

GERARD gives BOY IN WHITE and GIRL IN BLACK a few notes.

DORIS: You heard? Where'd you hear that?

The couple move off, exiting in search of other willing appreciators of living art.

LUCILLE: Oh, around. You know, how you hear things. Around.

DORIS: I never hear things, you always hear things, Garkon hears everything.

LUCILLE: All true.

GIRL IN BLACK rushes back and snatches up one of the beer glasses and the tin cup. Off she goes.

Scene 3: Immediately following.

LUCILLE: Let's look in the box.

DORIS; Only if you promise to talk of something else.

LUCILLE: Okay, then. How's Pamela?

DORIS: She's sent me another one of those miniature tele-phones.

LUCILLE: They're called cell phones, I believe.

DORIS: She should be locked in a cell for sending it to me. She just can't get her mind around the idea that her mom is, in her view of how life should be, a nutcase. But if she's so smart, like she thinks she is, why is she sending me another one of the damn things when I don't answer the first one?

LUCILLE: What color is it?

DORIS: What?

LUCILLE: The new telephone. What color is it?

DORIS: (*Looking in her pocket.*) Purple.

LUCILLE: Well, maybe that's why.

DORIS: Why what?

LUCILLE: I don't know.

DORIS: Enough about her. Pick another subject.

LUCILLE: The box. If we open the box, we'll have something new to talk about. Not your unfeeling daughter or my aging hands.... Have you seen these lately? Looked? (*Holding her hands under DORIS's nose.*) I mean really looked?

DORIS puts on her magnifying glasses, takes one of LUCILLE's hands in one of her own. Brings it close to her eyes. Turns it over and over.

DORIS: Okay. I've looked. What am I supposed to see?

LUCILLE: They're so old!

DORIS: Well, so's the rest...

LUCILLE: (*Interrupting.*) Don't... Do not finish that sentence, Doris. I am an artist's model!

DORIS: Were. That's the lie. You were an artist's model.

A pocket in DORIS's clothing gives off a few beeps then stops.

LUCILLE: Pamela sounds angry. At you.

DORIS: How can you tell?

LUCILLE: Whenever you're mean to me, a telephone goes off.

MISTRESS rises, in a huff, GERARD quickly follows her as she starts exiting. They pass by LUCILLE and DORIS' table.

LUCILLE: (*Cont'd.*) Au revoir, Monsieur, A bientôt.

DORIS: That's just goofy. My phone doesn't ring because I tell you some home truths, it rings...(*DORIS's pocket rings again.*)

LUCILLE: See?

DORIS: Screw the phone.

Scene 4: Immediately following.

DORIS rises, fetches the box, brings it to their table. LUCILLE, meanwhile, rises and angles the chairs in to the other two tables. Their 'area' is now secured. Both women remain standing and consider the box. DORIS reaches out a hand to remove the lid. LUCILLE stops her with an eyebrow question. Then, DORIS spits into her tea cup, pours a few drops onto the box lid. LUCILLE follows suit, then lifts the box lid.

LUCILLE: Ah.

DORIS: Oh, hell.

LUCILLE: (*Pulling out a pair of pumps.*) Satin, Doris. They're turquoise satin! Oh, how lovely!

DORIS: They're like new. Look, hardly scuffed.

LUCILLE: Mother of the bride's shoes?

DORIS: Middle-aged matron on her second or third marriage shoes? Brides maid? Maid of honor?

241

LUCILLE: Prom shoes, or graduation pumps. Special, one-time shoes. Oh, don't you wish they could talk? Tell us their story?

DORIS: What if one of the beggar women left her shoes in this box when all her money and hopes were gone?

LUCILLE: I think they're my size.

DORIS: Don't you dare. Don't you even begin thinking about putting these shoes on. It's too, too, what's the word I want…?

LUCILLE: Start in the middle.

DORIS: L… (*Pause.*) M… Ma-ca-ber. That's it. Macabre. (*Bad French pronunciation.*)

LUCILLE: No, no it's not. Don't you see? It's my something new.

DORIS: Mine, too.

LUCILLE: But I saw the box first. That makes it mine.

DORIS: I hate when you're right, I love when I'm right, and I'm ambivalent about anyone else being right.

LUCILLE: Those are all true, obviously. (*Hand walking the shoes across the table. Sighs.*) We have to create a new game. This one's getting too predictable.

During the following, GERARD returns, alone. He rights one of the tilted-in chairs and sits quietly at "his" table. His gaze is at first inward, then on LUCILLE.

DORIS: We've just gotten to know each other too well, that's all.

LUCILLE: Is there such a thing as too well between friends?

DORIS: I think so.

LUCILLE: Or do secrets keep friendship alive and thriving.

GERARD removes an artist's sketchbook from his carry-all.

DORIS: (*Taking shoes off LUCILLE's hands.*) So. About these shoes. (*DORIS's phone rings. She grabs it up, stands, looks about for a likely place to hurl the thing.*) This one's going in the Seine like its cousin.

GERARD catches LUCILLE's glance; she smiles slightly at him. He gestures toward her and his sketchbook and is understood by her. She nods ever so slightly.

LUCILLE: Why not answer it? Once, maybe.

DORIS: You know what'll happen. I'll just get yelled at. By someone half my age. By my own daughter. Pah.

LUCILLE: Then give it to me. I don't care if it rings or not. (*LUCILLE stands and opens her bag/basket.*)

DORIS: (*Tossing in phone.*) Thanks, Lucille. You're a good friend, you are.

LUCILLE gives DORIS a quick kiss on each cheek, gathers up her things, reaches for the shoes. DORIS quickly puts them in the box and clutches the box to her chest. LUCILLE sighs, slowly exits, moving very gracefully. After a moment, GERARD also leaves, following LUCILLE at a discrete distance. DORIS does not see this procession, this seduction about to occur. Instead, she rises, fetches the abandoned beer, returns to her table, and drinks.

BLACKOUT.

Scene 5: Next day, 4 pm.

LUCILLE and GERARD enter. He carries his sketch book. He escorts her to her table. They sit. She is beaming, and wearing antique lace gloves and a gauze summer hat. He opens and hands her the sketch book. She considers what she sees.

LUCILLE: Ah, Gerard, such a way you have avec le crayon. This line, here… (*He looks, nods.*) You've captured my soul in that line.

He stands, bows, kisses her hand, takes back his sketch book.

LUCILLE: (*Cont'd.*) When next you show it to me, will it be finished? Will all of me be there, on your canvas?

GERARD gives her a gallant bow and moves to sit at his own table. LUCILLE sits calmly for a moment, seemingly satisfied. GERARD lights up. LUCILLE removes DORIS's cell phone from her basket when it starts RINGING. She puts it on the table, looks at it with disdain. DORIS enters, clutching several pieces of official-looking mail. She is highly agitated. She calls out for GARÇON as she plops down on her chair.

DORIS: Garkon, if you love me, show mercy. Show me a pot of tea. For mercy sake. Tay! (*She wipes her brow with an 'official' envelope, stuffs another down her front.*) My daughter doesn't understand me. I've been widowed twelve years. Now I'm broke!

LUCILLE: I know the first two are true, and I know you're a

243

rich woman of property, so the last is the lie.

DORIS: No! It's not!

DORIS removes reading glasses from her front, hands them and one of the envelopes to LUCILLE, snatches them back, peers at the envelope, frowns, throws it on the ground.

LUCILLE: Doris, whatever is the matter with you?

GARÇON enters carrying the tea tray. Simultaneously, BOY IN WHITE and GIRL IN BLACK enter together and sit at their table. MISTRESS enters from opposite direction and sits with GERARD. All four light up. GARÇON sets out LUCILLE and DORIS's tea things, nods at others, exits. DORIS' phone rings again. DORIS lifts tea pot lid and jams phone in.

LUCILLE: *(Cont'd.)* *(Taking phone out; shaking it.)* Doris. Stop. You're scaring me.

GARÇON enters balancing two trays with beers, wine & glasses, and puts these out on the correct tables as DORIS grabs up phone, throws it. BOY IN WHITE and GIRL IN BLACK duck. DORIS rips up the last envelope as if shredding an enemy. LUCILLE slaps DORIS. Everyone stares at them. DORIS slaps LUCILLE. LUCILLE slaps DORIS again.

DORIS: Lucille! Garkon! We're going to need another pot of tay! And the rest of you! Quit smoking!

MISTRESS slaps GERARD's face. GIRL IN BLACK slaps BOY IN WHITE's face. These four exit in opposite directions. GARÇON gathers up wines and beers through until he exits with full trays.

LUCILLE: *(To GARÇON.)* Garçon? Why, umm… toute le monde…(Making slapping motions.) …pourquoi? Hmmmm?

GARÇON: Zo you are not alone, Madame.

LUCILLE: Ah. Merci, merci Monsieur. Garçon. *(GARÇON exits.)* *(To DORIS.)* You. Start at the beginning.

DORIS: A…

LUCILLE: No, your beginning. About all of this. *(Indicating the 'all'.)*

DORIS: A is where it starts.

LUCILLE: Proceed then. A…

DORIS: *(Noticing.)* What've you got on your hands?

LUCILLE: Antique lace.

DORIS: *(Examining with magnifying glasses.)* Woolworth's, more likely. Where'd you get them?

LUCILLE: From a street vendor. On the steps of the Louvre. Aren't they beautiful?

DORIS: (*Taking closer look.*) Good grief, they are antique. This is the real stuff. No street vendor ever has goods like this... (*Dawning.*) You got these from a beggar woman. From one of the old crones selling off her life. How could you?

LUCILLE: I don't see the harm. She needs a few Euros, I wanted the gloves, to go with the shoes... where are the shoes?

GARÇON, as if awaiting his cue, returns, this time bearing a tray on which resides the shoe box. He crosses elegantly to LUCILLE and DO-RIS' table and, very out of character, pulls up a chair from one of the other tables and sits with them. He opens the box and removes the shoes, displays them, during

GARÇON: I zink zeese are ze chues of a lost ladee. Une femme perdu. Non?

During his lines, BOY IN WHITE and GIRL IN BLACK enter from L. BOY IN WHITE takes the shoes, holds them in front of his body as if in supplication. GIRL IN BLACK slumps, becoming GARÇON's lost lady. During their pose being struck, GERARD and MISTRESS have entered, R. She runs over, takes the shoes, twirls and holds them above her head. GERARD follows in her wake.

MISTRESS: Zeese, ze chues of une belle ballerina. She vears zem ven she taks off her toes. Non?

GERARD: Non, ma petite. Zey are ze chues of a brilliant spy who gave her yoot to dreams. Non?

LUCILLE frowns; DORIS laughs.

GIRL IN BLACK: (*Rising; striking new pose.*) Non. Ze heels, ze toes, zey aire simply old. So? (*She shrugs, skips away.*)

BOY IN WHITE: (*Taking shoes from MISTRESS.*) Chues zis bleu, zey sing, non? Love songs—chanson d'armour. I like zeese chues. I take. Yes?

LUCILLE: No, oh no, I'm sorry, but, no. I saw them first, you see.

BOY IN WHITE: (*Speaking very good English suddenly.*) Then they must be for you, Madame.

BOY IN WHITE bows, puts the shoes on the table, rushes off after GIRL

IN BLACK. MISTRESS loses interest. GERARD follows her off. GARÇON is summoned by off-stage customers.

Scene 6: Immediately following

LUCILLE: So. A…

DORIS: A… Oh. A. A is for Alan who put the house in my name. A for Alan who died too soon and left D for Doris in charge. D for Doris who's always late—to tea, for her daughter's wedding, paying the bills. B for bills that D for Doris doesn't pay. T for tax bills that D for Doris doesn't pay. P for Pamela trying to call me to tell me that the T for tax bills that D for Doris doesn't pay have come and gone past due…

LUCILLE: Doris, just tell me.

DORIS: I couldn't stand it, faced with having to be on time about money. Money. Pah. So, things seem to have slipped.

LUCILLE: Define slipped.

DORIS: I'm broke. No dargent, dargent? what kind of word is that? money, money in my account. The house has been foreclosed, whatever that means, all my savings are going to be garnished. I'm left with my flat here, my furniture, my cigarette smoke fans. I'm done for, Lucille, done for.

LUCILLE: No, you're not. We'll think of something.

DORIS: I'm going to end up like one of those crones on the steps of the Loover. You'll come by one day in your lace gloves and satin shoes and you won't recognize me. My teeth will be gone…(*Making a toothless grimace.*)…my fingers crippled, my back bent, my hair falling out from eating cat food, oh God, I can't be poor. I just can't!

LUCILLE: You're not. You just said, you have your flat.

DORIS: So?

LUCILLE: So, you sell your flat.

DORIS: Oh, no, I couldn't…

LUCILLE: Yeah. Yes. You could. You'll sell your flat, that should give you a little nest egg to see you out, if you're careful, if you share expenses with me. We'll start something new and different together. Maybe read people's lives from the soles of their shoes.

246

DORIS: We're gonna do that here. Here? All we're gonna see on shoe bottoms is smashed dog poop and cigarette butts. They won't all be showing up in boxes, you know, these shoes you want to 'read'.

LUCILLE: Think Parisian, Doris. Look below the surface. See the cobbles. Feel the history.

DORIS: And live with you.

LUCILLE: Of course.

DORIS: I don't think so.

LUCILLE: Why ever not?

DORIS: I'll tell you why ever not. Toilet paper over or under.

LUCILLE: Over.

DORIS: Wrong. Tea or coffee in the morning.

LUCILLE: Coffee.

DORIS: Wrong. PJ's or sleep nude.

LUCILLE: Nude.

DORIS: Well, that one's right. Sleep walk?

LUCILLE: Talk in my sleep. My turn. What does clean mean to you?

DORIS: Able to see the table top.

LUCILLE: Right. How many folds of your bath towel on the rack?

DORIS: Two.

LUCILLE: Wrong. Three. And on Tuesdays, between two and four, you'll have to go somewhere. Else. Out for a walk, maybe. A walk on Tuesdays will do you a world of good.

DORIS: Ooooh, sneaky. Just why do I have to go somewhere else on Tuesdays between two and four?

LUCILLE: I have a standing appointment then.

DORIS: Standing appointment.

LUCILL: Yes.

DORIS: You mean you're standing around somewhere in your birthday suit being oggled by a bunch of... of ogglers.

LUCILLE: I told you. I'm an artist's model.

DORIS: At what school?

LUCILLE: The School of Life, Doris, the School of Life.

DORIS: So this is how I end up. Sharing a pensi-onn-e with a

247

deluded, wise-ass, has-been model who has standing appointments. And seven cats.

LUCILLE: Talk about sneaky. I'm going to ignore the first part of all that and go right to the part where I'm allergic to cats, so you'll have to give yours away before you move in. Or have them put to sleep.

DORIS: I'm not putting my cats to sleep!

LUCILLE: (*Standing.*) Let's go and start packing you up.

DORIS: Now?

LUCILLE: You have a better idea?

DORIS: Well, don't I have to put an ad in the paper? A sign on the door? Find a realtor? Do all those things that D for Doris isn't very good at?

LUCILLE: All in good time. First we pack. (*They wait each other out.*) It's me with no cats or keeping the cats and joining the beggar women.

DORIS: That's no choice. I love my cats, I hate you right now, and I will never beg for my bread.

LUCILLE: You love me. And you'd be begging for your daily baguette.

DORIS: With sliced ham.

LUCILLE: There's a good butcher near my pensionne.

DORIS: Something different, huh. (She thinks.) What makes you think tourists on a time schedule are going to sit down and upend their shoes to us?

LUCILLE: (*Starting to leave.*) We'll tell them we're really gypsies who were put under a spell when we were very small and only recently, here, in the Tweeleries, have come into our power. That's a good word these days, power. We'll make it sound so appealing, no one will refuse. Come on. We'll have fun.

DORIS: Dog poop and cigarette butts staring us in the face.

LUCILLE: We'll become part of the Parisian scene, known far and wide for our wisdom and mystery. (*Her voice fades off as she exits.*) One of those beefy gendarmes with steely eyes and an itchy trigger finger will haul us down to the dungeons below the Metro…Far and wide, Doris, far and wide.

They are gone, and have left the shoe box behind.

248

<u>Scene 7: 4 pm, another day</u>

GARÇON enters, carrying a cleaning cloth. He swipes these over all three tables; then he moves the shoe box and places it gently on LUCILLE and DORIS' table. LUCILLE and DORIS enter together, running lightly, out of breath. LUCILLE, whose hair is now dyed bright orange, is laughing; DORIS glowers, seems emotionally pulled in on herself. LUCILLE sits and removes a handful of postcards and a pen from her shopping bag/ basket. She chooses one postcard and begins writing. Stops, signals DORIS for a pair of glasses. DORIS hands them over, pouting.

LUCILLE: Sit down, Doris, and you sign this one too.

DORIS: Not until you promise to stop needling me about selling my flat.

LUCILLE: I'm only trying to help. The longer you put it off, the worse it'll get.

DORIS: I know. Just quit, okay?

LUCILLE: (*Holding up postcard.*) Don't you just love Degas dancers?

DORIS: (*Sitting; taking postcard; reading the back.*) "Share may-man."

LUCILLE: Mah-mah One doesn't pronounce the n, Doris.

DORIS: Oh, one doesn't. Okay. "Share May-may." Wait a minute. Your mother's been dead for… how long?

LUCILLE: Since nineteen eighty six.

DORIS: You send her postcards.

LUCILLE: Yes.

DORIS: And she's been dead since nineteen eighty six.

LUCILLE: Yes.

DORIS: Did you send her postcards when she was alive?

LUCILLE: No.

DORIS: Pamela needs to meet you. (*Resumes.*) "Share May-May. Today, oh-jurdey-hooey…

LUCILLE: (*Correct French.*) Aujourd'hui.

DORIS: Oh-jur-duh-hooey. Uh, "Today," I'll just skip the next word, "my share Amy…

LUCILLE takes the postcard and finishes reading it, all with correct

249

French.

LUCILLE: "Chère Maman. Today, audjourhui, ma chère amie Doris et moi took thé in the Tuileries. The Rive Gauche is awash in painters, the Louvre is swimming avec les touristes, Le Tour Eiffel is ablaze in August sunlight. Je t'aime, Collette." There. Now you sign.

DORIS: Who's Collette?

LUCILLE: It's my new name. My new Gypsy name.

DORIS: Why? Why do you need a Gypsy name?

LUCILLE: For the tourists.

DORIS: I thought we were going to read shoe bottoms.

LUCILLE: I like this idea better. We'll be Gypsies who send postcards to dead ancestors. We'll write whatever people want to say to their dearly departed, but haven't the… the…

DORIS: Balls?

LUCILLE: Doris. J… K… F… Finesse, that's it, haven't the finesse, to say themselves. And we need one for you.

DORIS: What, an ancestor?

LUCILLE: No, a name.

DORIS: I'm sticking with Doris.

LUCILLE: How many Gypsies do you know named Doris?

DORIS: How many Gypsies do you know?

LUCILLE: This isn't getting us anywhere. Just pick a name.

DORIS: Claude.

LUCILLE: Claude?! That's a man's name.

DORIS: Then you pick. What difference does it make? The whole thing's a house of cards anyway. *(Throwing LUCILLE's postcards in the air.)* This isn't real, this isn't going to change anything.

LUCILLE watches the postcards flutter around. After a long beat, she puts her thumb to her ear and pinkie finger to her mouth, mimicking a telephone receiver.

LUCILLE: *(In a peculiar, stretched-out, heavily-accented, e.g., Bronx, Appalachian, or Southern, voice.)* Hello, Doris' daughter?

DORIS: Now what are you doing?

LUCILLE: I'm afraid I have some bad news for you. Your mother is living in the streets. In Paris.

DORIS: Stop it. I don't like this game.

LUCILLE: She wouldn't listen to her friend Lucille, wouldn't go along with Lucille's postcard idea, now your mother is living on pigeon feathers and gar-bage. She needs your help.

DORIS: Stop, please.

LUCILLE: She needs you to rescue her.

DORIS: No, I don't. (*Removing LUCILLE's hand from her face.*) I don't need anyone to rescue me.

LUCILLE: (Her own voice, again.) Yes, you do. We all do, now and again.

DORIS: Well, Pamela agrees with you. She's here.

LUCILLE: (*Such a mystery.*) She got the call!

DORIS: (*Nothing mysterious about it.*) She's determined to take me back to Cedar Rapids with her. She's going to make her husband build me a room, push out a wall, shove me in a closet… all to keep me safe, she says.

LUCILLE: Surely she won't put you in a closet.

DORIS: I can't go back there, Lucille. I can't!

LUCILLE: It sounds like she's handing you a life line, Doris.

DORIS: She's handing me a sentence, a prison sentence. It doesn't matter how pretty she makes the room, it'll still be one room, in her house, it'll still be me stripped down to her vision of me…(*Winding up.*)…it'll be me having to make nice at the dinner table or having to sit and watch Jeopardy with them at night or worse retreating to my room hiding out like some sort of outlaw waiting for my days to wind down but they won't they'll just spread out in front of me like my own personal version of hell never ending days and nights staring at the same four walls with no…

LUCILLE wraps DORIS in a bear hug and holds on until DORIS calms down. BOY IN WHITE and GIRL IN BLACK enter, see LUCILLE holding DORIS, take up a pose echoing. Slowly, DORIS calms down, allows LUCILLE to seat her. BOY IN WHITE and GIRL IN BLACK mime LUCILLE's gentleness toward DORIS. They put their heads together when DORIS starts talking again.

DORIS (*Cont'd.*) When I came here, my soul finally unpacked. I never felt at home before that. In my parent's home, that was theirs. My marriage house, even after Alan made it legally mine, it never was mine. I never felt that feeling of home until I came to Paris and moved into my flat. Then I met you, and we started our teas at four pee-em in the Tweeleries, every day, Sunday no exception. I'm happy here, Lucille. I don't want anything to change. I don't want to start something different, I don't want boxes of turquoise shoes or any other color shoes showing up. I don't want to lose you. I don't want to lose me. I love you, you're my friend. And I don't want to live with you.

LUCILLE: You may not have to after all.

DORIS: I won't go back to Iowa.

LUCILLE: No, that's not it. It's just that, well, I'm not staying at home very much these days. In fact, I'm hardly ever there, so it will be as if you are still on your own, here in Paris. We'll pass each other occasionally, and still always take our tea together. So in a way your life won't be too different after all. Except for these shoes. I know. Let's decide about the shoes now. Then you won't have to think about them. No worries. Easy, graceful, together we'll slide into our next wonderful adventure.

DORIS: You're hopeless. You live in some sort of dream world…

LUCILLE: Yes. It's lovely. Come join me here.

DORIS: What about the shoes?

LUCILLE: (*Reaching for the box.*) I think they should go high up in my closet.

DORIS: (*Taking the box away.*) I think they should go high up in mine.

LUCILLE: Yours at my pensionne?

DORIS: I'm presuming there's going to be a closet for me?

LUCILLE: The place is practically all closets.

DORIS: Good. Then the shoes go in mine.

LUCILLE: Let's let Garçon decide.

Both release their hold on the shoe box. They wait. No sign of GARÇON.

DORIS: This is nuts. I'll go get him, or we'll be glaring at that box and each other all day.

She rises and storms off in search of GARÇON. MISTRESS enters by herself, in a snit. Spies LUCILLE sitting, stalks up and slaps LUCILLE on the cheek once, sharply. BOY IN WHITE and GIRL IN BLACK stand as if to come to the rescue, or echo the slap, until DORIS and GAR-ÇON enter as MISTRESS haughtily exits. LUCILLE covers her cheek with a gloved hand. GIRL IN BLACK and BOY IN WHITE both signal to GARÇON and are, for the moment, ignored.

DORIS: You talk to him, Lucille. He told me he won't do it. You convince him. (*Noticing her odd posture.*) What's the matter with your face?

LUCILLE: Nothing. Tooth ache. Ah, Monsieur, we require your assistance. Asseyez-vous, s'il vous plaît.

He folds himself and sits.

LUCILLE: (*Cont'd.*) You see, cher Garçon, we cannot, ma chère amie and I, we simply cannot decide who shall be the keeper of this box of beautiful shoes. We do not want to argue, such old friends as we are, you do not want us to argue, do you. (He responds with facial movements.) Non. C'est ça. Therefore, could you please find a small box-like space somewhere there in the far reaches of your café, in an office, perhaps?, where our little, unimportant to everyone, yet so very important to Doris and myself, where our little box of beautiful turquoise satin shoes might rest until we decide. Yes. Until we decide. Until it is decided. Monsieur? Garçon?

GARÇON unfolds himself, rises, takes the box as if it were the Crown Jewels or a newborn babe, cradles it underneath one arm, and swans off.

DORIS: (*Sitting.*) I don't know how you do it, but I'm sure glad one of us can still pull it off.

LUCILLE: What's that?

DORIS: The helpless girl thing.

LUCILLE: Nonsense. I was appealing to his masculine protective thing. Now the shoes are safe. Until we decide.

DORIS: Until I decide about moving in, you mean.

LUCILLE: What are you going to tell Pamela?

DORIS: I'm going to tell her to go home. (*Long pause.*) Don't give me that look. I'm going to tell her to go back to Cedar Rapids, without me. (*Pause.*) Okay, okay, and, I'm going to put my flat on the market. Satisfied?

LUCILLE looks a question.

253

DORIS: (*Cont'd.*) And ask you to help me pack. Now?

LUCILLE: Now. Oui.

LUCILLE and DORIS exit, arm in arm, passing GERARD who enters alone and sits at his table. GARÇON returns carrying a loaded tray, goes to BOY IN WHITE and GIRL IN BLACK's table, unloads it, nods at GERARD, exits. Life goes on at the café in the Tuileries.

Scene 8: 4 pm, another day

LUCILLE enters, now also attired in a jeune fille floaty dress along with her antique lace gloves and dreamy hat. She sits. In a moment, GERARD enters carrying a medium-sized canvas (e.g., 16x24) covered in brown paper. At her table, he bows, then begins unveiling LUCILLE's portrait. We see the back of the canvas only. LUCILLE's reaction moves from open curiosity through despair—she's aghast—to tears. She sees herself as she truly is, a woman past 60 years of age. As she looks, she touches her face with her fingertips, her neck with the back of one hand. She then hugs herself, as if frozen by the truth of GERARD's vision, and turns her face to him.

LUCILLE: (*Embarrassed; mortified; sorrowful.*) Say it isn't true, monsieur. Some sort of cruel joke, no?

GERARD: (*Softly.*) No.

LUCILLE gasps, pushes the canvas away from her eyes, and runs off. DORIS, entering L, bumps into LUCILLE exiting.

DORIS: Hey! Lucille! What's going on?! (*She sees GERARD and the canvas, rushes to table.*) You? You're one of her standing appointments? (*Looks at the portrait up close. To GERARD.*) Oh, hey. This isn't nice. Not nice at all. You didn't have to do this. She thought her standing appointments appreciated her, loved her a little, even. But this. You could've, what's the word I want, softened, that's it, softened the lines. This...this is...

GERARD: The truth, madame. My art re-, how you say, re-shine? Bounce back?

DORIS: Reflect.

GERARD: Ah. Oui. Reflect. Mon art reflects truth.

DORIS: Yeah? Your art, mister, reflects your twisted view of life. You wouldn't know the truth if it bit you. If it stood up on its hind legs and took a chunk outta your... your brushes, you wouldn't know. Lucille is kind and generous and beautiful. This is the picture of a hag, one of the street crones.

GERARD: I paint what I feel, Madame.

DORIS: How can you do this to her? She comes here every day, it's important, this place, you people...how can she sit here knowing you see her like this? You've ruined four o'clock in the Tweeleries for Lucille. How could you? How dare you?!

GERARD: (*Surveying her.*) Now you? You I'd paint au naturel.

DORIS: Au natur...

GERARD bows, exits slowly.

DORIS: (*Cont'd.*) (*Calling after him.*) You mean, naked? NA-KED??

A small breeze blows the brown paper bits around.

BLACKOUT

Scene 9: 4 pm, another day

The tables are empty. The following action occurs like a ripple disturbing the usual rhythm of the café. We are to notice it subliminally. GIRL IN BLACK enters, on her own, and sits at GERARD's table. MISTRESS enters and sits at BOY IN WHITE's table. BOY IN WHITE enters and lays himself gently down on the ground in front of LUCILLE and DORIS' table. GERARD enters and leans against a tree, just outside the circle of tables. DORIS enters, something heavy on her mind. LUCILLE enters a beat later as if wishing to be invisible.

They both slide onto their seats in silence. GARÇON enters and places the shoe box on LUCILLE and DORIS' table. He starts to exit. DORIS grabs his arm.

DORIS: Garkon? A beer for me and a, what, gin and it for Lucille.

GARÇON: Madame?

DORIS: I read it in a book...gin and it?

LUCILLE: Garçon? Gin avec un soupçon of tonic water. Very soupçon.

He nods understanding and exits.

DORIS: (*Grabbing at LUCILLE's basket.*) Gimme one of those postcards. (*DORIS writes rapidly on a postcard. Reads what she's written, passes it to LUCILLE, who reaches for the reading glasses on DORIS' front.*)

LUCILLE: (*Reading.*) "Doris needs you to come back from wherever you are. Signed a friend."

DORIS: Lucille? Talk to me. You haven't said a word in a week. Is it me? Something I've done? Is it because I haven't moved in yet? Just tell me. Tell me anything. I can take it. I'm not afraid to hear your words. What I'm afraid of is your silence. There's a pair of shoes, a pair of turquoise satin shoes in your silence, and that terrifies me.

GERARD goes to sit with GIRL IN BLACK. BOY IN WHITE goes to sit with MISTRESS. GARÇON enters, puts the drinks on LUCILLE and DORIS' table, leaves the tray behind, goes to lean against the tree GERARD just vacated. All this is done again in silence, in an ebb and flow. We are to feel as if the previous mise en scène is shifting itself and then resting, albeit slightly changed. Throughout LUCILLE's next speech, she will slowly float around. DORIS remains planted in her seat.

LUCILLE: I don't sleep anymore. I lie in bed and watch night cross my ceiling in greys and blacks, silvers and greys again. I have no words for you, Doris, because I have no words for myself. My thoughts these days are like odd buttons that don't match, that go nowhere, that bump up against each other inside their trap of a box, that can't escape into what they were once useful for, because they're disconnected, unattached, lost hopeful buttons, not sewn down to anything. (*Pause.*) Do you know, I haven't looked in a mirror since I turned forty-five? It's true. One day I passed a store window, I think it was Bloomingdale's, I saw my reflection, and didn't recognize myself. What I saw was my mother the year before she died. I was forty-five, standing looking at a woman who was sixty-five. One and the same woman. (*Pause.*) I turned sixty four today, Doris. (*New position.*) Do you know about dementia, Doris? Dementia is a cruel joke life plays on some of us. My mother slipped into its grip on her sixtieth birthday. She forgot who she was that day. (*New position.*) Do you know what happens when you're in dementia? It isn't a place you can visit and leave when you've had enough. It's not a life threatening disease, no prognoses given, no, you've got ten months to live. You can live forever with it. You can outlive everyone you care about. (*New position.*) And while you're doing that, living forever, you know you don't know you know you're not here, even though you are here. You pinch your skin, raising welts, to make sure you're alive, when inside your mind, in that place where you truly live, you're floating around like, like, a box of stray buttons, your thoughts like odd buttons that don't match, that go nowhere, that bump up against each other inside their trap of a box, that can't escape into what they were once useful for, because they're disconnected, unattached, lost hopeful buttons, not sewn down to anything. (*New position.*) That's what happens to one's mind in dementia, Doris. That's what happened to my mother. I watched her change from a strong, raging woman to a creeping husk that kept asking me, "What am I supposed to do?" I finally, after three years, I finally figured out what she was asking. She was asking me how she was supposed to die. She had no disease she could point to, could ask to kill her, she had no life-threatening ailment, no hope there for death. Just lingering in a half mind, less than half life, her body useless, her mind betraying her,until the day when she asked me, "What am I supposed to do?" and I said, "You can stop. And I can help you."

DORIS: (*Whispering.*) Did you? Help her?

LUCILLE: (*Sitting; ignoring the question.*) I turned sixty four today, Doris. One year younger than my mother when she went to dementia. It's not a place I want to visit. The doctors may not agree, but to me dementia is life threatening. My life is threatened by my mother's death, just as if I had to spend my years feeling for cancer lumps, just the same, from mother to daughter dementia can go.

DORIS: Can go?

LUCILLE: Yes.

DORIS: Not, has to go?

LUCILLE: Perhaps not.

DORIS: Then don't go. Stay out of dementia. I don't want to get a postcard from you from there.

LUCILLE: If I get it, will you help me?

DORIS: (*Ignoring the question.*) So. That's what it's about. (Pause.)

I know, let's have a party. Let's make all the blues and greys and blacks and silvers go away with a party filled with reds and greens and yellows. We'll throw away the shoes, that's our decision, good, yes …bye-bye shoes…and have a party. I'll buy you, no I can't buy you, but I'll find, maybe I'll find, a box of fabulous antique buttons to go with your lace gloves…(*Saddening.*) I can't buy you anything ever again. Or me. I can't buy me or you anything pretty ever again. No more trips on the Mondo Social tour bus… soon, no more tay in the Tweeleries…

LUCILLE sits with DORIS. Everyone else shifts their positions such that they are all part of a living tableau arcing around LUCILLE and DORIS' table.

LUCILLE: Why did you stay here, Doris, in Paris?

DORIS: You're changing the subject.

LUCILLE: You wanted me to talk. This is what I want to talk about. Why Doris, girl from the breadbasket of America, came to Paris and stayed.

DORIS: (*Slightly pausing.*) I wanted something different. You understand.

LUCILLE: Oh, I understand. All too well. (*Silence for a beat.*) But you had a home, a married daughter, a certain rhythm to your life there in Cedar Rapids. Why change it?

DORIS: Why did you?

LUCILLE: A question for a question?

DORIS: Maybe you're right. What you said about secrets between friends.

LUCILLE: I know you're holding one now.

DORIS: Am not.

LUCILLE: Are too.

DORIS: Name it.

LUCILLE: You have cat hairs all over your sweater.

DORIS: So?

LUCILLE: So? Do you also still have the cats that go with the hairs?

DORIS: No. Yes. Well. I. Listen. I can't do it.

LUCILLE: Do you still have a flat where the cats and their hairs and you all live?

DORIS: I won't have my cats put to sleep. I feel guilty just thinking about it, about telling the vet to give them all injections—the plunger thingy has a purple band around it, did you know that? I went to do it, and he said they wouldn't feel a thing, but how does he know? How does anyone know? All I know is how I would feel without them, knowing I made them be dead. Part of me feels dead, too, just thinking about it.

LUCILLE: Have you sold your flat yet?

DORIS: Now I'm changing the subject. It's Tuesday. Why aren't you standing somewhere? (*LUCILLE doesn't answer.*) (*Dawning.*) You only stood for Gerard.

LUCILLE: I don't want to talk about him.

DORIS: No. Me, either. Except…

LUCILLE: Doris…

DORIS: Except, why did he say he'd paint me naked?

LUCILLE: When did he say such a thing?

DORIS: That day, when I saw, when we saw, the painting, I yelled at him…

LUCILLE: You did?

DORIS: Sure. Told him he wouldn't know beauty if it bit him, and he told me he'd paint me au naturel, naked, right? What did he mean?

LUCILLE: The man sees entirely too much.

DORIS: Naked, like, exposed? Like something bare?

LUCILLE: For my birthday present, Doris, you can throw away our glasses. (*Taking a healthy swig of her gin and it.*) Let's never see clearly again! Let's only see our dreams of beauty and leave the ugly, ordinary, past behind. Let's become profound old women, riding the carousel in Montmartre forever…

DORIS: But my past is all I am, Lucille. And part of me is already missing me, missing my single life… the thought of never being able to walk through rooms filled with my sights and smells and sounds again… I know this doesn't make any sense, but I can't stand the thought … talk about thoughts these days … the thought of being dependent on you…

LUCILLE: You won't be. Or, if you are, then I'll be dependent on you as well.

DORIS: It's different. It's your home. I can't help but know that. I feel like I have no choices anymore, life in a prison with Pamela or with you or bedding down on the Champs duh Lee-say.

LUCILLE: There are all sorts of prisons, aren't there. (*Pause.*) Perhaps I came to Paris to die here. Perhaps some forgotten part of me remembered that one day I'd be old and unwanted and useless and came here to live in beauty before I turn my face to the wall.

DORIS: Not before me you won't. I didn't come here to die. I came here to live. (*Pause; asking LUCILLE.*) What did I do wrong?

LUCILLE: There is no shame in asking for help, there is shame in refusing help, the shoes are rightfully mine. Which is the lie?

DORIS: The last. The shoes go with me. (*Putting her hands over one end of the box.*)

LUCILLE: You will not abandon me. (*Putting her hands over the other end of the box; rising.*)

DORIS: You won't leave me. (*Rising.*)

At once, all hands reach for the box of turquoise satin shoes.

BLACKOUT.

Scene 10: 4 pm, another day

LUCILLE enters an empty stage. The top of the shoe box is *lifted and placed crosswise over the bottom of the box. LUCILLE crosses to it, removes the top, sees the box is empty, takes it in one hand. Goes to sit at their table, empty shoe box dangling from one hand. GARÇON approaches, stands, waits for Madame to give him her order. Today, her request is quite different.*

LUCILLE: (*To GARÇON.*) Ma chère amie Doris is never late. (*Pause.*) I will always be young. (*Pause.*) Tomorrow, as usual, Doris and I shall together take thé, here in the Tuileries, at 4 o'clock. (*Pause.*) Which is the lie?

GARÇON, well-trained Frenchman that he is, smiles briefly at LU-CILLE's question. LUCILLE watches the air in front of her with an expression of wonder on her face. She's waiting for an answer to her question. Which is the lie? She brings the empty box up and places it on the table.

LUCILLE: (*Cont'd.*) Which is the lie.

GARÇON, slowly, formally, pulls out DORIS' chair and sits. He will wait with LUCILLE.

CURTAIN.

Properties

Well-worn shoe box

Turquoise satin pumps, 3" heels (ca. 1958)

Two table fans

Packages of filterless cigarettes

Postcards

Pen

Official looking envelopes and contents

LUCILLE: Clutch bag, coat, hat, woven bag/basket, dresses, high heels; antique lace gloves, gauze summer hat, jeune fille floaty dress

DORIS: Sweaters and pants, running shoes; three pairs glasses; purple cell phone

GARÇON: Tea tray (two tea pots, cups and saucers, cream pitcher, sugar bowl, spoons wrapped in paper napkins); wine and beer trays (wine carafe, two wine glasses, two glasses containing beer); cleaning cloth

GERARD: Sketchbook; 16x24 canvass, brown paper wrapping

Music: Very subtle, very French, e.g., theme from Amelie, Paris Café Music, etc., only as overture at rise and coda at curtain

Scenery: Backdrop painted as Montmartre 1920s scene

Furniture: One tree, bare branched, Three round metal tables, Six metal chairs

Beans & Franks

(Revised February 2005)
© 2004 Jessie M Page

Characters

MARGE JENSEN: Forty-two, petite, compact, athletic body, short spiky hair, MARGE is an avid deep-sea diver; she stinks at it, but perseveres. MARGE is spunky and honest. Her favorite meal is beer, beans and franks, hold the ketchup. MARGE's greatest desire is to someday dive down to a forgotten wreck, find a treasure, move to Greece, live off her findings. Her greatest fear is that HORACE may want to change their living arrangement.

HORACE JENSEN: Foxty-six, large, burly, sloppy body, long scruffy hair, HORACE, a kind, somewhat vague man, is an actuarialist. Nobody really knows what his job is, maybe not even HORACE. Something to do with insuring numbers, he thinks. He's been doing it for twenty-five years, all the time he and MARGE have been married, and likes the linear monotony of the job. HORACE's greatest desire is to convince MARGE to move back to North Dakota with him. He wants to be married close to and in person. His greatest fear is junk food taking over the world.

FRED JENSEN: MARGE's landlady/lord, hers and HORACE's daughter/son, twenty-two. FRED is more creative than ambivalent. She made a killing on the dotcom market, got out at the exact right time, now owns property up and down the California coast, including the building containing her mother's studio apartment, and has become a performance artist. FRED's greatest desire is to find the exact right thing to wear each Halloween. Her greatest fear is that her parents will finally live together, close by, and muck up her life.

MATILDA CROSLEY: Forty, almost as tall as HORACE, MATILDA has the come-hither that grabs men, and women. Her allure comes from within; on the outside, MATILDA is a lanky, rather plain looking and speaking woman. But inside? Sensuality oozes from behind her eyes, her smile, even her subtle way of standing, often contradicting her words. MATILDA's greatest desire is snagging HORACE in marriage; her greatest fear is facing another Fargo winter without a broad back to warm her feet upon.

Setting

A small contemporary studio apartment somewhere in Southern California, decorated in a very particular, Salvation Army style. It is obvious one person lives here. Out the window on the wall UC, behind a pull-down shade, a dried-up hanging plant can be seen. Against the kitchen wall, L, two bookcases are stacked one on top of the other. The room contains a sofa bed, one end table, larger round table with one diner-type chair, a wooden dresser free-standing (or against R wall), standing lamp behind a comfy reading chair with ottoman. In one corner stands a store mannequin, missing one arm and hand, somewhat draped in bright-colored scarves, wearing only combat boots and a fatigue cap, and, somewhere on the floor, a diving bell with hoses. There is an entry to an off bathroom, UR, through a beaded screen; to the off kitchen, UL, through a swinging door; to the hollow wood door to the building corridor and stairs, CR.

AT RISE: Magazines litter the floor around the chair; the sofa bed is open and bedding is tossed; a set of barbells are on a pillow; leftovers of a beer, beans and franks meal remain on the table; serviceable underwear is draped over the table chair. A suitcase rests open on the bed. The window shade is pulled half-way down. We HEAR a SHOWER running from the bathroom, and MARGE JENSEN SINGING a John Philip Sousa March very off key.

Scene 1: Afternoon

We HEAR KNOCKING on the door. No one comes to answer it. Then we HEAR the SNICK of a key fumbling in the door lock; the door opens, hesitantly. HORACE JENSEN puts his head around the door jamb; his hair is tucked up under a used Fedora. He moves into the center of the room, taking in its ambience with furrowed brows.

HORACE: (*Calling.*) MARGE? You here? Got anything to eat? (*Moving to the table, sniffing.*)

MARGE's Sousa March segues into something louder, something Russian perhaps. HORACE exits into the kitchen.

After a beat, the water turns off and MARGE enters from the bathroom wrapped in a bath towel, scrubbing her hair dry with her fingers. She pulls the dresser drawers open, starts flinging clothes out in the general direction of the case on the bed. The towel drops; MARGE is wearing a tank top wet suit peeled down to the top of her breasts. She takes a swig of the stale beer and HEARS a THUMP from the kitchen. She stands stock still, waiting. The refrigerator door CLUNKS SHUT. MARGE looks around for a weapon, snatches up one of her barbells, sidles up to the side of the kitchen swinging door, barbell raised over her head. HORACE pushes the door open. MARGE beams him. He falls. She jumps on him, is about to mash his skull in. He gasps, rolls over, taking MARGE with him. They grapple around. Eventually, they roll to end up facing each other.

HORACE: Hell, Marge.

MARGE: Hell yourself.

HORACE: That's a hell of a way to greet your husband.

MARGE: Well, I wasn't expecting you. I'm packing to come to you.

HORACE: Well, hell.

MARGE: Ditto.

They get up, arrange themselves, sit—she on the table, he on the floor.

MARGE: I didn't recognize you.

HORACE: (*Removing hat; shaking out hair.*) I'm trying it out. (*Putting hat back on; tucking hair up.*) What do you think?

MARGE: I wouldn't have wasted a good hammerlock if I'd known it was you.

HORACE: No? (*Rising, tosses hat on the bed.*) I couldn't find anything to eat.

264

MARGE: Like I said, I wasn't expecting you. It's not your turn.

HORACE: No. Well…

MARGE: So why're you here?

HORACE: I don't know how you can eat that stuff, what is it, anyway?

MARGE: Franks and beans. Beans and franks. Beer chaser.

HORACE: Franks? Do you know what they put in those things? I don't want to even think what's in those… snouts, toe nails, feathers, snot, I heard this story about workers in a Frito plant in San Antonio who spit in the Frito batter, can you imagine, and then there's rumors of bits of butt…

MARGE: Horace.

HORACE: MARGE.

MARGE: Forget the franks. We could go out to eat. Maybe then you'll tell me why you're here. Huh? How's about it?

HORACE: You still have the body of a young girl, you know. But what's that thing you've got on, uh, half on?

MARGE: It's a wet suit, and you look like you've got on a few extra pounds.

HORACE: I can still get into my wedding suit.

MARGE: Why do you want to?

HORACE: What?

MARGE: Why do you want to get into your wedding suit?

HORACE: Just to see if I can still fit in it.

MARGE: Liar.

HORACE: Why don't you have any decent food in this place? And why don't you tidy up? And water that plant? Here…
(*HORACE starts picking magazines up off the floor.*)

MARGE: Why are you here out of turn? Summers, I come to you. Winters, you come to me.

HORACE: Don't you ever want it to change?

MARGE: No.

HORACE: (*Advancing on her.*) How's that thing come off?

MARGE: Unzips down the front.

MARGE closes the distance by leaping up on HORACE and wrapping her legs around his back, locking her ankles. They start frantically kissing. He swings them both around so he can grab the window shade pulley

265

ring and pull it down. She reaches out and pulls it up. This goes on a fews times, then HORACE heads them for the bed, mouths still locked. They fall on it, hard. The sofa bed GROANS, THUMPS on the floor. HORACE grapples with MARGE's wet suit. She struggles with his shirt buttons. He unzips and catches her skin. She YELPS, loudly.

Scene 2: Following

The door bursts open. FRED (wearing a tube top, extra-large striped boxer shorts, combat boots, cowboy hat) stands in the doorway swinging a base-ball bat. Sees the situation, misreads it, grabs at HORACE to peel him off, MARGE grabs at FRED to stop her/him, HORACE swings at FRED.

MARGE: (*Shouting in FRED's ear.*) It's dad!

FRED: (*Stopping to look at HORACE.*) Well, hell.

HORACE: Ditto.

They all stay on the bed.

MARGE: (*To FRED.*) What on earth have you got on?

FRED: I can't decide how to go for Halloween.

HORACE: It's March.

MARGE: Fred…

HORACE: (*Overlapping.*) Fred?

MARGE: (*Overlapping.*) … likes to get an early start on things.

HORACE: But it's March.

FRED: (*To HORACE.*) So. You're dad.

HORACE: That would be me.

FRED: Would requires an if, that would be me if something.

MARGE: Fred…

HORACE: So I should say, that would be me if I had been really a dad and not an absent father when you were growing up. Right? Better?

FRED: Not better, but true.

HORACE: You had a play thing once, I remember, I was here for that, what was it, you were some kind of pirate?

FRED: Peter Pan. I was Peter Pan.

HORACE: Oh, right.

MARGE: Anybody hungry?

A KNOCK comes at the door. They all look at each other. HORACE and FRED stay on the bed, MARGE opens the door.

266

Scene 3: Following

MATILDA stands there, wearing some sort of material that swoops across her lean body, a wide-brimmed hat, and high-heeled sandals.

MATILDA: Hey.

MARGE: Hey?

MATILDA: You got a HORACE Jensen in here?

HORACE: (*Getting off the bed.*) Matilda? Is that you?

MATILDA: (*Moving into the room.*) Can't be anybody else, can it?

HORACE moves to embrace MATILDA; MATILDA moves toward HORACE; MARGE inserts her body between them.

MARGE: Hey.

FRED slowly uncoils off the bed, stands by it as if stunned.

FRED: (*Breathing it.*) Ditto.

HORACE and MATILDA angle their heads at each other, but MARGE is a wedge between them.

MARGE: (*To HORACE's belly.*) Anyone care to introduce me? Horace?

HORACE: Matilda. It is you.

MARGE: Well, now that's settled. I'd like you to meet my daughter, Fred. Fred? Come on over here and meet this nice lady who seems to be a friend of dad's.

MATILDA: Dad? Since when have you been a dad, Horace.

FRED: (*Moving closer, hand extended to shake or touch.*) Since nineteen eighty-two.

MATILDA: (*Looking down at MARGE.*) And what'd you say your name is, honey?

HORACE: Why are we still standing like this?

MARGE: Anybody hungry? I've got twelve cans of beans, three packages of franks, and a six-pack of beer. Should be enough.

FRED: (*Touching MATILDA's arm.*) You'd be wonderful in our show. You'd out shine them all.

MATILDA: Horace?

Hearing his name causes HORACE to break the circle by ducking backwards, as if he suddenly sees himself from a great way off, trying to kiss his girlfriend with his wife sandwiched between them and his offspring hovering around the hoop they make.

MARGE: I think it'll be enough. (*MARGE exits into the kitchen.*)

FRED: (*Considering MATILDA's outfit.*) But you'll need something a little, something that, I know, I've got just the thing in my apartment downstairs. Have you considered even higher heels? Don't go. Don't move. You won't move, will you? Just stand right there and I'll be right back. Dad?

HORACE: Show? What show?

FRED leaps out the door.

Scene 4: Following

MATILDA does a little tour of the room and stops in front of the mannequin. She adjusts the cap, returns to the bed, and sits.

MATILDA: So, Horace. You have a daughter.

HORACE: That I do, although she seems a bit ambivalent about the daughter part these days. According to Marge.

MATILDA: And a wife.

HORACE: One of those, too, yes.

MATILDA: Marge.

HORACE: Marge. Yes.

MATILDA: And a Matilda in North Dakota.

HORACE: Well, but, literally, Matilda, we don't have each other, I mean, we're not married or anything.

MATILDA: You definitely led me to believe we might be. Some day. Soon. Didn't you, Horace. Tell the truth now, didn't you?

HORACE: Oh, I, well, uh… you see, I was going along like always, seeing but not seeing my everyday world around me, you know how you see without seeing, even down to not noticing when seasons start to change until they've gone and done their changing…

MATILDA: Horace, come and sit down here. By me. Come on. (*He does.*)

MATILDA: (*Cont'd.*) That's better. Isn't that better? Now, Horace? I'd like to talk about Marge and Fred and Matilda and Horace and see if we can't separate some and put some together. Think we can do that, Horace? Ummmm? It's real important to me that we do, Horace, otherwise…

A long silent pause.

268

HORACE: Otherwise what?

MATILDA: North Dakota winters get mighty cold, Horace. I'm not going to live through another one without someone's back to warm my feet on. You have a nice, broad back, Horace. And I have such cold feet.

HORACE: You should wear socks to bed.

MATILDA: Yours?

HORACE: I wonder what show Fred meant?

MATILDA: How do I know? I'm just the girlfriend.

HORACE: Again, not exactly correct, Matilda. You're a girl, and I guess we're friends, neighbors really, but to say girlfriend implies, or is that infers?... (*Beat.*) How did you find me here?

MATILDA: Every time you leave Fargo I follow you, Horace.

HORACE: You, uh.

MATILDA: And you always come here. June, January, January, June. Suddenly you take off in March. I wondered about that, you taking off in March. So I came. To see why.

HORACE: You follow me here?

MATILDA: I always guessed you had another girlfrfiend tucked away in this crappy dump. And that was okay.

HORACE: This building is not a dump. It belongs to my daughter and she takes very good care of it. So Marge says. (*Beat.*) You follow me?

MATILDA: How like you to defend your kid. But here's the thing, Horace. What I didn't figure you for was a man with a wife AND a kid. I don't know what I thought you were doing in here, a whole week, twice a year, but I went along with it because it made you more interesting. Almost dangerous. Definitely mysterious.

HORACE: You've followed me here. Twice a year.

MATILDA: A man with two girlfriends in two different states is much more intoxicating than a man with a wife. And a kid. That's just boring, Horace. How old are you?

HORACE: You've followed me here, twice a year, for how long? No one's ever followed me anywhere. Ever.

MATILDA: You sound like a woman who's never gotten flowers. Knock it off. I like you better mysterious.

HORACE: What do you want, Matilda?

MATILDA: Huh?

HORACE: From me. What do you want? You came here, so what do you want? You must want something. Did you ever look in the windows? When you followed me before? (*Calling off.*) Marge! I might be wanting a divorce.

MARGE shows up in the kitchen doorway.

MARGE: You might be wanting a divorce if what.

HORACE: If you'll give me one.

MARGE: Why would I do that?

HORACE: Because she's been following me here for… (*To MATILDA.*) …for how long?

MATILDA: Couple years. And no, I never peeked. I'm no peeker. Cripes. Why would you think I peeked? Besides, all your other life is on the second floor, so how could I peek? I just had to guess.

HORACE: You hear that, Marge. A couple of years. Following me. Me! I'm suddenly worthy of being followed. Have been for a couple of years!

MARGE: (*Thinking.*) I think you should go somewhere else and think about this, Horace. Think long and hard. Somewhere else.

HORACE: Why can't I think here?

MARGE: I think you all should go. Somewhere else. My beans are boiling over.

FRED darts in, carrying an iridescent feather boa. She picks up HORACE's Fedora and tosses these both at MATILDA who puts them on and preens a bit.

FRED: Now you're ready. Come on. We're starting rehearsals in ten minutes, but we can just make it if we run. Can you run in those heels? I know I said you should try higher, for the look, you know, but those look like they'll trip you up?

MATILDA: Honey, I've been running in heels since I was twelve.

MATILDA holds out her hand to FRED, who grabs it and starts to haul MATILDA out the door.

MATILDA: Horace? Honey? I'm gonna go do this rehearsal,

you go do some thinking…

FRED: (*Overlapping.*) And we'll all be back for supper. Okay, mom?

MARGE shrugs, still standing in the kitchen doorway. FRED and MATILDA exit on the trot. We HEAR their footfalls hit the stairs and these and their voices fading away.

MATILDA: (*O.S.*) So what're we rehearsing for, honey?

FRED: (*O.S., fading.*) It's a revue, you'll love it. You'll be great! You ARE great!!

Scene 5: Following

The room feels suddenly empty with just MARGE and HORACE there. MARGE doesn't move from her spot halfway in and out of the room.

MARGE: I followed you once, but you seem to've forgotten.

HORACE: When did you follow me?

MARGE: Twenty-five years ago, I followed you out of the Piggly Wiggly Market and bumped my cart into yours.

HORACE: I always thought we met by accident.

MARGE: Well. We didn't.

HORACE: Guess I'll be going, then.

MARGE: I think that's a good plan.

HORACE: See you for dinner? Later?

MARGE: You better knock first. If you come back.

HORACE slowly exits, as if torn between going and staying. Going wins out. He's gone.

BLACKOUT

Scene 6: A little later

HORACE enters to find MARGE in a yoga head stand against one wall. He moves the diner chair so it's in front of her. Sits. Stares down at her.

HORACE: What are you doing?

MARGE: Have you noticed how we only talk to each other in questions? Like we've taken twenty-five years getting to know each other? And we're still not there? At knowing each other?

HORACE: Why are you standing on your head? Oh, hell. Well, okay, so it's a question. So what?

MARGE: I can't talk to your feet.

271

HORACE: Come up and talk to my face then.

MARGE: I think better like this.

HORACE: What are you thinking about?

MARGE: I've been thinking, no, more like asking myself, if I want to prepare myself to forgive you.

*After a beat, HORACE swivels, swings his legs up over the chair back, lowers his torso backward, letting his head dangle. His and MARGE's eyes are now at a level, both upside down.*HORACE: You can definitely come up, then. Nothing to forgive, no preparing to be done. I've behaved like a fool, but I haven't been unfaithful.

MARGE: Ever?

HORACE: Never.

MARGE: So explain Matilda to me.

HORACE: It's one of those things you forget to get out of the way of. You know? Like you're starting out your door one morning, same as you've done for a whole lifetime of mornings, and maybe because you've started out your door for so many mornings you're innured to starting days like this, or noticing what goes on around you when you're starting out your door each and every morning...

MARGE: Horace.

HORACE: Right. The point. The point is Matilda moved in next door to me and sort of became part of the scenery, something I see every day and before I knew it she was...

MARGE: Where.

HORACE: Well, sort of standing on my stoop.

MARGE: How did she sort of stand?

HORACE: Well, she more like leaned.

MARGE: Leaned.

HORACE: Leaned. Into me.

MARGE: On your stoop.

HORACE: On my stoop.

MARGE: One morning.

HORACE: Last week. One morning last week. Thursday, I think. Maybe Tuesday. Two weeks ago? January?

This brings MARGE's feet down. She sits on the floor.

MARGE: Sit up, Horace. Your face is getting all red and

blotchy.

HORACE: (*Righting himself on the chair.*) Whew. Little dizzy there.

MARGE: She leans into you for months, comes here looking for you, acts like you're going to marry her, I mean, admit it Horace, the woman thinks she's headed for a marriage, I mean, you left here with her, well, right after her. I mean.

HORACE: (*Shaking his head gently.*) I'm better now.

MARGE: What's up, Horace? What's your plan? See, as your regular wife? I'd like to know if I have to cancel my deep-sea diving trip?

HORACE: When is it?

MARGE: February.

HORACE: It's March now. Didn't you miss it?

MARGE: Horace.

HORACE: Can't say as I've thought far enough ahead to formulate any kind of plan.

MARGE: But you must have. Remember, you left here full of plans—getting divorced from me, running away with Matilda, her planning to marry you, those are plans, Horace, plans.

HORACE: Once we were driving away together, and Matilda was talking a blue streak, I saw her words sort of string together and slide out the window.

MARGE: Oh, how poetic.

HORACE: No, really, like she was melting. I looked at her and she seemed dull, all her inner glow gone, where did it go, do you suppose? Do you suppose she put on a personality like make up and once she got what she wanted…

MARGE: And that would be you.

HORACE: And that was me, I guess, she just washed off. There was nothing left. That's why I don't have a plan. That's why I dropped her at the bus depot. That's why I came back here.

MARGE: Liar. You're a linear kind of man, Horace, always have been, always will be. You had a new plan the moment your other plan fell apart, and I'm guessing it fell apart because…

HORACE: Because Fredricka showed up.

MARGE: Fred.

273

HORACE: Do we really have to call her…

MARGE: Yeah. So Fred showed up, where were you, really?

HORACE: Sitting outside in the car.

MARGE: Horace.

HORACE: Well, you know. So there's Fred and Matilda, making eyes at each other through the window…

MARGE: Eyes? Making eyes? Really?

HORACE: I don't know, making eyes, signalling, what do I know. What I do know is, Matilda got out of the car and walked off down the sidewalk with Fred. So.

MARGE: So your new plan was to come back inside. To me.

HORACE: Not a good plan?

MARGE: Well, you're presenting me with a new plan, and I haven't decided if I'm going to prepare myself to forgive you for your other plan yet.

HORACE: There isn't any other plan. I don't want any other plan.

MARGE: How's about asking me what plan I want?

HORACE: You don't like plans.

MARGE: See how little we know each other? I love plans. I love planning how many beans and franks I'll need a week, how many times a year I can sneak away to go diving. I like planning to visit you. I like planning for you to visit me.

HORACE: How much planning do you do? When I'm scheduled to come here?

MARGE: I change the sheets. (Beat.) You don't know anything about me, Horace, not really, and I don't know the real things about you, not really. Twenty-five years married, and this is all we know.

HORACE: We know we don't know how to be married. Or, we know we know how NOT to be married.

MARGE: Yes. That's what we know.

HORACE: Twenty-three years.

MARGE: What is?

HORACE: You keep saying twenty-five years, when it's really only twenty-three. Years.

MARGE: First time, after I bumped my cart into yours at the

Piggly Wiggly, you said yes and we got married.

HORACE: That was a nice day. I always think of that as one of my nicest days.

MARGE: And six months into it we split up. Oh, I see what you mean.

HORACE: Not a nice day. Not a nice day, at all. One of my least nicest days, that was.

MARGE: And then, two years later, we hitched up again.

HORACE: That time I bumped into you.

MARGE: With that Rambler you drove. Right into the side of my Datsun wagon.

HORACE: That time I asked you and we've been married ever since.

MARGE: Twenty-three years.

HORACE: Do the years make any difference in how well we do or don't, well, uh…

MARGE: I think the smartest thing we ever did was to agree to live apart. To visit twice a year. To jump in the sack. To not talk too much. Seems this visit we're talking way too much.

HORACE: I came out of turn to ask you to come back to North Dakota with me. (*Recognizing the look on MARGE's face.*) But I guess that won't fly. (*Trying it on.*) Even if I said I couldn't live a split life anymore? Would you come then?

MARGE: Horace.

HORACE: No. So we're left with our original plan.

MARGE: Twice a year?

HORACE: Do you have to stand on your head again? To think this through? Think it out? Think it in a circle? Think it up? Think it down?

MARGE: Horace.

HORACE: Marge.

MARGE: What do we do about other possible Matildas?

HORACE: No more Matildas. You?

MARGE: No Matildas for me, either. One Horace is enough for me.

HORACE: Twice a year?

MARGE: Yeah. Let's start now.

MARGE and HORACE hurl themselves at each other. They clutch at each other passionately, lots of grunting and fumbling with clothes. They manage to maneuver themselves to the bed and flop down on it. It GROANS with their weight. Their machinations cause the bed to THUMP, THUMP, THUMP on the floor. HORACE gets the wetsuit zipper down into another patch of MARGE's skin. She YELPS. The door flings open.

Scene 7: Following

FRED stands there, baseball bat once again in hand. She takes in her parents, going at it like people in heat. Or love. Or maybe even both.
FRED: Again!!!???
MATILDA stands behind FRED, with an arm around her waist.
MATILDA: (*Calling out.*) You got anything to eat in here?
HORACE: (*Facing into MARGE's chest.*) We're having beer…
MARGE: (*Breathing hard.*) …beans and franks…
HORACE: (*Breathing harder; looking up.*) Twice a year. (*Groaning in pleasure; back to business.*) Forever.
BLACKOUT

CURTAIN

Crocodile Waltz

Running Time: 40+ Minutes
Intermissions: None

Time: The Present.
Place: Anywhere in urban North America.

© 2015 Jessie M Page

Characters

FERN FANSHAW: A woman of a certain age (60-70), FERN
FANSHAW'S mood is usually sharp and biting. A bit stand-
offish in her manner, she is actually a well-preserved, happy-
to-have-been-there Hippy with the soul of a wanderer and the
heart of a warrior. Loves spending her social security checks on
more bad art for her walls, another trinket for her bookshelves,
etc.. Hates bureaucracy. Doesn't tell about her past or present sex life. Best friend is her neighbor through the UP wall,
SOLLY.

TAMZIN POOLE: Stunning redhead; bears no physical resemblance to FERN FANSHAW. Could be 25 or 45, but she's
actually 32. Has an edge to her, which is like FERN'S personality. Thrice married; she's obviously not very good at it. Owns a
consulting firm that's fallen on hard times because she's never
figured out what to consult. Perhaps she's also failed because
she sports 14 gold earrings along one ear, favors nonmatching
clothing, far too young for her plump body, and her hair looks
as if she cut it herself with pinking shears. Her secret passion
is really bad boys.

SOLLY GREENE: Lives next door to FERN FANSHAW;
he's an artist who once-upon-a-time taught art; celibate and

proud of it; scruffy in appearance, all his clothes have paint on them somewhere; intelligent; witty; hard to tell age (is actually 63). This play, that was stolen by PRODUCER one drunken afternoon in the nearby park, was originally his idea. SOLLY's abiding dream is to return to New Mexico where he hopes to capture the light there.

DIBELS: His true nature is that he is a hunter, a man who got his first Bambi kill at the age of 3. He believes he owns the building FERN and SOLLY live in because his grandfather built it; off-kilter mentally, lives in a combination of steampunk and camo clothes.

DIRECTOR: Absolutely no sense of humor nor tolerance for actors; is obviously in the wrong profession (knows it? hides it?); exhausted all the time. Would love someone to come and take care of him. Wearing a long-sleeved T-shirt with the word DIRECTOR painted on it, front and back.

PRODUCER: Very out of his league; falls hard for DIREC-TOR. Wearing a long-sleeved T-shirt with the word PRO-DUCER painted on it, front and back.

DELIVERY: Delivers its speech with as if it's the last thing it ever wants to say. Wearing a long-sleeved T-shirt with the word DELIVERY painted on it, front and back.

ANNOUNCER & LIGHTS: Voice over.
NOTE: DIRECTOR, PRODUCER, AND DELIVERY CAN BE PLAYED BY EITHER GENDER

Setting: A rundown, one-room apartment.
Sofa sort of CENTER with adjoining cheap looking pole lamp and side table, rag rug underneath severely scratched wooden coffee table in front of sofa. UP wall is covered on either side of a shaded window with amateur paintings and photos, mounted with push pins. A low cabinet with an early model portable CD player/radio sits in front of this wall. Kitchen door is UP LEFT.

Door to outside the apartment, to the hallway where there's an overhead light that constantly goes out, is CENTER RIGHT. On both sides of the outer door are loaded bookcases; books, manuscripts, magazines, odds and ends spill out onto the floor in front of them. Against the LEFT wall is a single bed covered with a madras spread, circa 1965, and almost hidden by pillows. An unshaded bulb hangs down from the ceiling over the bed by a heavy metal chain. Lighting changes, as seen through the UP window, indicate shifts in time, day to night, etc.

Properties

FERN
Long shifts, vests, skirt, heavy socks.
Beat-up backpack.
Stained white butcher apron.
Canvas shopping bags.
Shoulder bag.
Filled laundry basket.
iPad.
Work suit, high heels, briefcase.
Scissors, laminated pages.
Toothbrush, Swiss Army knife, passport, soap, body cream, socks, underwear, sweaters.
Long, floaty, white garments (dress, shawl, etc.) - last scene.

SOLLY
Pendleton flannel shirt, tattered jeans, socks, Birkenstock-type sandals.
PJs, dressing gown.
Cell phone.
Well-worn duffel bag.
Loose, white floaty shirt and pants for last scene.

TAMZIN
Shirt suit, tennies, baseball cap.

DIBELS
Steampunk/camo gear clothing, belt.
Cell phone.
Carpenter's measuring tape.

DELIVERY
Clipboard, form.

TIME Magazine
Toe nail clippers.
Newspapers.
Books, magazines, posters, photos.
CD player/radio, CDs.
Sofa.
Rag rug.
Pole lamp.
Radio cabinet.
Coffee table, folding card table, folding chairs.
Single bed, madras spread.
Wine bottle.
Coffee mug, china tea cup, crystal bud vase.
Empty bowls, wine containers, mismatched plates, silver, Chianti wine bottle, burnt-down candles.
Deck of playing cards.
Pads, pencils.
Apple.

AT RISE: Scene 1.
SOLLY and FERN are sitting on the sofa. She's wearing a mish- mash of long things—shirts, vests, skirt, and heavy socks; is reading an old, beat-up copy of TIME™ magazine. He's wearing his usual paint-splattered out-fit—a well-worn Pendleton flannel shirt, slightly tattered jeans; his socks and Birkenstock-type sandals are on the floor by one foot. The other foot is up on the sofa; he's cutting his toe nails. She swats his hand; he grins and stops, picks up a newspaper from the floor and flips it open.
FERN: (*Looking around.*) I hate this place, really hate it. I wish

we'd never come back from England.

SOLLY: (*Heavy sigh; they've been down this road before.*) Fern, my erstwhile friend. My contract wasn't renewed at the Slade, your bank account ran out of money, we had no choice. Remember? (*Reads.*)

FERN: Yeah, well, I can still hate this place, can't I.

SOLLY: Always have a choice.

FERN: Doesn't feel like it, stuck in this pit. I guess I'll have to go back to work. Ugh.

SOLLY drops the newspaper, starts cutting nails on the other foot.

FERN: Hey, we agreed. You do your personal grooming in your apartment and I'll do mine in mine. So there. Huh. Maybe you should go to work and keep me in a style to which I've yet to become accustomed.

He ignores her, keeps cutting his toe nails until they're done.

FERN: (*Cont'd.*) Hey, Solly! You listening to me?

SOLLY: You got any zucchini? Thought I'd make us a squash mash.

FERN: I dare you to say that three times without laughing.

SOLLY: (*Folding paper; reading.*) Squash mash squash mash squash mash.

FERN: You win.

SOLLY: You bet. But, you got any?

FERN: (*Indicating kitchen with a wave.*) Nothing in there but some cheese pretending it's a science experiment.

SOLLY: (*Referring to newspaper.*) Here's one. Look.

FERN: (*She does.*) No good. It's sure as hell not for me and you'd be dead inside of a week. (*Pointing to it.*) When was the last time you lifted 50 pounds?

SOLLY: Forty eight?

FERN: Like I said, no good. See if you can find one in there for me.

SOLLY: Want to be an elementary school tutor? All you have to do, it says here, is fill in an application form and...

FERN: Egad, no. No more forms! But I do want to feed myself before too much more time goes by.

SOLLY: Yeah. So do I. Let's go out, then. (*Putting on his socks, standing.*)

SFX overhead of heavy things dropping repeatedly, rhymically.

FERN: Okay. (*Getting up, jerks head upwards.*) Have you heard him up there?

SOLLY: They can probably hear him in Chatanooga.

FERN: What do you think he's doing?

SOLLY: Whatever it is, I don't think it's benign. Got your keys?

FERN digs around in her pockets, comes up empty.

FERN: I got a better idea. I've got fixings for a cake. I'll make us one. You go back to yours and get us some candles.

SOLLY: I don't recall a celebration coming up? Did I forget something?

FERN: Just that a cake needs candles. Now, go!

SOLLY steps into his sandals and exits with the newspaper and his classic grin. The SOUND above stops.

BLACKOUT

Scene 2. Two hours later.

LIGHTS UP. A KNOCK comes at outer door. FERN enters from KITCHEN, hands buttery and flowery. She's added a stained white butcher apron, miles too big for her. She crosses and opens the door. TAMZIN POOLE stands in the doorway, broadly smiling, holding out a hand to shake. She's dressed in a skirt suit and tennies, sporting a baseball cap.

TAMZIN: (*V.O.*) Mrs. Poole?

FERN slams the door shut. The KNOCK comes again, this time with more vigor. FERN ignores it.

TAMZIN: (*Cont'd. V.O.*) (*Yells through door.*) Mrs. Poole? You can't ignore me! I'm your Granddaughter!

FERN glares at the door; if it were sentient, it would burn. She has a brief inner conversation, adjusts her apron, and opens the door a crack (curiosity has gotten the best of her.)

FERN: You say.

TAMZIN: (*Huge sigh of relief; rushes speech.*) Oh,I do say and I'm so glad you're going to open the door because I've come such a long way and tried so long to find you and here you are and now...

FERN: What makes you think I'm going to open the door?

TAMZIN: Because we're related, I'm your blood, your bones, your...

FERN: I am none of those things to you, young woman, and before you get any more graphic about what I am to you, you'd better get your foot out of the door unless you want to lose it.

TAMZIN: (*Doesn't get the reference.*) My foot?

FERN: (*Starts to slam door again.*) Get all your parts out of my door!

FERN SLAMS the door, stomps over to UP wall, POUNDS on it.

FERN: (*Shouts it.*) Solly! (*No response. Again, even louder.*) SOLLY!!!

Scene 3. Following.

SOLLY: (*From audience, aisle seat, front row.*) Here.

FERN: (*Looks around for his voice.*) Where?

SOLLY: Here. HERE.

FERN: (*Locates source of voice.*) But you're supposed to be on stage, HERE.

TAMZIN opens door and joins FERN, looks down at SOLLY.

TAMZIN: You should be up here.

FERN: Well, clearly he's not up here, he's down there.

SOLLY: I'm not down, or there. I'm here.

FERN: Yes, but the fact of you being there causes a problem for those of us up here.

TAMZIN: So why are you down there?

SOLLY: This isn't how my original play opened, so I'm pouting. Besides, I've wandered onto so many stages of life, across so many sets of humanity, that I've forgotten my lines. So I'm sitting this one out.

FERN: Oh, shit. Existential angst. Just what we don't need.

TAMZIN: But you can't sit out your own play.

SOLLY: Can and am.

FERN: Get your ass up here.

TAMZIN: And what happens to our parts if you're out there?

FERN and TAMZIN ad lib a beat until

DIRECTOR: (*Shouts from audience.*) STOP!!!

DELIVERY KNOCKS on open door, walks in, unaware that something's wrong. Delivers speech tiredly.

DELIVERY: Someone needs to sign this form. It's the form changing your other address form which unfortunately got wet in the last rain storm we had. All the forms got soaked. Sorry about that. So I inform the boss and hafta have a new form to replace the old form. So who's gonna sign? Sign this form? (*Holds out clip board hopefully*).

SOLLY: (*Climbs up onto stage.*) If a butterfly farts in Papua New Guinea, the climate changes in downtown Carlisle.

FERN: No, that's not it. It's, if a polar bear farts in the Arctic, bananas won't ripen in Santiago.

TAMZIN: What happens if a boy farts in Los Angeles? Or York?

FERN: Oh, boys are always farting, just ask Solly, and nothing ever changes.

BLACKOUT EVERYWHERE

Scene 4. Following.

DIRECTOR: (*V.O. from audience.*) I'm not going to put the lights back up until you all behave. Have you got that?

FERN (*V.O.*) And I'm not going to play in another play inside a play inside another play. Such old hat, don't you all think?

MUMBLES from the cast: "Noises Off, best ever, no, Six Degrees of Separation, Hamlet, of course," etc.

DIRECTOR: (*Ignoring cast, heavy sigh.*) Let's try again. From the top. Lights up, curtain up, on your marks, ready, get set, and go.

LIGHTS STAY DOWN.

DIRECTOR: (*Cont'd.*) Aaarrrgghghghh!! Lights, you up there? Or are you sneaking a smoke, picking your nose, or WHAT???

LIGHTS: (*V.O.*) End of scene. Says on my sheet, lights down. You wanna change that?

On a profound silence from DIRECTOR, LIGHTS come up over the house, briefly, then fade.

Scene 5. Later Same Day.

Stage LIGHTS up. FERN and TAMZIN are squared off on opposite

284

sides of the coffee table; they circle as they talk.

TAMZIN: Why do you keep on denying me?

FERN: Oh, that's the easy one. The hard one is who you think I am, might be?

TAMZIN: No, that's the easy one. Your name's Poole.

FERN: Nothing fancy in that. Lots of Pooles here and there if you just look for them. And I haven't gone by that handle in eons.

TAMZIN: Says so on your mailbox.

FERN shrugs this off. Sits down.

TAMZIN (*Cont'd.*) My late uncle's name was Poole.

FERN: Was? Aren't you a bit young to be having a late uncle?

TAMZIN; Well, mom told me, he kind of, um, disappeared, like, once.

FERN: Just once? That doesn't seem too careless.

TAMZIN: Um, like more than once, like, more like every third Friday.

FERN: Like? Like? You're too old to chucking like around like it was, well, I don't know. Like every third Friday or every third Friday? Make up your mind, girl. If you're my granddaughter, you speak your mind, you don't wander around in like.

TAMZIN: My name's Tamzin, not girl. So you admit it!

FERN: Oh-h-ho. Tam-zin, is it.

SOLLY enters from kitchen, licking his fingers, wiping his hands down the front of his shirt. He sits on the sofa.

FERN (*Cont'd.*) Says her name's Tam-zin, Solly. Did you ever.

SOLLY: Well, not so's you'd know, Fern, no.

FERN: Neither did I. Don't, neither.

SOLLY: But then, does it matter?

FERN: Don't suppose it does, one way or t'other. Since she isn't. Can't be, can she?

SOLLY: Not so's you'd know, no.

TAMZIN: What are you two babbling about?

FERN: (*Sits on sofa next to SOLLY.*) You can't be because I never was a begatter.

TAMZIN: I'm sorry, what?

FERN: Offspring. No babies sprung off these bones. No blood

285

lines trailing after me like so much spoor to be tracked. Tracked down. Like you coming in here, telling me I'm your grandma. Hah!

FERN and SOLLY go to 'high five' each other, but miss, hit each other's shoulders instead which they shrug.

TAMZIN: But you have to be! I need a grandmother! Desperately! (Dramatically, she flops down onto the floor.) More to the point, I need a Poole grandmother! (Starts exaggerated weeping.)

Scene 6. Following.

SPOT light on PRODUCER in the audience.

PRODUCER: (*Pops up.*) You're changing all the lines! You can't do that!

SPOT light on SOLLY on stage.

SOLLY: We're going back to my original script, you thief.

LIGHTS UP over house.

DIRECTOR: (*Gets up, walks toward stage.*) Just get going with something. Honestly. Actors.

PRODUCER scuttles after DIRECTOR who jumps up on stage and vanishes backstage.

PRODUCER: (*V.O.*) (*Whines.*) But, Sam, you can't let them do that!

LIGHTS OUT over house, UP on stage.

SOLLY: I vote we keep on and be in my script. Whaddya think?

FERN: Well, we better be in something, because there's an audience out there and they're waiting. Confused and waiting. (*Addresses audience.*) Right audience?

Audience claps, etc.

TAMZIN: I said, I need a Poole grandmother, desperately!

SOLLY and FERN look at each other, then over at DELIVERY, who seems to realize where it is and ducks OFF. A beat.

Scene 7. Following.

FERN EXITS to kitchen, returns with a folded card table. SOLLY follows, returns with three fold-up chairs. The three actors put the table up, set out the chairs, and sit. TAMZIN repeats her line, this time pulling out a form from her pocket.

TAMZIN: I need a Poole grandmother. Desperately! (*Waves the form at FERN.*)

FERN: (*To SOLLY.*) I'm going to need wine for this conversation. (*Continuing; ignoring the form.*) I've decided that, instead of a job, what I need is to start a granny gang. Or maybe that should be a Crone Crew, since I am not, contrary to the Tamzin's person's...

TAMZIN: (*Interrupting.*) Hey! I'm sat right here!

FERN: (*As if not interrupted.*) ...Tamzin person's belief, anyone's grandmother, never been, never will be. So there. (*To TAMZIN.*) Poole was those people's names, those nice but aimless folks who reared me til I was old enough to take on the job myself. I'm Fern Fanshaw 'cause I like the sound of it.

SOLLY: What's your manifesto going to be?

FERN: Hmmm. You're right. A manifesto. We're going to have to practice something, something not bound up in anything else, no structure or shape.

SOLLY: Formless springs to mind.

FERN; Formlessness, that's it, too many bloody forms in the world. We're going to meditate on formlessness, sing formless praises, out motto will be, never fill out a form, be shapeless. But I need wine to do it, Mister! And a piece of that cake!

SOLLY grins at her, gets up, EXITS to KITCHEN, returns with wine bottle and one coffee mug, one china tea cup, one crystal bud vase, sets these out, uncorks the wine. FERN takes a swig directly from the bottle.

TAMZIN: (*Intrigued in spite of herself.*) You'll have to live off the grid.

FERN: We'll be so so far off the grid we'll form a new grid, a formless grid. We'll never again have forms to inform forms informing other forms. Our formlessness will become all the rage. Everyone will want in. They'll form lines to join us, which will destroy the entire concept so we'll have to smash our pocketbooks down on their heads.

TAMZIN: Pocketbooks?

FERN: Oh, yes, we're going to have our own brand of granny-sized pocketbooks like grandmothers used to carry, over their arms, like the Queen still does...

SOLLY: (*Quiet interruption; takes a swig of wine from the bottle.*) How can you be for formlessness when you're in a form?

FERN: (*Ignores him: swept away by her own rhetoric.*) ...pocketbooks filled with enough heft to knock out a mugger if one ever dared attempt to snatch said pocketbook. All a granny crone needs is a good swing and, smash, the point is made.

SOLLY: (*Thoroughly enjoying himself, the wine, the silliness that isn't.*) How will people know how to find you in your formlessness?

FERN: By word of mouth, shapeless words flying away on a summer's breeze.

TAMZIN: What'll you do in autumn, or winter?

FERN: About what?

TAMZIN: Your formlessness thingy.

FERN: Good question.

SOLLY: Who's got an answer?

There is a KNOCK at the OUTER DOOR. FERN, SOLLY, and TAMZIN look at each other, TAMZIN grabs the wine bottle.

TAMZIN: The way this is going, it'll probably be the White Rabbit. (*She pours wine into the bud vase, downs it, pours again.*) *Another KNOCK.*

FERN: Enter at your peril!

Scene 8. Following.

DIBELS, dressed in a combination of camo and steampunk gear, EN-TERS by pushing the door open, stands in doorway as if waiting for permission to do something. A very long beat while they all wait until "Strangers In The Night" issues from the region of DIBELS' pants pocket. He takes his Smartphone out and starts texting, ignoring everything and everyone else. FERN and SOLLY choose to ignore him.

FERN: (*To TAMZIN.*) So why do you need this grandmother Poole? (*FERN is pointedly not looking at DIBELS.*)

SOLLY: What we really need are jobs. I'm tired of trying to eek out any reasonable existence on food stamps and a bus pass. And I'm feeling like an old crock. (*Takes a swig of wine.*) Maybe I will go back to teaching art.

TAMZIN: At the high school?

SOLLY: How do you know I taught there?

Overlap

FERN: About this grandmother?

TAMZIN: (*To SOLLY.*) I took a stab. (*To FERN.*) If I can find a like viable grandmother Poole, I inherit a bundle. See? Like it says on this...uh, sorry...form...

FERN: Viable? As in living?

SOLLY: Probably more likely reliable, as in DNA tested.

FERN: (*An idea hatching.*) Well, those tests can be knobbled, can't they Solly?

SOLLY: (*To FERN.*) Not so's you'd notice, no. Besides, you're the one with the ear to the criminal gossip mill.

FERN: (*To SOLLY.*) Well, honestly, just because I took a shine to that burglar 'cause he kept falling over my furniture in the dark. All I did was help direct him to the nearest food bank. (*To TAMZIN.*) Whaddya mean, took a stab? What does that mean?

SOLLY: All you did was adopt him for a week and learn a few tricks of his dubious trade.

FERN: (*Loves it.*) I do know how to open just about anything now, I'll grant you that. (*To TAMZIN.*) About this stab?

TAMZIN: (*Shouting.*) I can't go on living like I'm in a cardboard box or something. I need that inheritance and couldn't find any Poole grandmothers who look like the right age until I came across you and here you are and I need that inheritance, damn it. (*Holds out form for FERN to sign.*)

FERN: (*Shouting back, ignoring form.*) Whaddya mean??? Came across me??? Why do you think I'm a Poole person???

TAMZIN: (*Defensive.*) It's on your mailbox. And you look right?

FERN: (*Furious.*) So you've been stalking Solly and me?

Deadly silence. DIBELS stops texting.

DIBELS: Uh, Missus.? Got an extra pan? My goods don't arrive 'til Friday and I ain't got no way to heat up my Spaghettios.

FERN, SOLLY, and TAMZIN look at DIBELS like he's something they dragged in on the bottom of their shoes.

FERN: I hear you up there, you know.

DIBELS: Yeah? So?

FERN: So, sounds like you're bowling at three in the a m.

That's what so. So, what're you doing?

DIBELS: (*Tries to shrug it off.*) Practicing.

SOLLY: For what, the hammer toss?

DIBELS: So that's a no on the pan?

FERN shakes her head, 'no'. DIBELS shrugs, turns on his heels, and leaves FERN's apartment. He SLAMS the door behind him.

Scene 9. Following.

SOLLY: (*To FERN.*) Like I was saying, I need a job. So do you. Your bank balance is just as pitiful as mine.

FERN goes to turn on her CD player, puts in a disc. Holds out her arms to SOLLY as a Strauss waltz comes out the speakers.

FERN: Come here, you old crock.

He does, they waltz around the room, not as lovers, as loving friends. TAMZIN stands up, wanders into kitchen with her empty wine container.

SOLLY: All this exercise is making me even hungrier. (*Spins FERN out and back.*)

FERN: Me, too.

FERN spins SOLLY out and back. They execute some fancy dance steps through:

SOLLY: (*Dips FERN.*) Positively half starved.

FERN: Famquished.

SOLLY: Positively ravishing.

He pulls her up; facing each other, they say

FERN: Craving...

SOLLY: Craving...

SOLLY AND FERN: Mashed zuccini patties and pears!

They stop dancing. TAMZIN wanders back in, licking her fingers. FERN goes over to the front door.

TAMZIN: Hey? There's a cake in there flatter than yesterday's pancakes. But the icing's good.

FERN: Damn. (*Digs through one of the bags hanging on the back of the door.*) Double damn. Solly, I can't find my EBT card, or my bus pass. Lend me yours.

SOLLY: (*Removing his wallet, EBT and bus pass; hands them to her.*) I've only got forty-three dollars left on the EBT, so watch yourself in the candy aisle.

290

FERN takes the card and pass along with one canvas shopping bag and, with a cheerful nose thumb at SOLLY, EXITS. SILENCE for a beat or two.

Scene 10. Following.

SOLLY: Sit down, Tamzin, or whatever your name really is. (*Sits on the sofa.*)

TAMZIN: (*Trying to look offended.*) What's wrong with Tamzin? And who're you to talk, what kind of name is Solly?

SOLLY: The fact of the matter is that I don't actually give a damn what you call yourself. What I do care about is how you treat Fern. I will not have you mess her around.

TAMZIN: (*Silly giggle.*) You sound like that old woman on Brit TV, you know the one, that amateur detective, Hatty something. She's always saying, I won't have you, blah, blah, blah.

SOLLY: This isn't TV, and I'm not kidding. You mess with Fern and you'll be in big trouble from me.

TAMZIN: Oh, boy, am I scared.

SOLLY: You should be.

TAMZIN: (*Unfazed.*) So, what, you're threatening me?

SOLLY: Nope. Just telling it like it is. Fern is my best friend, bar none. She drives me crazy more often than not. She can never remember where she's put her food stamps card or her bus pass, she forgets her keys and we have to break in at least once a week, she's feckless and lazy and probably the most genuine person I've ever met. She's whimsical, lives in a fantasy world, could grow prize-winning zuccinis if she only had a green patch, and has to put spiders outside rather than kill them.

SOLLY picks up the old TIME™ and starts flipping through it. TAMZIN starts prowling, looking closely at things around the apartment.

SOLLY (*Cont'd.*) (*From behind the pages.*) I wouldn't snoop, either. Especially after Fern takes you in.

TAMZIN: You think she will?

SOLLY: What I know is that she's a sucker for a hard luck story and yours is a beaut. I'm sure you'll find a way to wheedle her into keeping you for a while. Inheritance, my ass.

TAMZIN: It's true!

291

SOLLY: Whatever. Point is, she'll let you camp out here and try to help you find a grandmother. You'll be on the premises and I don't want you...

FERN ENTERS, carrying a full canvas bag and her shoulder bag. She drops these on the card table.

FERN: You don't want her to...what? Solly? From the looks of you two, something's up.

They stay mute.

FERN: (*Cont'd.*) Whatever it is, or was, it can wait. I'm running on empty here! Let's get cooking! (*FERN EXITS to the kitchen.*)

TAMZIN: (*Sotto voce, with a sneer, to SOLLY.*) I bet it's really Solomon. Solomon Greene. Maybe once was Greenburg?

SOLLY: (*Glaring, threatening low voice.*) Tamzin, my backside.

<u>Scene 11. Following</u>.

TAMZIN: It's no good, you know.

FERN: (*Standing in kitchen doorway.*) What are you on about now?

SOLLY: I think Miss Poole is just leaving.

TAMZIN: No, I don't mean...you...never mind.

FERN 'gets' that something's bothering TAMZIN. She moves to the sofa, sits, and put an encouraging look on her face. SOLLY stays where he is, clearly disapproving.

FERN: I'm listening.

TAMZIN: Oh, I can't tell you.

SOLLY: I think you'd better. Or get the hell out.

FERN: Solly! Give the girl a chance.

TAMZIN: (*Picks up stool, perches on it.*) Okay then. It all started when... (*Jumps up.*) No, I can't. I just can't. (*Shoves form back into pocket.*) Thanks, both of you, you've been so nice to me, thinking that, well, but I just can't any more...you see, it's because... no. I gotta go.

FERN: Wait a minute, Tamzin. (*She gets up and joins TAMZIN at the outer door.*) You just come in here, claim you're my grand-daughter, and then you bolt like a scared rabbit. What's the matter with you? What's the deal here?

TAMZIN doesn't speak; grabs the door open and runs out.
BLACKOUT.

292

Scene 12. Two hours later.

SOLLY and FERN have finished their meal at the card table. An empty couple of bowls, wine containers, mismatched plates, silverware, and a burnt-down candle stuck into a Chianti wine bottle are all that is left. SOLLY and FERN are drinking cups of something. They clear the table and return to set out a game of cards.

SOLLY: (*Dealing for Gin Rummy.*) I called about that job while you were out shopping.

They start playing, FERN drawing first.

FERN: And?

SOLLY: And, you were right, as usual. I'd have to lift 50 pounds a day, every day, on that job, and, besides, the arrogant punk I talked to suggested the job would be too much for me. Kid must've been all of twelve.

FERN: Twelve? You sure? Not thirteen? Hey, I thought you were collecting ten's.

They play for a while more.

FERN: Have you looked at my hands lately?

SOLLY: Not so's you'd notice, no. Too busy noticing mine turning into claws.

FERN: (*Dangling one hand to make her point.*) My skin looks like yesterday's crepe paper. Look at that! And the skin around my eyes! I go to put on eye makeup in my magnifying mirror and could swear I'm looking at an elephant's eye. Look!

SOLLY: (*He peers at her eyes.*) Nope. An elephant's eyelashes are longer. And why are you still putting on eye makeup?

FERN: Habit, I guess. Have done since high school.

SOLLY: Look much more like you without it.

FERN: Since when did you see me without, oh...

SOLLY: New Mexico.

FERN: Ah, now that was a time, eh, Solly? We both of us just being ourselves out on that desert.

SOLLY: I still wish I could've caught that light.

FERN: You need to start painting again.

SOLLY: You need to start being you again. Harvest your own zuccini.

FERN: I know. I've not been me lately, have I? No, don't an-

293

swer that. It's just that I feel like I'm in some in-between place.

SOLLY: Which is…(*He lays his cards down.*) What're you holding?

FERN: (*Looking at her cards.*) Forty five. (*Beat.*) It's some in-between age, not middle-aged anymore, and not ancient yet.

SOLLY: Not ready for the drool cup, then.

She deals.

FERN: Or the diapers.

SOLLY: Getting strapped in a wheelchair…

FERN: …and left to rot in a urine-soaked hallway.

SOLLY: Not for us, my girl. Not for us.

FERN lays down her cards.

FERN: So what is this in-between time? And what do we do about it? What do we do, full stop? What've you got?

SOLLY: A mere twenty two. (*He gets up.*) I don't know what we do. All I do know is that I still want to be doing something. Not sitting on my ass, toothlessly smacking my porridge, waiting for the end like a decrepit, leftover, forgotten piece of yesterday's news.

FERN: (*She also gets up.*) I'm with you. Still do feel useful, inside, but no one wants to hire us, outside. We're too old for one kind of life and too young for the other. Bah.

SOLLY puts on a CD and holds out his arms. WALTZ MUSIC UP. FERN steps into them and they WALTZ around the room.

FERN: What do you suppose that woman really wanted, that Tamzin person?

SOLLY: Nothing good, I guarantee it. (*He dips FERN.*)

FERN: (*Dips SOLLY.*) Do you think any of that was real, about the inheritance? I mean, it could put us on easy street if I went along with the deal.

SOLLY: (*Steps out of her embrace, bows to her; goes to outer door.*) Don't even get anywhere close to that. (*Opening door.*) Promise?

FERN: Okay.

SOLLY: I mean it. Promise me you won't.

FERN: Okay, okay! I promise. Now get out of here, I need my whatchamacallit sleep!

SOLLY goes, shutting the door quietly behind him. FERN waits a moment, then picks up a pad and pencil from the bookcase, returns to the card

table, sits, and starts making notes.
BLACKOUT.

Scene 13. Following.
One SPOT on PRODUCER scurrying behind DIRECTOR as the two cross L to R on the apron.
PRODUCER: (*Desperate, sputtering.*) They've changed it too much, Sam. It's all over the place now. You have to stop this, this, before...
DIRECTOR: Too late now, Ray. This is a whole new play, a play with its own force. These characters are running the show, and I'm real curious to see where they're going to take us next. And if you're smart, you'll shut up and watch what happens. And if you're not...
DIRECTOR's voice FADES out as the two vanish from the stage.
BLACKOUT.
LIGHTS UP.

Scene 14. Next day, Sunday morning.
SOLLY wanders into FERN's apartment from outer door; wearing PJs and a dressing gown, eating an apple, carrying the Sunday paper. He sits and flips the paper open to the Classified section. FERN enters, carrying a very old wicker laundry basket, filled with freshly laundered clothes and linens. There is an iPad on top, which FERN removes as she plunks the basket down on the sofa.
FERN: Look!
SOLLY: (*Looks up; frowns.*) What's that, as in, what's that you've got that you've got no right to having?
FERN: I didn't nick it, if that's what you're thinking.
SOLLY: Who me? Perish the thought. It just occurs, with our pensions, one does not rush out and purchase expense generation millenial toys.
FERN: I didn't! Dibels give it me, yesterday night, when I saw him out by the recycle bins.
SOLLY: Why on earth would that slime bucket give you anything?
FERN: Oh, he's not so bad once you get talking to him. And

another thing. Did you know his grandfather used to own this building? (*Takes the iPad over to the table, sits next to SOLLY, and starts fiddling with it.*) Trouble is, I can't make it work.

FERN fiddles more with it, gets angry with it, tosses it. SOLLY retrieves it.

SOLLY: It might come in handy with our job search at that. I hear we have to get on craigs list, whatever the hell that is. Who's Craig when he's at home? And why's he got a list?

FERN: That's why I borrowed it when he offered. I told him we were looking for jobs, he suggested we might need to get online to do just that, and handed me the thing. (*Beat.*) Anyway, it all sounded so plausible, down there by the rats and the rubbish bins.

SOLLY: I love it when you talk English—nick, give it, rubbish bins—reminds me of those phenomenal fish and chips in Whitby, that Atlantic light, our whole England time. My teaching at The Slade. Your orange marmelade cat.

FERN: He was only ever a visitor, never ever stayed the night. They are silent a moment, floating on memories.

SOLLY: (*Getting up, grabbing iPad and FERN.*) Well, since we're not hooked up here, let's go down to the public library and use their electricity.

FERN: Great idea! Let me just get my library card... (*She rummages in her bag without result.*)

SOLLY: (*Smiling.*) We'll use mine, woman. Come on.

FERN: The librarian might prefer it if you were wearing something a bit less casual, and my name is Fern.

He laughs; they EXIT.

A long beat.

Scene 15. Shortly following.
We HEAR scrabbling noises in the keyhole of FERN's outer door and scuffles and then DIBELS' voice intrudes.

DIBELS: (*V.O.*) What the hell are you doing?

TAMZIN: (*V.O.*) Hey!!! Let go of me!

TAMZIN and DIBELS enter, him pushing ahead of her, her rubbing an arm. DIBELS takes out a carpenter's measuring tape.

296

DIBELS: I told you to stay away until I give you the heads up. Gimme back those keys.

TAMZIN: Oh, chill out, Dibels. I'll go anywhere I damn well please.

DIBELS: Not when you're in my building, you won't.

TAMZIN: It's not your building yet, you know.

DIBELS: Mine by rights. (*He goes around measuring the walls.*)

TAMZIN: Why are you bothering with that? Once you get all the oldies out, you're just going to knock it all down.

DIBELS: There's money in reclaimed brick. These walls are solid. A fortune if my guys are careful. Each apartment measures 20 x 20, times six apartments on each floor, times...Why am I telling you this? I've cancelled leases on four apartments already. Your job is to hook granny and land her somewhere else.

TAMZIN: (*Going up to him, wrapping a hand in his belt, pulling his hips to hers.*) Don't worry yourself about granny. I've got plans for her.

DIBELS: (*Responding.*) Ditto her scruffy boyfriend.

TAMZIN: I'm not sure what to do about him. But I know what to do about you.

TAMZIN walks them both to the bed, pulls him down. He starts to give in, then roughly pushes her off, stands up.

DIBELS: I'll make sure he never sees the light of day. (*Indicates she should tidy up the bed and holds out his hand for the keys.*)

DIBELS and TAMZIN leave after she smoothes the bedspread, she still pulling on his belt.

BLACKOUT.

Scene 16. Later: LIGHTS UP.

FERN and SOLLY return, looking a bit worse for wear.

FERN: Honestly, what a mess. We're screwed, Sol, flat out screwed.

SOLLY: Maybe we need to take a class in how to figure out how to make this webby thing help us find jobs.

FERN: Maybe Tamzin can teach us?

SOLLY: You go near that woman and I'm off. Seriously.

FERN: Oh, yeah? And just where are you going to go?

SOLLY: Back to New Mexico?

FERN: On what money? We need jobs and now. Where's that ad you showed me before?

SOLLY: The tutoring gig?

SOLLY finds the newspaper and the ad and hands it to FERN.

FERN: Yeah. (*Takes the paper and reads.*) "The Charter Reading Program seeks experienced K-12 literacy teachers, retirees encouraged to apply." And a phone number. (*Beat.*) Lend me your phone, Sol, mine crapped out last week. (*He does, she starts dialing, EXITS into kitchen.*)

KNOCK on outer door.

SOLLY: (*Calling out.*) Who goes there?

TAMZIN: (*V.O.*) Tamzin.

SOLLY: (*Opens door an inch.*) What do you want?

TAMZIN: Aren't you going to let me in?

SOLLY: Haven't answered my question.

TAMZIN: I want to tell Fern my good news. And you, of course.

SOLLY: News from you can't be good.

FERN enters from kitchen, closing SOLLY's phone, tosses it to him, goes to open door fully. TAMZIN bursts in.

TAMZIN: It's such good news, Fern, you'll never guess.

FERN watches SOLLY and TAMZIN verbally spar.

SOLLY: Still haven't answered my question.

TAMZIN: (*Ignoring SOLLY.*) I've just rented an apartment here! Isn't that great news? Now I'll be here all the time and we can do grandmother and granddaughter things together! Bake cookies? Play pinochle? What's pinochle anyway?

SOLLY: Don't you have a job to keep you busy?

TAMZIN: (*Waves it off.*) Oh, I bagged it.

SOLLY: Fired, more like.

TAMZIN: Oh, my boss was always in my face, demanding I get everything right. You should've heard him when I shredded that twenty grand check! Talk about a freak out! You'd've thought I shredded his cat or somethin'. He went ballistic and then the sunuvabitch canned my ass.

FERN: (*Quiet interruption.*) There aren't any apartments for rent in this building.

TAMZIN: A studio, well, more like a bachelor's pad, in the basement, So I can hang with you, all the time!

SOLLY: You're young. Get another job. No age discrimination for you. And get yourself an apartment somewhere, anywhere, else. Get your shit together and leave us alone!

ABRUPT BLACKOUT.

Scene 17. Two Weeks Later.

LIGHTS UP. FERN's apartment has an uncared aspect to it; magazines and newspaper and opened/unopened mail tossed on the floor, dirty dishes, glasses, utensils, etc., on the card table, the bed unmade, CDs and their covers scattered around. FERN enters. She's wearing sensible work-type clothes and a pair of high heels and is carrying a well-worn leather briefcase. She drops briefcase and kicks off shoes. She disappears for a beat into the kitchen, returns with a bottle of wine. She unscrews it, takes a slug. Sits on the bed, still in work clothes. Slumps her shoulders in resignation. Looks to be settled in for some serious drinking, but shakes herself and gets up. Crosses to briefcase, removes large sheets of laminated pages, finds a pair of scissors on a bookshelf, puts all these on the card table, shoving aside the detritus there. She gets up again, gets her wine bottle, takes another swig, and starts cutting laminated forms apart. A KNOCK is heard followed by SOLLY entering the outer door. He sees FERN's activity and starts straightening up the apartment. FERN watches, frowning slightly.

FERN: I wish you wouldn't do that.

SOLLY: I know.

FERN: Makes me feel a right slut.

SOLLY: (*Finishes tidying up, joins her at the table.*) It's been two weeks since you started that crap job...

FERN: The Charter Reading Program. CRP.

SOLLY: Right. Anagram, crap.

FERN: All my years of experience, acquired knowledge, street smarts up the yinyang, and this is what I've been reduced to... (*indicates pile on her lap with scissors*) ...slicing up laminated progress forms. Well, no more. (*She hands the scissors to SOLLY, the laminates drop to the floor. She takes healthy swig of wine.*)

299

SOLLY: So it's a crap tutoring job and it's been hard on you, but not damaging—until now. What's happened? And no wine while you're busy whining. (*He puts the wine bottle on the floor and starts to pick up laminates.*)

FERN: (*Prowls during.*) I was evaluated today. And leave those alone! And put evaluated in quotes. "Evaluated." Been on this grusome job for two lousy weeks and they told me I wouldn't do, to go away and never come back.

SOLLY: I doubt they said the latter. But wait a minute. Why wouldn't you do? What did you do or not do that they didn't like?

FERN: It's a reading program, right? which means scripted, have to follow the script, keep to the time table, fill out the assessment forms. (*Beat.*) I used to be a teacher, but what's happened to education while I was gone? It's all testing and filling out forms and has little to do with educating it seems to me or else it's all education by intimidation, by loud voices, by over the top political correctness politeness, oh, he's just having a bad day instead of walloping said him with some straight-edged discipline.

SOLLY: You're wandering. Not that it isn't fodder for a good argument at some later date, but the point is...?

FERN: The point is that I wandered off the script because the girl I was tutoring, during this so-called evaluation, asked me a question. A good question. A question about what we were reading, but sort of going in another direction. I thought a good enough question to answer, to follow for a minute or two, couldn't hurt, might even help her appreciate reading more.

SOLLY: Sounds great to me, a real value for that kid, so what's the problem?

FERN: The problem, as you call it, was and is that I veered off the script to follow that girl's mind onto another road, and they, the they who've hired me, think that's wrong, that my delivery is too slow, their words, can't keep the kid on task, put that phrase in quotes too, please, on task. (*She takes a breath and puts her face right up to his. Anger building.*) Sol? You're an artist? Right? Doesn't creativity come from curiosity? From getting off task?

Isn't it more important to respond in the moment than stick to some lines on a bloody form?

He puts an arm around her shoulders.

FERN: (*Cont'd.*) Maybe it's this twentieth first century stuff. Interwebby stuff and common core education. I was happy in the 20th century, could maneuver, navigate, find my way around. I feel like a dinosaur.

SOLLY: Take a breath.

She does.

SOLLY: (*Cont'd.*) (*Knows what's coming; not best pleased.*) So what'd you do?

FERN: I quit. What else? I mean, taking that job ranks as the second biggest mistake I've ever made.

Flops on sofa. SOLLY joins her.

SOLLY: The first most obviously that dark day in two thousand two when you turned down my proposal.

FERN: Dark day, my ass. You should've seen the look of relief on your face when I said no.

SOLLY: You laughed, then made me some shortbread cookies. And you were right, we're better as we are.

FERN: Neighbors and occasional partners in crime. Speaking of which...

SOLLY: Tell me I won't hear you agreeing with Tamzin's plan. It's fraud.

FERN: I know. But...what're we going to do?

SOLLY: I guess I'll have to go to work.

FERN: There's a chance?

SOLLY: A local private art school. Interview tomorrow. And now, (*He pulls her to her feet.*) I'd rather ask you to come next door to look at the painting I started today.

FERN: Well, I want to moan about K-12 education, or lack of it. School these days is just another bottom-line business.

SOLLY: Tell you what. (*He gets up.*) You stay here and have your moan. (*SOLLY gives FERN an affectionate pat, and goes for the outer door.*)

FERN: (*Calling to him as he EXITS.*) Glad you're painting again. *That's a good thing.*

After a beat, she gets up, carrying the wine bottle and spreads out on her bed, all set to drink the night away.
The light outside starts getting dark.
LIGHTS fade into

Scene 18. Hours later that night.
After a moment of darkness, we HEAR FERN softly singing "Go Tell Aunt Rhody" (American Folk Song).
FERN: "Go tell Aunt Rhody/go tell Aunt Rhody./Go tell Aunt Rhody/the old grey goose is dead. (Sings third Verse in its Minor key.) She died in the mill pond/she died in the mill pond./ She died in the mill pond/a-standing on her head."
She gets into it, backs up to the second verse, gets louder. We HEAR SOLLY pounding on the dividing wall. She gets louder, keeps singing, he keeps pounding. Pretty soon, they both are singing about the poor old grey goose, he on his side of the wall, she on hers.
LIGHTS slowly up, as dawn approaches.

Scene 19. Next day.
FERN is still in bed. SOLLY enters without knocking. He looks dreadful.
FERN: (*Lifting up on an elbow.*) I'll get up, come look at your painting.
SOLLY: Don't bother. (*He sits at the table, drops his head down on it.*)
FERN: What's up, Sol?
SOLLY: (*Muffled.*) It's gone.
FERN: What is?
SOLLY: The light AND the dark AND all the shades in between.
FERN: (*Getting up, shaking out her clothes.*) You're just talking like an artist. Want coffee?
SOLLY: I don't want coffee! I've just lost my reason for living, woman! Will coffee fix that? (*Sits up, shouts.*) Will it!?
FERN: (*Shouting back.*) Don't you dare call me woman! It's not my fault you're stuck!
SOLLY: I'm not stuck! I'm a mess!
FERN: Ah. (*She crosses to him, puts her hands on his shoulders. Talks quietly.*) We're born screaming, gooey and messy, we live messy

302

complicated possibly boring lives and then usually die in some crusty mess. That's what humans do and it's our jobs to make the most interesting mess we can. NOTHING is perfect, heaven sounds REALLY boring to me, nirvana as well, so slap your mess around and make something difficult, uncomfortable and beautiful. (*Beat.*) You're the one who told me that on one of my dark nights of the soul.

SOLLY: I won't teach what I can't do.

FERN: Maybe silly putty would help?

SOLLY: (*A small grin at that.*) So we're both unemployed and broke. Is that it? All we get? All there is for us?

FERN: (*She sits.*) I'm going for it. With Tamzin.

SOLLY: I won't be party to that.

FERN: I know.

SOLLY: You're on your own.

FERN: I know.

SOLLY: I told you what I'd do if...

FERN: I know.

SOLLY: You're throwing us away.

FERN: I don't know what else to do.

SOLLY slowly, sadly walks out of FERN's apartment. FERN stares at his retreating back. The die is cast.

BLACKOUT.

Scene 20. Next day.

LIGHTS UP. FERN and TAMZIN are seated at the table.

FERN: Okay. I'll do it.

TAMZIN: You will? Honestly?

FERN: I don't know about honestly, but I'll do it.

TAMZIN: Why'd you change your mind?

FERN: Because I can't stand being broke one more day. So I'll do it, but here's my condition: I get fifty percent of the inheritance.

TAMZIN: No deal.

FERN: I'm risking my liberty for you, you know. What we're talking about here is fraud. Jail time.

TAMZIN: You get twenty-five percent and you and I go live

303

somewhere other than this dump.

FERN: I'm not going anywhere.

TAMZIN: That's the deal. Take it or leave it.

FERN: (*Long thought.*) I'll take it, but you and I don't live any-where near each other.

BACKOUT.

Scene 21. Following.

FERN is finishing tidying up her apartment. She takes a well-worn back-pack off a shelf, lays it on the couch, and goes into the kitchen with a sense of purpose. We HEAR a slight CLICK at the front door, then TAMZIN and DIBELS enter softly. At first, they're whispering. Then their talk gets loud enough to be heard both by FERN in her kitchen and by SOLLY through the wall in his apartment next door. The scene is played quickly up until the denouement when SOLLY bursts in.

TAMZIN: It's all but a done deal, Dib baby. I've got her right where I want her.

DIBELS; She's going along with the inheritance scam?

TAMZIN; She can't wait to get her greedy hands on some of my money.

DIBELS: How much?

TAMZIN: Twenty-five percent.

DIBELS: (*Louder now.*) Twenty-five? Way too much. You stupid bitch. I should've taken her out.

FERN comes to the kitchen door. Can't believe what she sees/hears.

TAMZIN: It's all good, I promise. Come here, honey. Get some honey.

DIBELS: Don't want any honey, I want the money. What about the old guy?

TAMZIN: Ummm....

FERN's about to interrupt when

DIBELS: (*Almost shouting.*) What's the matter with you? Do I have to do everything? I gave you the gun. All you had to do was shoot the sunavabitch when he came out to the dumpsters.

TAMZIN: (*A whimper.*) I don't like guns, baby. Couldn't we push him in front of a bus or something?

DIBELS: (*Full shout.*) You're useless! Get that old lady and her

304

boyfriend outta here!! Use the gun, you useless piece of crap.

FERN leaps out of the kitchen and launches herself at TAMZIN.

FERN: (*Screaming.*) Not Solly, you...

FERN and TAMZIN have a physical fight. It starts verbally (Ad. Lib. insults) and then escalates. It's all about FERN feeling betrayed by TAMZIN and protecting SOLLY. DIBELS lunges at the women. SOLLY crashes in with a duffel bag which he uses to knock DIBELS out. DIBELS is on the floor. TAMZIN ends up flopped on FERN's bed; only FERN is left standing. Simultaneously, we HEAR police sirens in the distance.

SOLLY: (*To FERN, as he's pushing DIBELS out the door.*) Tell me goodbye?

FERN: Not until you say it. (*FERN shouts at TAMZIN.*) To hell with you and your crazy, and I do mean certifiably crazy boyfriend—what kind of a name is Dibels, anyway? (*Now to SOLLY and everywhere.*) And to hell with the Charter Reading Program alias crap and art schools and all this stuff in the apartment.

FERN grabs up the backpack and stuffs in a tooth brush, her passport—just in case—soap, body cream, two changes of travel underwear, Swiss Army knife, and extra socks and a couple of sweaters. During her packing up, SOLLY sits on the bed and forces himself not to grin, TAMZIN sputters a bit, then SOLLY shoves her out the door.

SOLLY: (*Dusting off his hands.*) That's the trash out. Now. Clearly you're coming. No need for goodbyes.

FERN: Not this time around, anyway. So. Greyhound bus? Amtrak? Hitch?

SOLLY: Yeah, been there, done that, got a gazillion Tshirts and burned 'em. Or, we could just walk to my bank and close out my account. Buy a camper van. Head for New Mexico.

FERN: You could get the light back.

SOLLY: You could grow stupendous plants. Take off the eye makeup.

FERN: Yeah, well, nice to dream, but a dollar ninety five ain't gonna get us far, unless we add it to the three hundred I've got left from that crap job.

SOLLY: More like fifty K.

FERN stops shoving her gear into the backpack.

FERN: You what?

SOLLY: Nest egg. For a time like this.

FERN: Why, you old crock. Why'd you never let on... Why not until now? (*Beat.*) Mind you, I don't suppose it matters much.

SOLLY: Not so's you'd notice, no.

FERN slings her backpack across one shoulder, turns on the radio. MU-SIC UP: "Waltzing Matilda" (Banjo Pasterson). FERN takes SOLLY's arm, and they waltz out the door. The police SIRENS get closer, then stop. BLACKOUT.

Scene 22. Following after a beat.

LIGHTS UP. The cast comes on for their bow. First, DELIVERY, who trots out and extends an arm towards the wings for PRODUCER, who trots out and extends an arm towards the wings for DIRECTOR, who trots out, etc. for DIBELS, and lastly comes TAMZIN who extends an arm towards the wings. No FERN, no SOLLY. Cast doesn't quite know what to do; start fidgeting, someone starts to ask DIRECTOR, when from the radio we HEAR

ANNOUNCER: (*V.O.*) We interrupt this broadcast of aboriginal and original Australian music with a traffic update. All traffic, in both directions on the Maclin Road southbound out of town, has stopped due to a fatality accident just south of the Maclin Bridge. According to police on the scene, the driver of a U.S. Government Printing Office van delivering a load of obsolete forms to the shredding office suffered a massive heart attack, lost control of the vehicle, and plunged headlong into a delapidated camper parked by the Maclin River.

Everyone looks at everyone else, confused, wondering, staring at the air the announcer's voice comes from.

ANNOUNCER: (*V.O. Cont'd.*) The driver of the van and the two senior citizens in the camper were killed instantly. The pathologist on the scene remarked that at least the two campers died happy. In a lover's embrace. Stay tuned for more weather, news, and sports, after this.

CLICK as radio turns itself off. Long silence.

DIRECTOR: (*Shading eyes, looking towards Sound Booth.*) Lights? This some kind of joke?

306

FULL UP LIGHTS ON STAGE AND AUDIENCE. Cast stares at each other, dumbounded, then all look out to the audience in wonderment, as if asking, "What the ef just happened?"
FULL BLACKOUT. The Waltz music is still gently playing.
Cast all EXIT silently.
SOFT SPOT on empty stage. MUSIC swells.
Slowly, followed by SPOT, draped in white floaty garments and barefoot, the 'ghosts' of FERN and SOLLY waltz across the stage and off.
MUSIC fades. SPOT dims and goes to black.

DIRECTORIAL NOTE: If needed/wanted, a fan in the wings could be used to help create a floating sensation by the actors. If used, FAN goes silent when music fades and light goes to black.

CURTAIN

Merrily, Merrily

© 2011

Characters

MARGARET: The matriarch of the friends who gather at Silas' Diner daily. In her early 70's, her hair is white, her posture and manner upright.

FIONA: MARGARET's long-time friend and housemate, FIONA is of mixed heritage. Also in her early 70's, her hair is jet black, and nothing about her gives away her age.

IMOGENE: A tall, lean 40-something, IMOGENE wears her auburn hair long, is long suffering, and only wants out.

MARYELLEN: Robust, grey curly haired MARYELLEN (mid-50's) is the frequent peacemaker of the group. She likes to underscore moments with a strum on her ever-present autoharp.

AGGIE TRENT: AGGIE TRENT (mid-60's) is the fixer: she can fix anything mechanical or practical, and many things metaphysical. All of 5 feet tall, she wears her long white hair loose.

ELDERLY MAN: Rather bent yet still spry, rumor has it that he's over 100 but nobody knows for sure.

Properties

For Sale sign, Pewter urn, framed photograph, two already-burned white candles, black crepe paper, moving boxes, four cardboard cutouts sit at another booth one wearing a feather boa, one a beret, one a turban, a black wreath, suitcases.
AGGIE TRENT: denim coveralls, tools sticking out of her pockets, paint-splattered coveralls, a 'save-the-otters' T-shirt,

cowboy boots, large cloth tote bag, screwdriver, battered pa-paperback, shriveled orange, wrinkled tissues, roll of Duct Tape.

IMOGENE: Bandage, purple garments, wooden clothes pins, black dress, shoes, stockings, gloves, hat, and coat.

FIONA: vested trout stream waders, black woolen dress, white stockings, lace-up brown shoes, a grey, thigh-length, cable-knit-ted cardigan, grey fedora.

MARGARET: vested trout stream waders, a full-length, navy-blue silk dress, pumps, and a full-length fake-fur coat.

MARYELLEN: autoharp, orange tent-like garment, flaming red flowers, purple and turquoise caftan, golden Ankh, Afri-can bone jewelry, elaborate silver and malachite roach clip sus-pended on a black silk cord, exotic silk flowers, Birkenstock™ sandals.

ELDERLY MAN: three-piece suit, spats and brogues, a splen-did fedora, a dog leash complete with studded collar but no dog.

Setting

The entire action takes place in the kitchen of Silas', a diner in the 1950's style situated in a small village on an island in the Pacific Northwest. Along the Left wall are the freezer and refrigerator, pantry shelving, and a door (interior) to the pub. Along the Right wall are cupboards, a door (exterior) leading to an alley outside, wall phone, light switches, and a largish win-dow through which we see the edge of a green metal dumpster. Against the rear wall are the stove, griddle, ovens. In a corner stands a coat rack with a few outer garments hanging from it. In the cupboard and on the shelves are a minimal number of kitchen supplies haphazardly stacked or just lying about: cans of food, an old radio, kerosene lanterns, candles, pots and pans, odd plates and flatware, cooking utensils including a car-rot peeler, rolls of foil and wax paper, cotton towels, boxes of foodstuffs, and the like. There is a circular wooden center table. A ceiling-fan-cum-light and fly strip hangs from overhead. The lighting is flat, allowing for little shadowing.

Scene 1

AT RISE: The diner is empty, has an abandoned air. MARGARET and FIONA appear outside and peer through the window. They are dressed in matching vested trout stream waders. MARGARET's white hair is cropped close to her head. FIONA wears her jet black hair in a long braid. They enter from the street door, ignore the boxes piled up against the window, cross to a booth, sit, and wait. IMOGENE, draped in purple garments, long auburn hair flying, clutching a "FOR SALE" sign, rushes onto the stage from the up left door. Back and forth she careens, between the kitchen, the counter, the side booths, navigating round the circular center table. Her progress is slowed by a massive bandage covering her left foot and ankle. It is an unproductive rushing; moving for the sake of movement.

IMOGENE: (*Under her breath.*) Damn fool. (*Louder.*) Damn fool. (*Full bore.*) Damn fool. Damn fool. Damn fool. Damn fool!
(One more sweep across the diner and she flings the "FOR SALE" sign up in the air. It catches on the dangling fly strip and hangs.) Damn fool. (*She lurches into the kitchen.*)

MARGARET: What do you suppose it is this time?

FIONA: Hard to tell with white women. But I like watching her when she's all wound up like this. Let's sit.

MARGARET: It just seems like such a waste of…(*Glass breaking is heard off-stage, followed by pans crashing and simultaneous*)

MARGARET: (*Cont'd.*) …uh, oh.

IMOGENE : (*O.S.*) DAMN FOOL!!!

MARYELLEN enters from the street door on the trot, carrying her ancient autoharp, dressed in an orange tent-like garment which accentuates her girth. Flaming red flowers sprout out of her grey curls.

MARYELLEN: Hoo boy! Harold is hungry-making work! I need me some refueling! Imogene, honey! Some of that corned beef and cabbage from yesterday, with a little sauerkraut and boiled potatoes to keep it company, and a strawberry malt to wash it down. (*Notices MARGARET and FIONA and O.S. commotion.*) Hey, Mags, Fiona. What's all the to-do today?

MARGARET: I told you to stop calling me that.

FIONA: From the pitch she's reached, I'd say this one's a 10-point Silas.

MARGARET: Sounds like some sort of shaggy four-footed

creature who can't find her way home.

MARYELLEN: Well, hell, honey, if the shoe fits…(*Strums a chord.*)

MARGARET: At the very least, use a new cliché. Honestly. Shoe fits.

FIONA: A good fitting pair of shoes is worth more than good fitting sex. Which reminds me, I'm hungry.

IMOGENE lunges out of the kitchen, stops in her tracks at the sight of the three other women.

IMOGENE: Go away. I'm not opening. Today, tomorrow, or any other day. I've had it. I'm leaving.

FIONA: Sure you are.

IMOGENE: No, I mean it. This time he's really crossed the line. And so I'm really leaving. Leaving…this, this fly strip, this one-horse town, this, this… Oh, shit.

FIONA: This snake-spit Sunday.

MARYELLEN: Hey, I like that. (*Strums a chord.*) Can I borrow it?

FIONA: I'm giving it to Imogene. Seems she needs it.

MARGARET: Imogene, pull your hair up. You'll feel better. (*She sits at the center table.*)

IMOGENE: Quit mothering me. (*She pulls wooden clothes pins out of a pocket and winds her hair up. She paces.*) I told Uncle Silas I'd run this diner for six months. Six months. The end. And what happens? He starts wandering off all over the place after six days. And then six months turns into six years. (*Pause.*) And I'm still here. (*Pause.*) Damn fool.

FIONA: Who you mad at, you or him?

IMOGENE: Go away, old woman.

She slumps down at the center table. FIONA sits next to her, rubs IMO-GENE's hands. MARYELLEN rummages behind counter; comes up with glass of water, ketchup bottle, and saltines. Joins the others at the table; makes soup-in-a-glass.

MARYELLEN: At least with Silas you've got some good stories. Remember that time he went down to California to that Renaissance Faire, all dressed up like a hunched-back pirate? And he put the moves on that woman with a hump costume?

Only it turned out hers was real? Shoot. Now that's a story. With Harry, all my stories start and end with pill bottles.

MARGARET: I always liked the story of Silas losing his dead grandmother.

FIONA: The dead don't like it if you roll them up in a rug and leave them on the top of a Volkswagen van while you take a piss in the woods. They get cranky and disappear when that happens.

MARGARET: She was found, wasn't she?

IMOGENE: Listen, I don't care about dining out on Silas stories. There's all that life out there…(Waves hands about, out there.) …and I'm missing it.

FIONA: (Pokes IMOGENE in the chest.) What about what's in here?

IMOGENE: (Pushing finger away.) I'd rather be on the road. And right now I'd really rather be alone. I've got some things to sort out…like, who's better at selling retail properties, anyhow. Hannah Thrang or Vern?

MARYELLEN: Would you buy anything from a man named Vern? (Strums for emphasis.)

FIONA: Don't you have to wait till Silas wanders back 'fore you sell his diner out from under him?

IMOGENE: Fuck Silas.

MARYELLEN: (Loud chord.) Ooooohhhhh.

FIONA: Uh huh.

MARGARET: Thrang isn't too up on it, either. And, I'll think we'll stay. (She's up and moving for the kitchen.) Surely there must be something in there we can heat up or mash or pluck or…

The street door flies open and AGGIE TRENT pops in, all 5 feet of her, in denim coveralls, her long, white hair trailing down her back, tools sticking out of her pockets. She rushes over to the table. Hangs on to a chair.

AGGIE TRENT: Imogene! Sit down!

IMOGENE: (Leaps up.) What!

MARGARET: (Moving back to the table.) Oh, god, now what?!

AGGIE TRENT: Imogene!

312

FIONA: Hold on! We're in it!

MARYELLEN launches into a peculiar rendition of "Go Tell Aunt Rhodie."

IMOGENE: Stop that! Aggie Trent, don't just stand there, spit it out.

AGGIE TRENT: It's Silas!!

IMOGENE: Well, of course it's Silas. It's always Silas. What the hell's happened this time?

AGGIE TRENT: He's DEAD!!

IMOGENE: Oh, perfect!!

BLACKOUT

Scene 2

LIGHTS UP: There is now black crepe paper draped across the counter and stools. More moving boxes creep up the window by the street door; several empty ones are in a booth. Four cardboard cutouts sit at another booth; one wearing a feather boa, one a beret, one a turban. A black wreath hangs inside the street door. The diner is empty. IMOGENE enters carrying a pewter urn, a framed photograph, and two already-burned white candles. She wears black—dress, shoes, stockings, gloves, hat, and coat. Her long hair is skewered on top of her head with clothes pins (revealed when she removes the floppy hat). She kicks the door closed, crosses to the communal table. She places the items there in an altar arrangement; the urn in front of the photo flanked by the candles. She removes gloves, coat and hat, drapes these on the naked cutout, and disappears into the kitchen through the swing doors. The street door opens and MARGARET enters wearing a full-length, navy-blue silk dress, pumps, and a full-length fake-fur coat. Her head is bare. She carries a clutch purse. She walks to the communal table, shrugging out of her coat. Coming close on MARGARET's heels is FIONA; but she stays put at the doorway. FIONA is dressed in a black woolen dress, white stockings and lace-up brown shoes, and a grey, thigh-length, cable-knitted cardigan. A grey fedora perches on her braided hair. Her face is tight with doubt.

MARGARET: For heaven's sake, Fiona. Come here and close the door. You're letting in the night air.

FIONA: And letting out the ghost.

MARGARET: What's that?

FIONA: Let's go.

MARGARET: We're not going anywhere. I'm hungry, you're hungry, we're here, we're going to sit and…

FIONA: I'm going. (*She pivots and starts out the door.*)

MARGARET moves to FIONA's side amazingly quickly. She takes FIONA's arm and pulls her inside the diner. FIONA allows herself to be tugged a short distance; then she digs in her heels and folds her arms across her chest. MARGARET lets go; she tosses her coat into a booth and stands behind a chair at the communal table, leaning on it occasionally.

MARGARET: And leave us not forget we are here to lend Imogene our support.

FIONA: (*Snorts.*) Your version of support is to feed your fat face.

MARGARET: Our community has lost a respected…, well, a member. And it's the least we can do to…

FIONA: Lies will kill you faster than fried potatoes, old woman.

MARGARET: I am not lying. I never lie. (*Pause.*) But I am hungry. I wonder where she is? (*Pause.*) If you don't sit down soon, I'm going to be up all hours rubbing your feet.

FIONA: I am not sitting in here with, with that… (*Points at the urn on the table.*) …and that crazy business… (*Points at the cutouts in the booth.*)

MARGARET: What? These? (*Goes over to look at cutouts.*) Not very traditional, I grant you, but harmless nonetheless. (*Crosses back to table.*) Come on, sit with me.

FIONA refuses to budge; shakes her head, 'no'. MARGARET scans the contents of the table.

MARGARET: (*Cont'd.*) Is it the urn? On that we agree. I think it's absolutely tasteless to present an artificial burial motif when one has just buried the body in the ground. When she comes, we'll insist that Imogene move this Silas to a more appropriate locale. Like out back with the other trash.

FIONA: (*Shakes her head again.*) You can stay here all you want. I know what's in there. And I will not stay in a room with a too-soon death. An' you can't keep me here, neither. I'll wait in the car for you. Gimme the keys.

MARGARET: You're behaving like a child.

FIONA: Takes one to know one.

MARGARET: (*Pause.*) Last week, you bet me I couldn't go for seven whole days and nights without eating fried potatoes and ketchup. Made me promise, remember? Well, old friend, tonight is the seventh night of my abstention. I kept my promise to you and I won the bet. And as I recall, that entitles me to a dinner right here. I'm calling in your marker.

IMOGENE enters from the kitchen. She goes to retrieve her coat, hat and gloves.

IMOGENE: Listen, Margaret, I don't think this was such a good idea. So if you don't mind…

MARGARET: Nonsense. It's a splendid idea. And some part of you must agree since you left the door unlocked.

IMOGENE: I had my hands full.

MARGARET: We never do anything we don't intend to. There is no such thing as happenstance. You left the door open, you want us here, we're here. Now. What shall I have? (*She crosses to the counter.*)

FIONA: (*From her position at the doorway, arms crossed.*) Imogene? What about those shadow people sittin' there and that business on the table?

IMOGENE: (*Picks up her things and walks toward the door.*) Surely you can understand that I might want to be alone tonight…

MARGARET: Worst possible thing for you, being alone. (*Picks up counter menu.*) Now then. In a way this is sort of a celebration, so I'll have a steak, very rare. Fried potatoes, and champagne. (*Goes to sit at the communal table.*)

FIONA: (*Moves toward the table.*) Now that wreath and the drapings, they make sense. It's this other business that needs explaining. And she'll have a green salad and mineral water. I'll have me some of that good bean soup you made last Sunday. (*She sits next to MARGARET, folds her arms across her chest.*)

IMOGENE: (*Exasperated.*) Well, for heaven's…

The street door flings open and AGGIE TRENT enters, hollering. She is wearing paint-splattered coveralls, a 'save-the-otters' T-shirt, and cowboy boots. Her long white hair is loose and flying. A large cloth tote bag is slung from one shoulder.

AGGIE TRENT: Damned idiot son of mine forgot to put my gas can back and my auto club card's gone missing! (*She almost crashes into IMOGENE, still standing by the door.*) Honey! What are you doing?!

IMOGENE: I'm trying to leave, but…

AGGIE TRENT: Go sit, you look peaky. (*She gives IMOGENE a quick hug.*) Can I use the phone? Maybe I can convince the garage to fetch me without my card.

IMOGENE: (*Frustrated.*) I'm sorry, Aggie Trent, but the phone's out. Uncle Silas forgot to pay the bill this month.

MARGARET: True to his nature until the end.

IMOGENE stares out the window.

AGGIE TRENT: Well, that was real smart. Damn all men, anyhow. Toads, the lot of them. (*She winks at IMOGENE's back; shrugs.*) Margaret, Fiona. (*She nods in their direction.*) What d'you all suggest I do now?

MARGARET: We have decided to have dinner. It seems appropriate.

FIONA: I am not eating until it's explained to me.

AGGIE TRENT: (*Sitting down next to FIONA.*) What's explained? (*Spies the centerpiece.*) Oh, isn't that nice!

FIONA: It doesn't bother you. And… (*Waving in the direction of the booth.*) …those?

AGGIE TRENT: (*Taking it all in.*) Gosh, I dunno. Maybe it's part of some sort of funeral rite they had in the family. Looks like it might be, what, pagan? or witchcraft? I wouldn't have thought it of Silas, but then, you never know with men.

On the word 'witchcraft' FIONA is on her feet. MARGARET grabs on to her skirt.

AGGIE TRENT: (*To IMOGENE.*) Honey? You fooling around with spells and magic? You want to be careful, that stuff can be tricky. (*She sits and starts digging through her massive bag.*)

MARGARET: (*Looking up at FIONA.*) A more plausible explanation is that Imogene has created this ambiance as part of her thesis on tribal rituals. Now sit.

FIONA: No self-respecting tribe ever created a ritual like this. It's nonsense. Let go of me.

316

MARGARET doesn't.

IMOGENE: Good lord. (*She tosses her belongings in the direction of the counter and marches over to the table.*) Uncle Silas never spent a day alone in his life. That's the main reason he opened this diner, and kept it open twelve hours a day, every day, no matter what was going on out in the world. And when he started wandering, well, he always came back, usually bringing some stray with him. You remember. (*All the women remember.*) I figured his spirit was here. So I made those cutouts and put them in the booth. They're here to keep his ghost company.

FIONA: So you're staying? (*To MARGARET.*) I said, let go.

IMOGENE: I didn't say that. Now the altar...

FIONA: Is a pile of...

MARGARET: (*Quick interruption.*) Is a centerpiece, to honor your uncle. No more, no less. (*Stands to push FIONA down in her seat.*) Imogene? I think food is in order right about now.

AGGIE TRENT: Oh, that's a good idea. Anytime my old Mercedes craps out on me, I always get a hankering for pie ala mode and beer. (*To IMOGENE.*) You got any Dos Equis? (*To herself.*) I know that card's gotta be here somewhere. (*Starts digging in her overall pockets, to no avail. She removes a boot and peers inside.*) Imogene? After I soak my thirst, I'll tackle that stool for you. (*She indicates the tilting counter stool with her head.*)

IMOGENE: (*Sitting down with the others.*) Leave it. I wouldn't recognize it straight.

AGGIE TRENT turns her tote upside down on the table. MARGARET stares down her nose at the contents of that huge container. IMOGENE idly pokes at some items; a screwdriver, a battered paperback, shriveled orange, wrinkled tissues, a roll of Duct Tape. FIONA shakes herself, folds her arms across her chest, and glowers.

MARGARET: Of course, when Arthur died, I selected the appropriate decor...a few discretely placed Calla Lilies at the church, a tasteful spray of Gladiola for the reception...

IMOGENE: Right. And we all know what a saint your husband was...

FIONA: Best leave it alone.

IMOGENE: Walking off and leaving you with two small girls.

317

If it hadn't been for Fiona, you'd have…

FIONA: ou're just feelin' raw 'cause you lost your uncle. Best not say more.

MARGARET: h, I demand that she does. I'd have what?

IMOGENE's response is cut off by the strains of the autoharp being strummed outside the street door, heralding the arrival of MARYELLEN. The door opens and she pushes in. She is wearing a purple and turquoise caftan; her ample bosom is strung about with a golden Ankh, African bone jewelry, and an elaborate silver and malachite roach clip suspended on a black silk cord. She has exotic silk flowers stuffed in between her curls. She attached to the autoharp by a well-worn leather strap; on her feet are Birkenstock™ sandals. She trots right over to the communal table.

MARYELLEN: Hoo boy! Funerals do get my appetite up and running! Hungry work, grieving. Takes a body clear out of herself. I need me some serious refueling! Imogene, honey! Triple cheeseburger, side of curly fries, slaw, plenty pickles, cherry pie. (*She sits down at the table next to AGGIE TRENT.*) Margaret, good idea of yours, this, to come here after. And, hey, where'd you get off to, Fiona? What's for drinks?

AGGIE TRENT: Dos Equis for me.

FIONA: I wasn't takin' part in no farce.

MARYELLEN: Good plan. Imogene? Maybe a beer to get it all working? (*She settles herself and her autoharp more comfortably. To FIONA.*) Which farce would that be?

FIONA: Huh. You all standing around a hole in the ground and then pretending the man's right here. (*She nods toward the urn.*)

MARGARET: We've settled that, Fiona. (*She turns to face IMOGENE.*) I'd like Imogene to finish what she started to say about Arthur. At least I had the decency to acknowledge a man's death in a dignified manner.

IMOGENE stands abruptly. She pulls the clothes pins out of her hair with a frustrated jerk, and paces up and down, muttering to herself. There is a long pause before AGGIE TRENT speaks.

AGGIE TRENT: You think you could drive me home later, Maryellen? Damn Merc's dry, lost my triple A card, and the diner's phone is out.

MARYELLEN: Sure can, after I fill up. Where'd you put my pickup, anyway?

AGGIE TRENT: In the alley behind the shop. Say, I like your new window display…all those pink and green dishes. Reminds me of my younger days. Where'd you get 'em?

IMOGENE: Would you all please go away now?

She is ignored.

MARYELLEN: Old lady Witson croaked last week. Got her whole estate for a song. (*She strums a trill.*)

MARGARET: Oh, now there's a fitting tribute to the deceased. One I'm sure Imogene would approve of.

AGGIE TRENT: (*Passes MARGARET's remark by.*) Anyway, the generator's fixed, but you're going to need a new set of plugs. I'm going to town tomorrow, I could pick 'em up.

IMOGENE: (*Sits at the counter, and changes the subject.*) I've decided I'm going to write an article about you, Aggie Trent.

AGGIE TRENT: About me? Whatever for?

IMOGENE: It'll be a great human interest story. (*Sketches out the headline in the air.*) Reclusive artist, dot dot dot, small-town miracle worker.

AGGIE TRENT: What?!

MARYELLEN: Yeah! Like, 'the residents of our fair village know that if they break something, their lady of the screwdriver will fix it'! (*Strums a chord for emphasis.*)

IMOGENE: Nothing here stays broken for long…

MARGARET: …be it a toaster, or a tractor…

FIONA: …or a broken-hearted love song.

AGGIE TRENT: Now, wait a minute. All I ever… I mean…I just…

MARYELLEN: You just always gotta do something when things go wrong. You know you do, Aggie Trent. Know you do. Sounds like a song title, dfoesn't it? (*Fiddles with a chord or two.*)

IMOGENE: Besides, my Comp Lit professor said he'd let me skip the final if I could get it published. I think the *Record* would take it, don't you?

MARGARET: Why don't you try for one of the more authentic newspapers?

AGGIE TRENT: Well, I don't know…

MARYELLEN: He's cute, this prof, huh.

IMOGENE: (*She fusses with some counter silverware.*) Never mind.

FIONA: It's important to know why you're doing a thing… don't matter what anybody else knows.

MARYELLEN: Silas sure as hell didn't know what he was doing last Sunday, did he? (*She nods at Silas' urn.*)

AGGIE TRENT: Wait a minute. I want, I mean, I don't want. Imogene, about this article…?

MARGARET: I never heard the truth of how he died. Just gossip. What exactly happened?

IMOGENE: (*To AGGIE TRENT.*) I wouldn't dream of writing anything about you without showing it to you first. I just thought it might be a good idea. Sort of help, you know?

AGGIE TRENT: Oh. Well. Sure. Why don't you come over next week and we'll talk about it?

MARGARET: (*She gets up, crosses to the counter, takes some napkins from a holder, blows her nose, and returns to the table while talking.*) I remember when my father died. I looked at him in his coffin— a very barbaric and undignified custom, staring at a painted corpse—and wondered what it felt like. Death. Have any of you ever considered…?

AGGIE TRENT: I think we sail on the wind and live in the trees. After our bodies die.

MARYELLEN: Damn fool shot hisself. (*She strums a few cheerful chords.*)

IMOGENE crosses to the street door, locks it, removes the wreath, and pulls down the shade. Then she sits at the booth with the cutouts.

FIONA: Watch your words. (*Gets up, goes behind the counter, and pours herself a glass of water at the sink. She stays and drinks it.*)

MARGARET: I heard one of the other hunters shot him by mistake.

MARYELLEN: Damn fool got hisself shot, then. Six of one…

IMOGENE: Shut up, MaryEllen. (*Puts her hat back on; face in hands.*)

MARYELLEN: Oh, honey, I'm so sorry. I didn't mean any disrespect. But you gotta look at it. Silas had never been hunting

320

in his life. He always said he hated guns. So what he does he do, but go off with that good old bunch from the rifle club and get himself killed. I call that a damn fool thing to do.

IMOGENE: He didn't shoot himself. Or get shot. No shooting. *(Looks up; big sigh.)* Aggie Trent, tell it to me again. Loud.

AGGIE TRENT: *(Pause.)* Well. According to Sheriff Furst, he fetched up under the ferry cables round about three a m. Just wearing his old jeans. *(Pause.)* With the fly open. *(Pause.)* One tennis shoe on. *(Pause.)* No socks. *(Pause.)* Coroner figured he was drunk, wandering around on the fishing pier. Took a piss off the edge and fell in.

MARYELLEN: That don't seem right, somehow. I always figured he'd get hisself shot. In the end.

AGGIE TRENT: Apparently the BA content in his blood... *(On IMOGENE's quizzical look.)* ...blood alcohol. Was the highest she'd ever seen...

MARGARET: Silas drunk?

FIONA: How 'bout that obit? Silas Horner, pillar of the community, blah blah blah. Pillar. Huh! I could offer a few home truths about his pillar...

MARGARET clamps a hand over FIONA's mouth. IMOGENE doesn't register. She's lost in her own thoughts.

IMOGENE: I can't get my mind around any of this. I feel like I've gone deaf. I see you all moving your mouths—but where are your words? *(Looks around.)* What are we doing here? *(Looks at the urn.)* What was Silas doing on a fishing pier? He hated fishing. *(Pause.)* I better open up. Silas'll have a stroke if...if... Oh, hell. *(Gets up and exits USL door.)*

AGGIE TRENT: One of us had better stay with her. I don't like the idea of her being alone, not like this.

MARGARET: She's fading in and out. It's not like Imogene to be disoriented. Do you think we should consult someone?

MARYELLEN: No. I read this article about that said you don't want to encourage dependency. I know, let's take up a collection...send her to Athens for a week.

MARGARET: And which literary tract was it this week... Home Shopping News? The Executioner?

MARYELLEN: I'll have you know, Maggie…

AGGIE TRENT: Why Athens?

MARYELLEN: All those ruins. Don't they strike you as soothing?

FIONA: Let's go down to the beach.

MARGARET: There's a storm coming. (*To MARYELLEN.*) And don't call me that, either.

FIONA: The thing of it is, a man is dead before his time, and I for one won't believe he knew it was coming.

AGGIE TRENT: Oh, I'm sure he didn't. Just last month we put down our annual bet on this year's salmon run.

IMOGENE returns.

IMOGENE: You two were always betting on something or other.

MARYELLEN: 'Member that one they had about the Beatles? Silas bet Paul wrote "While My Guitar Gently Weeps," and Aggie Trent here said, no, it was George. Silas said, Paul. Aggie Trent, said, George. Went on for days.

IMOGENE gathers up her belongings, heads for the front door.

IMOGENE: Uncle Silas was furious when he found out you were right, A.T.. He burned donuts for a week after. Now if you'd all kindly leave? (*Unlocks door; holds it open.*)

FIONA: Margaret and I bet on things, on occasion.

AGGIE TRENT: Really? I somehow don't imagine you as a betting kind of woman, Margaret.

MARGARET: I find it adds a certain air of, umm, piquancy, to one's passing days.

FIONA: (*She starts back toward the table.*) Translated, that means, when she's bored, she bets.

MARGARET: Oh, not necessarily. I'm not bored now.

MARYELLEN: Well, lay one out here, Fiona. Let's see if it gets picked up.

FIONA: All right. Margaret? I'll wager that you're gonna have to bury me.

MARYELLEN: Whoa! Big one. (*Strums a chord for emphasis.*)

AGGIE TRENT: It's a joke, right?

FIONA: No, it's no joke. I've just bet Margaret that she'll outlive me. The question is, will she take me up on it?

MARGARET: You know the answer to that one, old woman.

FIONA goes back to lean against the counter, locked in silence.

After a long pause, IMOGENE puts her things down on the counter.

IMOGENE: You're not going away, are you. (*The women look at her, surprised.*) Okay, I give. I don't know how much food's in the pantry, but I'll do my best. (*She puts on an apron, picks up an order pad, and approaches the table. Writes down the orders.*) So it's salad for Margaret, soup for Fiona, pie for Aggie Trent, and everything else for Maryellen. Right?

MARYELLEN: After what Fiona just said, you can double my order.

AGGIE TRENT: And bring me three beers.

IMOGENE: I'm never surprised at anything Fiona says, or Margaret says, or you say, Aggie Trent, or you, MaryEllen. But I don't think I can hear any more just now. Burying Silas was enough. You all sort it out. I'll go get the food. (*She exits into the kitchen.*)

MARYELLEN: She didn't bury him. He's right here. (*Indicates the urn.*)

FIONA: God's teeth, the man isn't here. This here... (*She reaches for the urn.*) ...is a sick joke! (*She is about to up-end the urn when MARYELLEN quickly stops her.*)

MARYELLEN: You're gonna get one hell of a surprise if you do that!

MARGARET: Do you mean to tell us...

MARYELLEN: Yup. She buried an empty box and brought dear old Silas home.

FIONA: No, she didn't. You thought she had him fried, but...

MARGARET: Fried? You think 'fried' is an appropriate word at this precise moment?!

FIONA: Absolutely. (*Shakes out the urn; nothing comes out.*) What I want to know is, where's Silas?

MARYELLEN: Jesus Fucking Christ.

MARGARET: Saints Preserve Us.

AGGIE TRENT: Holy shit.

FIONA: And sing hosannah to the four directions. Doesn't tell us where he is.

MARYELLEN: (*Peering into the empty urn.*) How in hell did this happen?

FIONA: You asked me where I was at the funeral. (*MARYEL-LEN nods.*) I got bored so I went went for a walk. Ended up back of the crematorium. Saw that guy, what's his name…

MARGARET: The name of the guy hardly matters.

AGGIE TRENT: That'd be Hannah's boy Ernie, he helps out with the burials for extra money. (*On MARGARET's withering glance.*) Well, he does.

MARYELLEN: Never mind! What happened!!

FIONA: Well, old Ernie's carrying an urn under his arm, this urn. And he shakes dust and leaves out of it. And he wipes it clean with his shirt tail and he hands it, like it's got Silas in it, to your boy. .

AGGIE TRENT: Well! Surely Rex Jr. would have…(*The women know he wouldn't have.*) Oh, my god. We have to tell her!

IMOGENE enters from the kitchen, carrying a tray loaded with flatware, a full water pitcher, glasses.

IMOGENE: Tell me what?

FIONA: (*Holding urn upside down.*) Your uncle's gone walkabout.

IMOGENE stares at FIONA holding the empty urn for just a second before she crumples to the floor.

BLACKOUT.

Scene 3

LIGHTS UP: The women are sitting on the floor, cradeling IMOGENE, waiting for her to come around. FIONA holds IMOGENE's head in her lap; AGGIE TRENT gently unwraps her bandaged foot and strokes both feet; MARGARET has hold of a hand. MARYELLEN sits a bit apart, strumming her autoharp. IMOGENE opens her eyes.

IMOGENE: How long will it take 'till I can't feel this rock in my chest? (*Pause.*) It's cold down here.

FIONA: It takes as long as it takes.

AGGIE TRENT: You just stay quiet a while longer. (*Continues unbandaging IMOGENE's foot.*)

IMOGENE: Is there a song for this kind of thing?

324

MARYELLEN: Oh, probably. (*She mulls, then offers.*) Row, row, row your boat/Gently down the stream/Merrily, merrily, merrily, merrily/Life is but a dream."

IMOGENE joins in for a round, then switches to singing a chorus in French.

IMOGENE: I feel unsettled.

MARYELLEN: You look it, too. Sort of emotionally uncoordinated, if you get my meaning.

IMOGENE: I should be crying. He was my uncle, for god's sakes. (*Pause.*) And he's missing. (*Pause.*) But I can't. (*Pause.*) Why aren't we all crying? Washing away? Aren't we supposed to cry when someone we know dies?

FIONA: He hated tears. "Gravestones cheer the living dear, they're no use to the dead."

MARYELLEN: Nitty Gritty Dirt Band.

AGGIE TRENT: I don't know why I should be crying. He thought I was crazy.

MARGARET: There was a time when he didn't. And even if he did, you didn't care.

MARYELLEN: Look who's talking. The whole town gets up in arms—does she care? Nah.

MARGARET: And where were you the summer of fifty-six?

IMOGENE: What are you all talking, or not talking, about?

FIONA: We're not talking. We're silly women making silly noises. (*Her glare at the other two is fierce.*)

MARYELLEN: My belly's making noises. (*Pause.*) I don't suppose there's any chance…(*A long silence.*) No, no chance. (*She strums a minor chord.*)

IMOGENE: (*Sitting up.*) Well, I'm not crying. I suppose I should be crying because I don't know where he is. But mainly I'm not crying because last year I got pregnant and had an abortion and it was his. Silas' baby. (*Pause.*) And I haven't figured out what any of that means to me. Yet. (*Pause.*)I just know that now I can leave.

MARGARET: That's incest. (Pause.) Isn't it?

FIONA: Last spring, when you talked about staying put?

IMOGENE nods.

325

AGGIE TRENT: Oh, honey, I'm so sorry.

MARYELLEN: (*Spits it out.*) The summer of fifty-six Silas and I were shacked up on the Snohomish River.

IMOGENE: What?!!

AGGIE TRENT: (*Whispers it.*) He said I was crazy as an un-caught butterfly, that time, on Craggs Peak.

IMOGENE: Wait a minute.

MARGARET: Can I help it if we live in a backwater, unen-lightened village that can't see beyond its collective prejudicial nose? Noses?

IMOGENE: WHAT??!! (*To FIONA.*) All of you??!!

FIONA: (*Offering a Cheshire Cat grin.*) Quite the charmer, your uncle.

An ELDERLY MAN walks into the diner. He is wearing an impecable three-piece suit, spats and brogues on his feet, a splendid fedora on his head, and holds a dog leash complete with studded collar but no dog.

ELDERLY MAN: Well now. (*He doffs his hat to each.*) Imogene, Miz Trent, Mrs. May, I see Harold's looking pinker these days. Mrs. Thurston. Miz Crowfeather. (*Pause.*) Very nice funeral, Imogene. Quite suitable. (*The women stare at him while he rambles on.*) I think Silas would have been especially pleased with that site. Overlooking the town, and all. He was such a community spirited man. Always involved in…everything. (*MARYELLEN has trouble keeping a straight face.*) I hope my little remarks were helpful in your time of bereavement, my dear. After all, it's not everyone who knew how much your Uncle Silas was, at the end of the day, just one of the boys. Nothing extra special. Oh, not to say that he wasn't special, I mean. Well, you know. One of the boys. All that. (*IMOGENE's face is twitching now.*) As a matter of fact, I can remember a time when we all, the fellows in town that is, called Silas the man who not only would, but could! (*AGGIE TRENT and MARGARET have to look away.*) Well, girls. I'll leave you to your… Such a glorious night, isn't it? (*Thunder is heard O.S.*) Good night, then, good night. And, Imogene, don't hesitate to call on me if I can be of service. Anything. Anything at all.   (*He jerks on the leash.*) Come along, Alfie. Time for din dins.

326

The ELDERLY MAN and his INVISIBLE DOG leave. The women fall into rhapsodic laughter. FIONA stands up and howls at the ceiling. A crack of lightning is heard O.S.

FIONA: MaryEllen! Strike up the band! I feel like dancing!

FIONA grabs up MARGARET and the two cousins sashay around the diner to MARYELLEN's improvised waltz tune.

IMOGENE and AGGIE TRENT, still on the floor, sway to the music and watch.

IMOGENE: I've always wondered about those two.

AGGIE TRENT: They're not lesbians, if that's what you mean.

IMOGENE: No, no I don't. Anyway, I don't care if they are. That's not what I mean. No, what they have, it's something else. Something... better. (*Pause.*) They've lived together all those years... how many?

AGGIE TRENT: Oh, must be over twenty by now.

IMOGENE: Yeah. All those years. But the rule is, women get weird living alone like they do. You know that rule? (*AGGIE TRENT knows that rule.*) And yet they seem so... is content the right word? (*Pause.*) Maybe they're on to something good for women. You know? Like... Just drop the sex out of it. And be... Alive. I don't know. (*She starts rebandaging her foot.*)

AGGIE TRENT: I wish you wouldn't... (*Sees IMOGENE is determined; lets it go.*) Honey, shouldn't we be talking about things?

MARYELLEN hands the autoharp to IMOGENE.

AGGIE TRENT: (*Cont'd.*) I mean, didn't we all just confess to something kind of huge? And then there's the matter of Silas...

MARYELLEN pulls AGGIE TRENT to her feet.

MARYELLEN: Hugher than huge, Scarlett. Come dance with me. We'll talk about it tomorrow.

IMOGENE finds three chords she can strum and repeats them in a sort of jig. AGGIE TRENT and MARYELLEN dance over by FIONA and MARGARET. After a while, the four change partners. IMOGENE changes the tune and sings.

IMOGENE: "Row, row, row your boat/Gently down the stream/Merrily, merrily, merrily, merrily/Life is but a dream."

CURTAIN.

Mirrors

© 2002

Characters

YOUNG LAURA: An eight-year old version of LAURA CARMODY.

LAURA CARMODY: 48, strong-willed, solitary traveler, not a finisher.

CHARLEY CARMODY: Youthful 65, charmer, published (never-quite-really famous) poet. Can be mean when crossed.

KATE DEVLIN: First a painter, second a mother, lastly a wife. 50, one crippled leg.

OLIVER DEVLIN: Disappointed poet, 50. Fearful; a wanderer.

DULCINEA JONES: 33, pregnant and proud of it. Bossy, greedy, extremely self-involved.

Time: The present, afternoon.

Setting
The set is divided into two spaces—the living room, which takes up the major portion of the set, and an artist's studio—of a large, weathered Victorian house. The ceiling of the studio is a slanted sky-light. In the studio are huge canvasses, one of which is propped against the back wall. Some of the canvasses are blank; stretched and waiting. A few are finished works. The one against the wall is a work-becoming; one-quarter covered by bold, slashing colors that symbolically reach out beyond their rectangular borders. On the wall beside this canvas is a painted child's hand. Also in the studio is a paint-splattered wooden table, large cans of paint, a coffee can filled with brushes, one with turps, stained rags, and potted flowers in a myriad

328

of life stages. The wooden floor is also paint-splattered. The living room is filled with comfortable, well-worn furniture: a small couch and a rocker/recliner, overflowing bookcases, a steamer trunk for a coffee table, an old brass floor lamp with a fringed shade, and a wooden table with one attendant ladder-back chair. The table holds a telephone, computer and printer, its wires trailing across the floor to an UC plug. The table is mounded by papers, text books, notebooks. Battered carboard file boxes compete for leg space underneath the table. There is also, scattered about, a badly painted high-chair, a dusty exercise bicycle, a sad rubber tree plant, a forgotten hobby horse, and numerous pairs of shoes and boots for all sorts of occasions, in varying stages of wear, in three distinct sizes—men's, women's, child's. The floor is haphazardly covered by rumpled, patterned rugs. Smack in the center of the living room is a metal bucket; a steady drip of water from the ceiling lands in the bucket with watery regularity. Along the back wall of the living room are a series of framed photographs arranged around an old, large, oval wooden frame containing a mirror made of dimpled, beaten metal. There is a movable screen between the two "rooms," a door RC to the outside, and a door UC to the inner reaches of the house. The living room has an air of having been 'left' years ago; now it is just passed through. It is the studio that holds the tendrils of a work-in-progress life.

Author's Note: If stage space is restricted, much can be painted on backdrop, but several essential items need to be retained on stage, as follows. The lemon tree. The screen dividing the spaces. In the studio, the canvasses, paint supplies, potted flowers. In the living room, the computer table, boots, metal bucket, metal mirror, sofa, recliner, rubber tree plant, trunk, and rugs.

Properties

Lemon Tree and lemons
Basket (for lemons)
Two buckets
Stacked paintings, canvasses, brushes, paints, etc.
Pipe (OLIVER's)
Pitcher of lemonade
Two plastic glasses
Wooden-headed mallet
Red file folder

Various file folders
Telephone
Backpack, shower bag (LAURA's)
File and book boxes
Green towel
Soggy blue towels
Locket on a chain
For Sale signs on stakes
Paring knife
Three juice glasses
Folded piece of paper

Clothing
YOUNG LAURA's pj's, summer dress, overalls & T-shirt, man's
 overcoat, older-girl's dress
KATE's long-skirted cotton dress, lacy shawl
LAURA's shorts, halter-top, boots, sun visor
OLIVER's jeans, plaid shirt, old slippers
CHARLIE's Abercrombie & Fitch fatigues, safari hat
DULCINEA's turquoise ensemble

SFX:
Telephone RINGS
Doorbell RINGS
Assorted thumps and bumps

 Scene 1
*BRIGHT SPOT ON lemon tree at APRON, remainder of stage in dark-
ness. KATE sits beneath tree, sorting lemons into a basket. She is wearing
a long-skirted cotton dress with a lacy shawl draped over her shoulders. Her
long black hair all but covers her face. She is completely absorbed by her
task and hums lightly. LAURA appears from AUDIENCE and stands for
a moment, watching. She's wearing shorts, boots, a halter-top, and a sun
visor atop her curls, which are dyed rainbow colors. She shifts impatiently
from foot to foot.*
LAURA: Hello.
KATE: (*Looking up.*) Hmmmmm?

LAURA: Do you live here?

KATE: What?

LAURA: Do you live here?

KATE: (*Considering the question.*) I suppose you could call it that. (*Goes back to sorting lemons.*)

LAURA: This is your house?

KATE: Wouldn't it be wonderful? To live in a life. Not just in a house. (*Looking up.*) Sit down, won't you?

LAURA: No, thanks. I've been sitting too long. (*KATE sorts through windfalls; LAURA watches.*) How come you don't take the ones off the tree?

KATE: (*Pause.*) Do you know the secret of making lemonade?

LAURA: I'm not sure…?

KATE: I think there's something very important about getting lemonade just right. Last year I tried making it with medium ripe lemons. But that was sort of flat. Those up there…(*Indicates lemons still on the tree.*)…are too tart. So this year I'm trying the old ones. To see if it's true. Age improves a thing.

LAURA laughs, relaxing a bit.

KATE: (*Cont'd.*) Didn't I see you down at the market last weekend?

LAURA: Do you remember everyone you see?

KATE: No. (*Pause.*) Are you new in town? Or just passing us by on your way to somewhere interesting?

LAURA: I used to live around here.

KATE: You got out and now you're back?

LAURA: Maybe.

KATE: Are you some kind of crazy woman? Should I get nervous? (*She looks anything but.*) Call someone? Get a fire extinguisher for your head?

LAURA: (*Laughing. Stroking her hair.*) It's a road thing, I guess. Something like talking out loud to myself. Or maybe it's something I did to challenge my world, or fill up empty nights.

KATE: I like that. Challenge your world. I wouldn't know how to begin challenging my world.

LAURA: Making perfect lemonade from ancient lemons might just do it. (Shared laughter.) (*Pause.*) I noticed the vacant lot next

331

to your house is…vacant. (*KATE nods.*) Well, I was wondering if I could park there. For a while. Just until things sort of… shake down.

KATE: Here?

LAURA: Yeah.

KATE: Nobody ever wants to stay here.

LAURA: You're here.

KATE: That's debatable.

LAURA: I won't be any trouble. I'll even stay out of sight, if you want.

KATE: No one comes to this house voluntarily. Not even Fred's friends. I think one of Charley's students got drunk for love of a dead poet or some stupid thing and had to sleep it off…but otherwise…

LAURA: I could do some gardening. House repairs.

KATE: What about showers…a toilet…

LAURA: I grab plumbing wherever and whenever it's offered.

KATE: Where was your last shower?

LAURA: Wyoming.

KATE: And before that?

LAURA: Kentucky.

KATE: Time for another one, then?

LAURA: Something like that.

KATE: What's next, after you're here awhile, showering?

LAURA: Maybe Taos. Someday.

KATE: Is it really Willy Nelson songs, and dinners out of cans, and meeting dangerous strangers? Finding out of the way places you want to die in?

LAURA: Sometimes. And other times it's fixing flat tires, or pipes, or figuring out how to get dollars for gas and food. Just like living in a house. Only you're in motion.

KATE: And now you want to stop. For a time. (Pause.) Well, I guess we could try it.

LAURA: Okay. Thanks.

KATE: Like I said, no one wants to come here. So don't thank me yet.

KATE starts to rise; she has trouble. LAURA automatically offers a hand

332

up; KATE shrugs it off. LAURA stands back and watches as KATE struggles upright. She settles the lemon basket over one arm and extends her right hand.

KATE: I'm Kate.

LAURA; (*Shaking KATE's hand.*) Laura.

KATE: Come on then, Laura. I'll show you where things are.

The women exit to BACKSTAGE. KATE's dragging leg makes her lurch slightly rather than walk.

BLACKOUT

Scene 2: Interior house.

LIGHTS UP: The house is empty; a water drip hits the bucket loudly, surely. The RC door pushes open. KATE enters first, walks in a few steps, looks to the bucket, and halts.

KATE: Damn!

KATE drops the basket of lemons on the floor, does an about-face and exits through UC door, leaving LAURA at the threshold. After a beat, LAURA steps inside. She stands in the doorway, taking it all in. Her eyes find the metal mirror on the wall and hang on it. The same with the old hobby horse. She is drawn to move, to examine this. She steps around the bucket with an eyebrow raised. She crosses to peek behind the screen, into the studio space. She moves around in there as though she is somehow acquainted with it; it is both familiar and unfamiliar to her. Her eyes catch the painted hand on the wall. She crosses to it, and places her hand over the child's. LAURA freezes. LIGHTS DIM. ROSE SPOT on YOUNG LAURA, wearing pj's, as she skips in through the RC door, skips around in a large circle in the living room, skips into the studio. There, she skips in smaller and smaller circles until she falls in on herself. She picks up three objects and tries to juggle them. It doesn't work. Not upset, she shrugs off her failure. Then she mimes loading a brush with paint and, standing next to LAURA, paints an imagined outline of her hand on the wall. Finished, she drops the invisible brush in a paint can, and skips in reverse circles out of the studio, the living room, the house. All of this at a fairly quick tempo. LIGHTS UP, KILL SPOT. The door bell rings. Repeatedly. Angrily. A series of thumps is heard. Then silence. LAURA unfreezes. She rubs her hand against her leg. Her attention is then caught by the stacked paintings. She crouches down to see them better and becomes absorbed by their power. She doesn't hear OLIVER shuffling into the living room. OLIVER (jeans, plaid shirt with holes, old slippers, a pipe dangling from his mouth) enters the living room from the UC door, carrying a pitcher of lemonade and clutching two plastic glasses under one arm. He goes over to the table, sits, and becomes engrossed in something on the computer screen. LAURA strolls back into the living room. The two surprise each other.

LAURA: Help!

OLIVER: Help!

LAURA: (*Extending her hand.*) Hi. I'm Laura. Sorry I startled you.

OLIVER: (*Rising.*) I'm Oliver. I live here. (*Pause.*) Where'd you come from?

LAURA: I met Kate earlier.

OLIVER: Are you from the school? Is it about Fred?

LAURA: No.

OLIVER; Oh, good. (*Awkward pause.*) Well. Would you like some lemonade?

OLIVER bustles getting lemonade. Gets the pitcher as far as the steamer trunk and leaves it there.

OLIVER: (*Cont'd.*) I'm sure Kate's around somewhere…you say you saw her…?

LAURA: Picking lemons.

OLIVER: Oh. Good.

We HEAR thumping and muffled swearing coming from overhead, in the attic. LAURA looks up; OLIVER ignores it. Another awkward pause. Then OLIVER wanders back to his computer, leaving LAURA to her own devices. She shrugs, and is heading toward the UC door when KATE enters from the RC door, carrying a metal bucket. She pushes the almost-full bucket over and puts this new one down under the drip.

KATE: (*To LAURA.*) There's clean towels in the upstairs closet.

OLIVER: I don't need a clean towel.

KATE: Laura's going to camp on the lot.

OLIVER: Kate? (*Looks up from computer screen; to LAURA*). Camp? Camp how? In a tent? Or do you have one of those RV things? I don't want any RV parked out… no, it's not… no…

LAURA: I have a van. '83 Dodge. Converted.

OLIVER: A van. Well, that's not quite so big.

LAURA: Dark green. It'll blend right into the landscape. You won't even see it. Or me.

OLIVER: What do you do?

KATE: Oliver…

LAURA: I've been on the road, living in the van, for about five years now.

OLIVER: Really. On the road. Living in a van. Hear that, Kate?

KATE: I'm still here, Oliver.

OLIVER: Remember the hippies roaming all over the place. And Dead Heads…everybody in tie-dye T-shirts and VW vans with purple flowers painted on the sides… But only students or drop outs live like that nowadays. (*Pause.*) So which are you?

KATE: Oliver…

OLIVER: Maybe you're a psychologist on a mission. Or a spy. A sleuth? A photo-journalist on assignment? (*Hoping.*) A writer?

LAURA: No.

OLIVER: An antiques dealer? Communist? Schizophrenic? A terrorist? Anthropologist? What do you do about an address? How do people find you?

KATE: Oliver. Laura needs a shower.

LAURA: (*To OLIVER.*) My zip code is wherever I happen to be.

OLIVER: And you want to be here? Why? For how long?

KATE: Until she goes. (*To LAURA.*) You can have the blue towels.

OLIVER: (*To KATE.*) No. No, she can't have the blue towels.

KATE: Why ever not?

OLIVER: Because they're for guests.

KATE: Laura's a guest. The first we've had since umptee-ump years ago. Remember guests? Here's one. Laura. And she's using the blue towels.

OLIVER: She can't.

LAURA: (*To OLIVER.*) Uh, Mr., ummm…

OLIVER: (*To LAURA.*) Oliver.

LAURA: Mr. Oliver Oliver?

KATE: (*To OLIVER.*) And why can't she use the blue towels?

OLIVER: (*To LAURA.*) Oliver.

KATE: (*To LAURA.*) As in Kate and Oliver Devlin.

LAURA: (*TO OLIVER.*) Mr. Devlin.

OLIVER: Oliver. (*Pause. To KATE.*) Because I used them to plug up a hole in the roof. Last winter.

KATE: Then she will use the green ones.

OLIVER: Those're mine.

LAURA: Oliver. I get the feeling you don't really want me here.

OLIVER: No, no, it's just that I'd…I'd like to know more about you bef…

LAURA: That's okay. I'm suddenly thinking this wasn't such a good idea after all.

OLIVER: What wasn't such a good…

CHARLEY tromps in from the UC door, carrying a large wooden-headed mallet. He is decked out in Abercrombie & Fitch fatigues, complete with safari hat.

CHARLEY: Don't you people ever answer your front door? I had to climb that rotting trellis out back… Oliver, I thought you were gonna fix that son of a bitch last spring. And, listen up, that attic's a swamp. Hole in the roof bigger than two of my feet. You two wanna keep any of that junk up there, you'd better…(*He spies LAURA.*) Well. Things have improved in my absence, I see. (*He approaches her.*) If you're gonna be part of this crazy household, gorgeous, I may just have to come around every week so's I can see lots more of you.

CHARLEY winks at LAURA and extends his hand for a shake. LAURA doesn't move. She stares at CHARLEY as though she's seen a ghost and she's not sure what to do about it. The telephone RINGS and is, naturally, ignored.

LAURA: Kate? Thanks, but I'm gonna head out.

KATE: Have your shower first.

KATE takes LAURA's arm and starts to lead her to the UC door. LAURA resists gently.

CHARLEY: (*To LAURA.*) I'll bet you clean up real nice.

LAURA stops in her tracks; is about to retort. The phone keeps on RINGING. OLIVER scurries over to the table and retrieves a red file folder, waves it at CHARLEY.

OLIVER: Mr. C? Charley? This is the start of my epic poem…

remember I told you… well, I was sort of hoping you'd look at it… give me notes… it's just a… I know it's just a feeble beginning, but maybe…

CHARLEY: (*Shouts.*) Answer the damn phone!!

KATE: If it's anybody we want, they'll call back.

The phone stops RINGING. KATE and OLIVER watch it; CHARLEY leers at LAURA; LAURA crosses her arms over her chest. The phone starts RINGING again.

OLIVER: (*To KATE.*) Your turn.

KATE finally makes a move for the phone, taking LAURA with her.

KATE: (*Into phone.*) Yes? Oh, hello, darling. When're you coming home? No, I don't think…what? But you've been at Miranda's for a week now. Come on home. I know, but maybe we could do something together, for a change. Well, of course he's here. Fred? Fred, don't hang up. Damn. (*She replaces the receiver. To OLIVER.*) Empty the bucket.

OLIVER: You empty the bucket.

CHARLEY: I'll empty the goddamn bucket!

CHARLEY leaves his mallet, takes up the full bucket and departs via the UC door. OLIVER gathers up his file and hurriedly follows CHARLEY.

OLIVER: (*Flipping through the red file as he runs after CHARLEY.*) See? Here in the first line, I just love this first line… (*OLIVER exits UC door.*)

LAURA: (*Hurriedly.*) Kate, I've got to… take a walk. I'll be back later.

LAURA gently extricates herself from KATE and exits the RC door. KATE contemplates the fact that she is alone in the living room. She starts to go into the studio, reconsiders. Rather quickly she exits through the UC door.

LIGHTS DIM

Scene 3

ROSE SPOT follows YOUNG LAURA onto stage from the RC door. Still in pj's, she walks slowly and mimes holding someone's hand, swinging it gently. She sits on the floor of the living room and has a conversation with her imaginary friend.

YOUNG LAURA: Jane, Jane, plain old Jane, couldn't get

through the window pane. So she's stuck in the middle of the main. Street. I think. Or stores. Floors. Pours. Doors. Some-mores. Oooh, some-mores, Jane. I want some-mores! Let's go ask Mama to make some-mores. (She doesn't get up; chanting faster now.) But we can't ask Mama, can we? 'Cause she's sick. Again. And again. An' again, an' again, an' again, an' again, an' again, an' again, an' again, an' again. And daddy's no good for some-mores. He doesn't even know what's in 'em. Listen. (She listens intently.) That was the door. And that's the car. And that's daddy going. Away. And going. An' going, an' going, an' going, an' going, an' going, an' going, an' going, an' going. She jumps up; does rapid jumping jacks in place, alternating "an' going" and "an' again" on each jump until she's breath-less. (*Then she hears another sound, grabs her imaginary Jane by the hand and runs to the UC door. Calling.*) Wait for me!!!
BLACKOUT.

Scene 4

LIGHTS UP. LAURA enters from the RC door. She is sweaty, agitated, has a back pack slung across one shoulder. She flings her backpack down on the Lazy-Boy, takes a shower bag out of it, and starts for the UC door. Her attention is drawn to the mirror. As though entranced, LAURA drops her shower bag, removes the mirror from the wall and carries it into the studio. There she takes it directly to the wall with the painted hand. She strokes the wall, searching for a nail. Finding one, she hangs the mirror. She stares into it, long and hard. Then, with a sigh, she sits on the floor and angles herself around to be parallel to the RC wall. She stretches out full length as if reclining on a single bed. LAURA freezes.

LIGHTS DIM. ROSE SPOT on YOUNG LAURA, wearing a summer dress. She creeps barefoot into the living room from RC, darting glances over her shoulders, listening. Satisfied, she hauls the hobby horse into the studio and up to the wall and positions it underneath the mirror, humming. She climbs up on the hobby horse, balancing herself carefully. She sticks her face close to the mirror, she pats the reflected image, pats her face, strokes the mirror self, searching for something. She doesn't find it. She hops down, picks up the same three objects from earlier, as if to juggle, then drops them. Dejectedly, she exits RC door.

LIGHTS UP, KILL SPOT. As LAURA unfreezes, KATE enters the living room from the UC door. She crosses to the rubber tree plant, trips on the computer chords, and slides on one of the rugs. LAURA starts to get up, to join KATE, when she hears OLIVER also entering the living room from UC. OLIVER, red file under one arm, passes KATE by on his way to the table and his computer. LAURA stays where she is and eavesdrops.

KATE: (*Righting herself.*) Where were you last night?

OLIVER: (*Rummages through boxes under table.*) Poetry reading in town.

KATE: All night?

OLIVER: Film festival. Warhol.

KATE: Pick one. Poetry or Warhol.

OLIVER: Does it really matter?

KATE: (*Picks up some litter, puts it down in new piles. Strokes the rubber tree plant.*) Poor baby, you're all worn out. Just like us, and this house. No wonder Fred keeps leaving. This isn't any place to grow up. Oliver. (*Pause. Louder.*) Oliver!

OLIVER: It was Warhol. The twelve-hour, black-and-white toilet film. Camera watching a toilet for twelve silent hours until Warhol's hand enters the frame and flushes the thing. Satisfied?

KATE crawls under the table with OLIVER. She holds onto his shoulders, talks close to his face.

KATE: Oliver. Let's blow this whaddya call it.

OLIVER: Pop Stand.

KATE: That, too.

OLIVER: Kate, I haven't the energy for this today.

KATE: No, no. This is important, Oliver. We have to get out.

OLIVER: Charley's here and he's going to read my epic poem. At last. I can't go any where.

KATE: Forget the damn epic. Forget the house. Forget all of it. Let's go somewhere fresh. Where I'll be able to paint again, and Fred will stay home. And you… you'll write something new and sparkling, not that dried up old epic you've been hauling around since the dawn of time… Come on, Ollie.

OLIVER: You know we don't… This is crazy talk. We don't have enough saved. We can't just… Go.

KATE: Sure we can! We can borrow the damn money.

339

OLIVER: Who from? From whom?

KATE: I don't know. Sell stuff. Something. ANYthing!

Thumps and muffled swearing come from behind the side walls. The sounds are ignored.

OLIVER: But I'm comfortable here. I feel safe. Safe enough even, that maybe, maybe I can rewrite my epic. Bring it to life again.

KATE: (*Angry.*) If you feel so damned safe, why are you always wandering off?

OLIVER: Because I can come home.

OLIVER finds the files he was looking for and crawls out from under the table. KATE stays underneath. CHARLEY enters from the UC door. He walks around the living room with a sense of ownership, and yet is unattached. He thumps the floorboards with a booted foot; pounds on walls with a fist, shakes his head at the over-loaded electrical plug. OLIVER exchanges file folders for the lemonade pitcher and two glasses and eagerly approaches CHARLEY.

CHARLEY: Hell's bells, man. What've you been doing with my house? Or not doing? Look at this mess. (*Bending down at electrical plug.*)

OLIVER: (*Extending the pitcher to CHARLEY.*) It's kinda hard keeping up with everything, you know? My job at the college... and...

CHARLEY: (*On the move again.*) I wouldn't call preaching the same worn-out clichés to a bunch of intellectual morons teaching, I wouldn't. Try volleying real literature with some old guys playing chess down on a water front somewhere, or with a homeless guy in a food line. That's teaching.

OLIVER: This term we're using your last volume... *Poetic Sirens of the Sixties...*

CHARLEY: Whatever. (*Tripping over a pair of shoes.*) Doesn't Kate ever clean up in here?

OLIVER: She's not really into housework.

KATE: She's really into art. Instead.

CHARLEY: (*Peers under the table at KATE.*) Art, fart. It's all bullshit if you haven't got a roof over your heads and a clean space to work in.

340

CHARLEY straightens up and comes to the center of the room. He stops. Looks down at the bucket. Looks up at the source of the leak. Looks at OLIVER. OLIVER looks down at the bucket; then up, then at CHARLEY.

CHARLEY: Oliver.

OLIVER: Mr. C?

CHARLEY: (*Looking up.*) About this leak?

OLIVER: (*Offering pitcher.*) Lemonade?

CHARLEY: (*Hugely patient.*) Would you say it started about the time you began your epic?

OLIVER: (*Looking up.*) Probably.

CHARLEY: And when would that be? In round years.

OLIVER: Nineteen eighty five, thereabouts.

CHARLEY: Jesus. I need a drink.

He takes the pitcher and a glass from OLIVER, slops lemonade out, and gulps it down. KATE comes out from under the table.

KATE: Well, Charley. What's on your agenda this time? Oliver, fill up Charley's glass.

CHARLEY shakes his head, no; OLIVER fills the glass up. CHARLEY gives the glass to KATE. LAURA slips unnoticed around the screen. She moves quietly towards the UC door and stops on CHARLEY's line.

CHARLEY: I have to make serious decisions about this house. I don't think I can keep on resurrecting the old girl. Poetry market's down…

KATE: Hear that, Oliver?

CHARLEY: …and I need some quick cash. A bundle.

OLIVER: Are you going to sell it?!

KATE: You're going to sell it!!

CHARLEY: Well, I've been thinking about it. But now I'm here, shit, the state it's in, I don't know who'd want it.

OLIVER: We would, wouldn't we, Kate.

KATE: You fix that roof, you'll get a buyer. Now if you boys will excuse me…I have work to do. (*Sees LAURA.*) Oh, there you are. (*Crosses to her. The men watch.*)

LAURA: I just came to say good-bye.

KATE: Oh. (*Pause.*) I cleaned the shower.

LAURA: Okay. (*Pause.*) Then I'm gone.

The women exit UC door.

341

Scene 5

CHARLEY: Rotten shame about Kate's leg. She's a handsome woman, otherwise, under all that hair. And that other one. There's a package I'd like to unwrap.

OLIVER: (*Puts down pitcher, picks up files.*) I found my early drafts. These have all the original stanzas, bits and pieces I've rejected in this later version… but maybe you'd… if you had a look, and you could tell me… I'd put some of it back in if you think… if it'd work better…

CHARLEY: Where'd she come from, anyway?

OLIVER: What?

CHARLEY: That woman, Oliver. That woman.

OLIVER: She's using my towels… (*CHARLEY shoots him a look.*) …taking a shower, camping out… I don't know.

CHARLEY: You've got to know, Oliver. Be observant. Find out about what's going on around you. Find the passion, the guts, the hidden stories. Sitting on your ass at a computer is the smallest part of writing.

OLIVER responds by handing CHARLEY the files. CHARLEY sighs, sticks the files under his arm and continues his inspection; he avoids walking into the studio. After a beat, OLIVER follows him around.

OLIVER: Listen, Charley. You don't really have to sell the house, do you… I mean, I'd really like to buy, but… I can't, we can't. I, I don't know why you need the money, but… but I need this house, and if there's a new owner, well, we might have to go… and…

CHARLEY: Lighten up, Devlin. You never know what's gonna happen tomorrow. I could sell, new people could come in, you could stay, go. It's all a crap shoot.

OLIVER: (*Deflated.*) But I have my epic to finish.

CHARLEY: Yeah, yeah, yeah. (*Deep sigh.*) I'd better take a look at the foundation. Any surprises down there you want to tell me about?

OLIVER: Maybe a few dead mice.

CHARLEY: Poisoned by sour lemonade, no doubt. (*CHARLEY turns to leave. He picks up the bucket. The water drip hits the carpet. He exits UC door.*)

342

OLIVER: (*To CHARLEY's back, small voice.*) But I don't want to go.

OLIVER crosses to the table and sits. He stares at the computer screen, types out a few lines, yawns, puts his head down on his folded arms. KATE, ignoring OLIVER, passes through from the UC door to the studio. There, she lifts a blank canvass over the one painting in progress. She stares at the empty surface. LAURA enters from UC door with a green towel covering her hair. She crosses to the couch. She takes a locket on a chain from her pocket, opens it, and sits on the couch, looking at what's inside the locket. LAURA, KATE and OLIVER freeze.

Scene 6

ROSE SPOT on YOUNG LAURA (wearing overalls and a T-shirt) as she tiptoes up to the lemon tree (APRON), walking crouched over, one finger to her lips for silence. The other hand pulls along her imaginary friend, Jane. YOUNG LAURA sits under the tree and plays pattycake with Jane while she talks to her.

YOUNG LAURA: Daddy wants me to go to the hospital 'n see Mama. But I don't wanna go. There's too much going around here. People go and they don't come back. What if I went and I didn't come back? Where would I go? What would I be? Would I just vanish and not be me anymore? Even when Daddy goes now he goes for a long time. What if he doesn't come back... Ever. (*Rapidly.*) Pattycake, pattycake, baker's man. Bake me a cake as fast as you can. Put it in the oven and cover it with... huh. Put it in the oven with Hansel and Gretel and eat it up before they find us. Come on, Jane!

YOUNG LAURA jumps up and races off, dragging her imaginary friend behind her.

BLACKOUT.

Scene 7

LIGHTS UP, KILL SPOT. LAURA, KATE and OLIVER unfreeze. OLIVER stays asleep throughout the scene. He snores occasionally. KATE crosses from the studio directly to the telephone, picks up the receiver, dials, and speaks.

KATE: (*Into phone; pauses as appropriate.*) Oh, hi, Mrs. Colburn.

343

Can I talk to Fred? Thanks. (*Pause. Into phone.*) Hey, kiddo, I know you said you didn't want to come home yet. And I'm not going to push. I just wanted to tell you… Charley's gonna sell the house. For real…seems like. Anyway. New Mexico? Hmmmm? I know, I know. Think about it? You can call me and talk if you want. You don't have to come home and look at me. That's… What? Yeah. Fred? I love you, sweetheart. No matter what. Okay? Bye. I know. Bye. (*She hangs up and stands contemplating the telephone.*)

LAURA: (*Soft interruption.*) Fred is your daughter's name.

KATE: (*Crossing to sit next to LAURA.*) I named her Fredericka, after my favorite grandma. But our Fred likes things short and to the point.

LAURA: I think I'd like your Fred.

KATE: I'm sure you would. You remind me of her, somehow. (*Smiles at LAURA.*) Does the green towel mean you're staying?

LAURA: I don't think so.

KATE: We're not really so awful, me and Oliver. We just sound like it.

LAURA: It's not you, or Oliver.

KATE: Charley? (*On LAURA's nod.*) Don't worry about him, he's harmless.

LAURA: I'm not so sure.

KATE: Charley'll be out of here once he finishes his landlord routine. (*She gets up and heads for the studio.*) And who knows, maybe we'll be going on the road soon. In the meantime… I have got to get to work… There's food around… somewhere…

LAURA: Well, if you're going to bribe me with food… Uh, shouldn't we do something about that? (*Indicating drip.*)

KATE puts a boot under the drip and exits to the studio, where she starts working on the new canvass. CHARLEY returns with OLIVER's file folders still under his arm and two empty buckets. He picks up the boot, drops it in one bucket, puts the other under the drip. He swears under his breath. Puts the file folders on the trunk, takes up his mallet. He spies LAURA, still sitting on the couch, and crosses to stand directly in front of her.

CHARLEY: We meet again.

344

LAURA: (*Not looking up.*) Move away from me.

CHARLEY: Well, that's not very friendly, darlin'.

LAURA: I said, move away from me. Now.

CHARLEY: (*Moving in.*) Oooh, darlin', your lips say no, no, but your eyes…

LAURA slides along the couch and jumps up. She stands braced; looks ready to swing a punch. The green towel slides off, revealing dark hair—no more rainbow effect. CHARLEY, thrown off balance by her abrupt move, stumbles and backs into the water bucket. Water slops over his expensive boots. He looks down, then at LAURA. He steps right up to her. The two are almost eye-to-eye. CHARLEY's eyes cruise LAURA, head to toe. LAURA swings at him and misses. Before she can wind up for another blow, CHARLEY grabs her arm, pulls her close.

CHARLEY: Cunt. (*CHARLEY pushes LAURA away from him. He marches out the RC door, slamming the door behind him.*)

The crash wakes OLIVER who comes to with a start. OLIVER doesn't ask; he quickly follows CHARLEY. The house is silent. LAURA touches her arm where CHARLEY grabbed it, and freezes. LIGHTS DIM. ROSE SPOT on YOUNG LAURA as she comes tearing into the house wearing a worn man's overcoat. She runs back and forth, into the studio and out; deep into the house, back into the living room, like a thing possessed. She runs back to the RC door.

YOUNG LAURA: (*Screaming, over and over, loud, fast, until exhausted.*) Don't leave me! (*YOUNG LAURA races out the RC door.*)
BLACKOUT.

<u>Scene 8</u>

LIGHTS UP, KILL SPOT. LAURA unfreezes. She catches her breath by shaking herself until she is calm. Then she slides around the screen into the studio, and stands quietly watching KATE paint. KATE attacks her painting. She loads a wide brush with paint, starts at the left edge of the canvass, and lurches across to the right. The paint follows in a jerking stream. KATE seems to be in rhythm with her art. But as quickly as inspiration comes, it leaves. Paint slithers down the canvass to the floor. KATE slumps. LAURA slips out of the studio, into the living room. KATE shortly follows.

KATE: I should've listened to my mother and become a disco

345

queen.

LAURA: Not going well?

KATE: Understatement. Did I hear shouting earlier?

LAURA: Nothing important. Charley found something he didn't like. (*Pause.*) I used to paint. And I remember how it would come and go.

KATE: Used to. What happened?

LAURA: Oh, things. You know, things. That get in the way.

KATE: Yes, I know those things. (*Pause.*) Fred's only fourteen and already she's learning about "things." (*She picks up LAURA's locket, still laying on the couch, and absently strokes it.*) I wish I could help her.

LAURA: Is there still a hole, like a cave, in the blackberry vines out back?

KATE: When we first moved here, I was pregnant with Fred. And that place, in the berry vines, drew me, became my sanctuary. (*Pause.*) Do you have children?

LAURA: No. I… No.

KATE: Fred found the same place when she was about eight. She said she knew someone had made it just for her. A hidey hole. I never told her I used to talk to her in there, when she was in my belly. But I keep the vines trimmed and available. Just in case.

LAURA: Tell her. That's how you can help. Tell her. (*Moving around the room.*) Where'd you find the hobby horse?

KATE: In the attic.

LAURA: The little girl who lived here used to…

KATE: Yes?

LAURA: Nothing.

KATE: Laura. Why did you come back?

LAURA: I was looking for something. Lost. Or left.

KATE: What would you do if you found it?

LAURA: Isn't that the question of a lifetime. (*She considers; makes a decision*). No. Some questions are better left unanswered. (*She stands and extends her hand to KATE.*) Thanks for the hot water and the company. But I'm going.

CHARLEY and OLIVER re-enter from the RC door. CHARLEY is tot-

346

ing hand-painted 'For Sale' signs on stakes.

OLIVER: Kate! Talk to Charley!

KATE: I like your sale signs, Charley. (*To LAURA.*) I'll walk you out.

OLIVER: No, no! Convince him to stay! We got to discuss this… What're we having for dinner? Hamburgers? Spaghetti? Curry? What do you like, Charley? Whatever's your favorite, Kate can make it.

KATE: Kate can not.

CHARLEY has been slowly and steadily approaching LAURA. She doesn't back away, even when he gets very close.

CHARLEY: (*Just for LAURA.*) Anything. As long as it's hot.

LAURA hauls off and slugs CHARLEY in the face. Hard. CHARLEY drops and crashes into the rubber tree plant. He staggers up. The timing speeds up from here to end of scene. Actions and speeches overlap as appropriate.

OLIVER: (*Rushing to CHARLEY's aid.*) What are you doing?! Do you know who this man is? Charley, you okay?

CHARLEY pushes OLIVER away.

KATE: (*Arm around LAURA.*) Are you all right?

LAURA pushes KATE away. CHARLEY is on his feet; LAURA is moving for the RC door; KATE and OLIVER stand, stunned. The RC door crashes open and DULCINEA enters. She storms up to CHARLEY.

DULCINEA: So, you're just going to leave me sitting out there? In that ratty old thing you call a car? I don't like being left alone. I am B-O-R-E-D. And you know how I get when I'm B-O-R-E-D…

CHARLEY: Oh, shut up, Dulce.

LAURA is almost out the RC door when KATE grabs her and holds on.

LAURA: Let me go.

KATE: You can't drive like this.

DULCINEA: (*Poking CHARLEY in the chest.*) In case you forgot, big boy, I'm preggers. Got your bun in my oven. You're not treating me nice, a girl in my condition. Where's a toilet, anyway? I gotta pee somethin' fierce. (*Looks around.*) Thought you said the place was empty?

LAURA: I can drive any way I damn well please. Let go.

OLIVER: This is my house. Who are you? (*Points at DUL-CINEA. To CHARLEY.*) Mr. C? What's going on?

KATE: (*To LAURA.*) No, Laura. I won't let you.

CHARLEY: (*Warning.*) Dulce… (*To KATE, moving to the two women.*) Laura. Did you say Laura?

LAURA tries to bolt.

KATE: I'd keep my distance, Charley.

CHARLEY: (*Staring at LAURA.*) It can't be.

DULCINEA: (*To OLIVER.*) Well, if it's your house, sugar, how's about you find me a toilet before I let fly right where I'm standin'?

CHARLEY: (*Staring at LAURA.*) I don't believe it.

OLIVER: Kate, do you know what's going on?

KATE: Shut up, Oliver.

DULCINEA: I gotta wee!

CHARLEY AND OLIVER: Shut up, Dulce.

KATE: (*To LAURA.*) Laura… ?

More or less in unison.

LAURA: My father.

CHARLEY: My daughter.

DULCINEA: Here goes nothin'!

OLIVER: Use the bucket!

KATE tries to put both arms protectively around LAURA. A high level of confusion reigns accompanied by ad lib dialogue as appropriate. OLIVER quickly leads DULCINEA through UC door. LAURA runs out RC door. CHARLEY starts to go after her, gives up, paces. KATE stumps toward the RC door, the UC door, the studio, unable to settle. OLIVER and DUL-CINEA return via the UC door. KATE goes out the RC door. CHARLEY goes out the UC door.

Scene 9

DULCINEA wanders around the living room. She tries to squeeze her bottom into the high chair; to rotate the exercise bicycle's foot pedals; shakes off her shoes and steps into a pair of man's boots. OLIVER follows her around the room. He doesn't speak until DULCINEA heads toward the studio screen.

OLIVER: That's my wife's art studio.

348

DULCINEA: (Peering around screen.) So?

OLIVER: She doesn't like people in there.

DULCINEA: Including you?

OLIVER: Especially me.

DULCINEA: And people ask me why I don't want to get married. You got anything to eat around here? (*She heads back to living room.*)

OLIVER: (*On her heels.*) How about an egg?

DULCINEA: An egg? You're offering me an egg? As in one?

OLIVER: Yes.

DULCINEA: Do I get any toast with it? Butter? A little grape jelly? A glass of milk, maybe? You're dealin' with a fragile pregnant woman here, buster. What'd you say your name was?

OLIVER: Oliver.

DULCINEA: Oliver. Eggs. Three. Toast, also three. Milk. Large. Enough butter for a heart attack. Plenty salt. Okay?

OLIVER: How about some ravioli?

DULCINEA

Okay, bud. Throw it in a pan, heat it up, and bring her on out here. I don't care. Just feed me!

OLIVER exits as CHARLEY enters the UC door. The two collide, then break up. OLIVER continues off UC. CHARLEY is carrying an arm load of soggy blue towels. He seems bewildered, shocked. He goes to and stands in the center of the living room, uncertain what to do next. Finally, he lets the towels fall at his feet. As though in a trance, he walks into the studio and stands in the center of the space, drinking it in. DULCINEA follows him into the studio.

DULCINEA: You know, baby cakes…

CHARLEY grabs her arm roughly and drags her out into the living room.

DULCINEA: (*Cont'd.*) Hey!! (*Shakes CHARLEY off.*) Don't ever do that to me again! I mean it!

CHARLEY: Forget it, Dulce. Just… go away somewhere.

DULCINEA: No, I will not forget it. And I'm not going anywhere! Hey! Look at me! (*Grabs CHARLEY's face. He jerks backwards. She pokes him in the chest.*) We got things to discuss here.

CHARLEY: I can't do this right now. Leave me alone. I mean it. (*But the force has gone out of his words. He flops down on the recliner.*

DULCINEA sits on his lap. CHARLEY all but disappears from view.)
DULCINEA: This is the way I see it. You told me we was coming to look at your house. Your empty house. The house you and me's gonna live in once junior here makes her appearance.
CHARLEY: Wait a minute, I never promised…
DULCINEA: But no-o. Not only is this place loaded with people, it's falling down. Look at it! Uh-uhh. We gotta have big re-thinks about this one. And then there's the liddle bittie fact about your daughter waltzing around the joint. Your daughter? How's come you never mentioned this monster news item? Huh? Charley?
CHARLEY: (*Pushes her off.*) I can't talk with you sitting on me.
DULCINEA goes to perch on the edge of the table. Pause.
DULCINEA: Okay. I'm off. So talk.
CHARLEY: I don't know what to say. (*Pause.*) I don't even know why I kept this house. (*Gets up, paces. Pauses where appropriate.*) God, it was all so ago. When Mary and I met… So, so young. We got married because she wanted to be respectable and I wanted this house to write in. She insisted the house be in my name. Owning a house is a manly enterprise, Mr. Carmody. Can you believe it? Mr. Carmody. Called me that, for real. She was like a ghost from an eighteenth century poem, for crissakes. Long white dresses, white gloves, even a white hat. Drifting from room to room, arranging flowers, or sitting still for hours. Always in white. Then she wanted a baby. Mary was so tiny, bones like a little bird, I was always afraid I'd break her. I'd stopped going to her bed after the honeymoon… but she was determined. She got pregnant, and her doctor wanted to take it. A clinical abortion, he called it. But she was driven. She stayed in bed six, seven months. And giving birth to Laura almost killed her. Later, I'd come in the kitchen, and she'd be washing Laura in a bowl on the sink. Crying. Weeping, her back bent over, her hair hanging down in the soapy water. She cried because she was afraid. Afraid she'd drop the baby. Lose the baby. Drown the baby. I could never do anything. I couldn't stop the damn crying. I started to go away. Come back, try again. One day I just kept going. After Mary died, her sister

350

wrote. Asked what I wanted to do with the house. Should've sold it then. But no, I got all romantic about the damn place. Talked myself into calling it an investment. And hell, the rent I get from the Devlin's barely covers the taxes.

DULCINEA: Wait a minute. Your daughter walks back into your life and all you can talk about is money?

CHARLEY: I'm just talking out loud here. Okay?

DULCINEA: You started talking. Then you shifted into crap about what the house is worth and all. What I wanna know is, what about Laura? How does she figure in with our plans? What are you gonna do about her? She's your blood. Your first born. Unless you've got some other kids I don't know about. Does she get the house, or what?

CHARLEY: Leave Laura out of it. She's got nothing to do with you and me.

DULCINEA: You think not?

CHARLEY: I know not.

DULCINEA: I'll tell you what I know, what's gonna happen here. Your Laura's gonna be real mad at you. For a while. Then, she'll take a look around, see a falling down old house with some potential, come to know she's got a daddy with a lot of bucks in the bank. She'll plant her ass. Right here. Claim her right of progen... pro... progenitals...

CHARLEY: God. Progenitor. That's me. Not her.

DULCINEA: Whatever. Her inheritance, then. I can just see her. Lording it over me, her younger, prettier stepmother. Jealous, you know? Oh, what a time we're all gonna have. Not.

CHARLEY: For godssake, Dulce. You haven't got a fucking clue. Laura is probably not going to want to have a thing to do with me. (*Pause.*) And I'm beginning to wonder what you and I are doing.

DULCINEA: And I don't think I like your attitude. You're taking her side where you should be taking mine. I can tell. You're more worried about her than me. I'm the big mama here. (*Nasty.*) Or did you maybe knock up your little girl, too. Is all this meeting her for the first time just a big old pretense...

CHARLEY grabs DULCINEA's arms and holds her. His tone is fright-

351

ening.

CHARLEY: I've killed men for less.

DULCINEA: Okay, Charley. Okay. I didn't mean it. I'm just… (*Pulling away.*) Well, put yourself in my place. I'm all alone. We're not married. You've never talked about marriage to me. I'm gonna pop out a kid soon. Hell. A girl's gotta look out for herself. (*Pause.*) 'Cause I guess you're not gonna, are you, Charley. 'Cause you're not really the daddy type, are you. Charley?

CHARLEY: No.

DULCINEA: Well, that's okay. 'Cause maybe this ain't your kid, anyway! Whaddya say about that?

CHARLEY: Get out of my sight.

DULCINEA: And just… Well… Where am I supposed to go?

CHARLEY: (*Counts off each word with his fingers opening up.*) Get. Out. Of. My. Sight. (*Then makes a fist and puts it close to her face.*)

DULCINEA doesn't linger. She scurries out the RC door. We HEAR Charley's car roar off. CHARLEY sits on the couch. He looks around the room, then covers his face with his hands as though willing the room, the house, his life, to vanish. CHARLEY freezes. LIGHTS DIM. ROSE SPOT on YOUNG LAURA (wearing her older-girl dress) as she walks slowly into the house from the RC door. She comes directly up to CHARLEY, touches him lightly. Then she quickly hides behind the couch. LIGHTS UP, KILL SPOT. CHARLEY unfreezes. Uncovers his face, looks at the place YOUNG LAURA touched. Puts his hand over it. The TELEPHONE RINGS. After several unanswered rings, CHARLEY gets up and snatches up the receiver.

CHARLEY: What! Oh, sorry. Your mom? Is that Fred? Yeah, Charley. How you… Oh, sure. Okay. I'll go get her. Keep your pants on… (*Putting receiver down, muttering under his breath.*) Women. (*CHARLEY exits UC door.*)

Scene 10

After a beat, KATE enters from RC, OLIVER from UC. OLIVER goes to sit at his computer table. KATE rests in the recliner. There is a long silence while OLIVER stares at the computer screen. Their conversation has a resigned tone; even the yelling lacks passion.

OLIVER: Look like you're going to get your wish.

352

KATE: Which one.

OLIVER: We're going to have to move.

KATE: Where do you want to go?

OLIVER: That's the whole point. I don't want to go. Anywhere. Why don't you hear me say this?

KATE: People only hear what they want to hear. You don't need me to tell you that. You're the smart one.

OLIVER: Yeah, smart. Look where smart's gotten me.

KATE: I want to go to New Mexico.

OLIVER: I notice you didn't say, let's go. As in, we're going. See how smart I am.

KATE: Do you really think that once we walk out of this house we're going in the same direction?

OLIVER: What about Fred?

KATE: She'll go with me, until she finds her own road.

OLIVER: She'll miss her friends.

KATE: You know she doesn't have any friends. Just Miranda.

OLIVER: She won't forgive you if you break that up.

KATE: Maybe Miranda will go, too. (*Pause.*) Where will you go?

OLIVER: Don't ask me.

KATE: Okay, I'll rephrase. Instead of, where would you go, who would you like to be with?

OLIVER: Charley. People like Charley. Poets and other writers who have passion about their work. Larger than life. I want to be able to walk into a room like Charley does and sock a hole in the wall if I feel like it.

KATE; Will that help your writing? Is that what you've been missing here with us? I wish you'd've told me years ago. You could've punched out all the walls, I wouldn't've cared.

OLIVER: Right. But, you see, I want to care. I want you to care. I want us both to get all crazy with caring.

KATE: You want us to care about beating up the walls?

OLIVER: No, I don't mean that. I mean… (*Getting up; paces.*) I always wanted to be the kind of man who was a little bit scary. Just right on the edge between ordinary and extreme. I had an uncle like that. I couldn't wait to see him, to be with him, and

353

all the time I was, I was in a state of agitation, waiting for his fuse to light, for the top to blow off. Not that he'd ever do any real damage to anyone or break up furniture. But he had this, spark, no, bigger than a spark, a firecracker, inside him. And you were always watching for it, knowing it was coming. And that's what made him so exciting to be around. You knew, if you waited long enough, there'd be a show brighter than any galaxy. I wanted, still want, to be like Uncle Zacharias. (Pause.) The Ernest Hemingway of poets. The Carl Sagan of teachers. The Don Juan of lovers. (*Pause.*) Instead, I'm Wally Cox reincarnated.

KATE: Oh, honey. (*She goes to hold him.*) I always loved Mr. Peepers.

OLIVER: (*Shrugging her off.*) You're missing it.

KATE: No, just trying to make it easier. Cox committed suicide before he was fifty. I'd like to have you, if not in the same bed, at least in shouting distance well past your fiftieth.

OLIVER: My birthday was last week.

KATE: Another wish come true. Must be my lucky day.

OLIVER: Maybe if we'd been able to yell at each other.

KATE: Let's try it now.

OLIVER: What'll we yell about?

KATE: (*Pointing.*) Those.

OLIVER: The blue towels?

KATE: Hmmm.

OLIVER: What're they doing down here? They're supposed to be stuck up in the roof.

KATE: I thought you brought them down.

OLIVER: Not me.

KATE: Maybe Charley.

OLIVER: Are we yelling yet?

KATE: MAYBE CHARLEY!

OLIVER: MAYBE CHARLEY WHAT!!

LAURA walks in the RC door, does a quick turn and walks back out. KATE runs after her and drags her back inside.

KATE: Don't go, we're just yelling at each other.

OLIVER: Mr. and Mrs. Peepers at home, practicing being

alive.

LAURA: I forgot my backpack.

KATE: Is that all?

OLIVER: (*Picks up blue towels.*) Kate?

KATE: Oliver, Laura's back. We can practice later.

OLIVER: When did I become a walking dead man? Was it when we got married?

KATE: Oh, Oliver…

OLIVER: When Fred was born? When I started teaching? No, I think it was when we came to live in this house. Must be! This place has sucked the juice out of me. Us! That's it. That's why I can't write. Kate. You've been right all along! It's the house! We have to get out of here! (*Starts rushing around.*)

KATE: You can't blame the house, Oliver.

OLIVER: You're always.

KATE: It isn't the damn house. It's us. We've killed us. The house hasn't.

OLIVER: No, no, you're right! We would've been fine, just fine, anywhere else! Thank God Charley's selling the place! Now we can go!! We stand a chance, now! Gotta start packing. Right away. You call Fred, get her back here. Where are my maps? You said New Mexico? Too hot. What about Maine? Or Montana. Yes, Montana, all that big sky country. The Dakotas! Come on, woman, shake a leg! Let's show a little enthusiasm! Your biggest wish has just been granted! (*OLIVER bumps into LAURA on his rush for the UC door.*) We're packing! You can't stay! Boxes, I need boxes! (*OLIVER dashes through the UC door. KATE and LAURA stare at OLIVER's back.*)

KATE: Why is the phone off the hook?

KATE crosses to phone and hangs it up. LAURA crosses to the couch and slings her backpack across her shoulders. The phone starts RINGING again. LAURA starts for the RC door, but stops, mid-room. The phone stops RINGING. KATE disappears through the UC door and reemerges carrying the lemon basket, a fresh glass, and a paring knife. The phone starts RINGING. KATE slices a lemon and plops the slices into the pitcher of lemonade still on the table in the living room. She pours out some into the fresh glass and hands it to LAURA. LAURA takes it and drinks, as though in a dream. The phone stops RINGING. Rings again. Once. Then twice. Then KATE picks it up.

KATE: (*Into phone with appropriate pauses.*) I'm sorry, darling. Your father seems to have lost his mind and I just couldn't face talking to anyone. Thanks for using our code. Huh…? Oh. No, it's good. Yes, I know the place. Little park on the bluff. Bye. (*Hangs up.*)

LAURA: Has Oliver really lost his mind?

KATE: I don't imagine so. He's probably put it somewhere out of reach. (*Pause.*) I have to go meet Fred.

LAURA: Is she all right?

KATE: She's in love with her best friend Miranda, and confused, and still sounds better than you look. Will you stay put till I get back?

LAURA: I make no guarantees, at this moment.

KATE: Fair enough. If you go…

LAURA: I'll send you a postcard. (*Pause.*) From Taos.

KATE exits the RC door.

Scene 11

LAURA doesn't have time to think before CHARLEY enters the UC door. He picks up his mallet, makes preparations to leave; all the time ignoring LAURA. LAURA makes up her mind; puts her backpack down and confronts him.

LAURA: Leaving? So soon? Oh, wait. I forgot. That's what you do best, isn't it. Leave.

CHARLEY: I don't have to defend myself to you.

LAURA: Don't you?

CHARLEY moves to stand in front of LAURA. The two are within touching distance but keep very much apart. Both are keenly wound and neither lets down their guard.

CHARLEY: No.

LAURA: Bastard.

CHARLEY: All I did was walk out a door.

LAURA: You left me completely alone.

CHARLEY: You had Mary. I was the alone one.

LAURA: You were the grown up. I was eight years old. And

356

mama was dying.

CHARLEY: Girls are better off with their mothers.

LAURA: You as good as killed her when you left for the last time. She never got out of bed again. (*Pause.*) I was eight years old.

CHARLEY: I wrote to your Aunt Aggie... I knew she'd come... Look after you both.

LAURA: Putting Aggie in my life was the only decent thing I remember you doing for me. (*Pause.*) I WAS EIGHT YEARS OLD. (*Pause.*) Did I ever cross your mind? Did you think about me... going to school, being afraid of boys, climbing in a tree? Missing you? DID YOU THINK I WOULDN'T MISS YOU?

CHARLEY: I sent money.

LAURA: (*Stepping back now.*) Oh, that's just perfect. What a great cop out. Well, fuck you. Just fuck you, all right? (*Prowling.*) I saw a letter you sent to Aggie. She didn't show it to me until the day I left...my eighteenth birthday. Oh, sorry, I keep forgetting. A letter makes it sound like we were all regular happy little correspondents. The letter. This single piece of paper that reminds me who I am. (*LAURA takes a many-times folded piece of paper from her backpack and tosses it at CHARLEY.*) My favorite line starts the second paragraph. And I quote. I'm keeping the house in my name, but I don't want to live there anymore. You make a life for Laura. If you want to stay in the house, fine. But don't look to me for any other kind of support. End quote.

CHARLEY: Jesus. Let it go. History is so deadly boring.

LAURA: Boring. Wow.

CHARLEY: Do you know what some men do to their daughters?

LAURA: I could've handled incest better than abandonment.

CHARLEY: You don't know what you're saying.

LAURA: And I suppose you do. (*Pause.*) With a rape, there's something tangible to point your anger at. With being left, there's nothing. I wasn't even good enough to be beat up or raped. I was nothing. No thing.

CHARLEY: You can't go on hating me.

LAURA: What I do or don't do is none of your business.

CHARLEY: Aren't you exhausted by it?

LAURA: Keeps me alert to pricks like you.

CHARLEY is on the prowl now, too. Occasionally LAURA and CHAR-LEY cross paths during the following.

CHARLEY: You got any money?

LAURA: What?

CHARLEY: Since you want the familial connection, you buy the house.

LAURA: What?

CHARLEY: I just want out. Finally. (*Beat.*) Although, it might be a kick in the ass to hitch up with you.

KATE returns via the RC door, unnoticed by LAURA or CHARLEY. She sidles over to stand behind the rubber tree plant, becoming almost invisible.

LAURA: Hitch up? (*She halts.*) You didn't just say, hitch up.

CHARLEY: Yeah. Write to each other, talk on the phone. Get to know each other.

LAURA: You gave up the right to know me forty two years ago. (*Pause.*) And accidentally colliding with you, on home turf, doesn't change that. (*Pause.*) Buy the house? You unredeemable bastard. You should GIVE me the damned house.

CHARLEY: I don't give anybody anything, sweetheart.

LAURA: Sure you do, Charley. (*Face to face with CHARLEY.*) You gave me a hefty legacy… of not being able to attach myself. I can't stick anywhere, to anyone. I've never held a job longer than a year, or lived anyplace longer than two. I'm a gypsy without the gypsy's soul. People talk about trying to find themselves? Hell, I've known all along there's never been any me to find. Because if there was, you never would have left.

The RC door pushes open; it's OLIVER, toting a book box. KATE grabs his arm and pulls him behind the plant with her.

CHARLEY: You can't blame me for how you choose to live your life.

LAURA: You take no credit?

CHARLEY: No.

LAURA turns on her heel and storms into the studio. CHARLEY, KATE, and OLIVER freeze. In the studio, LAURA crumples to the floor, and freezes. BLACKOUT.

Scene 12

LIGHTS UP HALF, ROSE SPOT on YOUNG LAURA (still in her older-girl dress) as she emerges from behind the sofa and runs into the studio with LAURA. She wraps her arms around her older self and rocks. LIGHTS UP, KILL SPOT. LAURA and YOUNG LAURA rock as one. After a beat, LAURA gets up and prowls the studio. YOUNG LAURA hides behind the stack of canvasses. KATE joins LAURA, puts her arm around LAURA's waist. CHARLEY falls back on the sofa. OLIVER comes to start packing up the litter on the table, sweeping things into the box. Lighting SPLITS the stage. When the women are speaking, LIGHTS UP in their portion of the stage during their speeches. When the men begin talking, LIGHTS DOWN over studio, UP over living room section. The men are motionless while the women speak and vice versa. LIGHTS UP over the studio, DOWN over the living space. LAURA disengages from KATE. She goes to place her hand over her small painted one.

LAURA: I painted my hand here when he started leaving... trying to hold on to something...

KATE: (*Leaning against her paintings.*) How do you think it would've been different, if he'd stayed?

LAURA: We'd have been a family... I'd be connected to some... thing, some... body...

KATE: Think so?

LAURA: Crap. No, you're right. No, you're not. I don't know. I just know I never got the chance to find out.

KATE: Every little girl's dream of perfection... daddy and me against the world. (Starts looking through paintings.) Mine threw me down the stairs before he left. (*Holds up a small painting.*) What do you think of this?

LAURA: (*Taking the painting.*) I like it, I think. But...

KATE: But... ?

LAURA: I feel nervous looking at it, sort of stirred up.

KATE: Oh, good. I thought you were going to say it's tired.

LAURA: Tired? No.

KATE: I painted that one this morning, early, just before you got here, so you could say it's yours. For stirring things up.

The women consider the paintings, LAURA the small one in her hand, KATE all the rest. LIGHTS DOWN in studio and UP in living space.

359

OLIVER finishes up packing his box. Starts moving things around on the table. His enthusiasm for this move wanes; he walks around the room, looking at his life, and grows weary. CHARLEY opens and closes the locket several times; watches OLIVER.

CHARLEY: Oliver?

OLIVER: Charley?

CHARLEY: What are you doing?

OLIVER: Trying to figure out what to take, what to leave…

CHARLEY: Where are you going?

OLIVER: (*Stops moving; flops into recliner.*) I don't know.

CHARLEY: Perfect. (*Pause.*) I never felt connected to Laura, or to Mary, in the way a man's supposed to feel for his family. Like he'd die to protect them. When all's said and done, blood doesn't mean shit. (*Pause.*) Christ, seeing her now, I probably would have made a pass at her when she hit thirteen. And she probably would have killed me.

OLIVER: Then we wouldn't be sitting here.

CHARLEY: No, Oliver, we wouldn't. We sure as hell would not. (*Pause.*) Do you, Oliver? Have that drive? That instinctive drive about Fred?

OLIVER: I did have, when she was little. But then she started wandering and just kept going. Kate blames me. I don't think that's fair. Do you? Think that's fair?

CHARLEY: Whattdya call fair?

OLIVER: At least you've got another chance.

CHARLEY: Say what? Oh, damn… Dulce…   (*Gets up and drops the locket into a pocket.*) Listen, I gotta get outta here. I got some things to think about, plans to make. (*Pats his pockets.*) Where's my keys? Oh, hell, she took the car. Oliver. Give me your keys.

OLIVER: What?

CHARLEY: Keys! Give me your keys!

OLIVER: In the last boot.

CHARLEY picks up one of the men's boots, shakes out a set of keys, and exits RC door. OLIVER watches him go and sighs.

Scene 13

LIGHTS UP in studio. DOWN in living room.

KATE: (*Indicating paintings.*) How many of these will fit in your van... if it's still going to Taos?

LAURA: How many do you want?

KATE: (*Considers.*) The one you're holding, and that big one. (*Pointing to the canvass she was working on earlier*). *LAURA tucks the smaller painting under her arm; the women pick up and carry the larger one out into the living space. LIGHTS FULL UP. While LAURA waits near the RC door, KATE goes back into the studio, gathers up her favorite brushes, and takes the metal mirror. She returns to the living room. CHARLEY enters RC door. He carries one of his 'For Sale' signs that has been vandalized with red lipstick. He tosses it down next to the bucket. He walks around the living room, as if seeing it for the first time.*

OLIVER: (*To KATE.*) If you hadn't turned Fred's bedroom into a painting studio, maybe she'd have stayed home more.

KATE: She goes like her father. To find something better. Maybe she'll find that with me and Laura in Taos. Maybe we all will. (*Long pause.*) And maybe now that old lemon tree will start producing really sweet lemons.

OLIVER: Then you'd have a reason to come back. If you ever wanted...

KATE: Well...

CHARLEY: Kate?

KATE: Yes, Charley?

CHARLEY: You're leaving?

KATE: Yes, Charley.

CHARLEY: Oliver?

OLIVER: Charley?

CHARLEY: Dulce's let me know in no uncertain terms (*Pointing at the sign*) that she doesn't want me around, your wife's up and leaving you, you gotta get up and go one of these days, what say you and me make it today. Take a chance. Head south. San Francisco. Give Ferlinghetti a run for his dead ass. See what the new hot shot poets are up to down by the Golden Gate.

OLIVER: What?

CHARLEY crosses to LAURA and holds out the locket. After a beat, she takes it.

361

CHARLEY: (*Nodding at the locket.*) You look a lot like her, you know.

LAURA takes the mirror from KATE. She holds it up and looks at her reflection. Then she turns it to CHARLEY, mirror side facing him. He ducks his eyes away from his image.

LAURA: I look more like you. (*She lowers the mirror and pockets the locket.*)

CHARLEY: I loved your mother… and you…

LAURA: Too little, Charley. Too little and…

CHARLEY: … too late?

LAURA: …too late.

LAURA shakes her head and walks out the RC door.

KATE: (*To OLIVER.*) Make sure you eat something sometime, Wally. (*Her hand on the RC door.*) We'll let you know our new zip code. (*KATE exits RC door behind LAURA.*)

OLIVER gets out of the recliner.

OLIVER: San Francisco?

CHARLEY: (*Staring at the RC door shutting behind the women.*) Why not?

CHARLEY spins around, as if looking for something. His eyes fall on OLIVER's epic folders on the trunk. He picks the red one up and, in spite of himself, starts reading. He leans against the computer table, engrossed.

OLIVER: San Francisco.

OLIVER goes through the UC door and returns with two new glasses full of lemonade. He hands one to CHARLEY and takes one for himself. He wanders up to the studio entrance and peers in without seeing. The telephone RINGS and is ignored by the men. As OLIVER turns back into the living space.

CHARLEY: (*Making a face after taking an unconscious swallow of lemonade.*) Gods, teeth, Oliver, don't you ever put sugar in this stuff?

BLACKOUT.

Scene 14

LIGHTS UP. The stage is empty. After a long beat, YOUNG LAURA emerges from her hiding place behind the canvasses. YOUNG LAURA skips gaily around the living room, through the studio, back again. Skips out through the UC door and returns in a moment carrying a full fuel can and a box of kitchen matches. She puts the matches in her pocket. She then splashes fuel all over everything in the living room and the studio. She goes to the RC door and opens it. She lights a match and watches it burn. She looks in at the house, then out the door.

YOUNG LAURA: *(Calling out RC door.) Wait for me!!!*

YOUNG LAURA tosses the match into the living room as she darts out the RC door. INSTANT CURTAIN/BLACKOUT. BRIGHT SPOT on lemon tree on apron. LIGHTING EFFECT on scrim shows/gives effect of house burning. The lemon tree, then, is all that is left.

BLACKOUT.

END OF PLAY

R-i-i-i-ring

©2001

Characters
MOTHER: Late middle-age, verging on elderly with flair
DAUGHTER #1:   Haughty, smooth, distant
DAUGHTER #2   Flighty, edgy, emotional

Setting
MOTHER's bedroom with DAUGHTER #1 and #2 positioned DSR and DSL.

Time: The present.

Properties
MOTHER: Single bed, metal frame, headboard only Coverlit, pillow Bedside table, small, wooden Black dial telephone, Lace doily, Red flannel nightshirt, full-length mink coat, man's Fedora, Wellington boots, Baloney sandwich

DAUGHTER #1: Easy chair; Push-button telephone on small table

DAUGHTER #2: Bar stool; Cell phone

SFX
Modern, touch-tone telephone and cell phone RINGS (high pitched)
1950's, dial telephone RINGS (lower and louder)
Modern telephone receiver hanging up
Cell phone slapping shut

At Rise:
Scene 1. *A single bed, with headboard only, sits center stage, perpendicular to apron. A black dial telephone rests on a small table next to the*

364

head of the bed. On the bed lies an almost elderly woman, MOTHER, dressed in her red flannel nightshirt, her feet pointing toward the audience. A small table with a push-button telephone sits at DSL next to an easy chair. DAUGHTER #1 sits in the chair. DAUGHTER #2 perches on a bar stool positioned at DSR. When MOTHER is speaking, she is in spot; the rest of the stage is dark. When DAUGHTER #1 and DAUGHTER #2 are speaking, they are in spot; the rest of the stage is dark.

LIGHTS UP on DAUGHTER #1 and DAUGHTER #2 who removes a cell phone from a pocket and punches in a number. DAUGHTER #1's telephone RINGS three times.

DAUGHTER #1: (*Picking up receiver.*) Hello?

DAUGHTER #2: Hey.

DAUGHTER #1; Hey.

DAUGHTER #2: Listen, we have to DO something about Mother.

DAUGHTER #1: Why?

DAUGHTER #2: Because she's getting older now, REALLY old, and, she could fall down and break something, and, there she is all alone in that big drafty house five miles from ANYone, and she's getting so vague and skatty, she keeps on getting herself LOST, for chrissakes… you should hear the PHONE calls I get…

DAUGHTER #1: I got lost last week. The traffic engineers are crazy here. The street signs are too far off the road, or point you in the wrong direction, or wait until you're somewhere you don't want to be before letting you know you're somewhere you don't want to be.

DAUGHTER #2: Be serious.

DAUGHTER #1: You be serious. I'll be roebuck.

DAUGHTER #2: Sis…

DAUGHTER #1: I don't see what the big deal is.

DAUGHTER #2: The DEAL is, Mother simply can't go on living alone anymore.

DAUGHTER #1: Why not?

DAUGHTER #2: One of us is going to have to take her in.

DAUGHTER #1: You're supposed to. You're the younger one.

DAUGHTER #2: No, you're supposed to. You're the older one.

DAUGHTER #1: She's not living with me.

DAUGHTER #2: But we have to do something!!

DAUGHTER #1: Why?

DAUGHTER #2: You're making me crazy!!

DAUGHTER #1: If you're just going to shout at me down the phone, I'm hanging up. (*She starts to do this.*)

DAUGHTER #2: No! Wait!

DAUGHTER #1: Waiting.

DAUGHTER #2: I'm scared.

DAUGHTER #1: Of what? Her dying? You having to take care of her?

DAUGHTER #2: I'm hanging up now. I'm going to call mother.

DAUGHTER #1: Good plan. (*She hangs up.*)

LIGHTS DOWN on DAUGHTER #1 and DAUGHTER #2.

LIGHTS UP on MOTHER in her bed. Her telephone RINGS five times. She reaches out for the receiver, still lying down, and listens, making mm-hmm noises occasionally.

MOTHER: That's nice, dear. Have a good time. Bye bye, now.

MOTHER lets the receiver drop on to the bed spread, then gets out of bed and exits SR. LIGHTS DOWN on MOTHER. LIGHTS UP on DAUGHTER #2 and DAUGHTER #1. DAUGHTER #2 punches in a number on her telephone. DAUGHTER #1's telephone rings. She picks up the receiver after several rings.

DAUGHTER #1: Hello?

DAUGHTER #2: Hey.

DAUGHTER #1: Hey.

DAUGHTER #2: Well, I called her.

DAUGHTER #1: And?

DAUGHTER #2: And, she didn't really say yes or no.

DAUGHTER #1: And that surprises you? You're forgetting who she is.

DAUGHTER #2: She's MOTHER!

DAUGHTER #1: She's a loner, always has been, even when we were around. Besides, what's the worst that could happen. She drinks too much one night, falls in the pool, and drowns.

DAUGHTER #2: Good grief. I can't talk about that.

DAUGHTER #1: What else are we talking about?

DAUGHTER #2: But we're family!

DAUGHTER #1: Family doesn't automatically make us the same.

LIGHTS DOWN on DAUGHTER #1 and DAUGHTER #2. LIGHTS UP following MOTHER, who enters from SR. She is wearing a full-length mink coat over her red-flannel nightshirt, Wellington boots, and a man's Fedora. She carries with her a bulging baloney sandwich from which she takes healthy bites. She crosses to her bed, sits, hangs up phone briefly, lifts up receiver, puts it aside, and dials. She waits, chewing. Then picks up the receiver when it starts squawking at her.

MOTHER: (*Pauses as appropriate.*) Hey, Sadie. Guess what. No, nothing's wrong. Just guess what. Well, hold on to yourself and I'll tell you. My youngest called me this morning. And guess what. HEY!! No need to yell. I think she's getting ready to put me away in one of those assisted living joints. Whadaya think of that? Yeah. Well, what're you going to do. 'Course, I never would've dreamed of turfing out Grandma Willis…she was a one, remember her? Last of the Tough Old Broads, she was. Huh? No, I didn't tell her anything. What do you think, I'm crazy?! I just let her ramble on, made encouraging mother noises now and again… The older one? Nah, I don't think she'll go along with it. But you never know, you never know. These girls these days. You just never know. What am I gonna do now? I'm gonna finish up this sandwich I got going here, then maybe you and I can catch a movie?… Oh, we did? You sure? We been to a movie today already? What'd we see? Oh, I didn't like that one. Let's try something else tomorrow. One I like. (Long pause.) Sade? I'm tired. Gonna lay my head down for a while.

MOTHER hangs up her telephone, her baloney sandwich forgotten. She stretches out on her bed and goes instantly to sleep. LIGHTS DOWN on MOTHER. LIGHTS UP on DAUGHTER #1 and DAUGHTER #2, still in their telephone conversation.

DAUGHTER #2: I hate it when you're right. (*Pause.*) But I think you're wrong.

DAUGHTER #1: I'll tell you what's wrong. What's wrong is even suggesting that I'd take in that woman.

DAUGHTER #2: She's your MOTHER.

DAUGHTER #1: Maybe so, but all she's ever done is criticize me. I publish a story, she says, well, dear, did you really mean to use that word? There? I teach a class at a community college, and she wants to know why I'm not making money running fancy workshops. I cut my hair, she likes it long. I leave it long, she prefers it short. I live alone, she tells me my heart is too closed up. I share my life, she tells me I'm too independent for that to last. So here's the deal. How's about we do nothing?

DAUGHTER #2: We can't just do NOTHING… we have TO DO SOMETHING!!

DAUGHTER #1: (*Long pause.*) Okay, okay. I'll get some brochures. I'll make some phone calls. I'll ask some questions.

DAUGHTER #2: It's a start. And after all, we've got lots of time yet. (*Pause.*) Hey, it's your turn to call Mother.

DAUGHTER #1: Yeah. Maybe later. Plenty of time.

DAUGHTER #2: Plenty of time. Bye.

LIGHTS DOWN on DAUGHTER #2. DAUGHTER #1 slowly dials her telephone. LIGHTS DOWN on DAUGHTER #1. LIGHTS UP on MOTHER in her bed, under the coverlit, wearing her nightshirt, asleep. MOTHER's telephone RINGS. MOTHER sits abruptly up in bed from the waist, fully upright, eyes popped open. One hand clutches her chest over her heart, the other reaches skyward. Her mouth opens in a huge 'O' and she smiles broadly, lets out her life on a long, satisfied sigh, and flops back down. Dead. MOTHER's telephone keeps RINGING. Slow fade of spot to full BLACKOUT.

CURTAIN

CPSIA information can be obtained
at www.ICGtesting.com
Printed in the USA
LVHW010234231220
674915LV00023B/240